For ... nt,
... J met you. ... win-in
these female characters as you
possess the beauty, strength,
courage & ferocity that I
have written these women
with. You are the storm.

♡

2022

SNAKE
OF THE NILE

THE AEGEAN SERIES

E.A. JACKSON

 FriesenPress

One Printers Way
Altona, MB R0G 0B0
Canada

www.friesenpress.com

Photographer: Jason Benson

Illustrator: Keith Tarrier

ISBN
978-1-03-913249-8 (Hardcover)
978-1-03-913248-1 (Paperback)
978-1-03-913250-4 (eBook)

1. Fiction, Historical, Ancient

Distributed to the trade by The Ingram Book Company

DEDICATIONS

For the constant echo of "never give up" that
resounds throughout my life in my father's voice;

For my mother, the living Greek Goddess of my imagination;

For Thomas, who sees me, who dares to look yet stands steadfast;

For Troy, whose midnight pancakes got me through sixteen-hour writing days;

For lovely Leanne, the Warrior Princess who began it all;

And for my sweet Sarah, who believed in me and
never wavered in the face of my ambition.

A tribute to David Gemmell:
one of the finest writers the world of fiction has ever seen,
whose work will always haunt and set the bar for my own.

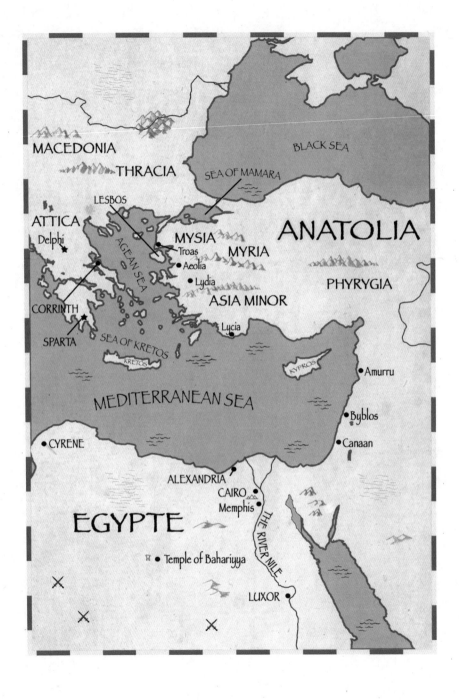

"And make death proud to take us."
—Cleopatra

(William Shakespeare's *Antony & Cleopatra*)

EGYPTE

DAUGHTERS OF THE NILE

— I —

Beams of sunlight streamed through the high stone arches, creeping like golden serpents across the palace terraces and over a sleeping girl's thin linen. The gentle breeze licked the sheer curtains, made from a fabric brought to Egypte by merchants from the East and so loved by the late Queen Kleopatra—the fifth of her name—that the entire palace was fitted with the fine golden curtains.

Somewhere amongst the linen of Egypteian cotton picked and woven by the slaves in the lower city, the girl stirred and squinted as she rolled onto her side, her hand finding and embracing the warm mound of fur that was Heba. Peeking through one eye, she grinned sleepily to see the magnificent spotted leopard peering at her with orange eyes. The cat had the docile temperament of a floor rug, but she was a beloved friend nonetheless.

Heba extended her hind legs leisurely as her whole body stretched the length of the large bed, fabric ripping softly as her hind claws caught on the delicate threads. Then she dipped her head forward to lazily lick the girl's closed eyes before giving up on the gesture in favour of more sleep.

The girl wiped the cat's saliva from her face and rolled again to her back. As her mind slowly roused, excitement surged in her. Her eyes snapped open, and with the speed of a desert cat, she sprang from her bed, wrenched open the heavy-set wooden door, and burst into the hallway. Her nightgown hung to her knees and swam loosely around her chest, still flat like a boy's. She raced down the stone-paved hallway, which was lined with tall, marvellously carved pillars and thriving plants propped upon stone mounts. She darted around two servant women carrying large baskets of linen, her cropped, dark hair brushing her shoulders. She skidded around a sharp corner, maintaining her balance with ease, and sped toward a large wooden door with heavy iron settings on its hinges, bare feet slapping against the ground. Without losing speed, she reached out her hands to put her full weight against the door, but on her approach, it suddenly opened. As her knees buckled under her, a man stepped forward, colliding with her. She bounced backward, her weight no match for his tall frame, and found herself sitting on the stone floor, blinking up at him in mild confusion.

The man gave a low, warm laugh as she scowled up at him. He was holding his tunic around his waist, but his muscled chest was bare, and he did not carry sandals.

His black hair was cropped short and his eyes deep-set with long. dark lashes. He was beautiful, yes, but her stare was cold and uncertain. He smiled, his face full of warmth and mischief, and when he spoke, his voice was low and confident. "Good morning, Princess. She's all yours once more."

She scowled some more at the man as he once again chuckled, darting his eyes around the hall before stepping lightly yet swiftly away, attempting to dress as he slipped out of sight and into the sleepy halls of the palace.

The girl pulled herself up, the excitement returning, and pushed through the door into a tastefully decorated room. Beautiful tapestries woven from silk hung from the walls, gold goblets and wine urns littered the enormous table by the balcony, and a large candelabrum hung low above wooden chests inlaid with copper, with intricate carvings on their lids of scenes, from far across the seas, of savages fighting their wars and worshipping their silly gods. How strange, the girl thought, that there were those who believed their gods would have need for animal sacrifices, when truly the divine only valued the sacrifice of humans.

She pounced from the floor onto the large, messy bed and landed on a sleeping woman. The woman awoke with a start, her beautiful face a mix of surprise and amusement, her dark features pulling together to form a radiant smile. "Is it time already? Does no one in this family need sleep anymore?" With a large exhalation from her chest, she wrapped her long, slender arms around the girl on top of her and leaned her head back, closing her eyes once more, but the girl protested.

"Yes, it's time, sister! There will be baked figs and honeyed meats!"

The woman, with her eyes still blissfully closed, mumbled lazily, "You and your figs. One day you will be queen of figs. Kleopatra, the Queen of Figs."

"What a terrible title." Kleopatra frowned sourly.

"All the figs in the land will tremble at your insatiable hunger for their flesh." The woman smiled into her pillow.

"Berenice, get up! Father will be furious if we're not dressed."

"Father will be furious whether we are dressed or not." Berenice sighed. "We still have to make it through the ceremonies before the feast, you know."

"There will be fresh breads and wine through the formalities, and Auletes said Father has brought jesters to the palace for the guests!"

"I forget that you haven't suffered through as many of these ceremonies as I have."

"Yes, you old hag, get up!"

The door flew open, and in swept five women, all in beige floor-length tunics, lengths of fabric sweeping their hair into twisted bundles atop their heads. They dispersed into a flurry of activity, filling the water bowl by the far wall from large steaming urns they carried, pulling open thin woven doors to reveal a large garment room filled with beautiful fabrics and jewellery, then came to pull the blankets off Berenice. One of them, a distracted older woman with small eyes and sparse dark hairs on her upper lip and chin, relayed an order to Kleopatra. "Get back to your room, child; your maids are looking for you. You should be washed and dressed by now."

Kleopatra slipped off the bed while the old woman and a younger servant girl pulled Berenice out of bed, and another two brought a large steaming bowl to her feet and began dipping ocean sponges into the water, then wiping them across her naked body.

Kleopatra stood for a moment, looking curiously at her favourite sister. Berenice, a woman of seventeen now, the eldest daughter of the Pharaoh Ptolemy XII Auletes and known throughout Egypt for her beauty and wit, was the goddess Isis herself in the eyes of her little sister. Her every move and action and speech were studied by Kleopatra, from the style of her jewellery to the way she wore her beautiful dark hair. Passing men in the hallways, Kleopatra had often heard them discussing the pleasing shape of Berenice's body and her attractive face, and she herself considered her sister to be the most beautiful woman she had ever seen. She longed for the day when she, too, had breasts like the goddess and could wear the belted robes of the older girls—the day she would be rid of her boy-like body of ten years and become a woman.

Berenice patiently lifted her arms above her head, her small but firm breasts high on her chest with perfect dark rings around her nipples, as her long black hair was brushed to where it fell at her small waist, soapy water running down her long, slender legs. A servant girl squeezed her sponge, dipped it in the water again, and then began to scrub high up Berenice's thigh, where a white liquid had dried to her skin. *Odd*, Kleopatra thought. She had never woken with such a liquid on her skin. She wondered if it were perhaps a part of the womanhood she was yet to come to, which Berenice had told her would bring her many pleasures and many pains. Berenice, now fully awake, glanced over to Kleopatra and winked an eye cheekily, seemingly delighting in the disapproving glances between the servant girls scrubbing away at her thigh. The last servant brought a long red gown with a golden rope around its waist and a brooch in the shape of a golden scarab beetle pinned to the left breast.

"Your gowns are so much prettier than mine," Kleopatra said with awe.

The old woman snapped her head up, realising Kleopatra still stood watching. "Be gone, child! Dress in your threads!"

Without another glance, Kleopatra turned from the scene and took off at a sprint back to her room; as she turned the sharp corner, she saw three servant girls bickering outside her open chamber door. One turned to see her approaching at full speed. "Where have you been? Get in here quickly, child! You'll get us all whipped!"

🌼

A HEAVY KNOCK SOUNDED ON THE DOOR OF KLEOPATRA'S bedchamber. As she sprang from her chair, the door swung open, and she was ushered from the room by four palace guards in full military armour: dull white skirts tied around their waists; thick leather sandals reaching up their lower legs; and broad copper neckpieces—Usekh collars, adorned with closely placed rows of coloured stones and beads—resting around their necks like armour reaching out to cover their shoulders. Each held a tall, thin spear. They moved in unison and never smiled.

Kleopatra set the pace, scampering along the tall hallways, the air thick with heat as they drew closer to the growing chatter of a crowd. She turned the corner and strode happily into the busy hypostyle. The spectacular hall was legendary. A grand space, its ceilings decorated with murals, it was so tall she was sure the gods rested upon it when they grew tired of flying. The countless stone pillars holding up the ceiling spanned the entire length of the hall. The walls were carved with intricate hieroglyphics of the great pharaohs and their families, of the gods and their wrath, above scenes of the triumphant battles of her ancestors. The vast floor was paved with precious stones and mosaics crafted by the best stonemasons in Egypt. An architect from Thebe had even been brought to Egypt to arrange the designs in such a way that their full beauty could only be seen if looked upon from high above, by the gods themselves. The great room was filled with flourishing plants and unlit torches, mounted on the walls amongst the armour of conquered kings and artefacts of great worth. The display reached around the raised stage at the far end of the hall where, several steps up, sat the gold throne of the pharaoh, and next to it, the throne of his queen, both thrones stretching high and encrusted with jewels and precious metals. To each side were beautiful chairs for the members of the royal family, upholstered with green fabric and gold cord. One of these chairs belonged to Kleopatra. The fabric sometimes itched her legs in the heat, but she loved her seat between Berenice and her favourite brother, Theos, whose name day had been celebrated last, before the youngest child, Auletes.

Kleopatra made her way through the crowd of excited and chattering nobles and lords to her place amongst the thrones. As she ascended the small steps up to the chairs, she felt eyes on her and glanced up to see her sister Arsinoe regarding her with malice, as she often did. Kleopatra dropped her gaze, ever unsure of what she had done to cause Arsinoe's heart to sour towards her. It was clear that Kleopatra was not welcome in the presence of Arsinoe, who made a point of inflicting pain on her on every possible occasion.

Kleopatra braved a final glance at Arsinoe. The girl's vehement gaze felt like spears in her chest. The angular scars tracing the bones of Arsinoe's face were faint yet raised beneath the heavy application of clay and mineral paste. Her lips were reddened, her eyelids painted blue with dark kohl designs above them, and she wore a thick black wig that fell to her breasts in many tightly woven braids.

The malice hurt Kleopatra's heart. They shared a mother, and Kleopatra had once loved Arsinoe as only a little sister would: following her through the castle, doing everything she did, eating everything she ate, laughing when she laughed, and wearing what she wore. But those days had disappeared as Father had begun to make his plans for their futures, and ultimately, it was Arsinoe who had paid the heaviest price.

Once, Arsinoe had even taken a sword from a palace guard, and when Kleopatra had wandered into the room clutching a woven toy and looking for their servant, Rehema, Arsinoe had swung the sword at Kleopatra with all the strength of a seven-year-old-girl, striking Kleopatra's skull from the side. Claudius had brought Arsinoe to Kleopatra's bed to apologise, but Arsinoe had refused. She had simply looked up at Claudius with eyes of terrifying indifference and said, "Next time, I'll swing harder, so she doesn't wake up."

A hush fell over the enormous space, and the pharaoh's presence enveloped the hall; he was draped in a long golden skirt, his head adorned with the crown of Ra. He held up a hand to the watching crowd as he sat proudly on his throne of gold, ever stoic, maintaining his imperious gaze and rigid demeanour. "Our Queen Safiya is resting today as the children in her belly seem more frequently to rob her of her stamina. Today, my son Auletes becomes a man under the laws of our kingdom. In his ninth year, he stands before you now, a prince of Egypt, son of the desert, and lord of our people." The pharaoh gestured to the temple priests, who were dressed in long purple robes, their fingers heavily jewelled, to proceed with the ceremony. Young Auletes stood, and the priests began to flick oil on him from wooden bowls as they chanted, monotonous enough to lull Kleopatra into a gentle trance, staring at her brother Neos.

Neos, the second son, after Claudius, was a malicious and treacherous creature, and when Kleopatra dreamed of him, his dark, soulless eyes became pools of tar, and his body distorted into that of a serpent that began to squeeze the life from her. She would wake gasping for air, and she was certain that, as she sat across from him now, if he were to bleed, his blood would be black like his soul. He looked bored, in contrast to the sister born after him: Isis. She sat rigid in her chair with a curious look on her face that seemed to flicker between interest and impatience. Her features were a little darker as she enjoyed walking amongst the people, and the sun was known to darken the skin. Her eyes were often narrow and seemingly distant, though focussed, her chin small, and her face mouselike. She wore a tunic of light green, and her soft hair was held in place with many metal pins of copper, tipped with tiny precious stones.

Next to her sat Arsinoe, her face set in permanent disdain, beside the now-empty chair of Auletes. The pharaoh and the queen's chairs were flanked by Ptolemy Neos on one side and Ptolemy Claudius on the other, the tallest, most handsome, and eldest of the sons, ever-present, and focussed on their little brother receiving the rituals of their priests. Next to him sat Berenice, then Kleopatra, and finally, Ptolemy Theos.

The priests intoned passages from ancient texts and presented Auletes with equally ancient scrolls from which he read passages aloud before the audience. Kleopatra reflected on how relieved she was that these ceremonies weren't held for the women of the royal family. If she had to sit through one for each of her sisters, she would surely be whipped for falling asleep many times. She gently sighed in relief at the thought that this would be the last one unless Safiya gave birth to at least one boy, in which case, the next name day would be nine years from now and manageable.

Then she felt the nudge of a wet nose and glanced down to see Heba lightly sniffing her hand. Finding no treats, the giant beast lay her patterned body down lazily between the chairs, resting her head next to the small wooden bowl of drinking water that the servants kept full for the cat. Without dropping her gaze, Berenice softly lowered her hand to run it affectionately along Heba's fur, calmly stroking the animal, who welcomed the gesture, rubbing her head against her hand. Kleopatra's heart sank for her sister, who had been given Heba's brother by the general Ankhmakis upon his return from a western raid. The beasts apparently ran wild there and regularly tore apart villagers, but the general's men had killed a mother cat, and the two cubs, still too young to be on their own, had been brought to the princesses as gifts. Kleopatra recalled the delight in her sister's eyes as she hugged the spotted cub. "He shall be called Berenike, the one who brings victory," she'd declared.

Father had killed Berenike in a fit of rage. Kleopatra had been six when she had run through the hallways on little legs still wobbly and with knees slightly too big for her, soft feet slapping against the cool marble of the palace floors, giggling, with her brother Claudius in pursuit, playing the monster, his teeth bared and claws outstretched.

Sure of her escape from the beastly pursuit, Kleopatra had suddenly felt her feet slip beneath her, and she had fallen, her small body sliding across the marble, eventually coming to a stop. Her face still filled with the thrill of the chase, she had looked back toward her brother, whose own face had frozen in shock, his handsome, dark features and tall, strong body turned suddenly stone-like. She'd noticed her legs and her hands felt wet, and looking down, saw that the floor seemed to be painted red. How odd, she had thought, that paint would be so sticky, and the air would taste like metal.

She had pushed on her little arms, attempting to stand, only to fall forward once more and land on her stomach. Confused, she had turned her head to the side to find Mother lying on the ground; it seemed she had also slipped in the red paint, and Kleopatra giggled at their misfortune. But when her mother hadn't giggled then, or come to pick her up as she usually did, a strange feeling of uncertainty rested upon her like a mist. She'd pushed herself up a little, the red paint dripping from the side of her cheek, to crawl toward her mother, and as shouting sounded somewhere far within the palace, she had noticed that her mother was staring at her, not blinking, lying beautifully in her white tunic, ruined by the paint.

"Momou?"

Before she could begin her crawl to her mother, large hands had gripped her tightly under her arms and hoisted her from the sticky floor, one hand cradling the back of her head. She had hugged her brother's large frame as he carried her away down the hall, his breathing loud, sounding as if he were in pain. She had stared at the paint on the floor as she was carried away, watching Berenike walk quietly toward the pool of red and sniff it curiously. Before they could reach the corner, a dozen soldiers appeared, headed by her father, moving with the speed of chariot horses, their sandals echoing loudly through the corridors; then Claudius had carried her around the corner, and the scene was gone.

Claudius's rapid breathing had been all she could hear on that unusually still evening until a scream had pierced the silence, sending a shiver through her little body.

The sound had been so agonizing she was sure she was dreaming. Claudius had let out a groan as the guttural screams of their father echoed off the marble and Claudius pushed open a heavy wooden door, clasping the little princess close to his chest. He'd stood before the princes Theos and Auletes, both in bed, clutching hands and staring with wide, uncertain eyes at their brother. Claudius had spoken then, calmly and low. "Theos, fetch your washing bowl. Auletes, bring the sponges. Quickly now, men."

Theos had leapt from the bed to retrieve the large bowl, but Auletes remained on the bed, his wide eyes fixed on the blood that covered their little sister. Theos began pouring water from the table urns into the bowl as Claudius set Kleopatra down on her feet and started removing her clothes. "It's cold," Theos said.

Claudius had forced a smile at the little prince. "That's okay; here, take your sister's hand." As he had lifted her into the bowl, she had begun to cry.

◆

THEOS LOVED HIS LITTLE SISTER MAYBE MORE THAN ANY of his other siblings. He took Kleopatra's hand and talked to her, occasionally glancing at Claudius, who meticulously ran the sponge over her naked body, washing off the blood with an expression that Theos didn't seem to understand.

Theos ran to his bed and took a toy from the pillow—an old carved wooden horse—and brought it to the girl. "Look. Look here. What is this?"

Kleopatra focussed on the horse. Her face began to relax as he moved the toy in front of her, and Claudius moved to wash her legs.

Theos held the horse close to her. He pressed down on a small lever below the tail of the horse, and a compartment in its belly opened. The girl seemed transfixed by the contraption and happily dunked it in the red water, splashing a little.

Auletes began to cry quietly on the bed. Claudius stood, took a length of folded linen from the shelf beside him, and handed it to Theos, then moved to crouch in front of Auletes to comfort him.

Kleopatra looked up from the wooden horse at Theos, her brown eyes innocent. He noticed she was shivering and bent down to pull her up, holding her under her arms, his body hardly bigger than hers, as they were both lean, scrawny children. Theos helped her out of the bowl and wrapped the white linen around her, which was quickly soaked, an orange hue seeping through the cloth.

Theos stared a moment, knowing in his strangely aching belly that, after tonight, something would be different forever. He glanced to Claudius, and Claudius met his gaze, confirming that something in their world was very, very wrong.

Theos pulled the cloth tighter around the girl, who was still clutching the toy. He rubbed the fabric over the rest of her body, then took it from her. "Would you like to wear my favourite green tunic that mother likes?" She nodded and followed him to the small room where the princes' garments hung from the walls.

Theos tugged down the green tunic their mother had purchased for him one particularly chilly winter. It had red cord at the hems and fell longer than their other robes. "Arms up," Theos ordered, and Kleopatra's arms sprung up above her head. He slid the tunic onto her and fastened it around her tiny body, then took her by the hand and led her to the beds, where Claudius hoisted her up next to Auletes.

Servants suddenly burst through the door. Claudius flew to his feet, and his hand shot out before him, a distinct order to halt and stay silent. The women's eyes were large and full of fear as they assessed the children tucked tightly into the bed.

Theos would have that image in his memories for the rest of his life: his brother, the beloved Prince of Egypt, his hero, standing tall with his strong arm stretched out before him as if he could stop a sandstorm with the certainty in his stance. The women relaxed a little, then dispersed into the room, making themselves busy, emptying the bowl of crimson water and dimming the candles. Claudius reached for Theos and led him out of the room by the hand. Theos looked back to his sister, who peered wide-eyed at him, the blankets pulled up over her nose.

❧

THE PRIESTS' VOICES DRONED ON BLANDLY. KLEOPATRA noticed that she no longer had sensation in her right arm; she shifted her weight and felt feeling return. She stared at the empty seat where she had seen her mother sit for every day of her life until that night. Now it belonged to another woman—a good woman and a fine queen, as kind a mother to them as if they were her own children.

Kleopatra liked Safiya. She was a sweet-natured young woman with a kind smile and seemingly endless patience. She was the daughter of a modest family and youthful enough to produce many sons for Father. Safiya didn't seem as terrified of Father as most people were, herself included. Some said he was a complicated man, but truly, over the years, Kleopatra had come to the understanding that Father inflicted pain and terror on others for no reason other than that he wanted to. She did not understand the man except for the knowledge that he had loved her mother more than he had loved any of his wives or children or siblings.

After her mother had died with a knife clutched in her hand, the pharaoh had found Berenike near the body, paw prints in the blood. Although it was evident that the queen had taken her own life, in his rage and anguish, he had ripped the cat apart with the knife. Once, she had heard her servants whispering about that night. They had spoken of his heartache and said that he'd sat between the bodies of the beast and the queen, in the pool of blood, staring at the floor for two nights before servants could ease him from his place of grieving.

They had whispered of something called the "birth shadow," which they described as a cruel god who visited a mother after the birth of her child and filled her head and her heart with sadness and confusion. Berenice, through utmost heartache, had argued with Father that one beast had already died, regardless of the cat's innocence, and there was no need to murder the other out of spite and pain. He did not respond with kindness or reason, but whatever she'd whispered to him when she took his hand in hers and knelt at his feet had crumbled his resolve, something Kleopatra had never seen before and never seen since. And so, Heba had lived, and Berenice harboured much affection for the cat while taking a large red and blue exotic bird as her own pet, which squawked terribly in a shrill pitch, unsavoury to the ears.

As the hall erupted with deafening cheers, strangely, her memories remained with images of Berenice's tear-stained face as she stroked the fur of her still cat before he was carried away by servants on a flat board to be buried. She had cried and slept in Kleopatra's bed for many nights as they found solace in each other's broken hearts.

11

Entombing their mother still seemed like a dream. Her sarcophagus, elaborately inlaid with gold and emeralds the colour of her eyes, had glinted in the sun as it was carried by Egypteian warriors to the great pyramid tomb of their family. She had been followed into the darkness of the monument by ten servants to serve her in the afterlife.

A gentle hand rested on Kleopatra's arm then, and she snapped her eyes to her sister, who nodded across the room. Realising the ceremony was over, she stood and bowed to her little brother, Auletes, who stood proudly next to his father, donning the sceptre of their grandfather and the spear of Ra, brought from the sacred temple to welcome a royal prince into manhood. The crowd clapped their hands and waved ribbons of silk in the air as the royal family stood stoic and emotionless, as they were expected to at any royal ceremony. "*To show emotion is to show weakness,*" her father had said.

Finally, the ceremony was over. Auletes was allowed to sit, and as he sank into the chair beside Arsinoe, he seemed thankful for the chance to rest. The musicians were signalled to begin playing, and the members of the crowd took turns kneeling before Auletes, pressing two fingers to their foreheads and then to their hearts. They began conversations as some moved toward the banquet hall, and some moved before the pharaoh to offer their congratulations, the pharaoh making no attempt to hide his boredom as he yawned and beckoned for wine.

Most of the royal family had disappeared already, and Berenice was engaged in conversation with Claudius about matters that thankfully did not concern Kleopatra, when Theos turned to her. "Do you think we can eat now?" he asked, sounding as if he might devour the next servant who walked close enough.

"If we don't, I think the vultures will descend, and we'll have to fight for scraps."

"I'd like to see you fight for figs, little Dorcas."

She grinned at him. She thought for a moment that, if each member of her family was assigned an animal of Egypte, and she was best suited to the gentle and timid gazelle, then Arsinoe would surely be a hyena. She ripped her mind from the memory of watching a pack of hyenas rip apart a small gazelle, tearing the flesh from its bones as it spasmed, not yet having the chance to die before they had eaten its hind legs. The scene had stayed with her for many years, as had the sound of Arsinoe's chilling laugh as she watched the carnage. But that gazelle was with the gods now, and the present was a time for sweet figs!

Kleopatra looked into the crowd, searching the faces for the one she wouldn't start the feast without.

Theos followed her gaze. "Where is Akela?"

"I'm not sure; I thought she would find us before we moved to the banquet."

"Perhaps she's assaulting the kitchen maids to be sure there are enough figs to sate your obsession with them. Which sounds quite in character now that I think on it." Theos sounded bored, and Kleopatra knew he was eager to get to the banquet and enjoy the celebrations. He had met a certain lord's daughter days earlier, and when he had heard she would be attending the ceremony with her mother and father, he had disappeared to his room and been seen by servants lifting heavy buckets filled with rocks up and down the kitchen steps. How very like her brother to desire to impress a girl and not understand that his status could acquire him any girl in the kingdom, Kleopatra thought. She reflected on the gentleness and thoughtful spirit of her favourite brother until her gaze settled on a familiar face in the crowd. "There she is!"

Akela was a pretty girl, only slightly taller than Kleopatra, with skinny arms and wavy, dark-brown hair held back from her face by a band of green, embroidered leather. She bounded toward them, expertly navigating the moving crowd, pushing through people, then disappearing from sight for several moments before reappearing closer to where Kleopatra sat with Theos, her face consumed by her wide smile and her deep-brown, almond-shaped eyes wide and alight with excitement. She reached them swiftly, panting a little. "Come! Before that stampede gets to the honey cakes!"

Theos and Kleopatra grinned widely and sprang from their chairs, the three of them dashing down the steps behind the thrones and disappearing behind a long beige curtain, feeling their way along the wall, the loud chatter on the other side of the curtain lively and joyous. They slipped through a thin wooden door at the end of the curtain to spill quickly into a room with many tables and clusters of candles where servants were putting the finishing touches to the garnishes on large platters of fruits and vegetables. Theos snatched a handful of nuts from a bowl as they shuffled through the room, spilling most of them on the floor, laughing as they reached another door and gleefully charged through it to arrive behind tall chairs at the head of many long tables. The tables stretched the length of the hall and were laden with platters of cut, honeyed meats, colourful fruits, nuts and dried berries, bowls of marinated olives with mounds of spices for seasoning, chalices of wine and ale, corked bottles of fresh goats' milk, and jugs filled with fruit nectar. Amongst the larger platters were whole goats and pigs and fowl, roasted and stuffed with spiced breads and dates. Kleopatra's eyes narrowed as she spotted a large bowl of honeyed figs, and without a word, moved to swoop it up. The room was filled with noblemen and guests of importance who swarmed around like locusts, food and wine goblets in hand, talking loudly, some already enjoying the loosening qualities of the wine. Father favoured strong wine and refused to water it when the shipments arrived from Kretos across the sea.

Akela and Theos took seats beside Kleopatra and began to pile their plates high from the platters in front of them. Theos turned silently to hand Kleopatra a goblet below the table, out of sight of the crowd; Kleopatra sniffed the liquid and grinned as she swallowed large gulps of the wine, then handed it to Akela, who drained the cup. Giggling and happy-hearted, they began the best part of the festivities.

The pharaoh arrived, with servants close behind, helping a pregnant Safiya waddle to her place with him at the head of the table. Kleopatra looked up and smiled at Safiya, who grinned back and nodded to her. Her belly was swollen and round, and she looked exhausted, the lack of stamina evident in the bones of her face. She requested water and fruit nectar and ate only some vegetables and dried apricots. The pharaoh sat stern-faced and quietly sipped deeply from a goblet. He looked tired, and Kleopatra realised she could not recall a time when her father had smiled. The thought was fleeting but somehow unsettling.

The older royal children slowly emerged and mingled amongst the crowd, fulfilling their royal duties as ambassadors of the kingdom. Claudius was heavily immersed in conversation with a fierce-looking man wearing full armour, his belly wrestling with his scabbard belt, which clearly needed to be loosened a notch. They were talking loudly at each other, shouting brutishly but both smiling, so Claudius's business seemed to be going well. Berenice nodded politely as an older man, whom Kleopatra recognised from their royal council, spoke animatedly at her, brandishing his goblet in all directions, Berenice's eyes flicking toward the wine he was spilling on the tunic of the women next to them. Kleopatra grinned to herself and swept her eyes across the room to spot

Neos with a familiar scowl creasing his brow, leaning against a far archway, holding a goblet which he then drained and dropped to the floor. He turned and disappeared. *A sad thing,* she thought, *to be so angry all the time.*

As she chewed on a fig and scanned the room, her eyes came to rest on Arsinoe, sitting by Isis, next to Safiya. Suddenly, at the sight of her sister, she no longer desired the taste of her favourite fruit. Arsinoe sat still as stone, a goblet raised to her lips, her deep-set eyes boring into Kleopatra from across the room. Arsinoe swallowed her wine and put down the goblet, flicking her eyes away to the conversation Isis was having with a very boring-looking man whose hair seemed to be clinging desperately to his head.

On Arsinoe's shoulder sat a foul creature of utter evil. Kleopatra and several of the family despised this sneaky and ill-willed demon, a monkey from a merchant who traded in the marketplace and had acquired it from an exotic land in the west where a lot of the slaves came from. The beast's beady eyes spotted a fruit of interest, and with sickening swiftness, it scampered across the long table and retrieved the plantain, ripping it open and devouring it, dropping pieces on the table then defecating next to the plate of a seated guest before snatching a whole loaf of bread and bringing it to Arsinoe, who tore off pieces with her hands to dip in the bowl of Greek olive oil before her.

"Do you think she has fleas from the beast?" Akela breathed to Kleopatra.

"If not from the beast, then from the servant boy she drags around with her to carry the creature," she replied, and they giggled, attracting Arsinoe's gaze, now cold and malicious.

✦

THE NIGHT WAS MERRY—AS MERRY AS A TYRANT'S lavish celebration could be while his people starved to death a mere palm tree away. Safiya, the pharaoh's wife, had retired early from the feast and had needed to be carried back to her room on a cushioned litter by her servants. Akela looked at the pharaoh, whose demeanour suggested at this moment that he wished *he* were heavy with child in order to escape the boredom of such an event. She was sure he was also grateful that Auletes was the last son to be celebrated into manhood.

Such a stern man, Akela thought. Although she had known him since she could walk, he still commanded such fear in her chest, as he did for all who stood before him. He rarely spoke without reason and wasted few words on those who did not serve his will or his mood. The palace servants had said he was well-loved by the people, but Akela, being the troublesome wonderer that she was, had pondered if they understood love and fear to be one and the same, as there had been several slave revolts in Memphis and on the lower mainland that had been met only with force and violence. Her father rarely spoke of the pharaoh, Ptolemy XII Auletes, whom he served as the commanding general of the great army of Egypt, but then, her father rarely spoke much at all, his most common utterance being a stifled grunt when leaning on his right leg, where a relentless ache from a spear wound several years ago still haunted him.

The pharaoh held her father, General Ankhmakis, in the highest regard. In fact, Akela believed that their sovereign trusted her father more than any other in his kingdom. Ankhmakis was a stiff man, broad-shouldered and muscular. He rarely smiled, but when he did, it softened the sun-weathered skin of his cheeks and somehow brightened his light-hazel eyes. She enjoyed watching his gaze make guilty men uncomfortable and truly tremble at the sight of her father when he stood in full armour, his head held high and proud, adorned by the greying beard of a wise man, the poised calmness of his stance silently filling the men around him with confidence.

She often wondered, when staring into her father's eyes, if he truly felt the courage that he embodied. She had never known him to be scared or dishonourable, and he was renowned for loyalty to his pharaoh. All of Egypt knew the general's name, and many in the ranks of the army fought fiercely in battle like gods, with hearts full of hope to receive his blessings. Akela knew, as he had told her on occasion, that she was his whole heart, and that he loved her more than the owl loved the night.

He had taken her by the hand one cool night to the terrace of their apartment within the palace and extinguished all the candles so that they stood in darkness save for the light of the thin moon. As her vision adjusted, she noticed a set of glowing eyes peering back at her from several paces away, among the branches of a tall tree that reached the height of the terrace. The shape and colour of the bird were hard to discern, but by its beauty and majesty, she knew herself to be in the presence of an owl. Her father had spoken low and gently of the grace of such creatures, who seemed to know more than the living things around them. She had seen few owls since then; she suspected they had secret, ancient business under the cover of darkness.

Ankhmakis had been sent west to suppress several riots and rebellions from the slaves, erecting monuments ordered by the pharaoh but also assessing the rumours of military assembling in the foreign lands to the west. Akela hardly worried for her father as he had never lost a battle and he always returned to her, riding through the city upon his ebony-coloured horse, Appollodon, a gift from a southern tribe who wore fabric around their heads and robes that dragged across the sand. He had helped them settle a short dispute with a neighbouring tribe, and they had thanked him with the colossal animal. Akela knew he would return to her before the season's end but feared the way the ache in his leg deepened with each battle and new creases appeared on his brows from enduring the violence that must take a toll on his spirit—a spirit, Akela thought, already weighed down heavily by grief.

Many guests in the hall had departed or taken their seats to continue their conversations when Kleopatra turned to Akela and Theos and said, "Let us go; the torches are to be lit!"

She took Akela's hand, and they began their dash through the halls towards the highest terrace in the palace, moving slowly from the weight of the feast in their bellies. They ascended the stone stairs that seemed to climb almost to the gods and came to a wide balcony scattered with chairs and furs and low tables bearing jugs of wine and bowls of grapes. Neos lounged casually in the far corner in light conversation with a man dressed in a short greyish tunic, their sandals kicked off to their sides. Isis turned to the three children as they came to a halt, catching their breath in the balmy evening air.

"They haven't started yet; a slave knocked over a bowl of the dust." She rolled her eyes and went to pour herself some wine. The three approached the balcony to lean on the cool stone that overlooked the vastness of the kingdom. The dark desert spanned miles in all directions, save to the north, where the placid ocean rippled in the dim moonlight. Firelight and the glow of torches glittered across the land from houses, the busy night markets, and the many temples that faced the palace, their great statues holding urns alight with coal that burned through the night. It was a spectacular sight. The bustling city, a flurry of traders and slaves and military, seemed never to rest. The land of

Egypte itself seemed to be alive with the busyness of life among the scattered palm trees, the busy port along the great winding river, and the many crop fields to the east.

Below the terrace, Akela could see the vast length of stone that paved the entrance to the enormous palace, where several metal dishes the size of bathing bowls had been mounted, lining the north-facing edge of the stone foundations. They were blazing with fire, and servants, who resembled beetles far down below them, scurried feverishly around a cluster of urns and pots. The ceremonial fires were a symbol of honour to the royal family, and Akela—one of a select few royal companions, servants, and warriors who were permitted anywhere inside the palace—had the great privilege of witnessing the ritual.

Suddenly, a horn sounded, echoing mournfully across the land before them. Servants ascended the short ladders beside each large dish and threw handfuls of sand-like powder into the fires. The flames surged upwards in unison, flaring violently in the colours of peacock feathers, roaring as they reached for the land of the gods. The servants continued to feed the flames with the powder, and the fires burned brighter and higher, blue as the brightest sky.

There were no cheers, as there rarely were in Egypteian culture, but the delighted exclamations of children were heard from somewhere in the darkness before the palace as the magnificent sight competed with the stars for beauty. As the flames began to fade back to their orange hue and shrank back to the confines of the dishes, Kleopatra yawned. The night seemed to be drawing to a close.

Theos strolled over to Claudius, Berenice, and Neos, who lounged together in the corner of the terrace watching the flames glow, and Kleopatra turned to Akela with a sleepy smile. "I wonder what makes it blue."

"It is sand blessed by the gods," Akela said with certainty.

"Maybe that's why the sky is blue, if their sand is that colour?" Kleopatra mused.

"You are much too clever for the gods to fool!" Akela said with a grin. Kleopatra giggled.

Akela took her by the hand, and they made their way to Kleopatra's bedchamber, where they pulled back the linen of her large feather-stuffed bed and wrapped themselves up, facing each other, their heads resting on the embroidered silk pillows. Their tired young eyes were drooping, and their contented bellies were warm with the delicious feast. The entire bed moved slightly as Heba landed on top of the covers and settled between the girls. Akela reached down to stroke the beast's ears.

"How do you suppose babies breathe inside the belly?" asked Akela through a yawn.

"Maybe they don't breathe. Safiya said that might be why they sometimes struggle—because they've been holding their breath for so long."

"I couldn't hold my breath for that long. I would die."

"I suppose we all held our breath for that long, because we were born, weren't we?"

"You weren't. Didn't your father say you were brought by a hag in the night to curse his days?" Akela giggled.

Grinning back at her, Kleopatra replied, "He did. She was toothless and pox- ridden, and he only kept me because I could be married to an ally and be made use of. He was very angry that day."

Akela laughed. "When does his anger sleep?"

"Certainly not while any of his children breathe."

"Do not worry. At least you did not crawl out of his piss pot like a demon, as he told Neos when he fell from his horse."

They grinned as their eyes closed, and the night faded to the sound of Heba's contented breathing.

ROMA

THE APPIAN WAY

— II —

The monotonous tapping of metal pegs into wood echoed as soldiers hauled nails and lengths of pine and cedar along the great basalt-paved path of the Appian Way, surrounded by serene countryside. The sunlight trickling through the tall cypress and weeping sycamores, swaying gently in the breeze coming down from Rome in the north, bathed the momentous road and the crucified slaves that lined it as far as the eye could see in liquid gold.

Decimus stood at the edge of the road, watching the scene before him. It had been a long thirteen days for the remaining legions of General Crassus's army, felling trees and crafting a cross for each dead slave, including the children, purchasing the metal pegs from the surrounding cities, digging the grounding holes, and mounting the defeated rebels at the roadside.

Some bodies were beginning to ripen in the hot sun, and Decimus was tired, his armour digging into his sides and his sword shoulder aching constantly. Tall and dark-featured, with a strong jaw and wide shoulders, he was considered a young warrior but had fought in many more wars than the small legion of soldiers he commanded. He was proud to be a soldier of Mother Rome, a Centurion, and most thought him older than his years. Perhaps the mistake was made because of his constant composed frown or his skill in strategy and foresight. Whatever the reason for his soldiers' respect, he did not relish the position as most did.

He turned to look toward the valley below the road. Peasant settlements and small, well-travelled roads created patterns among fields where goats, sheep, oxen, and mules grazed peacefully—a welcome sight when the last three years had been nothing but death and decimation. He never seemed to experience the sense of victory as others did, the cheering and drinking and revelling in spoils after a battle was won. Instead, he could not help but sink under the weight of the colossal waste of life. A curious thing, he thought, for someone so skilled at killing.

His mind wandered again to his aching shoulder, and he turned back to his sword brother, Servilius, who lay sprawled on the shaded grass, shaggy-haired, enormous, and dirty. He sat beside his comrade.

"What will you do first when you get back?" Servilius asked.

The giant young warrior sat up, his large body propped up awkwardly in his restricting armour. He yanked at the neckpiece and growled. "Remove my armour and lie upon my feather bed," Decimus said with a yawn.

"You always were the most boring one. The smart ones usually are. You should strive to be more like me."

"Then who would keep you out of trouble?" Decimus saw Servilius' blue eyes narrow with the challenge of the jest.

"Aye, it is an asset to have such a philosopher as a sword brother, but therein lies the hindrance, also. Thinking before running into battle can open the mind to reason, and has there proved to be any reasoning in our career of war?"

Decimus stared at his friend, taken by surprise. In their many years fighting together, Servilius had barely had an intelligent word to say. In fact, it was a rare occasion when he made more than a grunt or a fart. He was a simple man. Decimus envied him. How much less for the mind to endure if life were simple?

Servilius was an excellent fighter, never beaten. He lived for battle, and truly, watching him cut down the enemy was a sight to appreciate. He had size and skill but was also gifted with the speed of a man half his weight. He was also a loyal friend and reliable sword brother, and Decimus could ask for no better man with whom to walk this life of carnage and glory.

"I thought I was the philosopher, Servilius?" Decimus said with a raised eyebrow.

Servilius relaxed, looking smug. "Smart ones don't impress the women. They like the handsome warriors, and so, I am a handsome warrior. That is most likely why they do not like *you*, my friend. The ugly ones do get the rough of the lot. Perhaps adopt some charm?"

"I suspect they like your gold more than they like your personality."

Decimus's insult fell on deaf ears. "I'm going to try to find that fat, big-titted whore I had that time we got into the brawl with Dominus and his idiot posse."

"That time *you* got *us* into that brawl," Decimus corrected half-heartedly.

"The details don't matter! We won, and you took that fine golden belt from the brute. He was too fat for it anyway. I reckon she'd remember me," Servilius said with a proud puff of his chest. "Squealed like a giddy child, she did."

"Are you sure she wasn't squealing at your face?"

"Due to position, she couldn't see my face at the time." He winked at Decimus and gave a toothy grin. "Wine, a hot meal, and some gambling. Yes, that's what awaits me if we ever leave this stinking cow field."

They sat in silence for a moment.

"I wish for rest. For peace," Decimus finally said blankly, then stood again and walked to look down the road, setting his eyes on an approaching rider, whose gold helm glinted brightly in the sun, its white plume dancing in the breeze as he rode tall and magnificent upon a white steed. "The commander approaches."

Servilius lay down again with a groan. "Maybe he's come to tell us we can have the slave girls."

"I doubt it."

"So do I."

⚜

JULIUS NO LONGER SURVEYED THE PROGRESS OF THE slaves' crucifixion; he had endured the sight and the smell of festering bodies from the road's beginning in Capua. He kept his gaze ahead, admiring the beauty of his country. With the slight breeze in his favour, the smell of death eluded him.

The Third Servile Wars were finally over. The revolt led by the slave Spartacus had been crushed by himself and his mentor, General Crassus, but just as the victory was won, General Pompey the Great had swept in with his army and claimed the victory had been secured by the arrival of his reinforcements. Julius was still fuming at the gall of the man. *His name should be Pompey the Pompous*, he thought. He did not trust the man but could not fault him if his motivations were purely ambitious, for he himself had done much to further his own success and would make the same decisions if he were to face them again.

At twenty-eight, Julius was a seasoned warrior, a decorated commander, and a celebrated symbol of Rome's glory and vitality, yet in quiet moments such as these, when he did not stand before his massive legions or before deafening crowds of Rome's cheering people, he felt just as much the weak, poverty-stricken child that had miraculously become the prodigy of General Crassus of Imperial Rome.

The memory of that child disgusted him. He had defeated the largest rebel force Rome had ever seen, and now every one of their bodies—6,572 in all—would be nailed to a cross, soon to stretch the length of the great Appian Way. Now all who travelled this road would heed the warning, and all who heard of the sight would abandon their daring desire for liberation before hope could even be born in their hearts.

The three years of fighting had come to a glorious end, and his armies could return home to be celebrated and bask in the praises of all. Julius enjoyed his home in the capital but dreaded the thought of returning to his wife, Pompeia; though striking in appearance, she had a penchant for wine and parties and a volatile nature that made her lack a wife's proper obedience.

Julius thought he would have rather married a goat for all the use his so-called wife had been. She had not given him any sons. Not that family in the matter of succession was a tradition, for Rome was mother to all, and all were family, unlike the barbarians he had defeated on all sides of Italia. Among the proud Greeks, the savage Assyrians, and the lumbering Gauls, succession was of their blood regardless of the actual intelligence and talent in strategy and politics that it took to propel a people into a great empire. But he believed he ought to have a child, a boy he could teach the art of the sword and the game of outwitting an enemy either on the battlefield or in the Senate.

He had spent much time at war and rarely found himself in the company of Pompeia for sex, but he would have mind-numbing meetings with the Senate when he returned and would have an excuse to avoid her. Surely, he could soon devise another enemy that he must leave Rome to conquer.

War was simple; marriage was not. His heart tightened in his breast as the memory of a woman's laugh filled his mind. His first marriage, to Cornelia, had been blissful. They were young and in what (at that age) they had assumed was love. She was beautiful, the tight curls of her long golden hair framing her round face, where her smile lit up her eyes. She was kind and gentle, the source of serenity in his early years of warfare when the screams of men would haunt his nights. She had just been confirmed pregnant with their child when plague had struck the capital, brought into the city on trading carts peddling livestock and grains. The disease had spread fast, many had died, and somehow, sweet Cornelia had succumbed to the poxy illness. The touch of Cornelia's hand would calm him, and he cherished those simpler times, but he found no such solace in Pompeia, only dishonesty and malice in her dark, beady eyes.

His daydreams of the distant past ceased when he saw the centurion Decimus standing on the road ahead of him. Julius liked the man, though his quiet nature seemed to unnerve many other soldiers and commanders; the stocky, seasoned soldier had proved himself a good fighting man and reliable with a small charge of men.

As Julius approached, his beast snorted loudly, no doubt in as much discomfort from the smell of rotting flesh under the heat of the day as the rest of them. "Ho, Decimus, how goes the task?" Julius asked.

A man relaxing next to Decimus laughed, and Julius's attention was drawn to him. "Do my words amuse you, soldier?"

The man sat up with effort. "Everything amuses me."

"You will address your Caesar formally, or you will lose your head, peasant!" spat Julius, and as though suddenly realising the severity of his disrespect, the man clambered to his feet and bowed.

"I apologise, Caesar. My regard was too familiar for the company."

"What is your name, soldier?"

"Servilius, my Caesar." Servilius straightened from his bow to face Julius.

"Ah, yes, I remember the face. I will now not forget the name." Julius turned once more to Decimus. "You have done well, Decimus. Your name has been spoken to General Crassus by many commanders; you will be decorated for your dedicated service. The regiments are marching north to Rome; once your charge here is completed, you will bring my men home, where they will be celebrated for their victories."

"Aye, Caesar, it will be done," answered Decimus with a bow of his head.

Julius dug his heels into his mount, and the beast took off at a run, its powerful legs thundering across the basalt road.

DECIMUS TURNED AND SHOT SERVILIUS A HARDENED glare, but Servilius merely shrugged and lay back down on the grass, complaining of the hunger in his belly before drifting off to sleep within minutes, his unpleasant snores joining the tapping of nails into wood.

Decimus sighed, once more digging calloused fingers into his shoulder in an attempt to ease the aching. Somehow, the commander's words of encouragement had not lifted his spirit. He dreaded the return to Rome. Although he relished time away from war, he was good at killing, fast and precise with a blade, and strong and fearless. For Decimus, relaxing was uncomfortable.

It had crossed his mind to join a sea crew during crusades and earn coin while keeping his mind and body busy, but fighting the pirates that swarmed the Mediterranean didn't much appeal to him. He was a sturdy land fighter and had no stomach for the sea or head for nautical warfare.

He recalled the first pirates he had encountered on his first campaign with Julius, in some godforsaken land he could barely remember now, where the primitive folk were weak and easily conquered. They had been victorious, and the legions sent back to Rome, but Julius had handpicked twenty men, all young faces unmarked by war—Decimus and Servilius among them—to accompany him on one last endeavour before returning home. Julius had been abducted by daring pirates many months before, and they had demanded twenty gold rings for his ransom, not knowing who it was that they had captured.

Laughing at their low request, Julius upped the ransom himself by forty gold rings and sent word to his army to pay the ransom and retrieve him. For several weeks, Julius had joined in the pirates' games and recited his political speeches for the outlaw crew, having them laughing at his stories, insults, and threats of punishment once his ransom was paid and he was returned to his troops. He·ate, slept, drank, danced, and jested with the filthy sea rats until his regiment had arrived to retrieve him. Then he'd bidden them farewell, stating that when he returned, he would hang them all for their crime.

Decimus and Servilius had accompanied Julius as part of his twenty men. The pirates had embraced him joyously. Then he had ordered his men to arrest them and build a wooden cross for each man.

Decimus recalled the strange interaction between Julius and the pirate leader, who was a rat-faced, greasy-haired, scrawny little man with a poisonous glint in his eye. The pirates had stood along the docks as a crowd gathered, their hands bound, uneasy panic on some of their faces and hardened defiance on others.

"Surely, you do not mean to kill us. We two are friends! We have sailed the seas, shared wine, and gutted our share of dolphin shaggers." The leader was beginning to look worried. "You've played a fine trick on us, sea dog. Your talk of capture was in humour and so doesn't hold you to your word. Remove this rope, and we'll be off with a new tale. Aye, it is a fine day to sail."

Julius had stepped close to the rat-faced pirate and spoke casually. "I am nothing if I do not keep my word, my friend. I will, however, do you the kindness of killing you before you are nailed to the wood as I am told the sensation is most unpleasant, and with that ugly face of yours, I imagine you have suffered enough unpleasantness for one lifetime."

Terror had swept over the faces of the doomed outlaws as they realised their impending fate. The men began to beg and plead, promising gold or service, but Julius had simply drawn his sword with graceful speed and dashed the blade through the pirate leader's throat. Retracting the blade, he'd then moved to the next. As his soldiers held the prisoners, Caesar had ended every life himself. Blood had gushed from the wounds of each man, their lives spurting and pumping out of them and spilling over the dock into the green ocean. He'd then had them crucified.

Decimus shivered at the memory of how his Caesar had greeted the pirates with warm embraces and friendly jests, then slew them and mounted them upon crucifixes lining the bay, a message to other pirates who frequented the docks. He could have had his men execute the sea scum, yet he took each life himself.

⚜

VALERIA DARED NOT LOOK BACK OR LET GO OF HER SMALL son's hand as she dragged him onward. They had fled into the night and through the rains until finally she could run no longer and had come to a stop on the outskirts of a small village. Her throat burned, her legs were numb, and her skin was like ice to the touch. It was only when she at long last gave in to the limitations of her body that she let the glimmer of safety creep into her mind.

She let go of her son's freezing hand and stumbled to dry-retch on the ground, propping herself up with her arms because her legs were shaking too violently to steady her. She turned to look at her son, who had sunk to the ground, chest heaving, wide-eyed in the half-darkness, his teeth chattering uncontrollably and a look of sheer fear in his innocent eyes. She crawled to him and pulled him closer to her, burying her face in his soft damp curls and inhaling his scent to give her strength. Her resolve renewed, she mustered her still-shaking legs to stand tall, her muscles screaming as they worked to steady her.

"We must keep going," she said, still trying to catch her breath. She took the child's hand to pull him to his feet, but he only slumped against her.

"I can't run anymore, Momma." The boy began to cry, his exhaustion overcoming him.

"Come now, Vitus, the son of Spartacus does not cry," Valeria said sternly, but he looked up at her with eyes that had seen more terror than a child should ever have to, and she knew his heart was breaking, just as hers was. "We mustn't stop, my love; it isn't safe." She hoisted him to her breast, and he clung to her tightly as she took off at a run once more.

🌱

THE SEARING PAIN IN HER LEGS WOKE VALERIA, AND AS she opened her eyes, she took in her surroundings. They had rested where they had fallen, huddled at the base of a sycamore tree, whose leaning branches and hanging foliage had somewhat sheltered them from the rain. Vitus stirred beneath her arm, which she eased from around him to stand, leaving him sleeping.

There were spectacular mountains to the south, with high ridges and snow-capped peaks; behind those mountains sat angry Vesuvius, watching over all of southern Roma, and she knew the mountains cut across the land straight to the sea, where a boat had been promised to wait for them until noon of the tenth day. It was early morning now on that tenth day; their journey had been long and perilous, and many days had been lost hiding from the swarms of soldiers who hunted them relentlessly.

Glancing around to assure herself they were undetected, she approached a small ridge of grassy rocks, from which she could see the terracotta rooftops of houses. Keeping low to the ground, she peeked over the ridge at the settlement below. The quaint fishing village's streets were quiet, but the marina bustled with trade. She could see merchants selling stews and bread and fruits, and her belly growled painfully.

She recognised the stretch of land that jutted out into the marina and believed the village was called Varcaturo. Her throat tightened as she realised their destination was still a morning's journey away. If they were going to make it to their sea passage, they needed to hurry. Surveying the scene more carefully, she saw what she needed. She looked back at her sleeping boy nervously, then slipped off the ridge and down into the village.

When she returned, she found Vitus awake and crying quietly at the base of the tree. Running to him, she comforted the boy. She presented a bundle of clothing with a small, hardened loaf of bread and a single pear and kissed his forehead, fear still in her heart. She stripped off her battered, torn dress and pulled on the new dress. Pale yellow, it reached the ground, enough to hide her dirty and bleeding feet.

"Papa said we didn't have any coins for clothes," said Vitus through a mouthful of bread.

Valeria stared at him. "When did you hear your father say that?" she asked sternly.

"I don't know." He averted his gaze.

"Well, we're just borrowing these ones for today. Arms up." He raised his arms, and she slipped a clean shirt down over his belly, then wiped both their faces with her damp, discarded dress.

"Did we borrow breakfast too?"

"Stop asking such silly questions, Vitus!" she snapped, and the boy fell silent. "I'm sorry, my love, but we cannot rest yet; the sun is rising fast, and we have farther to go to find our ship with the big sails that will take us on that adventure we talked about. You will be Vitus, prince of the seas, remember?" She pulled him to his feet. They stuffed the rest of their rations into the small cowhide bag that she slung over her shoulder, then she took the boy's hand and led him carefully around the ridge and down into the village.

They made directly for the marina, as it would be faster to travel around the busy marketplace than through it, and once clear of the docks, the road south to Cuma was straight and wide. She looked down at Vitus. "No one must suspect us; don't speak and don't touch anything. We must be quick and clever, yes?"

The boy nodded solemnly up at her, and clutching his hand, she led him onward, weaving through the crowd of colourfully dressed noble folk and merchants loading and unloading cargo at the docks. She glimpsed a town well and pulled Vitus to it. She retrieved the water skin from the bag at her hip and filled it from the bucket resting on the well ledge. She held it to his lips, and he drank deeply until he had had enough. She sipped sparingly, filled the skin once more, then took his hand, and they continued down the wharf.

She tensed as she saw three Roman soldiers talking quietly ahead of her; she glanced to her left to confirm that the marketplace was too populated for them to move quickly, and behind the soldiers, a short distance down the dock, was the road they must reach. She glanced at Vitus; then they both flicked their eyes to the ground, and she led the child closer to the soldiers, her heart hammering as she kept her head low, expecting a sword held to her throat at any moment.

One soldier looked up as they passed, and she felt his gaze sweep her breasts and her waist; dreading his advance, she pulled Vitus closer as a group of loud and smiling whores swept past them and approached the soldiers enthusiastically.

Finally, Valeria took a breath and hurried toward the road. It would take two hours at a fast pace to reach Cuma.

As they neared the exit of the road, the sight before them was truly beautiful. The bay glistened in the mid-morning sun, and lively music drifted across the town, no doubt in celebration of Rome's victory against the rebel slaves and their leader, Spartacus. She pushed all thoughts of her husband aside and looked to the marina on the far side of the port. They were losing the day, and they still had to find the right vessel: cypress-hulled boat with a green sail (her husband had said). Tmesios would be waiting for them.

Suddenly, with hope in her heart and fear at her back, she tightened her grip on Vitus and made haste for the marina. Along the docks, there were more soldiers, but her determination outweighed her fear, and she pressed on, smiling down at Vitus as a noblewoman with nothing to fear would on such a fine day of glory for Rome. She forced her face into sweet composure as she glanced casually over the vessels, searching for a green sail. There was one dark green and one light green, so she made for the first, Vitus's little hand tight in her grip.

Suddenly, a shadow stepped in front of her, and she held onto her feigned sweetness for dear life.

"It is a fine day for Rome, my lady. Have you rejoiced?" The tall, burly brute led with his chest first, his extra weight fighting against the armour of a Roman foot soldier, strapped over a faded white tunic. His face was weathered beyond his age and his teeth generously spaced; he had dark, unfeeling eyes, and one hand rested proudly on the sword pommel at his side.

"I have, sir. It is a fine day indeed." Her heart began to pound.

"I have lodgings two streets from here; we can rejoice together." His smile was far from as alluring as he seemed to believe, and his dangerous eyes swept over her breasts and then her hips.

"I suspect we rejoice in different ways; I must be on my way with my son."

She made to continue, but the man stepped in her path once more, his body close enough for her to smell the wine on his breath and the sweat beneath his tunic. There was a small dagger sheathed at his waist. She knew where to insert it into his throat for the wound to be fatal, and with the drink, his reflexes would be hindered, but she would only have a small window to make a dash for escape, and she still did not know which vessel was there to take them to freedom.

"Do you know who I am?" he asked, his voice cold.

"You are a soldier of Rome."

"Aye. I nailed those filthy godforsaken goat shaggers to the crosses myself, and they squealed like little pigs. I've saved you from their plague of horror. You ought to be grateful for my protection."

The threat in his voice was not subtle, and Valeria struggled against the fury within her to remain calm. "I am grateful for all that the great mother Rome does for her people."

"Then what better way to show your gratitude than to ride the warrior who killed Spartacus?"

"You killed Spartacus?" she whispered, feeling bile rise in her throat and her son's hand tighten in hers.

A soldier seated nearby at a tavern stool yelled out, "You didn't kill Spartacus, you lying cock stain!" The men around him laughed and drank from their cups as the soldier before her jeered angrily at them.

"What is your name, woman? And where are you going with your boy?" he growled, his patience wearing thin, and she panicked, searching for a vague answer, but none came to her.

"My darling! Over here!" They turned to see a lean man in a sea-battered tunic, with sun-bleached curls falling to his shoulders and the skin of his tanned face stretched tight, clambering over the side of his vessel toward them. He strode up and clapped the soldier on his shoulder.

"Ah, Septivus, I hear you fought well, my friend. Truly, you bring such pride to Rome. We are lucky to have such talent with a blade defending us." He turned to Valeria. "My love, are you ready? We must sail. My son looks tired, woman. What have you done to him? Get aboard, and let's be gone."

"Yes, husband." Valeria dropped her gaze to the ground in obedience and pulled Vitus to climb aboard the boat with the light-green sail.

"This is your wife?" Septivus asked with irritation.

"Aye, she's a beauty, is she not?" Tmesios said proudly, with a beaming grin.

"A little plain for my tastes, and skinny."

"More for me then," Tmesios said with a laugh. "I will see you next season, lad."

He turned and strode toward his boat, untied the mooring rope, and pushed the vessel from the dock with his foot before jumping aboard and busying himself with the sail.

ψ

HIS PASSENGERS SAT QUIETLY AT THE BOW, HUDDLED together against the sea breeze, as Tmesios guided the boat slowly out of the bay and around the cove. His heart ached for them; in these last few years, and especially the days previous to this one, they had suffered greatly and endured much terror. Looking at the boy was like looking at his father, and Tmesios put his thoughts to the journey ahead; it would be long and would require his diligence and wit. The wind was fair and favourable today. He lashed the tiller in place, and they sailed south with ease.

He approached his two passengers. The boy seemed to be asleep on the bow bench, a battered piece of fabric over his body, and his mother stood to greet Tmesios. Without a word, they embraced tightly; he held the trembling woman in his arms, and finally, her tears came. She was thinner and frailer than the last time he'd seen her, and the bones in her face pushed against the sunken flesh of her cheeks. Her dress hung from her frame. He shared in her grief until she stepped back from him.

"Thank you, Tmesios. We are truly in your debt."

"You are in no man's debt, Valeria. We are all in debt to your husband." He sighed, and there was sincerity in his rough voice as he said, "My lady, I urge you to avert your eyes. The coast is not a sight for a woman."

She turned toward the coast to see the small crosses lining the southern marina, corpses nailed to them, black birds circling above. Tears rolled down her cheeks, and her hand flew to cover her mouth. She was too far to see their faces, but Tmesios knew she would have spoken to those poor souls, broken bread with them, mended their tunics, helped their wives tend to their babes, and affixed flimsy armour of tree bark and clay to them before they ran into a battle they could not win.

"I will look upon them with pride so they will never be forgotten." Her voice trembled. "He has fallen, hasn't he?" she whispered, her question almost lost on the sea breeze.

"There was no escape, but his spirit will rest knowing that you and your son are alive and that he stood for those without a voice. No man will forget his name in this life or the next."

Vitus gently touched his mother's arm.

"I have food and blankets for you both," Tmesios went on. "You can rest below deck. I am sure you are very tired. It is not a large space, but it is sheltered from the wind and sun. It will be a long journey to the port of Idomenae."

He turned back toward the stern with one last glance at the corpses on display, and with a heavy heart, spoke under his breath. "Rest well, my brothers. You are free now."

GREECE

THE LAST SPARTAN

— III —

A rattling breath escaped the lips of the young girl who lay on the warship's heaving deck in a small pool of congealed blood. The first thing she registered as her senses returned was unbearable pain in her shoulder. She attempted to shift position, but a bolt of searing lightning shot from her shoulder down to her fingertips, legs, and back. She let out a sharp gasp, now alarmingly aware that something was very wrong.

Her wrists, she realised, were bound with rope that felt embedded into her flesh, her arms stretched up and over her head. Steeling herself, she gathered one foot under her and pushed back. Every part of her body flamed with agony, but the relief she felt as the rope slackened was heavenly.

Her dry, cracked lips were cut and swollen. She tried to lick them, hoping for relief from the stinging of the delicate split skin, but her mouth was dry. Every inhalation was of hot salty air. One eye felt bruised and puffy; she wondered if she'd be able to open it. For now, it seemed too much work to even try.

She lay on her back, the sun scorching her, gulls crying in the sky above her. The wood of the ship creaked lazily. From somewhere else on deck came the low voices of men. Below her, another man's muffled voice kept in rhythm with the beat of a drum.

She heard the quiet sobs of women nearby, and in an instant, every memory of the events leading to this moment flooded her mind, and her heart sank with the weight of loss.

Her name was Chrysanthe. She was sixteen years old. Her mother's throat had been slashed before her, and she had been ripped away from the dying woman, refusing to let go of her hand until forced to do so. The noble children who had hidden with her had been either cloven almost in two or carried away screaming by warriors with horrifying lust in their eyes. Buildings had burned, turning the sky red with fire, sacred temples had toppled into ruin, and women had screamed as they were raped.

Her father had been bound, and several warriors had taken turns peeling flesh from his body. As she was hauled away, he'd screamed only the name "*Kallisto!*" into the red night air. The last thing she remembered was seeing her home ablaze with flames that seemed to reach Olympus, the crops and villages scorched all along the coast, and the moment time stood still as a terror-stricken white mare galloped away from the desolated city, her chest red with raw flesh and her hide aflame beneath her powering legs.

The girl could not bear to relive the horrors any longer; instead, she recalled the image of her father dying, holding it in her mind, savouring his agonising screams like the sweetest flute chorus. She felt comfort and only wished she had been allowed to witness the torture further, perhaps even to take part.

In one last effort, she'd heaved herself backward again and felt shade touch her face. Finally, she eased open her eyes, pain from the swollen one throbbing through her skull. Her blurry vision focussed. As her eyes adjusted to the harsh daylight, she took in her surroundings.

She was tied to an iron ring that was bolted to the wooden railing of the ship. With enormous effort, she managed to pull herself to a seated position. The agony this engendered almost made her pass out again. Panting, she looked down at her body and saw that her legs were covered with cuts and several large purple and green bruises. Blood that she guessed must have come from her blocked nose stained the front of her simple ankle-length dress, which had been ripped in many places, torn up to her thighs, and burned at the hem. Spasms of pain that shot from her ribs through her back and chest forced her to take shallow breaths, and there was a deep ache in her belly, which must have taken a blow of great force.

She gritted her teeth and lifted her head to face her fate. The deck of the warship was a violent scene. Three Spartan slave girls were tied at the bottom of the mast, their faces smudged with ash. One was slim, with large, sunken eyes that only emphasised the horror in her stare. The second one's shredded dress barely covered her body, and a large amount of blood had dried on only one side of her face; her eyes were downcast. The third girl sat slumped on her side, unconscious. Her cropped, dark hair looked strange, and Chrysanthe realised it had been burned. A raw wound was visible on the girl's scalp, festering in the hot sun.

Several large men moved about the deck, performing their duties, some in simple chitons and others in bronze armour over deep-blue knee-length tunics, hands resting on the swords at their hips and eyes scanning the horizon in every direction. Though no one spoke to her, she felt the hunger in their glances, their eyes sweeping over her bare, beaten thighs.

Some men lay on the deck, sleeping in the shade of the monstrous black sail, which bore the symbol of a red snake wrapped around an infant on a shield of blue, the frightful reptile bulging in the strong northern wind. She recalled seeing the sigil once before, many years ago, in the bay of Helos. She couldn't remember the name of the king whose emblem it was, but she knew he ruled a kingdom in southern Attica.

In recent years, the alliances of Sparta had shifted rapidly. From the merciless decimation of her homeland, she knew this king was no friend of hers, and her life would either end soon at the hands of her captors, or what awaited her would make death seem a blissful luxury. There were only a few reasons to keep captives, and none were kind.

In the middle of the deck, upon the smears of blood, was a large pile of gold urns, elaborately decorated armour, bejewelled swords, heavy wooden chests, and other trinkets and trophies from her father's collection. A severed hand lay a little way from the secured pile, and as heavy footsteps approached her, a man's sandal-clad foot kicked the hand with gusto into the legs of another man nearby, looping rope, who laughed deeply from his belly and sent the hand tumbling back. The man with sandals—enormous, wide-bodied, and square-faced, with two raised scars trailing from his lip up past his callous eyes—booted the lifeless hand into her legs. As she recoiled, it bounced toward the man with the rope, who kicked it overboard.

A pair of feet in brown leather sandals stepped before her. Defiance surged in her, only to be overcome by another wave of pain through her body that caused her to squeeze her eyes shut and wish only for death to be quick.

But no mortal blow came. Instead, the man squatted beside her, dropping a waterskin at his feet, and reached out a large, dirty hand to lift her face. Ready to meet another man who would take something from her that was not his to take, she opened her eyes to see the huge ugly brute before her, strapped into impressive bronze armour, a short cape the same colour as his blue tunic draped down his back. His tanned face was dirty, the two scars pronounced beneath the filth. He had dark, heavyset eyes, a long, straight nose, and an unnerving grin on his jutting jaw.

"Welcome aboard, Princess. You'll heal in time." He smiled deviously, and she ripped her face from his hand. "Spartans always need the most discipline. Perhaps the gall can be bred out of them. You will learn, and if not, we will just have to beat the pride from you."

Despite the heat of the scorching sun, the coldness in his stare sent a chill along her damaged skin. Her fear of death having left her, she spat in his face and held his gaze, the pride of her people's defiance boring into him. Soldiers who stood near enough to witness the exchange fell silent, and strangely, so did the gulls. *Gulls,* she thought. *The ship is close to land.* Perhaps she would have a dignified burial rather than her body being simply tossed into the sea.

The man shot out a hand and slapped her with immense force. Her head bounced back and slammed against the wooden railing, and all things fell away into darkness.

☙

SEVERAL DAYS HAD PASSED SINCE SPARTA HAD BEEN razed to the ground, Chrysanthe had been bound and thrown onto the warship, and they had sailed away from the bay of Helos to begin this treacherous sea voyage. The days melted into one long fever dream of pain and misery, the heat of the sun, and the chill of the night.

Chrysanthe had faded in and out of consciousness as her wounds both woke her and drained her of spirit, but through her haze of dream-like memories, she had learned the large man was King Athanasios, so perhaps it was not a life of slavery that awaited her but another type of servitude.

This day, when she woke, she found they had changed course, and the black sail cast a shadow across her, providing her with some relief from the sun. Pulling herself carefully to sit, she wondered if the sun god, Apollo, ever looked down at the mortals suffering below as he chased his sister, Artemis, across the sky in his chariot that pulled the sun. Surely, having pursued her for so many years, he would become bored with the chase, look down to see the atrocities of man, and send a plague or famine to wipe evil from the lands of the innocents who worshipped him. *"Where are your gods now?"* a voice whispered in her mind.

She pulled herself to stand. Still unbalanced on her legs, she leaned her weight against the wooden railing and looked out over the great ocean, whose rolling motion made her stomach clench feebly. Her long, flaming-red hair whipped around her shoulders in the harsh wind coming off the sea, but she remained steadfast, taking in the sight before her.

The war galley was speeding toward land, mountains rising in the distance beyond the beach. Given the direction they had been sailing over the past few days, and with vast green sea in all other directions, she discerned from her studies that this must be the isle of Kretos. As dread seeped into her bones, she also recalled from her studies that the Kretan king had earned a reputation as a ferocious tyrant for his revival of human sacrifice, honouring the long-standing tradition of worshipping Thanatos, the god of death, with temples, rituals, offerings, and the sacrifice of any babies born on the eve of the winter solstice. She had heard her father speak of the kingdom of Kretos, and it was never a joyous subject.

Looking around at the hardened faces of the men working along the decks, she saw no warmth or benevolence in the soldiers and crewmen, only brutes who had raped her friends and murdered their children. Hatred rose in her throat like bile. She vowed to herself that, if she survived long enough for her wounds to heal and her strength to return, she would avenge as many of her people as Ares would allow before her own inevitable death.

Past the stern of the ship were a fleet of around twenty-six dark-painted war galleys, following in formation and flying the colours of their flagship, a revolting sight for any man with a shred of honour. A shadow descended across the galley as the mountains of Kretos loomed, blocking out the sun.

Chrysanthe could see a busy port, crammed with shacks and buildings and cargo being feverishly cleared by merchants making way for the army to disembark. As they approached the docks, she looked back to sea to notice that only their ship would be berthing. The remaining galleys had ceased their rowing and bobbed monotonously on the water outside the harbour. She surmised this would be a brief stop and not their final destination.

The timing of the oarsmen was exceptional and well-rehearsed; the hull of the ship nudged the dock gently as rope was thrown down to waiting men, who began to secure the mighty vessel.

⚘

IN THE COMPANY OF ATHANASIOS AND A PARTY OF OFFIcers and soldiers, Chrysanthe was led off the ship and onto the dock, which was crowded with sailors hauling large nets of fish from their boats and men stacking crates of fowl and spices and linens. The buildings were poorly constructed and simple in design. There wasn't a smile in sight on the faces of the villagers, who regarded Chrysanthe with no attempt to hide their hatred, indifference, disgust, and lust.

Athanasios appeared at her side and gazed at the trail ahead of them, which wove through the forest toward a large castle of grey stone and dark mortar. On the verge of a high cliff, it loomed over the town below, emanating an ominous wretchedness, its many oddly shaped towers casting long shadows down the hillside. There was a strange eeriness to the bay, and for a moment, she was sure she heard a faint song on the breeze, but a dip in the cliff face funnelled the wind up and back out to sea, carrying with it the elusive hymn.

"I do wish she'd die soon. Corinna has no redeeming qualities, and this formality is an exceptional bore," Athanasios said casually. Chrysanthe, keeping her chin high and feeling her jaw clench at his proximity, gave no reaction, which did not seem to bother the brute king. She knew kings, and she was no coward in such a presence.

A two-horse chariot emerged from the sparse, thirsty forest and halted before them. The short, stocky driver jumped off. "Get on." Athanasios said to Chrysanthe as he strode toward the chariot and took the reins.

She didn't move. This chariot might be here to take her to her death, but in her gut, she knew it was something worse.

Athanasios glanced at his two generals, who stood nearby, waiting for orders like obedient hounds, their faces harsh and detached. Quickly, forceful fingers seized her arms. The two generals brought her forward, lifted her in, then climbed aboard themselves. Athanasios cracked the reins, and the chariot began to trundle roughly up the rocky path toward the castle. The journey up the gravel road was sickeningly rough, and Chrysanthe vomited beside some dead shrubbery when they reached the top.

Now, standing in the odd-shaped megaron, grateful for refuge from the heat and salt air, Chrysanthe watched Athanasios furiously pacing as they waited silently before an empty stone chair embellished with bronze and mounted on a small platform. She felt a rumble in her belly and winced as a careless breath shot pain through her chest. Steadying herself, she thought how dull and dark the room was. The curtains were closed, and dust had collected on the sparse tapestries.

"The bitch disrespects her own brother. I refuse to be marooned here before sundown having to spend the night in the spinster's ruined hovel," Athanasios spat at his generals, who did not flinch.

Suddenly, a door flew open in the far corner and a tall, scarily thin woman moved toward them with lack of haste. "Brother King!"

"Dearest sister Corinna, it has been too long." Athanasios's voice dripped with forced charm as the woman stretched out her hand. He kissed it.

"Please do forgive me for my lateness. I was simply having too much fun." She smiled, but the sight was ghastly.

"It is forgotten."

"What have you brought me?" Corinna's violet eyes, like pools of venom, focussed on Chrysanthe, whom she assessed with spider-like regard. "This is the younger child?" There was disappointment in her tone, and Chrysanthe struggled to remain calm.

"It is."

"What is your name, little harlot?" The question dripped from the old crone's dry lips like poison into blood.

Chrysanthe felt her jaw tighten and her breathing quicken. She gave no answer but met the queen's gaze with defiance. Athanasios struck her from the side, his large hand thundering into her cheekbone, but somehow, she remained standing and breathed through the pain now throbbing behind her eyes to stare malevolently at the old woman again. Athanasios struck her once more, and this time, knocked from her feet; she fell to the ground and was wrenched upright again by both generals.

"I pray that the stubbornness of the Spartans will die with you!" Athanasios roared, raising his hand again, this time in a fist.

Chrysanthe recoiled in anticipation, but the hag raised a hand to stop him. "Everyone breaks, brother; it is only that not everyone's poison is the same." The queen inspected Chrysanthe, whose nose dripped blood down her lip. "You look just like her," she said with a vileness of which Chrysanthe could not discern the source, then looked back to Athanasios.

"The king?" she asked.

"Flayed, as you asked, sister," Athanasios answered flatly.

"The whore?"

"Slain, as you asked, sister."

"Mm." An invisible weight seemed to lift from the frail body of the woman, and she turned to sit on her throne, now with a strange, giddy air of girlish satisfaction. Chrysanthe could feel the seething rage from Athanasios as he watched his sister address him formally. "What of Sparta?"

"Desolated." He was clearly struggling to suppress his anger.

"And what will you do with the slut?" Corinna gave a sharp nod toward Chrysanthe.

"A gift for our brother. Demosthenes expressed his dispirit at having missed the victory over Sparta, and so I have brought him a Spartan wife to ride out his dejection."

The corners of the old woman's thin lips curled up into a hideous smile as Chrysanthe's heart sank through her stomach once more. "He will surely be pleased. Well done, brother."

The queen gestured a hand toward a servant standing against the wall, holding a carved wooden box, but the servant did not see her gesture. Without missing a beat, the hag queen grabbed her water goblet from the small table beside her and hurled it at the man; it missed him, and the clang echoed loudly in the small room. The frightened servant hurried forward to Athanasios and bowed low, presenting the box. Athanasios opened it to reveal a small, gold, jewel-encrusted goblet upon a pillow.

"To what do I owe such a gift?"

"You have granted me a great favour, and I pay tribute to your victory," his sister replied with no real gratitude in her voice. Having seen the greed in his eyes, Chrysanthe knew that this cruel king would have invaded Sparta on his own accord, but his sister's vendetta was the perfect excuse. "Though surely without my soldiers or gold, the outcome would have proved different."

The insult was a salted dagger to an already angry wound. Chrysanthe saw Athanasios bite his tongue. "I thank you, Corinna." He bowed half-heartedly and all but tossed the box to one of his generals. "Now, I must speak with Potimus before I return to my own kingdom."

"He is in the west hall." The queen gestured offhandedly toward a door. "But I will allow you to speak with him once he's finished his duties for today." She stared unblinkingly, still and stone-like, as Athanasios wrestled within himself to refrain from unleashing his rage at the spurn. Slowly, a malignant smile formed on the face of the pale-skinned queen. "Does it frustrate you that you cannot fuck the defiance from me, brother?"

The moment was odd, and Chrysanthe sensed another conversation was being had to which she was not privy. Athanasios stormed from the room with both his generals.

The queen, her eyes trained on Chrysanthe, rose from her throne and glided toward the princess, stopping only inches from her face. The wine on her rancid breath was pungent, and her personal smell was of rust and a medicinal paste whose unpleasant odour the girl had smelled before when she had cut herself playing with her father's sword.

"Come, child, I will entertain you while the bastards compare their cocks." She turned and walked toward the door, but Chrysanthe did not move. The queen stopped, turned, and gave her a cold glare. "Athanasios decrees I won't be killing you today, but I am not a patient woman."

Chrysanthe looked around the dull room and decided that if the crone somehow killed her on this venture, it would be a kindness, and so she followed.

The halls were long and cold beneath Chrysanthe's burned bare feet, and grateful for the soothing relief, she walked quietly. The queen, her long, dark, close-fitted dress dragging behind her, paused at a small table and poured herself a cup of wine, which she drained while the two stood in silence. Then she filled it again and continued to saunter stiffly toward the staircase.

They began their ascent up into one of the many strange towers. The stench of rot became overwhelming as they climbed, and faint echoes of moans bounced from the mouldy stone walls. The staircase had become dark, but Chrysanthe saw light ahead, and when they reached the last stone stair, catching her breath, she stepped into the small round room behind Corinna, who spun suddenly to face her, a faint smile playing on her lips.

"It is only natural that you should meet your new, loving family." The delight in her eyes was tinged with a strange, lewd thrill. She stepped aside to reveal a caged area behind her, where a skeletal creature lay despondent amidst a gruesome scene of true horror. Chrysanthe's hand flew to cover her mouth, and taking shallow breaths to avoid the reek, she stood frozen in shock as she struggled to comprehend the sight before her.

"This is your queen mother-to-be. Do not take offence if she is shy in her old age," Corinna said with an air of whimsy, perusing a vast table of tools and instruments.

As if compelled, Chrysanthe stepped closer to the cage to see the extent of the creature's suffering. Small cuts and burn marks were scattered across the skeleton-with-skin that lay in the muck of its own waste. There were several dirty human teeth scattered in the filth of the cage. The fingernails and toenails of the poor soul had been removed. Both ears were missing, as well as one eye, the gaping hole staring into the abyss from the sun-exposed peeling skin of the weathered face. In addition to fresh wounds, there were old wounds from what Chrysanthe knew were many years of abuse.

The creature that she now understood to be Corinna's mother shuddered absentmindedly, staring wide-eyed at nothing with her mouth agape, revealing rotting, toothless gums. There was a clamp on the living corpse's lower leg, two wooden lengths on either side with several holes in each, which seemed to have been crafted so that sharpened wooden pegs—like the ones that lay scattered on the ground amongst the muck—could be inserted through the holes in the planks on each side and hammered in to crush the bone, leaving the leg thin and distorted, with the knee swollen and several sharp, shattered bones protruding, to which medicinal herb paste had been administered.

Feeling faint and determined not to lose consciousness in the company of the mutilated queen and her insane daughter, Chrysanthe stepped toward the small window and sipped the fresh air as best she could, narrowly avoiding inhaling a fly that was coming in to feast on the rot.

Preservation instincts took over, and she engaged the unhinged queen, feeling that if she was talking, she was safe. No matter if that were true or not, it was all she had to cling to.

"What is the horn for?" Chrysanthe asked, keeping her voice calm and unaffected as she focussed on the large brass cone that opened like a flower toward the small window. Corinna spun around, her face alight with excitement.

"It is my executioner's design," she said gleefully, clearly delighted at the interest shown in her complex and unique torture methods. "The mouth is placed on the pipe, and when hot pokers are applied to the body, the screams echo out across the villages below. The shape of the horn allows the sound to carry a song, a beautiful melody for the people." She reached out and touched the brass horn affectionately.

Chrysanthe jumped as two rats scooted from one corner of the cage into clumps of straw near the body. She had seen starvation, torture, and sleep deprivation before, but the extent of this cruelty was astonishing. The woman's long matted hair had been ripped out in patches, leaving open wounds festering on the scalp. It seemed the barbaric depravity could not get any worse until Chrysanthe noticed the tight and discoloured skin between the victim's thighs and realised that her genitals had been burned. The skin was contorted, and the lower belly protruded. The princess felt bile surge up her throat, but she forced it back down. To appear weak in front of such savagery would bring dishonour to Sparta, and she wiped the sweat forming on her brow.

"What was her crime?" she managed to ask. Corinna giggled and gestured to two poorly built chairs by a small table upon which were jugs of wine and cups. Chrysanthe found herself obeying as if her body had taken over her free will out of shock. Corinna poured and handed her a cup of wine, fixed one for herself, and then the two sat. There was nowhere to look but at the unfortunate, cadaverous soul twitching in the muck with its one cloudy, unseeing eye.

"I take something for every day she took something from me." The queen's tone was suddenly frightening in the stuffy room, where the scent of death and decay hung thick in the air. Chrysanthe noticed her words were slightly slurred.

"What did she take?" The question had slipped out before she could stop it.

Corinna regarded her with repugnance, her demeanour insect-like. "I think you Spartans mistake not knowing your place for bravery."

Pride surged in the young princess, and with her jaw tight and back straight, she turned to confront the hag-faced queen, whose black eyes glittered with malice. But then Corinna's expression changed to one of vacant spite, and draining her cup, she turned her eyes on the filthy prisoner. "The woman who birthed me was a wretch of a harpy—a slut with many lovers. Once, when I was a child, she thought she saw the braggart she was fucking look at me. It sent her into frenzy. She took an iron poker from the fire and inserted it into me so that no man could ever have me, nor I ever have a man."

The princess realised that her mouth was agape with a level of shock she hadn't known possible.

The queen snapped from her distant memory to look at Chrysanthe. "But what use would I have for a man?" There was genuine disgust on her face. "So, I sealed the bitch's cunt, and I visit her in her . . . royal chambers." Corinna gestured to the walls of the room, then held her cup to the young princess, who left with no choice, touched it to hers.

Corinna waited for Chrysanthe to sip, but she could smell that the wine was not watered down and so could conceal an array of poisons. She felt fear warm her belly. She knew that if she did not drink, it would cause offence, and the mad queen would kill her regardless, or worse, toss her into the cage.

"It is not poisoned," Corinna said. "I do wish you dead—you are correct about that—but there is no sense in wasting energy on you when Demos will do that for me. He and I share the same affinity for the unsavoury. I suppose becoming our parents is inevitable." Corinna stared into her cup with a soft smile, lost in a memory.

A surge of defiance arched in Chrysanthe. Every threat made on her life, every unwanted advance, every moment of abuse, every time she had been used as a pawn in the plans of men who believed they owned her like an animal flashed through her mind, and rage warmed her skin. She raised the rim to her lips, locked eyes with Corinna, and drained the wine to its end. She paused, awaiting the sensation of her organs shuddering and failing in an excruciating death that did not come.

Corinna's lip curled into a terrible smile. "Most poisons go undetected until too late, some are fast, and some wait for the opportune moment." Her eyes were wide and dark but seemingly lost in visions of her own rage.

"I know of poisons and their perils," replied Chrysanthe, trying to sound strong as her eyes watered from the decay in the room.

"As your father's daughter, I'm sure you are."

"You speak as if you knew him."

"Oh, yes, I know the sheep-shagging son of a whore. It was proposed that we wed. I was offered to the king of Sparta by my father. The pig countered the offer, saying that if he wanted ugly children, he would marry a mule." She was quiet for a moment, then closed her eyes and whispered, "I would give all my gold to have heard his squeals as his flesh was peeled from his body." She opened her eyes again and looked at Chrysanthe. "I understand you were there, child. Did he squeal like a little piggy?"

Chrysanthe nodded slowly. The delight in the sickly queen's eyes was unnerving, and the protruding bones in her emaciated frame made her eerie.

"I'm glad what my mother did to me left me unable to soil my bloodline by breeding with that swine. I'm glad he married that Thracian bitch. You will understand soon enough that the ability to bear children is a curse. The desecration of your body to give them life does not ensure their allegiance. Still, that was not my mother's motivation for her actions, and so, she will suffer as I did."

The poor, mutilated creature laying in its cage gave a sudden sharp moan. An arm reached up to grasp the air then fell back to its side.

"I am tired of your company. We will go." Corinna stood, as did Chrysanthe. Corinna seized a poker resting in the small fireplace, approached the cage, and through the metal bars, jabbed the hot iron into the prisoner's side; the creature cried out with the hoarseness of a throat deprived of relief.

Chrysanthe could not take the sight any longer. She slipped out the door and descended the dark spiral staircase as fast as she could while being careful not to slip. She guided herself with her hand against the damp wall.

The only sound in the darkness was her shallow breathing, which seemed louder to her now, matching the pounding of her heart. Her belly rumbled, and she could feel the warmth of the wine; the urge to escape the queen's company and the stench of death had stunned her, but now, here in the darkness, reality bit at her ankles like fire to her skin. Seeing light, she pushed onward, and emerging into the small, empty receiving hall, made to run across the dark stone floor, her breathing erratic and her head becoming light.

As she reached for the door, a man's voice called out, and the room around her swallowed itself into darkness.

◆

CHRYSANTHE AWOKE LYING ONCE MORE ON THE DECK OF the warship, sweating in the sun, her mind cloudy. She felt throbbing in her cheekbone and brow where she must have landed when she'd fainted. She fought through the pain in her body, wincing at the deep searing in her pelvis. Using what little strength she had left, she hauled herself to her feet.

The warship was now berthed at a different dock in a different town. How long had she been unconscious?

Just as she reached to steady herself on the railing, large, rough hands suddenly grabbed her. Men were lowering themselves and cargo over the side. The sailor who had grabbed her passed her over the railing to seamen waiting below. A set of grubby, tight hands placed Chrysanthe roughly on the dock, and in mere seconds, the man had moved on to other cargo.

Chrysanthe found herself standing next to the three girls who had been tied to the mast. The unconscious one was now awake but barely coherent, and her weight was supported by one of the others, her own frame too thin. All of them looked around with nervous and weary eyes. Chrysanthe took the hand of the girl with the ripped dress and bloodstained face, and they grouped together, finding solace in their shared nightmare. The port was teeming with activity, and the colours here were brighter but somehow no more comforting to the heart. People shouted in the markets, and donkeys screeched as they hauled enormous loads of pottery, fabrics, trinkets, bread, sacks of wheat, and livestock.

Three dirty and spent-looking slaves stood on a small platform across the market, their faces sullen. Flies lingered around the raw wounds on their wrists from their shackles. Chrysanthe turned to see a small, fat, bald man drop a large pouch into the hands of one of the military generals, who nodded in agreement.

Then suddenly, a large, ugly oaf, hunched and missing his two front teeth, snatched the joined shackled chains of the three Spartan women, and the girls began to scream, clutching one another. Chrysanthe fought to keep hold of the other girl's hand, but they were hauled in opposite directions. She realised someone was holding her back, but at that moment, she didn't care. All she knew was that she did not want to be alone in this godforsaken place, and that to lose the last living Spartans was surely to lose herself.

The sweat on her palms from the beating sun compromised her grip, and the other girl's hand slipped from her grasp, parting them forever. Chrysanthe saw the terror in the young woman's eyes and felt the helplessness bleed through her. The girl was yanked forward and struggled to stay on her feet as the oaf lumbered away into the crowd with his screaming prisoners. Their cries echoed from the flat walls of the buildings.

Chrysanthe did not scream. She felt her face was wet with tears, but she did not scream. She had decided many years ago, before she had even become a woman, that no man would hear her scream. No man would have the satisfaction of forcing a scream from the princess of Sparta and the daughter of Apollia, the lioness queen.

She thought of her mother, and at that moment, wished she could go back to her city and pick the wild swamp flowers that bloomed only during the night. Her mother would hold her above the water on her hip as she waded into the lake, and they would pick the glowing blue flowers that lit up the land as if it were the Elysian Fields themselves. She remembered the warmth of her mother's skin and the scent of her hair and the safety in her embrace, an embrace she would never know again. She stood on the dock, the pain of so much loss overwhelming her, but was quickly shuffled onto a waiting cart with the king's generals and several crates of their riches from foreign lands.

The cart trundled away from the marina and made its way up through long streets of white-walled houses, past alleys where laundry hung above children playing under the watchful eye of nearby whores. Looking back as they ascended the hill to the palace above, Chrysanthe could see across the wide bay to the port, where many small boats bobbed lightly on the sea, trailing their fishing nets behind them. There was a clear sky, but the distance was too great to see her Sparta. *Would you wish to see the smoke of your people's demise billowing into the sky?* she asked herself. No, better to stride into the unknown than remember her home ablaze and her mother slain.

The wagon creaked to a halt before an enormous, sturdy gate built into a high stone wall that stretched far in both directions. Its curve suggested it enclosed the great palace atop the highest hill. Chrysanthe was pulled from the cart by soldiers and brought to Athanasios's side. He took the lead of her shackles, and as the mighty gate opened, nudged his horse. It strode forward into the deafening cheers that erupted at the sight of the king in his battle armour on his stallion. The streets were full as the victorious war party paraded their way through the city. People screamed and cheered, showering the soldiers with rice and salt, and young women darted forward to place flower wreaths upon the heads of soldiers. City folk whistled and waved the flags of the red serpent.

A soft tomato exploded on the side of Chrysanthe's face, and some other vegetable was pelted into her arm. Shocked, she stepped closer to the horse and raised an arm to shield herself from the hurled insults, spit, and rotten food. Athanasios waved to the elated masses, which reached all the way to the heavy, iron-reinforced gates of the palace.

Once those gates had shut behind the small war party of important soldiers and palace officials, the noise became only a dull pounding in Chrysanthe's head. Her lips were cracked and her throat dry, her arms ached from the position of her shackles, and her feet were bleeding from the coarseness of the hard city road she had walked. Athanasios dismounted, and a tall, thin, blonde woman wearing an ankle-length green dress and a hardened, unfriendly expression emerged from the high paved archways of the palace entrance, greeting Athanasios with a stiff, quick embrace.

"Welcome home, husband. You were missed," said the woman.

In response, the king laughed loudly. "Today is too fine a day for lies, Charis. Let us not waste air on false pleasantries."

The woman shot a hostile glance at Chrysanthe, then turned and disappeared inside the palace. Athanasios departed promptly with most of his guard. The packhorses were unloaded and dealt with as Chrysanthe stood in the courtyard before the great, ugly, and foreboding castle, staff and soldiers ignoring her as if she were part of the stone building. At that moment, she wished she were.

A slimly built young guard approached her, clearly uncertain of his authority. "Thianis, my lady," he said, introducing himself with an awkward half-bow. "I am to show you to your apartments." His eyes were bright blue, and the kindness in him seemed out of place in such a hive of callous souls. "Please gather your effects, and we will proceed."

She stared at him, wondering at what point in his life he would stumble upon an unguarded woman and use his strength to pin her down and violate her, or at what point he would begin to take delight in the cruelty of punishing another man before ending his life. The young soldier looked uneasy at her lack of response; he drew a quiet breath and puffed his chest before reaching for the chain of her shackles and tugging timidly to pull her forward, but she stood fast, her bare and bleeding feet planted to the ground, her stance one of unhumbled pride. Her stare remained hard on him. She watched the calculations move through his mind of how to proceed when dealing with a captive princess. Clearly, the boy had a good heart, but didn't they all when they were only boys?

"Food and clothing await you in your apartments, my lady," he said nervously. Part of her desired to stare at him blankly until he revealed the true animal nature that lived within all men and expose him for what he was so that he would be confronted with the ugliness lurking in his heart, but she was tired, and the boy was no threat to her today.

"Do you not wish to bathe and change your clothing?" He looked embarrassed and averted his eyes from the tattered dress that barely concealed her modesty.

"What I wish is to unleash a hideous violence upon you and your barbarian people, but I suspect that is not a desire I will be privileged to indulge." She spoke with venom but saw pity in the soldier's expression.

"No, my lady, it is not," he replied earnestly. "I have only heard what has happened to your home and your family. Such is the nature of war, but I believe you will be happy here. The gardens are green and the crops plentiful. The palace will be a fine home for a princess."

"A fine prison for a slave."

"It may feel like a prison, but in time, I think you will see you are not a prisoner. You are a princess of Kretos now. As many who have come here before you, you are to be wed into the royal family."

He watched her nervously as she sighed. "Such is the nature of war," she whispered as if only to the breeze, then nodded.

He returned her a cheerful smile, but as he turned to guide her into the castle, she yanked the chain from his hands. He spun around, ready to apprehend her.

She straightened her back, wincing at the pain somewhere deep in her lower spine as well as the base of her skull. "If I am not a prisoner, I will not be led." She gathered the chain in her own hands and walked calmly past him into the palace.

The palace walls were various shades of grey, and each hallway the same as the next: catacombs, her tomb, cold and devoid of life or light. The soldier directed her up several staircases to an enormous wooden door deep within the palace; he then released her from her shackles as maids silently swept from the room, their eyes flicking up only briefly from the floor to see the new resident. She stepped inside and heard the boy pull the heavy door shut behind her.

The apartments were spacious but smaller than her own in Sparta, the walls dully decorated with dreary, moth-eaten tapestries made with little skill. The sparse furniture was practical: There was a small robe closet, a small table and two chairs by the large arched window, a washbasin, and a moderately sized bed adorned with several coloured pillows.

She sat on the bed and stared out of the huge window. She could see a great deal as she was high in the royal quarters: The dry fields were barren, and beyond them, the vast green sea stretched to the ends of the Earth. To the left of the brown fields, she could see bustling villages and the marina where she had arrived, and she controlled her breathing as the reality swept over her once more that death or torture would find her in this dreadful place. It was only a matter of which came first. She prayed for death.

Ripping her gaze from the view, she looked around her. The candle lamps needed replacing, and the rug was coarse beneath her maimed feet. A small symbol caught her eye, and she leaned closer to the bedpost to see *Elpizo*, the Greek word for hope, carved deep into the dark wood. She pulled her legs up to the bed, lay back, and exhaled, but with her breath, she also released her composure, and shocking her, tears began to fall silently down her face, soaking the linen beneath her. Faces of the dead swam in her mind. The scream of her mother as she tried to protect her daughter echoed within her heart alongside visions of her home burning, red flames leaping high into the starlit sky, until the extent of her injuries seared through her body, sending blinding white light behind her eyes, and exhaustion drove her to sleep.

EGYPTE

THE SECRET OF THE NILE

— IV —

Safiya sat propped up in her bed against many soft pillows, sweat forming on her brow, holding her enormous belly in her arms. Large marks had appeared on the sides of her belly as the skin had stretched with the growing babes, who felt as though they were deliberately taking their time to rest inside her. *Wise*, she thought, for once they graced the world and took their first breaths, screaming in their uncomfortable new existence as royal children, they would hardly rest again. The world was filled with danger and hardship, and royal families were known for disposing of each other when grappling for power. How odd that a thing such as power could turn a sweet soul to murder and debauchery when there were so many other simple pleasures of life to enjoy that didn't involve the killing of men or the suffering of family.

Safiya had been the youngest daughter of a Thessalian king in lands to the east of Egypte and had been sent to Egypte to marry the newly widowed pharaoh. Egypte was warmer than her home but pleasant enough. The kingdom seemed to be thriving, and the people seemed as happy and loving of their sovereign as they were in her father's kingdom.

Safiya had ventured outside of her father's palace only three times in her eighteen years there. The first time, she had seen a peasant marketplace filled with dirty-faced children and thought it strange that they looked so skinny and sullen, but her father had explained that they ate modestly to respect the gods and refrained from smiling to avoid swallowing the flies around their mouths. The second time was only to walk in the lush gardens outside the palace wall, and the third was when her caravan had departed to bring her to Egypte, where she remained content inside the palace walls. How lucky she thought the people to have such freedom to wander near and far and lie by the oasis with their camels, snacking on grapes and cheeses until the cool air of evening came.

She sighed and reached for the bell on the small table beside her, ringing it loudly. Two servant women bustled in, and Safiya requested wet cloths for her forehead and a sticky balm to be rubbed on her belly to cool her from the heat and ease the aching in her back and hips. One servant applied the balm from a clay pot while the other lifted the linen at the end of the bed and gently rubbed her swollen pink feet. She moaned in relief at both comforts. Then the door creaked open, and in raced little Kleopatra and Akela, launching themselves onto the bed and throwing their arms around her neck, giggling loudly.

"Good morning, little ones. How did you find me?"

"Where else would you be?" asked Akela.

"I might have been riding a camel or swimming in the royal baths, or I could have been chasing Arsinoe's terrible monkey from the nursery." Safiya smiled, tucking Akela's hair behind one of her ears as the girls settled on the bed on either side of her.

"You couldn't do any of that," teased Kleopatra. "You're like the snake Father found in the garden. He had eaten a gazelle whole and couldn't move for days! He couldn't even get up the hill."

"Yes, I am indeed a fat snake who can't get up the hill. I *have* eaten two gazelles, and now I have a bellyache."

Kleopatra grinned, and the girls leaned forward to rest their ears on her belly, listening intently.

"Can they hear us?" asked Akela.

"I think they're sleeping now. Perhaps they can hear you in their dreams."

Kleopatra sat up and presented a bowl to Safiya.

"We brought you some figs! Rhema said that they help mothers with the aches in their bones when they have babies growing." Slight guilt crossed her brow, and she shyly added, "There were more, but I ate them."

Safiya laughed and thanked her.

The door opened again, and Theos wandered in, holding an old-looking sword with a worn leather hilt and a dull yellow jewel embedded in the pommel. He presented the sword to Safiya. Though confused, she asked warmly, "Dearest Theos, what have you brought me?"

"It is not for you, my lady. It is for the baby prince," he said formally, with a distant look in his eyes that was strange but familiar.

"So many gifts today! Thank you, Theos, that is very thoughtful."

"The babies can't hold swords, Theos. What is he supposed to do with it?" piped Kleopatra.

"When he can hold it, he can learn to wield it. I will teach him, and then, when he's strong like Father, he will already be skilled," snapped Theos.

"But there are two babies, young Theos. What will the other learn to fight with?" Safiya asked.

"Only one is a boy, and the other won't be able to hold a sword." Theos shrugged casually, then left the bedchamber without another word.

"Why is he so grumpy?" Akela asked, rolling her eyes.

"He must have to study with Father today." Kleopatra grinned.

"You shouldn't say such things," scolded Safiya.

Then the door opened once more, and the pharaoh stepped into the room, dressed magnificently in ceremonial garments. His kohl-traced eyes snapped coldly to Akela, who immediately slid off the bed in a panic and stumbled awkwardly to stand on the floor, her head bowed. Kleopatra froze where she sat and looked up at her father, whose eyes were narrow and trained on Akela, his lips pursed tightly and his nostrils twitching with anger.

Before he could open his mouth to speak, Safiya reached over to touch Akela's arm. "Thank you for bringing me the figs I requested, child. I'm glad you got to feel the pharaoh's babes moving. You may go now."

Akela dipped her head to Safiya, then again to the pharaoh, and quickly whipped past him out of the room.

When the pharaoh spoke, his tone was cool. "The tomb ceremony will begin shortly, and I shall be gone until sundown. The babes are well?"

"They are well, my lord," Safiya said sweetly, with a smile. "You may feel them if you wish?"

"As I said, I will be back at sundown." The pharaoh turned on his heel toward the door. He then paused and looked back to Kleopatra, who felt the cold gaze of his contempt creep up and sit in her throat. "You are expected for this ceremony, child. Your absence will not be excused, and it will be the whip for you."

"Yes, my lord."

With that, he was gone. Kleopatra took a deep breath.

"Best get yourself prepared, little one," said Safiya with a sympathetic smile.

◆

KLEOPATRA SLIPPED OFF THE BED AND MADE FOR HER chamber, where Akela peeked around the sandstone wall. Kleopatra rolled her eyes, and Akela grinned. "That was close."

As they left the pharaoh's residence, they saw the other members of the royal family descend the steps of the palace and make their way to the lower city. Kleopatra turned to Akela. "See you at dinner."

"I'll see if Heba will help me catch that demon monkey." Akela grinned back.

Kleopatra skipped to catch up with the royal caravan on foot. An enormous Afrikaan man, with skin as dark as night, fell in line behind her. Attempts on the lives of the royal family had been made before, and this ceremony presented the opportunity for an arrow shaft to be loosed silently and end her life in an instant. The giant Kohlis, in his thick leather armour and with one hand on the sword at his hip, swept his ever-serious eyes around their surroundings meticulously, and occasionally would place a hand as big as Kleopatra's head on her shoulder to pause their walk, then remove it when they could continue.

She felt very safe with Kohlis there, even if he wouldn't let her eat the fruits from the market stalls or try on the jewellery from the merchants. He trusted no one, and Kleopatra wondered if he had a family of his own, and if he was capable of relaxing at all. Kohlis was her favourite of the personal guards, and she often wondered how he could stand the heat in the leather military garb of his homeland. She delighted at the prospect of learning about his people and what they were like, if she could ever get him to say more than a single word.

Her nurse, Rhema—who was old and sun-skinned, with greying eyebrows and a pain in her hip during the rainy season—had told her stories of the different kingdoms across the great green waters and beyond the sand dunes of the south. She had spoken of spices that burned the tongue in delightful ways, spike-covered fruits the size of her head, and robes of such colour and decoration that kings from all lands sought to purchase them for their wives and daughters.

Kleopatra had dreamed of travelling to these magical lands, eating exotic foods, and meeting people so different from her. She wondered if they would understand her when she spoke to them. Kohlis had not, and she thought that perhaps he did not know enough Egypteian to answer her questions.

A giant of a man, stern-faced and stone-mannered, terrifying in a fight, his strength was frightening in its speed and stamina. Father did not care much for the Afrikan warrior, who seemed to not comprehend how to bow when Father addressed him, but his usefulness outweighed his lack of understanding of the royal custom. The pharaoh had assigned the giant to his least important children, clearly not caring if the brute and those offspring were assassinated. *Odd*, she thought, not that her father saw no value in her life but that he had such little faith in such a force of a man. But then, she had observed the ego of men and found the quality boring and tedious.

Content with her protection, she walked on, aware of the sweat forming in her sandals. Glancing ahead, she noticed the slender figure of Berenice draped in a long white dress, tied at the waist with a gold rope, her hair adorned with small white flowers. She was giggling to herself and smiling at the personal guard who walked beside her. Kleopatra noticed that it was the man she had seen leaving Berenice's bedchamber. He now wore the royal guards' uniform and was carrying an upright bronze-tipped spear in one hand. Kleopatra thought he must be a very trusted guard for Berenice to have him guard her through the night.

The caravan of the royal family was now entering the largest street through the city, which led directly to the Tomb of Pharaohs. The street was lined with trading stalls selling spices, dyed fabrics, and barrels of fruits and grains. Soup simmered on the low fires of a stall to her left, where a fat old woman argued with a peddler over the quality of the bread served with the dish. To her right, a child cried in the arms of a thin and tired-looking young woman, who gestured blindly to her tables of wares without looking up to see who passed. Strings of garlic and small dried red vegetables hung from the canopies of food stalls.

Most of the people they passed looked up to stare at the royal party as they passed with their accompanying staff. Some had looks of wide-eyed curiosity, taking in the details of Kleopatra's appearance as she smiled widely and waved to them. They did not wave back. *Perhaps that is not the custom of peasants,* she thought.

One man swept his dark, wide eyes over her young body. She felt his hungry gaze sweep over her flat chest and fixate on the end of her tunic; she realised her shoulders had tensed, and her heart suddenly felt small and nervous. The enormous shadow of Kohlis, an arm's length behind her, brought relief.

Some gave looks of contempt, glances flicking up toward the party with unfeeling eyes, which confused her, and some seemed to become nervous at their presence, but one elderly woman smiled, and without a thought, Kleopatra stepped toward where she sat propped up on a wooden stool against the sand brick of the wall behind her. She smiled as Kleopatra came to stand before her, and the princess noticed that though the woman's teeth were few and brown, and her cheeks were dirty, her eyes were kind. The woman's feet were warped and bare, and she held the smaller hand of the naked child sitting in the dirt beside her, flies dancing around its head.

"Where are your sandals, old one?"

"I traded them for bread, Your Majesty." Her smile remained. "For the little one." She nodded to the filthy child at her feet.

"Oh." Kleopatra did not quite understand why the woman would trade her sandals for bread and frowned. "Can you not buy more sandals?"

"The sandals cost coins that I do not have."

Kleopatra couldn't imagine having no sandals while walking on these harsh roads. "Oh. Well, I have coins; you may have mine." She reached into the small leather pouch tied around her hips, pulled out three golden coins, and held them out to the woman, who extended her frail hand. Kleopatra slipped the coins into her grasp.

The shadow of Kohlis stepped even closer to Kleopatra, so close that she could smell the sweat of the man. She suddenly became strangely aware that the scene around her had changed and glanced around to see several peddlers and stall owners staring silently at the exchange. The old woman closed her hands gently around the coins, and with a look Kleopatra did not understand—a mixture, she thought, of relief and unsure caution—the old crone thanked her.

Wanting to leave now, she turned her back on the woman and returned to the street, her pace fast and her mind uneasy as she hurried to catch up to the royal party far ahead, with Kohlis close behind her. She did not look up for the rest of the journey, and after what seemed a whole day of walking, she halted just in time to stop herself from colliding with Berenice, who had stopped in front of her.

She looked up to see that they stood before a magnificent monument, yellow in colour and perfectly flat on each of its four sloping sides, which came to a point at its top. Berenice had explained to her once that the point looked directly into the eye of Oriasis, and it allowed him to look upon the tomb and converse with the spirits of the past pharaohs entombed within. Each stone seemed placed perfectly upon the next—a marvel to see.

Ahead of them, she saw the pharaoh and his sons, Claudius, Neos, Theos, and little Auletes, ascend the small set of stairs at the entrance of the pyramid and disappear into the darkness. Berenice turned to look down at her little sister. "Do you remember the tradition once we arrive at the centre of the tomb?"

All Kleopatra remembered was that the last time she'd walked the dark, musty labyrinth of the strange building, for the funeral of her mother years ago, she'd wished she were anywhere else. She shook her head at her sister and took her hand, gripping tight.

"We follow the stairs and the tunnels lined with torches to the largest room, where the ancient ones rest; then we kneel to them as the scriptures are read. When Sebekem has finished, we stand and light the candles, then follow Father in laying a hand on each resting one. And remember, we must do it all in silence."

Kleopatra nodded.

A young man in a plain beige tunic appeared at the entrance to the pyramid and beckoned the remaining female royals to enter. Arsinoe followed Isis up the stairs, and Berenice held Kleopatra by the hand as Kohlis and the sunlight disappeared behind them.

Suddenly, all was dark, and they stood still for a moment as their eyes adjusted. The dimly lit hallway was narrow, and its ceiling sloped inwards; it smelled like wet soil and rotting palm leaves. They stepped carefully along the damp, sandy ground, following the torches that led deeper into the maze, and after a short while, stepped into a well-lit room much bigger than Kleopatra remembered. The room expanded through many pillars and was surrounded by walls covered with elaborately coloured and intricate hieroglyphs. One scene depicted the god Ra inflicting his wrath on the sand peasants for their ignorance in the matter of ritual offerings.

Torches shed light over the many jewel-encrusted sarcophagi, made of solid stone slabs, each of which had the living likenesses of the corpse it contained carved into the stone of its lid. There was a wall of several small stone boxes stacked on top of each other—deceased royal babies were a common occurrence. There were around thirty or forty large ones by her count, and she suspected there were more, deeper in the tomb, perhaps in other grander rooms.

Her eyes fell on one sarcophagus in particular. The slender stone box was covered in emeralds, and the face of the sleeping woman depicted on the lid seemed elegant and colourless, her hands crossed on her chest and precious gems inlaid in the garment above her brow. How beautiful she looked.

It was then that Kleopatra noticed that the hand of her father gently lay on the edge of the woman's tomb. His head sank, and for a moment, she saw the sorrow of his heart in his expression. As quickly as it had appeared, the moment was gone, and he turned his cold face toward his children, then gestured to the woven rugs before an empty, lidless sarcophagus mounted in the middle of the room. The royal family took to their knees on the rug and bowed their head, and then Sebekem, the priest of the sun god, began to recite in an ancient language from a stained, browning scroll stretched out before him.

Kleopatra did not know how long they knelt on the itchy old rug before Auletes was called to stand before the empty stone box and recite Sebekem's words. Then the pharaoh stood and dipped his fingers in a blue paste in a small wooden bowl held by the priest and wiped the gritty substance across Auletes's brow. Auletes then dipped his own fingers in the mixture, and both father and son began to smear it across the edges of the stone coffin.

The ceremony was concluded by more of the beady-eyed priest's unbearable spoken nonsense; then all the royals were invited to take turns to bow before Auletes. Kleopatra was last to arrive before her little brother, who already stood taller than she. He looked focussed and serious in his royal collar, with the blue paint on his face. She bowed low to him, then stepped aside to join her siblings, who were inspecting several open sarcophagi mounted around the room. Each of their names was carved into the undecorated stone of the box that awaited them upon their own deaths.

Kleopatra glanced toward where her sarcophagus sat in the corner next to Theos's, expecting to suppress the strange feeling she had experienced when gazing upon it many years before, only to see Arsinoe, dressed in a dark-red tunic with heavy gold jewels hanging from her ears, standing beside Kleopatra's tomb and slowly and gently, almost lovingly, tracing the edges of the stone. She flicked her eyes up to meet Kleopatra's gaze with such dangerous precision and terrifying intent that a chill rippled through the youngest princess, the hair on her neck and arms rising. The malice in Arsinoe's eyes was like a cold, sticky hand closing tightly around her throat. Dizziness touched her, and feeling an odd sensation deep within her belly, she found Berenice and scampered to her side as the party moved behind the pharaoh and began their exit.

Kleopatra was glad to step into the sunlight again, but the heat hit her fiercely, its touch overwhelming. The scene before her began to blur.

MYRIA

DAUGHTERS OF MYRIA

— V —

The grass hissed as Bremusa flew through the tall blades with Euryleia only seconds behind, unrelenting in pursuit. They crossed the field with ease, vaulted a gushing stream, and landed on its far shore. There, the two young girls stood frozen on the muddy bank before a thick, dense forest.

Bremusa kept her dark-brown eyes focussed deep into the undergrowth, her breathing controlled, the shaft of an arrow notched to the string of her sturdy bow, held tightly in place for a quick release. Behind her, Euryleia clutched her side, struggling to slow her breathing in the bright sunlight of the peaceful woodlands.

Her determined companion finally released the tension in her weapon and lowered it irritably. "He's faster than Apollo's stags themselves," Euryleia breathed, impressed with the animal's speed and nimble grace.

"Yet he is as mortal as we are," Bremusa growled.

Euryleia moved to rest her chin on Bremusa's shoulder and looked up to meet a dark, angry glare. "Let him enjoy another sunset. We will meet him again," she said sweetly, without a trace of disappointment.

"And when we can no longer enjoy another sunset because our bellies have withered and our bodies failed? His escape with his life could mean our death," Bremusa snapped.

Euryleia laughed loudly. She strode past her agitated companion into the forest. "Come, Bremusa. We may be no match for a stag today, but there never was a rabbit that could escape your snare."

"I wanted stag."

BREMUSA SLICED THROUGH THE BELLIES OF SEVERAL dead rabbits, releasing the wet innards onto the ground while their flayed pelts cured in the sun on the grass of the slight hill. Euryleia lay nearby, lazily ferrying berries to her mouth from a pile on a small cloth beside her.

"It is curious to me how the squealing and blood doesn't bother you," said Euryleia.

"The meat is to feed my sisters—to feed *you*. I take the rabbit's life to sustain yours. It is always a simple choice, much like in battle: the enemy's life or yours."

"You've never been to battle," Euryleia teased as she rolled onto her side and reached out to run a hand across the rabbit pelt beside her.

"Soon, we will all fight for the glory of the Amazon nation."

"So quick to rush to carnage."

"If we were not, others would be, and they would not show mercy because we are women. Quite the opposite!" Bremusa growled harshly, and Euryleia let out a sound of frustration, rolling to lie on her back once more.

"I hate that you can always smell them before you see them." Euryleia scrunched her face in distaste, eying the rabbit corpses.

"You don't make that face when they're in Karthdia's plum stew," Bremusa replied, turning back to her task, grateful for the reprieve from such a stagnant argument.

"Because you can't taste *anything* in Karthdia's plum stew! I believe she's put all manner of creatures in there without detection. She is a mistress of Bacchus. I am sure of it."

"There's no plum stew in Thracia, so begin your adjustment."

"I won't fight," Euryleia said, her voice certain.

Bremusa looked up again. "If the western allies fall, we'll have to either run or fight. If we run, we'll head north to join the queen on the Thracian plains and battle with the Gauls against Rome, and if we fight here, we will hold the valley. In either instance, battle will be joined."

"You are suited for this world, my friend. We both know I am not," Euryleia said with a soft smile.

"That is why we train. You think you are not equipped because you have not yet applied yourself. That is why the tournaments are held; that is why we prepare for them. It is our right and our purpose to defend our tribe. You will learn further, and then you will see," Bremusa said confidently, returning to the rabbit carcass.

Euryleia turned to look out across the meadows. High ridges of rock rose from the Earth, higher than their perch on the grassy hillside, reaching up toward Olympus and forming the walls of the valley that shielded them from the gullies beyond. The meadow was lined with thick trees and tall grass, grazing grounds for forest creatures, and water flowed from somewhere in the foliage to form a vast, clear lake at the meadow's centre. The sight was one she deemed near to the descriptions of the Elysian Fields. The everlasting blanket of sunshine cast over the land rested like melted gold on the surface of the lake.

"If I could will it, I would have us stay here always, picking berries and swimming. That would be true bliss. Olympus upon Earth," Euryleia said quietly.

"I doubt the gods would allow it. They commend battling, and victors are favoured. War pleases the gods."

"Does it please Aphrodite? Or the gentle Eirene?"

"Those are lesser gods; their favour does not matter. They fear the mighty gods of war and glory," Bremusa said proudly. "War is part of life. It is our way, the way of all those before us, and will continue to be the way of our daughters."

"What a thing to be feared," Euryleia whispered.

⚘

BREMUSA FROWNED AT EURYLEIA, WHOSE EYES AND thoughts seemed lost in the bright blue of the horizon. Moments passed, and Bremusa shifted uncomfortably, knowing that wherever Euryleia had gone in her mind, she was no longer sitting here with her friend; she was seeing scenes of wonder and awe, of life and death, of women and men and the sun and the moon.

Such things Bremusa knew she herself would never see. *Could* never see. The sadness that rippled through her as she watched the strangely unreachable friend beside her on this soft hill in the heat of Myria dripped over her spirits with the weight of Prometheus's boulder. How far she could feel from one so close—close enough to touch, yet oceans lay between them.

Then, swiftly, Euryleia rose, tugged at the leather ties of her skirt, and dropped it to the grass. As she removed the rest of her clothing, made of game pelts and soft under-fabrics, Bremusa felt the uncomfortable sadness contract to a ball in her stomach and a deep warmth stir in her. Her hands still deep in the meat of her kill, her gaze swept over the thin, bare legs beside her, then past Euryleia's slight belly and over her small but beautiful breasts before reaching where her slender neck met the most delicate jawline. Bremusa ripped her eyes from Euryleia to cast her vision anywhere else; she did not care where.

In a few graceful bounds, Euryleia descended to the crystal lake below and threw herself into its depths, disappearing, leaving Bremusa completely alone in the enormous valley. Shame sat as her companion on the small hill, as the true loneliness she felt seemed brought to life by the song of the forest birds themselves.

She does not love you that way. You are stupid to think so, even more so to hold hope in your heart for her affections. Bremusa felt her throat tighten, and immediately her back stiffened; there would be no betrayal of her true desires today. The sunshine had never brought her joy; she was the daughter of Artemis, and darkness was her preference, better cover for successful ambush raids, better for travelling unseen, better for training a warrior's senses and fighting blind in the dark.

Staring into the innards of the rabbits strewn before her, she wondered if the animals experienced desire as mankind did or if, perhaps, they just rutted at random at any chance presented. The latter seemed most likely, as their young heavily populated the many burrows of the forests. That suited her. *The more meat, the better, so let them rut as they wish*, she thought.

There was a small splash and then Euryleia surfaced on the far side of the lake, the crystal water glinting in the sun. "You better get in here. I won't listen to you moan of it tonight!" Euryleia called out playfully.

Bremusa felt the heat of the day on her neck and brow, the sweat soaking her garments, and the sticky blood that bathed her hands. She stood slowly, a resistance in her gut poking at her compliance. Removing her clothes, she took her blade down to the riverbank, and as she crouched to wash her hands and the dagger clean of blood, her reflection stared back. Her legs were thicker, wider, more muscular than a girl's ought to be at the age of twelve, and her shoulders were broad like a man's. The muscles in her arms and back had begun to define the shape of her neck, the physical manifestations of her devotion to learning the craft of warring. Her hands were rough and calloused, her upper arms bulged slightly, and tight braids pulled dark hair back from her face in Amazonian tradition. In herself, she saw no beauty nor any features of an appealing nature, but in Euryleia, she saw all that Zeus had intended for womankind: the grace of Euphrosyne, the kindness of Aglaia, and the enchantment of Thalia.

Their mothers had told the young Amazon girls that fair maidens of such renown and purity were born from Aphrodite's eyelashes as they left her and fell to the Earth. To find one was to have one's destiny revealed: to walk the Earth as the protector of Aphrodite's pearls—a great honour, though it came at the cost of the protector's freedom.

Euryleia was Bremusa's heart, and so the charge had been accepted without hesitation. Bremusa had told Euryleia once that she thought her to be a pearl of the love goddess, and Euryleia had laughed loudly at the suggestion. Bremusa then withheld her thoughts and feelings for fear of further mockery amongst the tribe, but in her heart, she knew it to be true and had accepted her destiny: She would protect the one she loved most until her own dying breath.

Bremusa stood on the riverbank, water dripping off her skin into the shallows around her knees. She could not suffer a moment longer the gorgon that inhabited her reflection and was grateful to hear splashing drawing nearer. She looked up to see Euryleia, belly to the sky, cease the kicking of her legs and simply glide along the surface of the water partially submerged, her eyes closed as if sleeping blissfully. How luxurious, thought Bremusa, to enjoy each moment with ease instead of the exhausting suspended alertness of warriors. *But why should she fear? Her eyes may rest, her sleep may be deep, her belly never go without. She is protected.* The strange creature of jealousy, or wounded hope, recoiled into its dark cave. *I could never forsake my purpose: Euryleia and her greater destiny,* Bremusa resolved.

She watched the floating goddess. Her hips were slim and her frame boyish, but the curve of her neck as it flowed into the perfect bones of her shoulders made it seem as if she were cast from melted copper and then made flesh, the work of Aphrodite and her blacksmith husband, Hephaestus, forged in the throes of wedded passion. Euryleia's hair floated around her head in perfect suspension as gentle ripples lapped over her small breasts and delicate nipples, their stiffness revealing the chill of the water.

Euryleia opened her eyes and brought herself upright, pushing herself from the water and letting it cascade in rivers down her skin. She pulled her hair to one side, and as she wrung out the water, she met Bremusa's gaze with a smile. *A smile to rival that of Helen of Sparta.*

Then the peace of the valley was cut by flickering shadows across the grass like a shower of arrows, accompanied by screeches from above. In a heartbeat, Bremusa lunged at Euryleia, bringing them both down into the shallows, thrust against a fallen log decaying beautifully in the reeds. The two looked to the sky, only to relax into relief as they climbed to their feet and stood naked in the shallows, watching a breathtaking display of several hundred larks circling, diving, plummeting, and swooping in marvellous grandeur. Euryleia laughed with joy and pressed her chest against Bremusa's back, throwing her arms around her neck and resting a gentle chin on Bremusa's shoulder.

The sound of the deafening theatre was merely a whisper, for Bremusa only felt Euryleia's cold skin against hers, her stiffened nipples against her back. *If only a moment were eternal.* The dark cloud of sky creatures began to disperse toward the ridge of the valley, where they disappeared. Although her senses were heightened, and her skin felt alight against Euryleia, Bremusa knew nature's displays of such magnitude and opulence were omens. There was danger on the wind.

"You're bleeding! Are you hurt?" Euryleia fussed about Bremusa's thighs, then stopped abruptly and sighed heavily, shaking water from her skin and collapsing grumpily onto the nearby grass. Bremusa looked down, swore, then waded further into the water and began to wash herself.

"The waiting is infuriating! I have no patience for the delay," Euryleia whined.

"You are the most patient I could name," Bremusa called back.

"You have been blessed with yours. I want it now," Euryleia huffed as Bremusa waded out of the lake and came to lie naked on the grass beside her friend.

"I would hardly call it a blessing, and if it were possible, you could have mine. I have no use for it."

"But you'd make a wonderful mother!" Euryleia teased. Bremusa's irritation clearly only amused her more. "Their little feet and little toes, their fragile necks, to feed them from our bodies, and the little sounds they make," Euryleia cooed.

"And the infection and the weeks of bleeding, the incessant wailing, and more so the immobility caused by the condition. Wielding any weapon is made severely difficult, and so a pregnant warrior is useless in battle."

"Do you think of nothing else?" Euryleia moaned.

"I do." Bremusa's voice was thick. "And to conceive such a small gorgon, there is the matter of rutting with a *man*. That a sister could stomach such a repulsive thing, and complete the task, must only be credited to the warrior within an Amazon."

"Karthdia says they don't hurt us during the ceremonies. It is a time of peace. The rituals are sacred and welcomed by both parties. A man is necessary to grow a babe, and thankfully, his involvement is required for mere moments." Euryleia recited this formally and with conviction.

The tense silence between them grew, swirling with quiet pain and longing, loneliness, the absence of acceptance, and the unspoken presence of love not returned.

"You are not a warrior, Euryleia. There is great kindness in your soul," Bremusa whispered. "Artemis will bring your blood, and you will make a fine mother. You may not wield a sword or hurl a javelin, but a warrior is woken each time an Amazon becomes a mother, and you will protect your child, your pearl, just as any sister would protect another."

"As you moved to protect me moments ago?"

"Yes."

"You worry for me; this I understand. The world of men is carnage and violence, yet life springs from their groin. It has no sense to it. I am sure that there could be peace if—"

"You trust too readily!" Bremusa snapped. "I fear your sweet wits are no match for the sly cunning of a man. There will never be peace in hearts of greed, and I am to protect you from their evil."

"Because I am your pearl?" There was a sadness in Euryleia's voice. "We two are destined for different paths, adjacent or not. It may be the same road but with separate purposes. We are joined. I know this, sister, but if I am not your pearl—"

"Be silent. I am in no mood to explain myself."

"You don't—"

Bremusa hissed sharply at Euryleia, and the two fell silent. Listening intently in the absence of their voices, Bremusa heard the faint sound of a low, resounding gong echoing on the gentle wind.

"The queen?" Euryleia asked, eyes wide, as the two sat up.

"Or the victor . . . the two may not necessarily be the same." There was caution in Bremusa's voice as her demeanour changed to that of a hunting wolf, the embodiment of alert vigilance. "We must go. Dress yourself with haste, sister."

🌿

THE VALLEY WAS FAR FROM THE VILLAGE. THE DAY'S hunt was heavy around Bremusa's waist as the two darted through the forest. The forests were Myrian territory, but that did not discourage thieves or foreign intruders, and they were always cautious.

Hearing a crash behind her, Bremusa stopped and turned to see Euryleia assessing the damage of her fall. Bremusa ran back and helped her up, and they began to run again, but it wasn't long before they could endure the pace no longer.

"Perhaps we're not needed," Euryleia said hopefully, clutching her side awkwardly. "Perhaps there is no need to rush."

"And perhaps there is every need." Bremusa surveyed the dense foliage surrounding them. A scream, raw and hoarse, pierced the air and echoed oddly through the trees, anguish in the cry. The young Amazons threw themselves to the ground, and on their bellies, pulled themselves carefully through the dirt and undergrowth to the ledge of the low cliff and peered over.

Below them was a sight that stole all words from their tongues. The wide trench, which showed signs of once being a riverbed, was used to travel quickly on foot and even on horseback, through the narrow, hidden gullies that protected the Amazon territories all the way south to the Lyrnessus and all the way east to the barriers of the Tarsius ranges.

A thin, dwindling line of women stretched in each direction, and to the north, the tail end of an army was disappearing at a steady pace around the curve of the trail, leaving behind a light river of blood. Those left in their wake were scattered. Horses struggled under the weight of poorly built wagons, piled with rotting and partial bodies, vacant eyes staring up unblinking to the sky. Injured women roughly guided emaciated animals and carts along the bloodstained earth past hunched figures clutching wounded limbs or carrying barely conscious sisters. They were what was left of the Queen's army, come back from fighting along side the Celts in Gaul as they defended their home-lands from Rome.

Another agonised scream sounded through the winding ravine, shorter this time and more desperate, drawing Euryleia's and Bremusa's bewildered atten-tion to an injured woman who lay on a thin, wheeled cart that jolted sharply as the horse pulling it struggled to navigate the sharp rocks of the former river bottom. The woman cried out once more.

An armoured warrior walked back and leaned over her. They spoke quietly, and then the warrior reached to peel back the blanket covering the distressed woman to reveal the source of her anguish.

The warrior raised a hand to cover her nose and mouth. The woman's belly had been gashed so deeply that it was unable to contain her organs, and the innards spilled from her gut as her emaciated, greyish hands held in what she could. The living corpse whimpered, one leg dangling from the cart. The warrior was silent and deliberate as she stepped closer to the mumbling creature, then gracefully drew a long, thin dagger from a scabbard at her belt, slipped a hand behind the woman's head, and cradled it against her. Then with jarring but merciful violence, she drove the fine blade behind the jaw and up as far as the hilt would allow. Quickly she retracted the blade, wiped it on the stained blanket, and returned to the front of the wagon to pull the horse onward. As the wagon trundled forward once more, a thick dark river flowed silently from the girl's limp neck, spilling off the wagon, and coating the ground.

Euryleia lay frozen on the precipice above the horror, seemingly too afraid to move a muscle or take a breath. Bremusa's thoughts burned with deflation, shock, and fear. As the stragglers pushed on, clinging to whatever strand of life they still possessed, some collapsing with their last breath amongst the corpses, there was no thought of war or glory in Bremusa's mind, nor could she imagine how there ever would be again. These pitiful, defeated weaklings did not seem to be the mighty warriors from the tales they knew so well—tales consumed eagerly by the light of the cooking fires—about the horde of fierce lions that had left Myria six years earlier to roar down the southern plains and devour the plague of besieging barbarians.

No, these were no such lions. They were barely even human.

EGYPTE

THE GAZELLE AMONG SNAKES

— VI —

Kleopatra opened her eyes to see the clear blue sky spread above her, and deep within it, a circling eagle ... or perhaps, a kestrel? As her vision sharpened and she looked around, she realised she was moving and sat up to find that she was held securely in the large arms of Kohlis, his other hand holding a small canopy of fabric, casting shade across them both.

The giant man looked down as Kleopatra roused and slowly turned toward a camel walking alongside them, where Berenice sat as tall and regal as if she were a goddess visiting the world of mortals. She looked down at her little sister with a grim expression, her mind seemingly elsewhere. She held out her arms to Kohlis, who passed Kleopatra to her and settled her in the saddle. "You scared me, little gazelle," said Berenice.

Kleopatra still felt weak and let her small body relax against the safety of her sister as the rhythm of the camel's step soothed her. She noticed they appeared to be travelling alone—the others must have already returned to the palace.

The view was higher, and from here, she could see farther than before. The tops of the huts were made of layers of fabrics and dried mud, the edges of the fabrics moving gently in the breeze. The air smelled of cooking meats and barley stews, a smell so delightful that Kleopatra felt her mouth become wet at the thought of her coming noon meal.

Down a small side alley to her left, she caught a glimpse of a group of people sitting and eating from bowls. A man with no hair, perched upon a stool, strummed a lovely tune on a stringed instrument. She smiled at the scene, but Berenice's arm around her tightened as the camel lurched left a little, continuing on its way

Kleopatra looked over to the right, where Kohlis walked beside them, to see a baby boy lying on the busy street, a pool of blood behind his tiny head. Her brow furrowed, and as her mind began to grasp the reality of what lay before them, she felt the quickening of her heart and sweat along her brow. The boy's small, naked body lay in an unnatural shape. His little fingers were curled into his palms, and dried blood painted a trail down his colourless skin from the large gash in his throat. The cut had been so forceful that the head seemed barely attached.

Kleopatra found her throat now as dry as the desert, and her breath shallow, she swept her terrified eyes to the wall behind the child to find the old woman to whom she had given three gold coins still propped up where she had sat, leaning against the wall, her eyes wide and staring at some point far beyond the sky. Her clothes were stained with blood from the wounds to her neck and chest, and flies swarmed around the corpse, whose feet were still bare. Suddenly the smell of the stew seemed putrid, and the faint music seemed a mournful tune.

The little princess was certain she would be sick, but when she leaned forward, a haggard sound was all that escaped her throat, a burning sensation up her dry gullet. Kohlis stepped over the babe as they passed, and the peasants and stall owners went about their business, seemingly unaffected by the bodies. She looked down at Kohlis, who felt her gaze and glanced up for a mere second, then away again, ever alert for dangers. He guided the camel by its thick leather bindings back into the middle of the road and moved his hand to the sword hilt at his hip as a beggar hobbled forward to address Berenice.

"Greetings, Princess. It is good to see you have visited your humble subjects on this fair day. Have you any coin to spare to feed my family?"

Berenice ignored the man as Kohlis placed a large hand on his chest and pushed past him. A moment passed before the man scampered in front of them once more.

"Perhaps a stone less precious to you, Nomen?" The man's eyes were eager and hopeful in his dirty face.

Kohlis extended his arm again, and this time, pushed the man harder, so he fell backwards to the ground. As he did so, a bright gold coin fell from inside his tunic—a coin bearing the likeness of the pharaoh's head, gleaming brightly in the hot sun. The man snatched it up and slipped it into a worn satchel at his waist, then stood again.

"Nomen, surely you could spare a jewel! No doubt, none of them shine as you do."

Attention on the exchange began to grow, and many eyes on either side of the road watched the princesses pass. The man's final mistake came in stepping toward the camel once more. In a single motion, Kohlis drew his sword, plunged it deep into the man's chest, and withdrew it again. The man crumpled to the ground, lifeless. Kleopatra felt her chest tighten at the sudden violence, which was over almost before she knew it had begun, but noticed that she felt no such tension from Berenice, who remained tall yet relaxed upon the camel, gazing toward the palace ahead without flinching.

Kohlis flicked his sword clean of blood, then returned it to the scabbard at his side and stepped over the body as they silently pressed on.

Kleopatra tried to regain control of her shaking hands. She glanced back to see several peasants swiftly scattering into the side streets, the man's body having been stripped of any valuables in mere moments. "Will someone come to bury him in his tomb?"

"No. He will feed the rats tonight, I think," Berenice replied.

"We could send Larbaris and his guard to bury them."

"We have far more serious matters to attend to, Kleopatra." Berenice's voice was heavy with melancholy and perhaps a touch of anger. The girl now feared what awaited them upon their return to the palace.

As they approached it, she saw that Akela sat in the shade of one of the pylons that lined the entrance to the great palace, her gaze fixed on the droplets of blood that formed a trail up the steps and across the long stone courtyard into the palace halls. Heba sat beside her, occasionally getting up to pace and huff anxiously.

Berenice and the worried Kleopatra dismounted at the bottom stair and ascended toward Akela. She stood as they approached. Berenice passed at a quickened pace and paid no attention to Akela as she disappeared into the palace. Kleopatra embraced her friend. The two looked each other in the eye and Kleopatra's heart sank. "What has happened?" she asked, truly wishing she did not need to know.

Akela looked as if she might cry. "Come, Princess." She took Kleopatra's hand and led her into the palace, Heba trotting close behind.

GREECE

THE PLIGHT OF CHRYSANTHE

— VII —

The rest of the daylight slipped away. The cities on Kretos celebrated the return of their sons and fathers and brothers and husbands. Lambs were slaughtered and roasted over fire pits, and lively music echoed through the settlements, where soldiers enjoyed watered wine and flirting whores.

It was dark when Chrysanthe woke with scalding pain in her ribs. Clutching her side, she felt the deep burning of her flesh fighting to mend itself. She sat up in the small and lumpy bed, her throat coarse and dry and her head pulsing hard. She looked around for water. A ceramic jug had been placed by the basin across the room, and slowly, she eased from her bed. She filled the basin and drank deeply with her cupped hand, then stared into the water, thinking how peaceful it would be to slip beneath the surface of the small dark pool and sink into the abyss.

The door opened, and in stepped an enormous man with the darkest and smoothest skin she had ever seen. The black hair on his head, matted together in bulky strands, trailed far down his back, tied together with a length of leather. He was sturdily built and stern-faced, with one eye missing, its socket scarred over. The eye that remained was the same eerie sapphire blue as the ocean shore; it showed no emotion, no sign of goodness or evil. His armour was that of the Kretos palace guards, and the deep-blue tunic looked godlike against his skin.

"Is it not customary here to announce yourself before you enter royal rooms?" she said with a scowl creasing her brow.

The man stared blankly at her, his expression hard as he towered over her and held out a pale-yellow garment. "You will change." His voice was low but commanding. It seemed to vibrate through the air, and some kind of deep knowing stirred inside her. His fate was tied with hers. She felt it with a deep certainty she could not explain.

"I will not be beckoned by a foreign king. If I am not a prisoner, I will not be summoned."

"Change."

"No."

He stood motionless for a moment before he took one effortless stride to her, grabbed her arm, and dragged her to the bed. Despite her resolve never to let a man hear her scream, she screamed loudly, feeling her damaged insides cringe as she fought against him with her remaining strength, but he thrust her onto the bed and ripped her tattered, dirty dress from her body as she struggled against his grip. She noticed his eye did not flicker to her young breasts or to her pubic hair. His expression did not change, not even as her bare skin spoke the truth of her horrific torture.

Surely, he will be punished for this! she thought. If she were meant as a bride for some royal brute, then where was this man's fear of the crown? Where were his decency and honour?

He pulled the dress over her head, then down her struggling body. His hand was close to her face now because he had adjusted his grip to deal with the gown. She turned toward it and bit down hard. He merely huffed and let go, but then a blow came to her face that sent the vision fading from her open eyes and made fresh pain ripple down her. He yanked her from the bed and dragged her from the room.

Her feet barely touched the ground as he pulled her through the palace halls, the sounds of loud cheers and a buzzing crowd mingling with swells of music and laughter. The giant pulled her into the enormous dining hall.

The scene before her was as she had expected. Masses of soldiers and men of importance conversed loudly with merriment, and the royal family sat in their decorated chairs, the head of a colossal boar mounted at the crown of the king's, where he laughed robustly and paid no attention to the wine spilling down his beard.

His impaired gaze fell on Chrysanthe, and he gestured to an empty chair between two drunken guests engaged in separate conversations. When she did not move, she found herself being lifted off the ground and placed in the chair by large black hands. Someone behind her greeted the vile warrior, calling him Markos.

In front of her were several cups, soiled cloths, platters, and a sharp, silver-bladed carving knife. It was within easy reach, but even as she wondered if she would have enough time to reach for it and drive it into her throat before her giant guard could stop her, his hand passed over her and took the knife, stabbing it into a hock of roasted meat on a platter just out of her reach. A swift death by her own hand would have been preferable to whatever she suspected was to follow.

The king stood, and the volume of celebrations lessened as he raised his goblet to the gathered crowd. "Tonight, we welcome a new princess of Kretos, Chrysanthe of Sparta. Her people fought well but were no match for the serpent warriors of Krete." He turned toward her. "Welcome to one of the greatest Grecian kingdoms on the Aegean Sea. May you finally find your place in a civilised society and amongst a people with honour, strength, and intelligence, which surely must be foreign to you, Chrysanthe of Krete!"

The crowd cheered and continued the festivities. The mockery in his voice had not been lost on her, and the glint in his eyes told her the humiliation she had been dragged here to publicly endure was far from over.

The king called to two men who seemed to be dancing near the long banquet tables. "Halt your sports, you dogs! Bring the princess the prize from our victories. She will celebrate with us." The thin smile that stretched his lips as he sank back into his chair stirred nausea in Chrysanthe's empty belly, and she realised the men whom she had thought were dancing were, in fact, kicking an object back and forth to each other, both barely standing as they stumbled about, grinning groggily. One bent down and retrieved the object, which he came to place roughly on the table before her.

She felt the bile rise in her throat. It was the head of her father, his vacant and colourless eyes staring blankly. The rounded flesh was covered in salt to prevent decay.

The room fell quiet. She sat straight and tall and knew that the king had not achieved the reaction he had wanted.

When it was clear that she would not entertain them with her reaction, several men stepped forward and retrieved the head. One held it close to her face with his fingers inserted through the neck to animate the jaw and began to taunt her with insults, asking her if she wanted to kiss her father goodbye. The other men held her in place so she could not move her chair backwards as the smell of her father's rotting flesh violated her nostrils.

She stared at the pale and puckered skin of the man who had brought her so much pain. Images of her mother's blood pulsing from her neck flashed through Chrysanthe's mind. Her thoughts became fire, and rage swept through her. With one hand, she snatched a carving knife from the guest's plate beside her and drove it through the skull, again and again and again and again, until the already decomposing innards of the head oozed out toward the silver platters of the banquet.

She became aware that the entire room was silent and mouths hung agape. She looked to Athanasios, who sat comfortably in his chair, holding his cup of wine and regarding her. She hoped he saw her eyes blazing, saw her as a filthy goddess of carnage, brilliant and radiant in chaotic death, the flesh of her enemies decimated before her.

"Long live the king," she said, then hurled the knife to the ground and swiftly left the hall, which erupted in deafening cheers, returning to the former celebration with gusto.

Eventually finding her chambers, she quickly closed the door behind her, slipped beneath the linens of the old bed, and rather than removing the spoiled dress, clung to it; the blood soaked into it was both the last remnant of her family and evidence that the world had at last been rid of her father.

❧

FOR SEVERAL DAYS AND NIGHTS, SHE REFUSED TO ATTEND the dining hall or leave her room. No maids came with food or fresh water with which to bathe and dress her wounds—a punishment from the king for her disobedience. She watched the sun move across the sky and the moon chase it, lost in her memory of days not filled with sorrow or fear.

Spartan children were taught honour and bravery as they were raised, and their strength as warriors came from discipline and knowing that fear was not something to be squashed—that bravery was not the absence of fear but the spirit to proceed with fear present.

She wondered what her mother would say to her now if she could see her daughter shed a tear over her misfortune. The former queen of Sparta, Apollia, was the most beautiful woman Chrysanthe had ever seen. Her long auburn hair fell almost to her hips in enviable ripples, and her green eyes, set in a face of strong but feminine bones, were deep wells of knowing, as if the tall, slim goddess could read the true hearts of men. Her calm yet forceful presence made many uncomfortable for fear she could read their thoughts.

Lying on the bed, Chrysanthe imagined her mother's lingering kiss on her cheek, and for a brief moment, was home among the barley fields that rippled in the breeze on a balmy night where the lanterns glittered, lighting up the palace, and the moon cast a silver snake across the northern river.

On the third or fourth day—she did not know nor care to count—a handmaid entered her chambers carrying jugs and filled the washbowl, then approached. Grasping Chrysanthe's foot, the maid yanked her from the bed, and she crashed to the ground. Dispirited, dazed, and indifferent to her fate, she looked up into the angular face of a thin young woman who couldn't be much older than herself. The harshness of her features did not match her youth; her black eyes were devoid of warmth under thick, dark brows and untamed curls of hair. She looked down her long, sharp nose at the girl on the floor, and her lips seemed to give away her delight in the act of humiliation.

"I am Isidora. You are to bathe."

Behind her entered another servant, plump and much older than Isidora, her hands calloused from a career of tending and her maternal demeanour evident. She carried fresh linens and a plate of food into the room, and after putting them down, began stripping the bed.

"I am Theophila, and I will be your handmaid. You look as though you could do with some hot water and breakfast, no?"

Before Chrysanthe could answer, Theophila had helped her to her feet and led her over to the hot-water basin, where Isidora was adding scented oils to the small bath next to a pale blue dress that hung upon a peg in the stone wall. Chrysanthe was weak, her eyes stung, and her stomach protested. What little resistance left in her faded quickly as the women dipped cloths in the water and began to move them over her skin. The sensation was glorious and comforting. She surrendered to the brushing of her long, matted hair into neat waves of deep flame and stood quietly while the two women fitted the blue dress, then added bracelets of gold and red stones to her wrists.

There was a knock on the door.

"A moment longer!" Theophila called out, and then she took a delicate, jewelled hair comb, decorated with three small white flowers, and pulling the sides of Chrysanthe's hair to the back of her head, used the comb to secure it. Then she placed a thin, delicate diadem, over-decorated with jewels, upon her head. *Worthless laurels,* Chrysanthe thought, the king decorating his property with jewels he'd slaughtered men to obtain.

"Beautiful," Theophila said, then called, "You may enter!"

The heavy door opened, and in stepped a man of Chrysanthe's own height, with a modest belly, wearing the many-layered white robes of the noblemen, his grey hair in tufts on the sides of his head. A boy of about ten, with fair hair and bright, eager eyes stepped in behind him, and both bowed their heads.

"Greetings, Princess, welcome to Kretos," said the older man. "I am Lysander, and this is my pupil, Timeaus. I am honoured to have been appointed as your personal adviser and will be assisting you in your adjustment to Kretan palace life, duties, and traditions. I am sure you have many questions. If you are ready, we shall begin." He smiled and gestured toward the open door, but she did not move.

"I do not wish to learn of your traditions or the duties you attempt to force upon me."

"Well, then, shall we return to that at a later time and simply enjoy a walk in the royal gardens to learn of one another? I am curious about your former culture and have a great desire to earn your respect. Please allow me the chance."

"The best bakery in Krete is just outside the palace gates," the boy blurted enthusiastically, "the most delicious honey cakes you have ever tasted! Lord Lysander said we might stop for some." The excitement and purity in his expression softened Chrysanthe's resolve. There was life and hope here in this wretched place. Perhaps these people were also slaves, and here was a chance to escape the castle.

"The best, you say?" she asked the boy, and his grin grew wide.

"I will wager on it, my lady."

"Enough! Princesses do not gamble," Lysander growled at the boy.

"Princesses, I believe, can do whatever they please," Chrysanthe said. She straightened her back and exited the room.

Lysander led her onward. The palace was bustling with activity. Servants carried large crates of wine jugs and barrels of spices, while others led pigs and goats on ropes. Groups of staff hurried through the hallways engrossed in conversation or light debate, not looking up to acknowledge the princess or her companions; some carried papyrus, and some sent others off in various directions with loud commands. Timeaus kept up the pace, seemingly thrilled at the activity around him. He skipped at Chrysanthe's side, staring up at her.

"You look beautiful, my lady. If I may say so, Grecian gowns complement your features."

Chrysanthe experienced, for what she believed was the first time, the strange sensation of male eyes assessing her with a total absence of lust or crude desire. Instead, the boy looked as though he were staring at a goddess in the flesh, wide-eyed and truly a child in his admiration. She decided she liked him.

Out of the corner of her eye, she noticed a large, dark figure following them several paces away and now understood she would be guarded at all times by the one-eyed brute.

"Hush, boy, before you irritate both me and the princess to our deaths," Lysander scolded, and Timeaus fell into silent step behind them.

They continued through the halls and emerged into an enormous courtyard filled with thriving flowers, citrus trees, vines, and berry bushes and decorated with a central fountain where a great stone eagle sat upon the arm of a carved maiden.

"I imagine you have many questions about your place here in the palace, and I am at your disposal." Lysander signalled to the soldiers stationed above them on the wall. The narrow gate began to open, and the trio strolled down to the small bakery only paces from the gate.

There, they sat watching the busy street, their cakes in hand, and Chrysanthe asked if the upper city was always this busy.

"It's for your wedding, my lady!" replied Timeaus. "The whole city is preparing for the celebrations."

Her stomach churned, and suddenly her appetite vanished. She handed the rest of her cake to the boy, stood, and walked briskly down the street toward the lower city.

"Your highness, wait!" Lysander quickly caught up with her. "It is not safe for you in public without an entourage."

"I am sure there is a thug somewhere nearby keeping a watchful eye."

"Please, my lady, we have much to discuss. I must insist you return with me to the palace at once."

"You insist, do you, Lysander? That sounds quite like an order. You and your fellow Kretens have a clever way of giving commands disguised as favours. I wish to lay eyes on my subjects, and an old man with an agenda will not stop me, especially if I am indeed not a prisoner as everyone is so adamant about having me believe."

With that, she spun and strode down the cobbled street into the crowds. She felt the proximity of Markos close by; his presence spoke loudly to her. Soon, Lysander and Timeaus reached her side and quietly accompanied her farther into the streets full of people. The scene was a flurry of activity and chaos as livestock moved in herds, guided by their shepherds, young women travelled in groups, giggling amongst themselves, and merchants and smiths hocked their wares beneath coloured tarps. An old, fat woman with a visible moustache stirred a great pot with a tree branch. The steaming contents smelled of mutton. Soldiers entertained themselves with drink and women at the many tavernas.

Chrysanthe wanted to know the calibre of people on this so-far-hideous island. Her father had once said, "To know the people is to know the manner in which to rule." However, his empty wisdom had never matched his cruel, calculated actions, and she doubted he had ever journeyed further than the comfort of the Spartan palace, let alone done what was best for the Spartan people.

She forced thoughts of her father from her mind. If she were to survive and find a way off this godforsaken rock, she would need allies, and seeing as no one in the palace could be trusted, she would need to make acquaintances beyond the palace walls.

Chrysanthe carried on past merchants' stalls and gangs of huddled gambling men, past street musicians and mean-faced whores, and past putrid outhouses next to bakeries, the entwined smells of the two assaulting the senses. She didn't know what she was looking for, but with each step farther from the palace, she felt the strength in her grow.

Turning down an alley, she felt Lysander's uneasiness but pressed on past the dirty-faced children playing on the ground and the drunk cripple sitting in his own urine against a wall. Then daylight hit her face as they cleared the alley and stepped into an open trading agora. The housing seemed to end here. Before them stood trading houses, an execution podium, and many stationary wagons fitted to horses and donkeys. There was a tavern to the left, presumably full of sailors and drunks, and men argued loudly on the small stools outside. The smell of animal faeces was thick in the air, and many of the peasants moved about their business with grim expressions.

Chrysanthe saw slaves on a podium to her right: five of them, two men and three women, standing shackled and filthy, staring at the ground as a man with metal shears snipped brutally at their hair. The princess took off with swift steps towards the podium, Lysander and Timeaus following closely.

"My lady, please! I fear your tender heart may lead you to unwise actions—"

"If my heart were tender, I would be dead already." She stopped before the podium. She looked up into the faces of the poor souls but found none familiar. "You, sir."

The large, heavy man looked down at her with uncaring eyes.

"What are you doing to these slaves?"

"Why do you give a shit?"

"I am a princess and do not have to provide a reason for my giving a shit."

The man bowed his head reluctantly, almost with an air of jest.

"Forgive my tone, Princess, I do not know your face. Lice. The swine are riddled." He gestured to the captives with the shears. "I treat the hair and sell to eastern merchants for a fine price." He cleared his throat and spat on the ground.

"I see. Tell me, sir, do you know of any Spartan slaves?"

He eyed her curiously with dark, beady eyes. "No, Princess, no Spartans here."

"There would be three of them."

"If they were here, they'd have any memories of their homeland shagged or beaten out of 'em by now." He laughed crudely and turned his back on her to continue cutting the hair.

Chrysanthe's heart sank. If she were truly the last Spartan, then what would be her purpose? Was she to marry and breed more Spartans? Was her purpose to scour the islands, looking for survivors, and carry on the name of her people?

Or was it simply that the time of the Spartan had passed, and all that remained was her own death?

The thoughts became overwhelming, but somewhere nearby, a dull shouting began, growing louder and pushing the thoughts away. She turned to look back toward the taverna to see a large woman beating a smaller man, striking the cowering slave with great force, intending significant damage.

Before Lysander could protest, she was standing before the enormous woman. "Madam, what is this slave's crime?"

"Madam? That's a first." The woman sneered, revealing her yellowed and slanted teeth. The men drinking nearby on stools snickered.

"His crime?" Chrysanthe pressed, stone-faced.

"The shit near brought the pottery shelf down on himself. If he dies, I gotta buy a new slave, and they ain't cheap, are they, boys?" She grinned at the men, who groggily raised cups to her in agreement.

"And the slave deserves to be beaten for almost causing his own death?"

"It's my slave. I do as I want, girl." The woman's several chins wobbled as her voice grew hostile.

Chrysanthe felt anger rise in her chest, but maintaining her composure, she slipped off a gold bracelet from her arm and held it out to the woman. "I wish to buy him."

The woman stared at the bracelet, her greedy eyes fixed on the shining gold jewellery. "He is a good slave, young and strong. He is worth two of those."

"He is worth barely a few silver coins in the condition he is in, and even less if he is as clumsy as you say. The gold is more than enough."

The woman licked her lips, smiled, and then pocketed the bracelet. "Very well." And without a beat, she waddled away back into her dwelling.

Chrysanthe, feeling eyes on her, bent to lift the injured man to his feet.

He met her gaze timidly, and the misery there reflected her own. "How may I serve you?"

He spoke with no feeling. She slipped a further two bangles from her wrist and placed them in his hand, closing his fingers over them. He looked up at her with stunned eyes.

"I have no wish for slaves. I have enough. You are a free man now. I suggest you buy passage from this place immediately."

"My lady, I—" His voice was shaky, but Chrysanthe shook her head.

"Leave now. That is your final command."

"Who may I thank for this kindness, my lady?"

"I am Chrysanthe of Sparta, and I wish you a life of peace that I shall never have." She turned away from him and made for the way she had come. She had no desire to linger in such a place. She felt her cheeks redden and sweat form on her brow, uncomfortable with the attention of the crowd though only moments ago she had entertained the urge to seek some sliver of control, perhaps righting a wrong in the world or showing the people that she intended to use her perceived power to help them.

Eager to escape the sea of watching eyes, she glimpsed Markos stalking in the shade of pavilions, his eye on her as always. Lysander's irritation was clear in his silence.

As she passed the men drinking at the taverna, one large soldier stood and stepped in front of her. The strange grin that spread on his face felt threatening. "I was there at the palace. We raped your whore mother as the life drained from her throat." He leered, and several of the other men laughed and jeered.

"Aye, her rear was enjoyable," one of the seated men said.

She knew Markos was only moments away from removing her from the agora, and as the rage in her broke its chains, she allowed it to consume her. The knife at the waist of the sitting man was suddenly in her hand and had been promptly plunged deep into the neck of the soldier standing before her; she had struck him twice, as swiftly as the bolts of Zeus, smooth and controlled. Before he hit the ground, the knife had flashed down several times on the back and head of the sitting drunk man.

Lysander gripped her arm. She collapsed all her weight and used it to escape his grip, then jumped on the downed man and stabbed furiously at his face and throat. Suddenly, she was pulled into the air. She thrashed and squirmed, biting at Markos' wrists, clawing to be released, but she was quickly hoisted over his shoulder and locked in place with a single vise-like arm. She continued to struggle, but soon her defeat was apparent.

Markos was striding away from the agora. Looking back at the scene, she saw drunkards and street folk clambering over the bodies, one of them still convulsing, picking them clean of loot. As a noisy brawl erupted, she registered the furious face of Lysander and the shocked one of Timeaus, following closely.

She had scared the boy, and for that, she was sorry, but given a choice, she would do the same again without hesitation.

Markos strode into the courtyard, Lysander and Timeaus close behind. Once released, she sat upon the ground. A strange lightness inhabited her body, and an intoxicating peace flowed through her bones and along the entire surface of her skin. The world before her melted away as she cast her eyes to the bright blue sky where gulls swooped, embracing their freedom. She was only vaguely aware of Lysander pacing furiously before her.

"Are you listening to me, girl?"

She turned her gaze to him; his face was red and flustered. "As a princess, the people look to you for leadership. Your duty is to protect the royal family name and reputation—"

"A reputation for being violent murderers and rapists?"

"You are a child, and your behaviour speaks to your immaturity. *This* is your life now. The sooner you accept that, the sooner your life will become less complicated."

"I will never accept *this*."

"You may think you've been through hell, but trust me, girl, this is just the beginning! However, it *is* survivable. I am here to teach you all you will need to survive in a palace like this and a position like yours." He struggled to calm himself, small veins protruding from his temples. "It showed weakness to give the slave gold, and it was rebellious to then free him." He stopped to rub his eyes as if the day's events had drained him of stamina.

As she watched the old man search for his patience, Chrysanthe wondered perhaps if killing those two men had been a stupid impulse. But she felt her mother's gentle kiss in the breeze through the gardens and knew in her heart that, given a chance, she would do it again.

"Two families will be without a man of the house today. Two husbands will not return to their wives," Lysander said sternly.

"Men like that? I would wager their wives would thank me."

"Not when their children starve, they won't! Did you give *them* gold rings? Did they get the coin purse their father carried, or his sandals, which would have fetched a fine price? No. You have robbed those families of their right to those means to feed themselves. The wives will no doubt become whores, and the youngest children will be sold for a low price out of desperation. Your actions have consequences, and you alone are responsible. You are a spoiled child with the blood on your hands of two Kreten war veterans who have fought and killed for this kingdom."

"Yes. They fought and killed *my* kinsmen. *My* queen. *My* mother. I will not honour them. I will celebrate their deaths."

Lysander threw up his arms and stalked away, calling back to Markos to take her to her rooms. Timeaus, with a sheepish glance at Chrysanthe, skipped after the old man, who continued to curse as he disappeared into the palace.

🌿

IN HER ROOMS, CHRYSANTHE STOOD NAKED WITH HER arms outstretched as Isidora and Theophila measured parts of her for her wedding gown. She stared blankly at the wall, trying as best she could to hold onto the feeling of peace the events of the day had brought her, but slowly, reality crept back into her heart and threatened her fading elation.

There was a knock at the door, and without waiting for a response, a small, grumpy man entered; he looked as though death could come for him at any moment, but he toted a heavy bag nonetheless. Chrysanthe scrambled to cover herself, but the man simply scuttled to the bed, lay his bag on it, and began to unpack apparatuses and strange-coloured vials of herbs and paste. "I've seen it all, stupid girl."

"This is Buchorus, the palace physician. He will be tending to your wounds, my lady. He is very good." Theophila gave her a small, encouraging smile, but Chrysanthe still held her dress to her body as the frail old man beckoned her to him impatiently. Once within reach, he pushed her to sit on the bed and examined her many bruises and cuts, from her injured feet up her legs to her stomach, her ribs and back, her arms, and her face. He applied an array of tinctures and strange pastes, some that smelled horrendous and some that stung fiercely.

"You've had your blood?"

"Yes."

"Then you are fit to be wed, and I am done here." He began packing his utensils. "Do not remove that gauze until it itches." He gestured to her forearm before hauling his large bag off the bed and waddling with a painful limp out of the room.

Theophila left after him. Isidora approached Chrysanthe and helped her into a plain dress without disturbing any ointments.

"Prince Demosthenes is returning to Kretos soon, and you will be wed on the day of his arrival. The celebrations are set for the day after tomorrow," Isidora said coldly as she tended to Chrysanthe's hair.

"I would prefer death."

"We would all prefer you died, but alas, the gods have not blessed us. Marrying a prince is a great honour, and you are extremely ungrateful."

"What is your personal stake in this matter?" Chrysanthe looked the girl in the eye with a challenge in her voice.

"I do not have one."

"I do not have one, *Your Highness*." Chrysanthe watched the maid's eyes darken before her.

"I do not have one, Your Highness." Hatred leaked through the words.

"I have reason to believe you do, Isidora, so tell me your stake. I wish to know why you behave with the disrespect of a harpy and a temperament as if I have wronged you." Chrysanthe remained sitting tall and watched possible responses wrestle one another within the girl.

"My sister was to marry Prince Demosthenes upon his return," she said at last. "If you had only died in Sparta with your kin, she would be sitting here being fitted for her gown instead of some filthy harlot who will soil the great bloodline of Kretos."

"I thank you for your honesty. If I could trade places with your sister, I would do so. Somehow it would be noticed, I think. Are they lovers?"

"Yes. Very much so."

"How many others does he have?"

"She is his true love. No others matter."

"Had he proposed to your sister?"

"It was to take place on his arrival."

"Is it possible that your sister confused his lust for a declaration of love and that your hatred of me is misplaced?"

"She is not confused!" Isidora caught herself before she could release her true rage. "There is no mistake. They were to wed. They love each other. You have robbed my family of our future, and I will not forget it."

"How curious. Queen Corinna implied that Demosthenes was far from capable of love. And if I were to rob your family of anything, be assured it would be all you had, not just the conjured romance of a deluded girl."

Isidora stepped back, her fury evident, and without another word, she stormed from the room.

❦

CHRYSANTHE HAD BEEN SUMMONED TO THE QUEEN'S apartments—it was tradition for a princess to spend the afternoon before her wedding with the reigning queen if she still lived. As she approached the queen's tower, Chrysanthe lifted her dress of plain white to ascend the stone steps, the heavy necklace that Theophila had chosen for her weighing uncomfortably on her chest in the thick heat.

Reaching the top of the stairs, she stepped into an enormous room, flooded with light and decorated elaborately with tall golden statues, assorted rugs, and luxurious lounges next to tables holding large platters of meats, cheeses, and breads, along with many chalices of wine.

Charis emerged from the far archway. Her unwelcoming expression did not change as she approached and gestured that they sit. She poured Chrysanthe wine, then filled a large cup for herself and drank deeply. Chrysanthe sipped her cup awkwardly in the silence, sitting stiffly in the queen's overpowering presence.

The queen exhaled loudly as she drained her cup, then filled it once more and sat back to lean on several pillows, eyeing Chrysanthe without warmth. "Demos killed his last two wives." Her voice was flat, and her posture did not change. "Did you know that?" She grazed the platter of food lazily.

"No, I did not. Why?"

The queen shrugged as she selected almonds and slices of dried apricot. "Why does Demosthenes do anything?" It was not a question intended for answering, and the silence grew as the queen chewed loudly and sipped her wine. Then her eyes fell on the princess again. "Have you ever fucked?"

Uneasiness nipped at Chrysanthe as she tried to remain sharp-witted. "No, your highness," she lied.

"Hm. Well, there's not much to it. You lie down, and it happens; that's the duty done."

"How long have you been queen?" Chrysanthe asked.

"I find that the more I count, the more I wish to throw myself from the window."

"But you are beautiful, and you are a queen."

Charis locked her intense brown eyes on her. "I am no halfwit, slut. Do not attempt to falsely flatter me. You will rue it." Her gaze on Chrysanthe was dark, and the princess saw the danger in the queen's spirit. "Your family is dead?"

"Yes."

"That is probably best. Hear me now, girl. Do not come to me with your concerns or predicaments. I will not care for your children should you become unfit. We will not be friends, and you will not proceed me in any royal matters. If an occasion demands it, you will lay down your life for me or my children. Do you understand?"

"Yes, my lady."

"Don't 'yes, my lady' me. I am your queen!"

Her words were slurred, and her head lulled groggily. For a fleeting moment, Chrysanthe's heart leapt with the hope that the food had been poisoned and the queen was dying, but quickly she discerned that, if the queen was murdered and she was the only one in the room with her, she would surely be to blame. Wouldn't she? Perhaps she could convince the king that it was by her hand and thus induce her own execution.

But poison was a sly death; he would ask her where she'd gotten the poison—she'd been guarded day and night since she'd arrived on Kretos, and those who'd interacted with her were trusted staff. Such a situation would bring only lengthy torture before the release of death, and the thought of more pain chilled her. No, if Chrysanthe were to force the king to execute her, the murder would need to be obvious. With the queen's eyes closed as she waded through whatever agent inhibited her blood, Chrysanthe took the thin, sharp cheese knife from the platter and slipped it into a fold in her dress.

"Are you feeling well, Your Highness?" Chrysanthe asked as she put her cup down on the table, poised to strike.

"Of course, I am, stupid girl."

At that moment, two children skipped into the room and threw themselves around their mother gleefully.

"My little centaurs!"

The girl was the oldest, perhaps twelve, and looked frighteningly like her mother, with golden hair, brown eyes, and thin lips; the boy looked close to nine years old and had dark hair like Athanasios but a shy demeanour. He eyed Chrysanthe sheepishly; she did not smile in welcome but remained where she was, indifferent to their presence.

"Who are you?" the girl asked, assessing Chrysanthe with a hostile stare.

"I am Chrysanthe of Sparta."

The queen giggled groggily.

"Aren't you going to ask who I am?" the girl asked with an entitled tone.

"I don't care who you are."

The girl seemed to struggle to process the response.

"You're very beautiful." the young boy said bashfully into his mother's dress, squirming at the interaction.

"She can't be beautiful, Athanis. She's Spartan. Everyone knows Spartans are diseased dogs infested with lice and evil sorcery," spat the girl.

"Now, Charissa, not *all* Spartans. This one only has lice," Charis said, entertaining only herself.

"Is it true?" Athanis asked meekly.

"Infested," replied Chrysanthe. "And if I'm not required to remain here all afternoon, I have lice to tend to." She stood and turned for the staircase.

"Uncle Demos killed both his wives, and they were prettier than you," Charissa called after her.

Chrysanthe turned back calmly to face the girl, who warily watched her, awaiting a response. "If husbands murder their wives based on beauty, then you will live a very long life." Chrysanthe watched the girl's face fill with anger. She smiled at the little witch, then turned and descended the stairs.

Her heart pounded; it seemed common knowledge that her betrothed was a blatant murderer, and it appeared that marriage provided no safety from that fate. It was strange to hold two conflicting desires within her heart—the wish to die and the animal instinct to live. The hopeless feeling returned as each scenario to escape her fate played through her mind with no viable solution.

Thoughts of suicide filled her. As she flew down the corridor as fast as she could get away from the queen's apartments, she stopped to inspect the balcony. She leaned over to see the height of the drop and assessed it quickly. She knew that the fall would likely not kill her, and so she continued with haste toward her own apartments.

The halls were like a maze designed to keep in a minotaur—or a captive princess—and she became lost very quickly, the thoughts in her head becoming loud, whispering that if she were to die, it should be in battle like a true Spartan, but there was no war here save the one that pitted her against all others. She decided that she would provoke one in which she could fight valiantly and join the fallen Spartan warriors at the eternal victory feast in Tartarus.

Rounding the corner of a hallway, she saw two armed guards standing lazily chatting and realised her chance had been presented. A plan formed quickly in her mind. If she had learned anything in her weapons training, it was to utilize her strengths; luckily, her size allowed for speed, precision, and surprise. As she recalled the night Sparta fell to Grecian savages and the screams of her people, cut down by soldiers wearing blue tunics, bronze breastplates, and black-plumed helms, the spirit of Ares filled her with his wrath.

The soldiers noticed her as she swiftly approached, their blue tunics and bronze armour echoing loudly in her memory; neither raised a weapon but merely regarded the princess, perceiving no visible threat. As she reached the first man, she slipped the cheese knife from her robe and rammed it with precision into his exposed, soft-skinned neck at an upward angle, retracting it with speed before turning to attack the second man. He had managed to raise his sword, but without pause or hesitation in her resolve, she simply sidestepped under the soldier's raised arm and flashed the knife up into his armpit, pushing it as far as the hilt would go, then snatching it away again as she stepped out behind him.

With no change in her expression, she turned to watch the lifeblood slowly pump out of the two fallen men, surprised to find that the ordeal was over so swiftly. She had not expected her training to take over so completely and had prepared herself to at least be stabbed—with any luck, fatally—but two enemies were dead, and she stood unharmed.

Dropping the knife to the ground, she looked around, realising that she hadn't expected she would need to plan for survival. She stepped forward to pick up the sword that lay on the ground; it was heavier than she recalled from the last time she'd held one, but the shape was familiar. And so it was decided: She would fight whoever came, and it would not be long before the strength and skill of fighting men would overcome her, and she would be free from this life.

She pressed her fingers into the pool of deep red that had spilled from the men, then wiped it across her cheeks; the first blood spilled in a Spartan war was a noble sacrifice. Seemingly, the tradition of her people would die with her, but she would honour it until her last breath.

The moment was odd. She had now taken four Kretan lives, yet she felt no relief and the anger remained. She had never excelled in her secret studies of Spartan warrior training, hiding in the shadows as she watched the young men fight, but she had a Spartan heart, anger, and nothing left to lose. If women were permitted to be trained as warriors, then perhaps Sparta would not have fallen, and she would not be standing in a Kretan palace hallway, preparing to face her swift end.

Someone shouted behind her, and she turned to see several more soldiers running toward her. She raised the sword, ready to embrace her death, but as they approached, a hard blow suddenly struck the back of her head. As the dull, heavy pain spread from the spot and down her body, she lost consciousness.

◆

WHEN SHE AWOKE, HER WRISTS WERE BOUND WITH ROPE, and she sat propped against the wall across from the dead men, their eyes staring blankly to the ceiling. She was aware through the throbbing in her head and strange tingling down her left side that there were men nearby, and as she roused, she was hoisted by large hands to stand, and with great force, pushed against the wall, where two helmed men restrained her tightly.

King Athanasios rounded the corner flanked by armoured guards, and as he assessed the two dead men, the cheese knife, and then the princess with evidence on her hands and dress, he burst into bellowing laughter. All present stood still, confusion on everyone's face, including Chrysanthe's. The king continued as if he were not able to stop. His face became flushed, and he turned to walk away, his chuckling continuing down the hall. All stood unsure of what to do as Lysander came hurtling to the scene with Timeaus close behind him; the old man assessed the dead men and then addressed the guards sternly.

"Bring her to her rooms. The bridal preparation is to begin. Do it now! And clean up this mess." His expression was dark as he stalked back the way he came, and the soldiers moved after him with a painful grip on Chrysanthe.

"What were you thinking, you stupid girl? The king could have had you executed without a trial!" screeched Lysander.

"But he didn't. Your king merely laughed at the death of two of his men. What kind of king is that?"

"*Your* king! I know it is difficult for a girl child to comprehend, but this is your home now, Athanasios is your king, and you are his property to do with as he wishes! And he wishes for you to marry his brother. It will be a glorious union, and your duties will be to produce heirs and serve your husband's wishes and needs."

"And what of my needs?"

"This is not a game! The duties that come with womanhood may not be ideal for you, but the gods have decided this to be your path. You will obey, and so you will survive; you will stop these treacherous antics and begin to behave like a princess of Krete." Lysander paused to catch his breath and fill a cup of water, which he drained. "Tonight will be the washing ceremony, and tomorrow morning, you will visit the temple of Hera and then attend your wedding to Prince Demosthenes. He is arriving in the bay as we speak."

Chrysanthe's heart lurched as once again the reality of her situation was confirmed. Her plan to force the king's hand had failed, despite her blatant murderous act; the chances to evade her fate were becoming fewer, and the time in which to carry out the final deed was ebbing away.

🌱

THE GIRL WILL BE DEAD WITHIN A WEEK, LYSANDER thought. *A pity: she has the hips for bearing many children with ease and seemingly the spirit to survive this wretched family of wolves.* He sighed; the princess was his last, fading hope to secure himself the position of king's treasurer, and with it, agreeable pay and spacious apartments within the palace, to which he could move his wife and still-unmarried daughter. He had watched his child suffer in the public knowledge that she was undesirable, though to him, she had the most beautiful face and nature—a reflection of her mother.

After Athanasios had murdered his father and taken the throne of Kretos, Lysander, among many other trusted royal staff who had been loyal to the crown since the early days of the late king's reign, were thrown from their positions and replaced with vile and thuggish men who would do Athanasios's bidding with no question. There was no reward for the years of loyalty and pride in the fine and intricate work of crucial palace roles, and although Lysander and his family had been kicked to the dirt, they had remained standing, heads held high with dignity.

He had sought suitors for his daughter, but with his sudden and severe demotion, the pool of eligible men of status had dried up almost instantly. He had worked for many gruelling years now in this position of adviser to the lesser royals, seeing his chance of restoring the pride and reputation of his once-established and well-regarded family, but this stubborn and arrogant child could ruin his plans to return to good favour.

♦

"I WILL NEVER BE A PRINCESS OF KRETE. YOU MAY BEAT me and restrain me, but I will not be a trophy of conquest for Grecian barbarians," Chrysanthe said in a low voice.

Lysander turned to her with a glare as the silent Timeaus kept his eyes to the ground. "Then all the strength of Sparta will die with you, for you will be beaten, Princess; you will be restrained, and I fear you do not grasp that those will be preferable to many other actions you will suffer if you do not embrace your new life. The day will come when you are beyond my help, and I pray that is not the day I attend your funeral pyre."

Lysander's gaze spoke more to Chrysanthe than his words. Peril lay ahead, she had more enemies than friends, and this was a game she did not know how to play, where defeat was inevitable because the game was designed by the enemy.

Lysander stormed from the room, followed closely, as always, by Timeaus, whose nervous eyes never left the ground.

Chrysanthe sat alone in the dusty rooms where time had eaten away at the tapestry threads and stale air had dulled the shine of the copper urns, looking out of the enormous arched window across the barren plains as the dying sun dashed its orange glow through the sky. The thudding in her head had eased a little, but in any event, she no longer felt pain. *What is pain?* she asked herself. *A bodily response? A reaction to violence inflicted? Or does it serve as a lesson?*

No, she decided, pain was a reminder that the world of men still owned her. Pain was used to control and bend one to another's will. Pain was only of the body, and she vowed her mind would know no such pain.

She jumped as the door opened once more and Theophila entered, carrying large pottery jugs, followed by Isidora, who held a large, heavy, woven basket. Chrysanthe returned her blank gaze to the setting sun as the maids quietly began pouring the warm jugs into the bathing bowl. After adding their perfumes and flowers, they pulled the princess to stand, her stare never faltering from the beauty of the sky, and she was gently bathed. Then oil was massaged into her skin and herbs applied to her remaining unhealed wounds. A long cloth of white was wrapped tightly around her, and her hair was wound into tight ribbons and secured with pins.

The night before a Grecian wedding, the bride was to fast, taking no food or drink, and so, once the linen was fastened and she felt trapped within the binding, the maids lay her on the bed and drew the covers over her body before dropping liquid from a small vial onto her lips and beginning silent prayers on either side of her.

Chrysanthe closed her eyes and prayed for death to come to her while she slept. The tingling sensation of the oil on her lips spread through her body before pulling her into a dreamless sleep.

EGYPTE

THE BROKEN PRINCE

— VIII —

The morning was balmy with a stronger wind than normal, coming from the north off the great churning sea. The palace was busy with Egypteian warriors and military generals frequenting the great war chamber in the west wing of the pharaoh's house, and he himself had barely surfaced from the military business being done with great diligence.

The halls were quieter, and there had been no royal duties since the ceremony of Auletes—now Ptolemy Auletes of Egypt. There had been news from the armies in the eastern Egypteian settlements that rebellions had ignited and grown large and troublesome. Fighting men were rallying, and although unorganised, their numbers were a source of great concern as the settlement military were too few to defend the land held there should the Assyrian forces attack. The land would be lost all the way to the mouth of the east river.

This weighed on Claudius as he made his way from the war chambers through the palace. The threat from the east was growing. General Ankhmakis commanded the eagle armies in the west, but he had sent word that the savages were strong opponents, hostile to Egypteian law, and their frequent livestock raids were proving difficult to thwart. Claudius also knew the southern tribes posed a threat that should not be overlooked.

The Assyrian tribes, if assembled, would tally in number close to fifty thousand fighting men, and the savage tribes in the west already slightly outnumbered the army of Ankhmakis. Egypt's only advantage on each side was that their military was trained and skilled in battle strategy and techniques, whereas the savages were unskilled farmers and labourers with no battle experience.

The military under Claudius's command numbered close to thirty-eight thousand trained warriors, and Neos commanded another thirty-five thousand, but they were to be divided between defending the southern settlements, where Egypte was making progress in taking over the lands, and keeping order in Memphis, including protection of the palace itself.

The thoughts circling in his mind were beginning a deep throb in his forehead. He thought of the days when he'd been a young boy running through these same halls, absent the worries of the world of men's duties and war.

Claudius rounded the corner to find his sisters Berenice and Isis arguing— Isis clearly the aggressor in the hostilities and Berenice pushing back admirably. "Sisters, what is the matter?"

Isis whipped round to face him, her eyes wide with rage and her cheeks flushed. "Father means to kill us all and ruin Egypte! Surely you have seen the battle plans for the east? We are outnumbered and to attack would certainly mean defeat against such a horde. Where will Egypte be should the eastern battle sour on us? The rest of the army is in the west, and the palace would be taken by the time of their return!"

"Father has a plan. That is why he consults his generals!" barked Berenice.

"His generals couldn't knot their tunics if deprived of their sight. Egypte would be better off being defended by a herd of sleepy camels!"

"Sister, you are right," Claudius said. "The numbers are against us, and the forces spread sparingly. But the plans are sound, and the eagle army of Ra will not fail us."

Claudius saw fury flick across Isis's face, followed by desperation. "We should be sending the captured western slaves to fight in the east; they are strong, with solid stamina, and their losses in battle would not matter. They are ten thousand in number. Father's ridiculous monuments can wait."

"And how would we feed such an army?" The irritation in Berenice's voice was apparent as she paced. "They are kept in the west because supplies are in the west."

"The slaves aren't trained, Isis. They're savages, just as the Assyrian tribes are," said Claudius. "They would be more likely to turn on themselves than fight and die for Egypt. The slaves would be an uncontrolled force and would take months to prepare for battle."

"So, you would send your thirty-eight Sand Eagles to Assyria in the hope that victory somehow prevails?" Isis sneered. "The supply line is a problem in itself. We would have to sail supplies across the great sea to Karkar if the banks of the Tarsus River were captured and our soldiers in Marqash cut off."

"I agree that the entirety of the strategy would have to be executed perfectly, but that is why the savages fear Egypt: Our generals are precise and fierce." Claudius spoke sternly, implying his desire for an end to the dispute.

Isis took a breath, her eyes narrowed and hard. "If you were pharaoh, would you prepare the same plans?" she asked Claudius.

"I would make adjustments, but Father's strategy is sound."

"You speak too carefully, Claudius!"

"And you not carefully enough, Isis!"

"You would change the strategy. I know you would, because you are clever, but you are too soft. Neos has explained what we are to expect in many scenarios, and he agrees, Egypt will fall under Father's careless decisions. And make no mistake, brother, we will fall with her. He will be the death of us." Isis was seething, and Berenice threw her hands up in frustration.

Claudius' eyes narrowed, and he stepped closer to Isis. A head taller than she and larger from his military training, he spoke low but with menace. "Quiet your tongue, sister, and steady your childish temper, for the words you spit smell of mutiny and foul sedition."

"Would you not welcome the sovereignty if it were presented to you?" she asked.

"That would be in the event of Father's death, and I speculate he does not intend to join the gods at any moment soon."

Isis smiled and leaned close as though to kiss his cheek. "We are not blessed with the mastery of our deaths, brother. Even you, the golden Sand Eagle of Father's pride, could fall at any moment to the bite of an asp or a fall from your beast." She leaned back to face him, her eyes glazed with the whisper of a mind unhinged, then turned to stalk away.

🜆

BERENICE AND CLAUDIUS EXCHANGED AN ANGRY GLANCE before she, too, strode away, still furious from the argument. Her mind was alight with questions. *Father surely wouldn't risk the security of Memphis or the palace. Would he?* If he departed with his army and left the city undefended, it would allow him to take both the armies under the commands of Claudius and Neos, which would ensure his victory in the east, but it would leave the southern flank of Egypt exposed to the hostile tribes that dwelt on the border.

Berenice cast an eye out across the lands to her right, and as she walked, a tightness crept inside her chest. She knew their father did not care for the lives of any of his children. Of course, none of his daughters were of value except as brides to foreign powers to bring alliances, and he had been clear that Claudius, although obedient, brave, and celebrated in his military achievements, was too mild-mannered to rule as pharaoh. Neos was too stubborn and undisciplined in his temper and selfishness. And Auletes showed more interest in his horses than he did in wielding a sword.

Father despised young Theos. Ever questing for his father's approval was a fruitless endeavour, as all but he could see. Theos was not a weak young prince by any means; he was quick with his blade and steady on his feet, smart in strategy, and patient with the matters of the city, but the boy was gifted with a sight. His veil was that of silk rather than stone, and he knew things he could not have any means to know, unnerving the pharaoh, who suspected evil within the child. But then Father, even if presented with another of himself, would find a reason why that child was not fit to rule his precious city of golden sand.

Bernice's mind was saddened with the thoughts of her beloved little brother and the violence he had suffered at the hands of his father, far greater than he had deserved. She turned a corner, her mind weighed down with her thoughts, only to be suddenly grabbed by her shoulders and pushed against the rough wall, a strong hand over her mouth.

A familiar scent settled in her consciousness, and she relaxed in the grip of the soldier kissing her neck with a lack of gentleness. She smiled and let his hands run across her body, gripping her buttocks firmly as he pressed his hard body against hers, pinning her forcefully, preventing her escape. "Salonious, someone will see."

His mouth found hers, and his kiss was deep and hungry. A rough hand found one of her breasts, causing her lips to part, kissing him harder. The hand made its way from her breast down past her navel, then slipped between her thighs and curled upwards. She let out a soft moan and felt his smile in their kiss. She took the hand and led the man quickly down the hall, both stifling their laughter.

◆

KLEOPATRA SAT WITH HER HEAD BOWED IN FRONT OF A small table adorned with small carved figures of beautiful men and women draped in robes, some holding weapons, one bearing a great owl on her arm. "Thank you, my lords. May your wisdom and glory reign in the hearts of man."

She raised her head to stare at the gods of Greece. Her mother had been a princess of Attica when she'd come to Egypt to marry the pharaoh at barely sixteen, and with her, she'd brought her faith. The pharaoh had seemed intrigued by her gods, which were not his but were widely celebrated and accepted across the Aegean, and she had been permitted to serve them still if she also accepted the gods of Egypt into her faith, to which she had famously replied, "I will fear all gods, but no more than they fear me." Such a religious compromise had been unheard of then.

Paintings and carvings across Egypt depicted the coming of Kleopatra V, who'd stood, veiled, before a young tyrant Pharaoh and presented to him the severed head of her sister. Egypt had been forever changed that day when Kleopatra V informed the bewildered Ptolemy Auletes of the fratricide of her elder sister, the bride the young Pharaoh had been expecting. The crowd present had heard that it was a demonstration of Kleopatra V's devotion to Egypt and its betterment. It was depicted and recorded that the tall, proud Grecian princess had tossed the leaking head aside, stepped to the Pharaoh, and with bloodied hands, pulled away her veil, then bent to take his hand and kiss the largest ruby adorning his long, bony fingers. The Pharaoh was said to have gasped in awe of her striking beauty, the only sound to penetrate the eerie silence of the stunned hypostyle audience. She then straightened herself, moved to stand at his side to address all gathered, and declared, loudly and clearly, "Because of my actions, my lord will have more handsome sons than my sister's homely face could provide. He will not tire of his queen as many do, for she possesses wit unmatched, the stamina of a boar, and the guile of a man.

My lord's dynasty will not be sullied by an ill-matched counterpart, nor will Egypt be kept from the heights of her greatness by a queen with no spine to lead such an empire. I have slain my weak and inferior sister to ensure the glory of Egypt, and I come in her place. She was no queen. I am." Kleopatra V then turned to look down at her new husband, her black, confident, almond-shaped eyes penetrating his stunned gaze. "You asked my father for a queen, and a queen you will have."

From that day onward, the whole of Egypt had rejoiced and reaped the bounty that generously flowed from the Pharaoh's adoration of and infatuation with his new queen. It was a time of celebration. Liveliness. Prosperity.

Those days were long buried in the memories of those who had lived them. This morning, Kleopatra prayed for her brother Theos and his fast recovery from the injuries he had suffered. His memory had returned, and his speech was almost audible but still impaired by his broken jaw. The technologies and contraptions of the physicians were truly fascinating. They used metal wires and wooden splints and cogs that turned loudly to retrain the bones and muscles all across his body.

Here, in the half-darkness of her chambers, Kleopatra took each deity figure one by one and brought them to her lips the way that Mother had shown them, and with each kiss, she filled her mind with love for her brother, knowing that she had so much love for him the gods would not ignore her prayers.

She stood and moved to the small table where the bowl of figs she had requested from the kitchens sat, ready to be taken to him. Her heart was always heavy before her daily visits. His spirit was as broken as his bones. She feared he would never be the same brother she had known. Something had changed within him. A light gone out, a fight abandoned, a presence dissolved. Not only did heartache cut her whenever she gazed upon him, confined to his bed, but there was a sticky anxiousness that crept into the air around him, for it was known he saw true visions of things that were yet to come, and the weight of his words that day had shocked all who knew of his gift.

Kleopatra stared at the figs as she recalled with chilling clarity the day of Auletes' tomb ceremony.

She had climbed the stairs to the palace, Berenice moving fast in front of her and disappearing. Kleopatra had approached Akela. "Something has happened. Tell me, Akela, if you love me. Tell me now." But her dear friends' mouth was too dry for words, and her cheeks stained with rivers of tears.

Akela took Kleopatra's hand tightly, and with haste, led her into the palace. It was unusually quiet through the halls, and there seemed to be an eerie lack of staff on guard or servants going about palace chores. She noticed even the animals were quiet.

Akela stopped at the bedchamber door of Theos, where two Sand Eagle warriors stood tall and stone-faced, spears in hand. Akela let go of her hand, and Kleopatra moved forward, the guards stepping aside and opening the heavy-set door for her. She looked back at Akela, who was quickly wiping a tear from her cheek. Akela turned to quickly walk away without another word, and Kleopatra stepped into her brother's room.

The chamber was dim. What little candlelight there was flickered over the bed and the small group of people huddled around it, speaking in low whispers. A servant dashed from the huddle, holding a large bowl, while another, holding steaming rags, dashed in to replace her. A strange scent of burning herbs and unsavoury oils permeated the air. The large terrace doors were closed and the thick winter curtains drawn, preventing the entry of any fresh breeze.

Then the familiar smell of wet metal found her and assaulted her mind. She knew it to be blood.

A man looked back at her from the huddle, and even in the dim light, she could see that Claudius's face was pale and his expression grim. He beckoned her to come to him, and when she approached, knelt to look into her face. "Be strong, child. The gods will come soon, and our time is precious. Prepare your nerves."

Her heart stopped and her body stiffened as she looked at the bed. Before her lay the gentle prince of Egypt, Ptolemy Theos, broken and dying. His face seemed to be in pieces, his features not where they ought to be. A surgeon, hands covered in blood, worked swiftly with skill and concentration to sew the flesh back onto the side of his head while another attempted to keep one of his eyes from falling from its socket. The other eye was swollen closed and black. There seemed to be a distorted mound of flesh where Theos's nose used to be, but his lips, although cut, bleeding, and swollen, were distinguishable. The swelling had caused his lips to part, and a small tube, made of a reed that grew in the swamps of the barley fields, was inserted between them. She could see that several of his teeth were missing. Steady hands rhythmically squeezed an inflated animal organ attached to the reed, and she somehow knew that it was only this contraption between Theos and the gods.

Unable to look upon her brother's face any longer, she cast her gaze down his naked body as the servants, healers, physicians, and scholars moved with precision in mostly silence. Several large gashes across his chest leaked thick streaks of blood. One surgeon, gripping the thinnest, sharpest dagger she had ever seen, gently pressed it to his flesh, opening one of the gashes. A swollen sack bulged out, releasing with great pressure a great deal of blood.

Kleopatra felt her head spin but gripped the wooden frame of the bed to steady herself. Her fingers suddenly felt sticky. She closed her eyes a moment to refrain from looking at his blood, now on her hand. When she opened them, she saw that the bone above his elbow on his right arm had speared through the skin, and two fingers bent backward. His abdomen seemed to turn purple, then blue, then black before her eyes in large patches that had suffered some terrible impact, and one leg seemed bent sickeningly toward one side.

A deathly wheezing sound began as one surgeon, with a hand half inside the boy's chest, jolted, and a small crack was heard. The man, his brow creased as it apparently had been many times before, spoke swiftly, with large words, to the thin, obedient man leaning in close beside him, holding out a piece of parchment covered with diagrams. The old man glanced at the parchment, then grunted; the thin man passed the parchment off, then reached for a small clay pot and several small, corked vials, grinding herbs and other things together in a bowl, then instructing the servants around them to apply the thick paste to certain places on the boy's skin. The old man then hissed orders to fetch more lengths of fabric and drizzled a clear liquid, with a smell that assaulted the senses, over open wounds.

Kleopatra had not noticed Berenice kneeling across the room before a small table, her head dipped toward a small wooden carving of the goddess Isis with both palms open and the goddess Aceso clutching a staff wrapped with a serpent. Kleopatra stepped back from the surgery bed with unsteady legs, her place taken immediately by a servant. She made it to Berenice before collapsing in her arms, wishing the gods would take them all so that they would never be apart.

❧

THAT NIGHT, BERENICE HAD LAIN WITH KLEOPATRA IN her bedchamber, Akela tucked in tightly with them. How plain Berenice thought the general's daughter to be, yet she possessed warmth and intelligence that made her joyous company. A good friend for her little sister to have, thought Berenice. Those were truly rare in life.

Berenice had explained as gently as she could to the children how Kleopatra had fainted just before young Auletes proclaimed that, when he became pharaoh, he would order a large temple erected to honour himself, and Theos had replied, "You do not need to linger on such thoughts. Father will be the last pharaoh of Egypte."

The pharaoh had heard Theos and had descended upon him with such rage and violence that, when some tried to step in to pacify their sovereign, he had screeched that any man who attempted to stop him would be executed where they stood. His other children had stood and watched the near murder of their gentle young brother, helpless and sickened.

GREECE

ONE GRAIN OF SAND IN AN ENTIRE OCEAN

— IX —

A small herd of chattering servants woke Chrysanthe as they bustled into her room, the morning light only just beginning to creep over the edge of the world. They had dressed and covered her head to toe in the white virgin's veils worn by the priestesses who worshipped at the temple of Hera and marched her down through the gates into the upper city below the palace.

The ceremonial pilgrimage to the temple was a bore, and the prayers were performed by old Grecian priests who looked as though they had been woken from their tombs to recite these passages. She thought the breathing corpse who struggled to read from the scriptures shaking in his grey hands might not survive the ritual, but alas, no Kretens had died today.

She had been guided through a secluded door by many servants, also dressed in white. They passed behind the walls of the palace courtyards down a narrow, hidden passage, the lively sounds of amassing wedding guests echoing through the royal gardens and musicians playing their instruments in the background of the loud exchanges. Chrysanthe knew from her time under her father's reign that only a small few cared for weddings. The rest came either to curry favour with the hosting king, to seek enhancement of their family's status, or to plot the downfall of other guests, even the king himself. How small-minded the world of men was! They were greedy, conniving creatures who, with their pedestrian aspirations, only sought their own demise, and the foreign kings invited here today would be no different than the noblemen who schemed behind their backs.

Now sitting at the small round and slightly unbalanced table in her rooms, she closed her eyes and breathed in the silence. The white dress was heavy and warm, and the veil made her itch. The thought of a brutish swine ripping the dress from her body and angling to mount her filled her mind, and she began to panic. If she could ply him with drink, surely he would sleep through the wedding night, and she could claim the consummation had taken place. It was easy to smear blood on linens but harder to feign a second time.

She could try to acquire a weapon at the feast and attack him as he stumbled drunk into her chamber, or she could try to pierce his throat at the wedding feast. With such an audience, the king would have no choice but to execute her. *Or else*, the voice in her mind whispered, *die in unwedded bliss and make it so that Sparta dies free of any man's chains.*

All fear fled from her, and she rose calmly to walk to the door, open it, and pass through the archway. Then, in two quick strides, she reached the high balcony that overlooked the gardens many levels below. Using the pillar, she pulled herself up to stand on the railing and extended her arms out beside her; her breathing was steady, and the face of her mother filled her mind.

Chrysanthe smiled and let go. Her body began to surrender to the forward lean, and the ecstasy of freedom filled her before something hard collided with her stomach, and suddenly, she was harshly yanked backwards.

As the realisation dawned that her freedom had once again been taken from her, she thrashed in the iron arms of Markos, who spoke no words but dragged her screaming into the room. Flinging her to the floor, he exited. She heard him lift a heavy wooden bar into place, sealing the door.

Slamming her fists against the wood, she hurled insults at the giant, unsure if he still remained but not caring. Her life had been hers, and now, somehow, it was not.

She slumped against the door and slid to the ground. The world seemed bigger, and she seemed smaller; she was glad Sparta could not see her now, a helpless child not even capable of dying with honour, screaming like a harlot, lacking dignity and the poised strength of royalty in the face of wickedness. If her mother were here, she would tell her daughter that men were slaves to their anger and greed, but the strength of a woman was quiet, like the olive trees in the groves, and ever adjusting, like the trickling streams through the grass.

But she was not her mother. Her mother was a queen and had fought in battles, killing men and women and raiding towns with courage and honour. She had been depicted in paintings throughout Sparta as a goddess of fire, her auburn hair glowing as though aflame as she laid siege against cities with her husband. Chrysanthe was the youngest child of a goddess and a demon, the child who had "brought evil to their shores," as her father had told her. Perhaps her life was indeed meant to be one of pain and suffering. Perhaps she was to pay for the wickedness of her father.

🌿

CHRYSANTHE WOKE TO THE ROUND FACE OF THEOPHILA only inches from her own. The servant smiled softly at her, then pulled the defeated princess gently to her feet. "The time has come, little one. You have made a mess of yourself. Come, and we'll fix you up."

Theophila guided Chrysanthe to the wooden chair and eased her to sit. The maid used a wet cloth to wipe the girl's miserable face clean and fussed over out-of-place hairs; she then removed the lid from a tiny clay pot, and using her finger, smeared a reddish powder on Chrysanthe's cheeks, dabbing with purpose, leaning back to check her work and adjust further. Then the dress sewn by the maids was slipped over her head and all layers pulled down in place at her feet.

The maid held Chrysanthe's face in her hands and stared into her eyes; the kindness emanating from the woman now felt foreign. "Today is one day in countless—one grain of sand in an entire ocean. You have survived the world thus far, and you will survive this. We have heard stories of the Spartans, the most fierce and fearless warriors the Aegean has ever seen. You will not fail them, child; you are all they have. Now, to your feet. It is time to depart."

She pulled Chrysanthe up and squeezed her hand as they exited the room to be greeted by a royal escort of soldiers dressed in full armour and crests. *One day in countless*, she repeated to herself and stepped on.

The ceremonial hall was filled with murmuring guests dressed in their finest robes and jewels for the occasion; the walls of the hall were painted with elaborate scenes of war and victory and of the historical glory of whichever debaucherous cretin had slain the past kings and taken Kretos by force. The many beautifully carved pillars stretched up to the high, domed ceiling, and light spilled through the intricately crafted windows along the east wall, showering the guests in streams of gold. The sight was devastatingly beautiful to behold, and had it been a day of love instead of one solidifying the slavery of a traumatised child, it would have been an enchanting celebration.

The temple was cool but the dress, thick and heavy, weighed on Chrysanthe throughout the service. She steadied herself, raised her chin with the pride of her mother, stepped before the scrutinising crowd, not misplacing a single step, and took her place beside the enormous figure who stood bent before the priests at the altar. She knelt beside him, the scriptures were read by the temple of Hymenaeus' senile priests, wine was taken on their tongues, and oil was dotted to their foreheads.

Chrysanthe's knees began to ache on the hard marble of the altar, and she could feel the callouses on Demosthenes' hands. The smell of wine and sweat lingered around him; he had obviously celebrated his return home into the early hours and most likely throughout the morning of his wedding. A length of dark-blue linen embroidered with gold threads was laid over the joined hands, and the marriage was declared.

The crowd applauded, and the royal couple stood. Demosthenes immediately turned toward his rowdy acquaintances, who greeted him with embraces and boisterous vigour, and seeing as no one knew or cared for Chrysanthe, she lifted the hem of her dress and gracefully strode down the length of the aisle and out of the ceremonial hall, making for the upper royals' gardens, where she knew she could be alone for many hours and avoid the crowds.

In the last of the fading sun, she leaned against a pillar with her slightly trembling hand and drew in several long, steady breaths. Once balanced, she collected the unnecessary layers of fabric of her gown and made her way through the palace, which bustled with rushing servants preparing for the night's festivities, and returned to her apartment.

Upon entering the dimly lit rooms, she was met by Theophila and Isidora, who had already tended to her bed linens and tidied the space. The basin water was clean, and fresh fruits had been placed in a bowl on the small table.

The maids began to remove her dress, and she was grateful for the release as it fell around her feet. Isidora then brought forward a simple, dark-blue chiton that came to her ankles, and she felt her body begin to relax under the loose, flowing garment.

Theophila had collected more small, white hillside flowers and began to pin them around the jewelled coronet she had placed upon the princess's head. Both servants were quiet, keeping their gazes low and busying themselves with their task of readying Chrysanthe for her wedding banquet.

A strange strength had come over Chrysanthe that she could not describe; some regal mask had fixed itself to her face to allow her to walk through this new life and protect her from the surrounding eyes of evil. Her mother had told her once how she had been sent to Sparta by her father, the king of Thrace, to marry the young Spartan king, Dorian. She had never met King Dorian nor been to the lands of Sparta. She had never travelled by sea either, and the journey had been long and the seas rough.

Apollia had spoken of the strange customs and surroundings she had needed to conform to with apparent ease and the grace of a princess who would become a queen, a wife, and a mother. She soon became fiercely revered, and the public gave her the respect due a warrior as she took an active role in her royal duties with her husband, and the kingdom was brought much prosperity and growth. While the king tended to matters of war and military strategy to protect the empire they had built, the people flourished under the social change and economic reform implemented by Apollia and her selected advisers. Under the reign of the young king and queen, Sparta grew into the ferocious legend that all had come to know across the great seas.

Although Dorian was feared, he was not loved as Apollia was. Perhaps that birthed the king's hatred for his wife. Although she'd endured his hatred with the elegance of her reputation, she bore him two beautiful daughters—who (she thanked the gods) reflected no trace of him—and taught them all she knew. Chrysanthe was the last Spartan princess, as her sister was now queen in a faraway land, her homeland forsaken. She was her mother's daughter, and the reverence of such a legendary queen would live through her. The tenacity of the Spartan blood would thrive in this cesspit of barbarism. Today, she became the woman her mother, too, had needed to become.

Unless she could find a way to die . . .

She stepped into the banquet hall, to a sea of celebrating guests. The space beyond the banquet table was swarming with unseated patrons, conversing, drinking, eating, and cheering, and before them all sat the royal family at their places. She saw her elaborately decorated seat among them, next to Demosthenes' empty seat. No one in the crowd noted her entrance except Lysander, who moved forward to bow before her, the drink in his hand untouched.

"Your Royal Highness." He smiled warmly at her.

She did not return it. "Lord Lysander, do you never rest?" She nodded to the cup.

"There is always business to be done, but one must embrace the show." His smile faded. "You must excuse me, Princess. You look an exquisite bride tonight. I extend my congratulations."

Before he could leave, she stepped around him and took her seat at the table. Immediately, goblets and jugs of wine were placed before her by servants, and small bowls of nuts, berries, carved sweetmeats, and cheeses were placed within her reach.

Suddenly, Markos's enormous hand appeared and removed the cheese and meat knives from the setting before her. She wondered how such a large man could function so discreetly, and she made a note that she would have to adjust her peripheral vision to track his ever-lurking presence.

She glanced up to find King Athanasios regarding her with relaxed contemplation; she gave no greeting. Beside him, Charis glared down the table at her over the king's shoulder. The woman was beginning to irritate Chrysanthe, and it was then that she decided that, if the opportunity came, Charis would die—her children too, if the gods willed it. Especially the girl.

She watched the crowd as they mingled. She could feel the king's eyes on her, but she remained stone-faced. Athanasios would never know her and thus would never know her capabilities. He would underestimate his enemy as most men did when their foe was a woman.

Seeing Lysander speaking with an old man and woman dressed in identical pale-blue robes, she noticed the absence of his shadow, Timeaus. Now would be the opportune moment for the boy to be introducing himself to the men of power and influence who were present, to enhance his prospects as all political men did, but the child was not with the adviser, and she found that bothersome.

She spotted two guests standing together: a shorter man with a bald head and a pointed, bright-red beard; and a taller, slender woman, whose raven hair trailed far down her back in a large, loose braid, glittering with slivers of silver hair. The woman wore a modest diadem and the man only a few gold rings and a fine jewelled belt; they seemed to be their own island floating in the sea of chaos but soon adjusted as a rowdy, fat, grey-haired man in a wine-stained tunic stumbled over to greet them boisterously.

Chrysanthe jumped in her seat as hounds ran past her chair and chased each other into the fray, testing the balance of several guests. Then her eye caught on another minuscule interaction, an exchange quick and almost unnoticeable to any who simply scanned the crowd without purpose. The dimly lit figure of Timeaus clung to the shadows by the far wall near the high, arched entrance, speaking with subtle movements of his lips to two men dressed in darker colours.

Strangely, she found no trace of the boy's usual childlike charisma in his face. His hand gestures were controlled and sharp, and he glanced around him as the two men kept their backs to the room. Something felt wrong—it was as if Timeaus had been cornered by these men, and if he called for help, he might be quickly and quietly overcome, perhaps stabbed, his killers merging quickly into the crowd.

Keeping her gaze locked on the boy, Chrysanthe placed her hands on the arms of the great chair and began to push herself to rise, but she abruptly halted as a monstrous figure collapsed into the large chair beside her with a guttural grunt, and she sank again into her seat. Her breath stuck in her throat as she turned to her husband.

The man was so like his brother king that the uncanny sight dried her mouth—he had the same strong brow, the same angular jaw and prominent nose. He had already assessed her face and body and had a dark grin on his lips that made her tense.

"So, this is what my wife looks like." He grabbed a roasted hock before him, ripping the meat with his thick fingers and stuffing the greasy chunks into his mouth, chewing loudly and spilling small flecks of the food down his thick black beard—where they caught—followed by wine that he gulped noisily. This, too, spilled generously down his front, and once the cup was drained, he banged it loudly on the table until a servant rushed forward with a jug and filled it once more. He then regarded her with dark, glistening, desolate eyes.

"You don't say much, do you? Did they take your tongue too?" he asked.

She hardened her gaze, and he chuckled lazily, sipping more wine and glancing around with boredom. "Good. I hate women who talk."

"Who talk, or who have opinions?" Chrysanthe said coolly.

"I already don't like you," he replied.

"It is good then that we are not required to like one another."

"Have you fucked before, Princess?"

She flicked her focus to the crowd, her lips pursed shut, dread creeping up her neck. She heard him laugh into his cup. A weak horn sounded, and she looked around for Timeaus, but he and his companions were gone.

Two guests had stepped before Demosthenes and herself, a scarily thin woman whose tired eyes looked as though they would fall from her face if she were bumped too forcefully, and a thick-necked man with small copper rings braided into his long, greying beard. Both bowed before the couple.

"Well wishes to you both. May your kingdom strengthen with this union," the man said with feigned sincerity. The woman simply nodded with no enthusiasm.

"My thanks, Midas," replied Demosthenes, almost as bored.

The well-wishing continued until Demosthenes engaged in a lengthy discussion with another king.

"Princess Chrysanthe," a man's voice said, and she looked up. A bearded man and a slender woman stood before her, emanating such a presence that she could only nod in acknowledgement. The short man's face was round, his head bald, and his beard flaming red. His kind eyes were deep pools of dazzling green, and Chrysanthe knew there was carefully guarded depth to the man.

The tall woman was surprisingly elegant in her fluid movement. Her face and nose were long, with untraditional beauty. Her cheekbones were prominent but complemented by the abundance of her long greying, ebony hair. She smiled down at Chrysanthe.

"I am King Aristokles of Zykanthos," the man said, "and this is my queen, Eirene. It is my honour to meet you, Princess. I have known your family for many years. Your mother would swell with pride to see you now."

The sincerity in his gaze pierced the dam of emotion within her, and with every ounce of her being, she wished to fall before the two foreign rulers and beg them to take her with them to wherever they wished to go, but the love in her heart for her dear mother wrenched her truest desires to heel. "You knew her?"

"Only for a short while, but her reputation spoke much to her character," replied Eirene, her smile emanating true sweetness.

"We feel your loss, and please know, you will always have friends in Zykanthos, should you desire to visit." Aristokles smiled warmly, but a trace of pity swam in his eyes.

"I thank you for your attendance here today," Chrysanthe said earnestly.

"I am sure you are tired and long to escape the formalities; we will leave you. Many blessings to your union, Princess." Eirene bowed gracefully.

"Aristokles, you dog! You survived the journey in your bathing bowl of a ship, did you?" Demosthenes jested with a familiar tone, and the Zykanthos royals moved to greet the drunken prince, their demeanour stiffening at the interaction. Chrysanthe noted the exchange and managed a half-hearted smile at the next plump couple who waddled up to greet her excitedly.

Slowly, the well-wishers waned. Chrysanthe was tired. Demosthenes had indulged heavily in the drink already, but even so, she signalled to a servant to fill his cup again. Then, when his attention was focussed towards a lord and his large-breasted companion, she pushed against the heavy chair and stood quietly to swiftly exit the hall, shooting a glance at Markos, who waited by the archway and slipped in behind her.

As she made her way through the deserted palace, she found peace in the stillness and silence of her dark and formidable prison. As she reached the door to her rooms, a hand grabbed her arm, and she spun to look into the harsh face of Markos. For a moment, she could not discern his intentions, but the moment passed when his hands patted her gown. He stepped back when he found no concealed weapon.

"Ever the attentive soldier," she whispered with venom. The words seemed to reach him, but she cared not for their effect on the animal. She turned and entered the rooms, closing the heavy door behind her.

Alone in her apartment, she undressed and took the jewels from her head, placing them on the small table, then slipping into the bed beneath thin linens, as it was a balmy night. She lay back and tried to relax into sleep; it was common knowledge that grooms often drank too much to rut on their wedding night, and Chrysanthe knew that much could be done in a single day to prevent consummation. Tonight, the groom would be sleeping in some hallway, still cradling a jug of wine. Tomorrow, she would apply her best tactics to turn the prince from thoughts of sex.

With plans in place, she drifted into slumber. Her sleep was restless and broken. Memories of a time long past crept in silently—a time when a man larger than she had entered her chamber, his cold, clammy hands had pulled back the blankets that shielded her, and he had violated her heinously, despite her begging for mercy. Her father's breath had been rancid with decay and unwatered wine, and the way he'd ridden her had made her wonder what she had done to make him hate her so.

The room was dark and still when Chrysanthe woke suddenly. She heard her door close, and she sat bolt upright, trying to adjust her eyes to the darkness.

A large figure stumbled clumsily into the basin table but remained standing. She swung her legs out of bed to stand, wrapping a sheet around her naked body, and stepped into the alcove of her garment closet. She knew Markos had been ordered to follow her night and day. If the intruder had taken down the one-eyed giant, no help was coming, but perhaps a guard nearby would hear her scream for help if it were loud enough.

Nervously, she watched the man barely keep himself standing as he grabbed onto furniture and stumbled forward. She was poised to scream when she saw his face in the sliver of moonlight.

It was Demosthenes.

With urgency and purpose, she moved forward to him. "You are in the wrong chamber, my lord. Come to the door, and a guard will escort you safely to your bed."

"I . . . need to piss." His breathing was heavy, and he reeked of wine. Leaning with one hand on the pillar of the bed, he wrestled with his belt, which fell to the ground. Lifting his tunic, he relieved himself on the floor. "Where is my pretty wife?"

He turned towards her, swaying on the spot. She didn't know what to say and remained silent, hoping he mistook her for a servant.

"There she is."

Panic rippled through her. "There is plenty of time to make babies, my lord. You are drunk, and you have enjoyed your wedding. Go to sleep, husband."

She reached to guide him to the door, but instead, he stepped in, taking her arms with his hands. "You think you're better than all of us heathens."

He grinned maliciously, towering over her. She could still see the lifelessness in his eyes, even in the darkness. "No. I do not."

"My brother says you have the spirit of a mare he bought years ago. A flighty bitch. I never liked the thing, but she proved useful once broken."

"My lord," she pushed against his grip, "there is much time—but you need sleep. Now that you have returned, you have many duties to tend to—"

"My duty is to make sons. Your duty is to give me them." He tugged at the linen, dragging it clear of her body and dropping it to the ground.

She pushed harder against his hold on her. "My lord, stop! You are not of sober mind. You will stop!"

The back of his hand lashed out and smacked her face. She fell forward onto the bed, her vision blurred, the sudden violence shocking her body. She felt him climb on top of her clumsily, his immense weight pushing the breath from her lungs.

"You give me no orders," he breathed in her ear as he adjusted his body. She felt him harden against her leg, and she began to thrash and scream with fierce effort, but he did not move to cover her mouth nor silence her, almost revelling in her terror.

His wide knee parted her legs, and pain shot through her like a red-hot spear. She screamed and cried out for what felt like hours, loud enough to wake the lower villages, but no one came. Finally, the heinous bastard's weight lifted from her, and he was gone, leaving the abundance of his sweat covering her body to cool in the night air.

Whatever strength she had felt on the evening of her wedding had dissolved. Staring at the small, carved symbol in the bedpost, she lay defeated and alone, in pain, and robbed of something so great she could not describe the loss.

ᴥ

THE DAYS THAT FOLLOWED WERE DARK. HE CAME AT night, and eventually, the pain seemed so familiar that it felt part of her. Women truly were only animals in the world of men, broken like the wild horses her father used to shatter. Once they submitted, the wild spark in their eyes extinguished, and they were ridden by men for pleasure and war until all worth they'd had was lost to time and injury.

Chrysanthe did not know the day nor the hour and had refused to eat or drink for many nights. Faces and voices came and went. Some tried to rouse the princess from her trance-like limbo, but slowly the visitors dwindled.

Isidora was in cheerful spirits each morning when she assessed the new wounds to be tended, humming as she jabbed at the painful bruises with herbal paste. Theophila, however, tended to the girl personally, cleaning the wounds between her legs, applying soothing pastes and herb tinctures, wiping down Chrysanthe's unmoving body, and gently brushing her hair.

The maid was tender with her, and her kindness was evidently deep, but the compassion was lost on Chrysanthe, who could not find salvation from the pain and the torture repeated without fail; the strength had drained from her, and the thirst for vengeance had spilled from her heart, beaten and crushed beneath the violent desire of a demon.

Night came as it always did, and so came Demosthenes as he always did, never faltering in his brutality. Time and time again, the searing pain in her groin screamed as flesh stretched and ripped with each thrust. She kept her gaze always on the small carved symbol, losing herself in the pattern, but hate for it was beginning to grow in her mind, so much so that she didn't notice clenching her fists so much that her palms bled.

"*When you forget hope,*" she remembered the whispers of the old maid in her ear, "*and accept things as they are, the pain becomes more bearable.*" It did not. She had forsaken hope. It had become only another word in a language that had too few words to articulate the decimation of her spirit.

One morning, as Theophila entered the rooms quietly and cleaned Chrysanthe with warm, wet cloths, a raw wound was nudged, and the pain suddenly lit up her body as it hadn't before; she cried out, and the old maid floundered, trying to comfort the princess. It was then that the broken parts were washed over by her grief and the first tears began to fall from her face.

The maid climbed upon the bed and pulled the child to her breast, stroking her mass of flame-coloured hair gently as Chrysanthe clung to her and wailed until her emerald eyes were dry.

On a cooler afternoon than usual, Chrysanthe spent the day in her rooms once more, wrapped in a thick sheep's fleece, her legs tucked beneath her as she perched in a large chair by the small fireplace. Lysander entered with Timeaus in tow, the ageing man absorbed in his papyrus and what seemed like the endless list of problems in the court. Chairs were brought and the table moved near the fireplace, and the two sat with the princess.

Timeaus greeted the princess silently with a gentle smile, though pity and shame swam in his eyes. Lysander, however, seemed ignorant of her despair and proceeded with the night's agenda. The princess sat quietly sipping wine as she observed the two discuss the issues at hand, wondering if perhaps Lysander merely required her presence as a formality, as since arriving, she had not made a single decree or decision for herself with regard to the business of Kretos.

The evening wore on as Lysander and Timeaus sifted through kingdom matters. A farmer in the western hills had lost three cattle to a sudden flood and so would have to marry off his daughter to keep his farm. The farmer was the source of beef for the palace as King Athanasios claimed his was the best beef he had tasted, and Lysander, seeing an opportunity to strengthen two useful corners of the large empire, planned to arrange a match for the farmer's daughter with a young-but-promising aristocrat.

Other issues on the agenda included solving a dispute between a blacksmith and a drunken palace guard, easing the unrest from the raising of tariffs in the main port, and arranging the construction of two new outhouses in the upper village to replace the two that had recently exploded, damaging many nearby businesses and killing two women.

Chrysanthe's attention drifted in and out as she stared into the waning flames. Lysander rubbed his tired eyes and sighed as he squinted at the papyrus before him. "Did we locate the witness to the slaying in the East Tolsa village?" he asked wearily.

"No, my lord. A small troop has looked for days now," Timeaus answered. He paused and then continued in a cautious tone. "Although, a body was pulled from the river mouth near his dwelling. The head was missing, but he matches the description of the witness." Timeaus seemed older in this light; the weight of hard decisions no doubt filled his young days now.

Lysander sighed. "I fear the wrong man was executed, lad, and now I carry the death of an innocent on my conscience."

"It could not have been the wrong man, my lord. The witness was sure of the culprit, and the murderer did not protest."

"Indeed, it was the correct man arrested, but the man to pay the price was not him, and with the culprit detained, it is too curious that the only witness should disappear and a body very likely to *be* that witness emerges only days after."

"Then it is true," Timeaus whispered, his gaze lost in the flames of the fireplace. "He truly cannot be killed."

"Hush, boy! He is only a man—a clever one, but only a man. He can be killed, and he will be brought to justice once his cunning is outdone by the finest soldiers of Kretos."

"A prisoner escaped?" Chrysanthe asked softly.

"She speaks!" Lysander threw up his arms and sat back against the chair, resting his aching back.

"Yes, my lady," Timeaus explained calmly. "A royal councilman was murdered in the lower village outside a brothel. The bastard was found and executed, but my lord believes the wrong man was put to death."

"Why do you believe this, Lysander?" Chrysanthe asked.

"It is a grisly matter, Princess, I don't—"

"I will pretend that you are weary and do not intend to insinuate that the violent depravity I have endured since coming to this wretched rock is not a 'grisly matter,' Lord Lysander, and we will proceed to where you answer the question your princess has asked—seeing as you insist on my inclusion in matters of the palace," Chrysanthe said, face cold, with no trace of the young girl she had been mere moons ago.

"I did not mean to offend, my lady. The . . . the two men were similar in height, build, and appearance, unshaven, with long unkempt hair, and thin-framed. When the man was arrested, I checked for a long scar down one of his legs—"

"Phrixos, he's the most famous assassin in the world!" Timeaus blurted excitedly. "He has travelled far, across the great sea. He has murdered thousands of men, women, and babies. They say he can never be caught as no one has seen his face! The legend tells of a great red scar all the way from his heel to his ear, from a fierce battle with a mighty sea titan, when—"

"Enough!"

Timeaus' eyes were alight with the thrill of the legend, but Lysander's deep, furious tone had brought the theatrical rendition to a stop. Lysander glared at his pupil, and suddenly, Timeaus looked like a small child again, cowering in the wrath of discipline.

The old man struggled to contain his irritation. "He is known by many names across the lands of men, for he never fails at his task."

"Ammon." Chrysanthe breathed the name. She had heard whispers of such a man in passing from Spartan guards in the dim palace of her father. He was a man of many names—a man of shadows.

"The hidden one." Lysander nodded.

"And you believe you captured this man?" asked Chrysanthe.

"I do. I saw the great scar with my own eyes, but when the man's body was loaded onto a cart to be buried, I saw his bare leg . . ." Lysander looked confused, then shook his head as if clearing his mind. "It was dark, and the hour late, and my eyes are not a young man's anymore. Perhaps I am mistaken." Lysander's perplexed expression lingered as he stared into the dying embers of the fire; then, suddenly, his sense of duty returned. "I am a man of integrity, and if the murderer has escaped, he will kill again. I am to protect the people of Kretos, and I intend to, but I was instructed not to pursue the matter further, and now that there is no witness, I fear there are no more cards to play."

"Athanasios instructed that you forget this concern?"

"Yes, my lady."

"And if the wrong man was executed, then the switch would have had to happen in the royal prison, where crimes against the crown are sentenced?"

"Yes."

"Does that not suggest that the assassin is in the employ of the king?"

"Such things, Princess, would be treasonous to suggest."

"Long, unkempt hair, you say? A beard and a slight frame?"

"Let us move on from the stupid suspicions of an old man." As Lysander continued on with his agenda, Chrysanthe glanced at Timeaus, who gave a quick nod before averting his eyes studiously to the papyrus before Lysander.

The night was long and arduous, and the embers of the fire were truly cooled before they could work no further. The two advisers prepared to make their exit from her chambers.

"I bid you goodnight, Princess," Lysander said, wearily standing by the door as Timeaus used all his strength to open it for his teacher. The two turned to leave.

"Lysander," Chrysanthe called to him, and the old man turned obediently to her, holding his old and aching frame. "How does he murder? Phrixos."

"Poison, my lady. Opus-bloom, I believe. Very rare but distinct in its lilac colour. An odd choice."

"Why is that?"

"It is . . . uh, I suppose you would say it is a cruel choice? The nature of the tincture is to paralyse the victim without dulling the senses to pain and consciousness and simulate death when, in fact, the organs take longer to slowly shut down. As I said, a cruel choice to force one to witness one's own agonising death."

"Cruel indeed. Goodnight to you both." She gave a nod to Timeaus, who grinned widely, and the two left, leaving Chrysanthe alone in the dim light of the few candles that still burned. A cold wind whistled as it surged through small cracks in the wood of the now-boarded-up window, and a memory danced in her mind of a servant boy writhing in agony at the feet of her father. The child, assigned to taste her father's food before consumption, succumbed to his fate and lay still, his wide, scared eyes staring blankly to Olympus, lilac foam seeping from his small mouth.

She shivered in the breezy darkness and pulled her shawl tighter around herself. "The shivering of skin from fear," she whispered into the darkness, her spirit revived. She rose from her seat, glided across the room, and stood before a thin stream of wind that poured through the largest crack in the window barricade. She closed her eyes as the cold sea air washed over her face and down her neck, and gentle bumps began to rise along her skin in response. She breathed in the freedom of the wind and knew that soon her spirit would ride the great flurries of air across the oceans, taking her far from this place.

EGYPTE

EVER-LOOMING DANGERS

— X —

Kleopatra and Akela spent the days following the assault on Theos keeping each other's silent company in the warm upper apartments, having their meals brought to them, and watching the slaves slowly erecting small temples beside the great Sphinx. To the south, they could see the construction of a large, new monument in the young, far-away city of Luxor.

On the third day, a small bird dropped onto the terrace, its neck broken. It twitched and tried to move its wings, but only one leg seemed to be within its control. Kleopatra let out a gasp and ran to it, kneeling immediately to reach down and comfort the creature. Akela stayed where she was, simply watching the bird struggle. *How strange flying is*, she thought, looking up to the cloudless blue sky, half-heartedly alert for further ill-fated birds. She watched her friend stroke the terrified bird's feathers gently as it flapped in panic, one twisted foot spasming and clutching.

Watching Kleopatra, Akela felt a sadness in her spirit. The warmth and compassion of the young princess were pure and untaught. Her mercy was admirable and innocent, but this was not a place of mercy. The pharaoh's temper and Arsinoe's hatred were ever-looming dangers. It was clear that Isis and Neos loathed their family, and their blatant contempt lent anxious uncertainty to the future of the dynasty and threatened the safety of such a naive princess.

Akela shook off the sticky feeling of unsavoury deeds brewing as Kleopatra ran to the door of the room behind the terrace and called for Kohlis, who stood outside. He rushed in quickly with his hand ready to draw his sword, only to stop when she showed him the bird. He responded with humility and solemnly replied *"No"* when she inquired if it would live. She hung her head sadly as he stood with the bird in his hands and turned to leave. She called out to him. "Kohlis?"

He stopped and turned toward her, patiently waiting for her question, his giant hands cupping the twitching bird.

"Those people on the streets. Why did they do that?"

Kohlis stared a moment before speaking with a thick accent in a deep, rumbling voice like thunder in the distance. It rolled like chilled water up Akela's spine. "People will do evil when the belly is empty."

Kleopatra turned away, seemingly trying to understand his response, and he exited without another word.

Akela liked the man; he saw what others did not, and she admired intelligence in any creature. *Father would like him too*, she thought. Then thoughts of her father flooded her mind and tightened her chest. She missed him dearly, and each day she could not reach out and touch him was a day she rued. He always returned before the rains, as sure as the sun rose and set. He had always made sure to return before the rains. He said it was poor battle strategy if a settlement was not secured or a battle not won before the rains came, but the whispers of rebellions in the west had set a fire below her heart, and worry had fanned the flame.

She looked to the west, a small part of her hoping to see the caravan of an army on the horizon through the blurred shimmers of the heat above the desert sand.

⚜

THE SURGEONS WERE A FAMILIAR SIGHT WITHIN THE palace halls for days more than Akela could count. The younger ones spoke fast and hushed in groups of five or so, debating competitively, wearing long white robes and no jewellery or adornments, while the older groups tended to huddle over large parchments and listen intently to the speaker. Healers and holy men had even come from foreign lands to meet with the modern physicians of Egypte, and Akela had heard that the recovery of Theos, though slow, was being revered as a miracle of the gods,—even though most of the damage was irreversible. Even though Akela's faith in immortal beings was suspect, she was glad Theos had lived. He was, after all, like a brother to her also.

She walked with Kleopatra from their scripture lesson, where they had studied with an old fat teacher of numbers and hieroglyphs. They could both almost read and write sufficiently in six different languages, which delighted them both for their plans to travel to exotic lands beyond the sea. Because of General Ankhmakis's highly regarded position and irreplaceable value, Akela had been allowed to attend scholarly lessons with the royal children, as were several of the other nobles' offspring, and the general had been given his own apartments within the palace where he and Akela lived, although most nights when her father was away, the apartments seemed cold and lonely, and she often slept with Kleopatra in her bedchamber.

Akela wondered if she would have made it through each season of her father's absence without her closest friend. They had become inseparable from their first meeting at the age of five, and rarely was one seen without the other. She glanced at her friend with her deeply tanned skin, dark hair and brows, and eyes a lighter brown than her own. Kleopatra's mouth was small and sweet, framed with soft cheekbones and a slight jaw. Akela loved that when the princess smiled, her face lit up with joy, and that her eyes were large with a wonder that only the innocent possessed. Akela smiled to herself, filled with happiness to have such a friend, and she entwined their fingers as they walked.

THE SUN HAD SET ALMOST TWICE BEFORE RHEMA entered the banquet hall, torchlit and set with tables laden with meats and fruits, at which many of the royal family were eating their evening meal with their various companions, while three war generals spoke intensely to the pharaoh.

The room fell silent upon Rhema's arrival. A light sweat glistened on her brow, and faint bloodstains marked the fabric tied over her long tunic. She bowed and addressed the pharaoh. "The babes have arrived, Your Highness, one boy and one girl, both healthy and already well-tempered."

Cheers erupted from the table, and the pharaoh threw up his hands with a triumphant expression, immediately turning to the servant beside him and ordering wine jugs to be brought in abundance. Berenice rose quickly with a smile and exited the hall.

Rhema spoke again. "The mother is well, Your Highness, and resting."

"You may go," the pharaoh said. "Tend to them."

❧

THEOS SAT A LITTLE WAY DOWN THE TABLE FROM Kleopatra and Akela, and as far from the pharaoh as the table allowed. He dropped his gaze at the news and stared down at his plate morbidly. Akela noticed the boy's discomfort, and her heart bled for him. His meat had been cut for him by a servant, for his right hand—once his promising sword hand—was beyond repair, the knuckles and joints bent unsettlingly in too many places. Half of his head was shaved clean of hair and displayed a grizzled, red patch of skin that stretched the whole side of his face, attached with raised but healing stitches of cotton and wire. He was thinner now and hunched to one side—no doubt, Akela thought, guarding several pained ribs.

She had watched him for many nights move his food around his plate, and she realised he must not yet be able to chew. Stew or soup would be more suitable, and of course, he would have it brought to his room to avoid the public attention.

Below his pale green tunic, terrible red lightning-shaped scars peeked out menacingly, and Akela wondered if he might be the only person to have ever had another man's hand inside their chest and lived.

Theos eased himself to his feet quietly to slip away with a limp while his father was well-distracted, and Akela turned to Kleopatra, who was munching on figs, her fingers red with the seeds. "Are we allowed to visit the babies?" she asked.

"If the servants let us. We can go after we finish eating."

"I am finished when you are, Princess."

"Don't call me that."

"Forgive me, Your Highness."

Kleopatra rolled her eyes. They stood, then dashed out of the hall and down the corridor toward Safiya's new chambers in the eastern apartments. She had requested them for the sunlight that streamed into them each morning;

the woman sometimes seemed to be sunshine itself, thought Akela as they approached the queen's room.

One palace guard, with scrutiny in his expression, pushed the door open for the girls, and they entered to hear quiet laughter. Berenice stood near the bed, smiling down into a bundle of fabric in her arms, and Safiya turned to see the girls as they entered, her smile beaming through the tiredness on her face. "Come, sweet girls, come see them."

Akela and Kleopatra stepped lightly closer, now with a sense of uncertainty. They rarely saw babies in the palace, and the creatures were still a mystery, helpless and unable to serve a purpose for many years. They crept carefully onto the bed, where Safiya lay holding another bundle of linen that seemed to be gurgling strangely. As they crept closer, she leaned toward them, and they saw the tiny babe, its skin light brown and spotted with dried blood. Its little eyes were closed and its tiny face scrunched into an ugly shape. Its little limbs twitched unpredictably.

"Would you like to hold your brother, Kleopatra?" Safiya said with a proud smile.

Kleopatra looked up at her, wide-eyed, and nodded excitedly.

"Sit back and cross your legs, and hold him like this." As Kleopatra readied herself, Safiya sat up awkwardly, wincing slightly, and placed the babe gently into the princess's arms.

"Sit back, Akela." Berenice had appeared at the bedside and held the second babe out to her.

Shocked and a little nervous, Akela scrambled quickly to sit and cross her legs next to Kleopatra, receiving the child from Berenice and settling into a tense and determined position. She looked down at the child, curiosity filling her mind, and found herself smiling. "This is a girl?"

"She is a princess of Egypt," Berenice answered, and Akela thought she heard worry in her tone.

It looked a little like the wrinkled hairless cats that sometimes would wander into the palace from the royal menagerie, ugly little things and dangerously delicate, thought Akela. The little beastie wriggled uncontrollably, and she fought to balance it in her arms. The fabric began to loosen, and the child started to cry, moving its body uncomfortably. Its little right arm escaped, revealing a stunted hand. There was a small ball of bent flesh at the end of a short forearm, and Akela noticed the babe's shoulder seemed distorted also. She looked up at Berenice, whose face seemed grim, but she spoke gently. "She is a special princess, touched by the gods."

"And will never hold a sword . . ." The whisper escaped Akela's lips without a thought, and the room was suddenly eerily hushed as servants looked up wide-eyed from their duties around bowls of soiled water and bloodied rags. The words foretold by Theos rang true. His gifted sight was becoming harder to ignore. Akela knew now that the child's hand would only confirm the gifts of Theos, and because of their truth, his life would be forfeit if the pharaoh believed such coincidences to be sorcery. Which he did . . .

It was then that Akela's gaze wandered to the child prince, Theos's words echoing like the cold breeze of winter across her neck: *Father will be the last pharaoh of Egypt.*

Berenice leaned in and gently took the child from Akela. "Time to be gone, young ones."

❧

THE MARKETPLACES WERE BUSTLING WITH THE HOT grind of morning chores, and the ever-rhythmic ticking of the slaves' picks on stone seemed almost comforting. Broths began to boil on small fires through the stalls, and the smell of barley bread wafted slowly down the streets where beggars moved to sit in their chosen spots and children ran undisciplined, carrying wide sticks upon their shoulders from which hung racks of studded leather sandals or animal-hide satchels.

Folissi was a humble merchant of salt-dried meats, and the sun-weathered man was generally content with his life; he earned enough to feed his plain-faced wife and their small daughter, whose sweet smile brought joy to them both. He climbed the narrow stone steps of his sand-paved home to the roof, where several lines of thin rope were strung tightly between wooden posts. He set down the wide reed basket his wife had woven for him to carry his marinated camel and goat meats, then began to hang the cuts from the ropes, keeping them in place with carved wooden pegs. He attached the last strip and took a step back to breathe in the delicious smell of the spices, then stretched his arms wide with a contented yawn.

He sank into his worn chair—the reeds of which had conformed to the shape of his body over the years—beneath a small cloth canopy to shield him from the harsh sun and settled in for a day's work. Almost immediately, a small falcon landed on the line next to a strand of drying meat, and Folissi sprang to his feet, grabbed a long staff of wood with thorny vines wrapped in a fan formation on its end, and lunged forward to swat the bird violently, but it launched away before the tool could catch it and was gone.

He swore loudly at the bird and thought to himself that the falcon would have been good for supper. It was his young daughter's favourite. He smiled at the picture of his little Khepri in his mind, a kindhearted little girl unaware of their poverty. Her happy nature pulled him from his bed each morning, and hearing her laugh eased the pain in his knees and shoulders.

Leaning on the staff, he cast an eye to the west. The horizon was a crisp line of gold meeting bright blue; he rubbed his eyes a moment to refresh his failing sight and confirmed that there was indeed a faint trail of ants marching toward Memphis.

ROMA

MARCH OF THE CENTURION

— XI —

The cheering from the people as Crassus and Julius rode into Rome at the head of their remaining legions was splendid and deafening. Every eye in Rome was fixed on the famous generals atop their brilliantly decorated war mounts.

Julius waved proudly at the excited faces as coloured rice rained down and bounced from shining golden breastplates embellished with scenes of victory. Crassus's face remained hardened and unfeeling; he kept his thoughts to himself, seemingly unmoved by victories or glory, a perspective to which Julius could not relate.

The army marched in unison through streets bathed in flower petals of white and red. The warriors were showered with gifts and affection by families and smiling children. A soldier broke formation, picking up a young woman and spinning her around before removing his helm and kissing her deeply to a slew of whistles and cheers. Julius smiled to show his approval of the victory returning home was in itself. Typically, the breaking of formation would be punished, but it was a happy day for Rome, and her happy people ensured his support.

The closer he approached Palatine Hill, the more elaborate the houses became, the more colourful the amphitheatres, and the smoother the cobbled streets beneath the hooves of his horse. He rode steadily onward, through the gates of the upper city, where the sight of his palace and the forums was truly spectacular.

Pompey's army had already arrived back in Rome after opting out of seeing the enemy nailed to their crosses, but word had reached the people, and they could not deny that Julius and Crassus had won the glory, which no doubt would enrage Pompey. Julius smiled at the thought of the pale-faced piss-for-brains idiot flushed red with rage.

Although a strength of his, Julius found politics quite boring. Crassus typically spoke for him at the Senate meetings or in his absence. Though Julius did love the spirit in the people when the entire city loved him, he was tired. It had been a long three years, and if he were to survive the debriefing, the victory feasts, and the obligatory conversations with each and every nobleman offering their congratulations, he was going to need rest. He decided that he would address the people now while affection was fresh in their hearts so that he might forgo the speeches later, and so, as he came to the top of the first forum grounds, he pulled hard and sharp on the reins of his horse and swung his beast to face the enormous roaring crowd.

Silence fell over the masses gathered before him. Julius' booming voice thundered clearly across the plaza. Even the breeze seemed to hush in his presence.

"People of Mother Rome, you put your faith in me, trusted me with your lives, sent me your fathers and brothers and your sons. There have been dark, uncertain times, but I have brought them home to you with riches beyond our dreaming, gold, stones, gems, furs, savages, precious metals, and expansion of our lands. Now we are united, people and state, bellies never to be hungry again and children to play without fear.

"War takes from every man, but those who emerge from it do so with wolves in their hearts and fire in their blood. Our fallen are the heroes of the ground we walk on with pride. To the sons who have returned, I say I am honoured to fight beside such wolves, and may you prosper in the glory you have sown for your empire. I will not forget your sacrifice! Glory to Rome!"

The sea of bodies erupted with exhilaration, and horns sounded, coloured rice was flung, and silk sashes filled the air, waved by cheering citizens. Beside him, his right-hand commander, trusted friend, and fellow senator Marcus Junius Brutus drew his sword and held it to the sky.

"Hail Caesar!" Brutus bellowed, and the crowd's crying only swelled further.

They turned their horses away and continued up the hill toward the far forums, where Crassus had dismounted, walking stiffly past the waiting senators in their long white robes.

"Are you prepared to return home only to be bored to death before the Senate, my friend?" Julius said sourly. "Epidus will surely have only criticism."

"He is only wise as far as his beard. You have exceeded the expectations of Pompey and Marcus Antonius, which surely must taste as sweet as victory itself. The Senate cannot deny your achievements, but it does not mean they will not try, my lord," Brutus replied.

"A pox on them all," spat Julius.

"It will not be long now until they all find blood in their piss pots."

"Not soon enough," Julius mumbled as he dismounted his beast and approached the waiting men, who greeted him with no warmth.

"Hail Caesar. You are fourteen days late to return. Your pointless crucifixion venture has cost the military further rations and pay. I suggest you prepare to share your solutions for this unnecessary expenditure."

"It is good to see you also, Flavius," Julius said with a bored sigh as he strode past them through the large carved forum pillars.

As Julius entered the lavish courtyard of the forum, he inhaled the familiar scent of the lavender bushes and ancient citrus trees that grew, twisted and warped, around trellises surrounding several grand water fountains.

A young boy appeared suddenly in the doorway ahead of him, and a smile lit up the child's face. "Julius!"

"Octavian, my boy!" Julius held out his arms, and the child flung himself into the general's embrace. Julius loved the boy as his own. Seeing him was one of the few things he looked forward to upon his return to the capital. The greeting was a rare display of affection from the child. Pulling away from the boy, he assessed Octavian. "You've grown two heads taller, and you've become a strong lad."

"I have practiced my sword work every day and have been strict with my studies, Uncle." Strangely, there was less child in the boy than there ought to be; his face was always serious, and he was disciplined beyond his years. *More useful to me than any miserable cripple in the Senate,* Julius thought.

"Come, let us endure the pointless gabble of old, whining men."

Julius and Octavian strode across the courtyard in silence. The debriefing took the rest of the day and was a sickeningly boring formality to endure. Julius almost drifted to sleep while resting his jaw on his fist but was beyond relieved that Marcus Antonius and Pompey seemed intent on disputing petty claims until the Senate guards had to physically pull them from one another. Thankfully, Crassus had spoken for Julius, as Crassus was his senior general, and Julius had no wish to navigate the nauseating, perpetual interrogation of the senators.

Glancing to where Octavian sat, however, Julius observed the boy's devoted attention to the council's debates and discussions. *A fine commander he will make when he is grown,* he thought. Pompey's shrill allegations ripped across the Senate chambers once more and were met with gusto by Crassus's bellowing swearing, and with that, Julius rose and exited.

The halls were quiet, and Julius was grateful for the peace until Pompeia rounded a corner and stopped abruptly upon seeing her husband. She wore a white dress with a purple sash draped over her thin frame, her spindly fingers wrapped as they always were around a cup of wine. Her curled hair was pinned with a fine, jewelled golden comb, and the angular, bony features of her face only emphasised her resemblance to a volatile and unpredictable insect that ate its young.

She sauntered like a brightly decorated animal, colourful to signal danger, with no female tenderness in her shifting eyes. She was violent, and he recalled the night she had struck him during an argument. Infuriated, he'd responded with a slap of great force that had sent her hurtling to the ground. It was then that she had looked up at him with hungry eyes alight with carnality, his entire mind and body pumping with rage and frustrated confusion as she'd slithered across the floor to his feet, climbed up his body, and pounced, clinging to him, her legs latching around his waist, her kiss deep and passionate. He'd been unsure of what he was feeling, but her persistence had turned his rage to lust, willing prey to her desire. She'd bit his lip, and he'd thrown her on the bed, maddened by the intentional wound, but when he'd looked at her, he'd found no repentance. Her fingers had reached between her legs, and her tunic slipped to reveal one small but firm breast. Julius had felt he had no free will. He'd felt bewitched by the sorceress, turned into an animal. They had ravaged one another until they could not any longer.

That had been the only time they had lain together except on their wedding night, out of ceremony.

"You've returned," she said.

"I have. It has been a long time. You look well."

"Do I?" She raised an eyebrow. "How curious. Do you know when I look unwell?" Sharp undertones he could not decipher lined her voice. How was it that he could predict the movements of an enemy army and slaughter all who opposed him, yet he could not understand the strategy of females?

"I suppose I would not."

"One of your hounds died," she said with a bored tone. "Welcome home, husband." She glided past him, and he felt the haze of his confusion leave with her. Eager to be alone, he pressed on toward his palace.

He had thrown himself into war to quell the grief he'd suffered when Cornelia died, and since then, he had known nothing but the numbness of deafening battle. He had relished it, found his solace in it, found himself amongst the blood and the dirt and the animalistic fight for survival. Crassus had not approved of his first wife due to her status bringing no high reputation or family wealth to their union, but Julius had not cared.

He thought perhaps the gods had frowned on him, Cornelia's death their punishment for choosing love over his duty to Rome. Crassus had urged him to marry Pompeia and bring their two wealthy houses together. Julius suspected Crassus had much use for her grandfather's gold and Senate influence, and he cursed Crassus for burdening him with this harpy of a woman and for how, every chance he found, he would remark upon the fact that she was not yet pregnant. *It must be done for offspring, I suppose*, he thought unenthusiastically and rubbed his eyes, his muscles complaining. Once finally alone in his rooms, he called for a bath to be drawn.

The noon sun had long passed, and the light began to drift into breathtaking orange and pink streaks across the sky. The perfumed bathwater had cooled, but Julius remained motionless, in some pensive state between consciousness and sleep. The killing did not weigh on his conscience and hadn't for some years now, but in the absence of war, there was only silence, forcing him to listen to the two wolves that clashed violently within him.

The elation from victory was fleeting in contrast to the years devoted to achieving it. He wanted prosperity for Rome and wealth for its people, for his place in history to be marked for generations after him, and for a child . . . he wanted a child. He knew he was ageing, and in his position as one of the wealthiest and most decorated men in the empire, there were few things he had yet to experience. *How ironic*, he thought, *that a man who can acquire anything he desires should be bored of life.* His male lovers had held his attention for many years, as the world of men was new and untapped, but he grew tired of that too and sought undiscovered affairs, anything to drown out the ripping growls and savage duels of his wolves.

The heavy wooden door opened, and a servant backed into the unlit room, her arms full of linens. She nudged the door off her hip and turned toward him, gasping in surprise upon seeing him and burying her face in the linens. "I am sorry, my lord. It was quiet, and it had been some time. I thought you had finished." She gave a small curtsy and made for the door.

"Stay. Go about your chores. Do not let my presence stop you." His voice was vacant and low, and she half-turned back to him, lowering the linens from her face. She stared at the ground, clearly unsure of where to look and how to proceed in the vicinity of a naked general.

He could see her now, and the heavy clouds in his mind cleared. "Hortensia?" She turned toward him but kept her eyes on the floor.

"Yes, my lord. I can return later and leave you with your thoughts."

"No, please, do not leave me with my thoughts. They are far from the company I wish to keep. Remain and speak with me. It has been many years, and I am sure you have much news for me."

The girl placed the linens upon a lounge and moved to sit in a beautifully made chair near the carved marble bathing basin. She did not relax or smile, still careful with her gaze.

"It is good to see you well, my lord. You have been much awaited," she said, her voice soft and sweet. Many had noted that this servant was ugly, plump and plain. She had a small mouth but full lips, a narrow nose, and large, light eyes framed by wisps of curly brown hair. *Beautiful*, he thought.

🌢

"HOW IS YOUR FATHER?" JULIUS ASKED.

"He has recovered, my lord," Hortensia replied. "Our family is grateful for your involvement in the matter; we thank you dearly."

"I am glad."

There was no enthusiasm in his voice. Hortensia sensed the mind of her master was troubled but dared not speak on it.

The silence grew as Julius stared into the bathwater; Hortensia started to believe he had forgotten she was there, but then he broke the silence once more. "What do the people want, Hortensia?"

She hesitated, unsure of what answer to give as speaking out of turn could offend and prompt punishment.

"Speak your mind, girl; there is no pretence of rank here. I see the cheering faces of many upon every return, but they are not the faces of all."

"Well, my lord . . . The wars have taken much from all, save the rich." Shocked by her own temerity, she fell silent, scolding herself in her mind, but to her surprise, no discipline came.

"Continue. My patience for delay is thin, and I wish for the truth."

She swallowed hard and continued. "Many of the poorer districts are hungry. There are many crippled or maimed veterans who cannot work to feed themselves; they beg on the streets but are often disregarded. In the insulae hovels, there is a lack of jobs, and men struggle to feed their families. Land is expensive with Pompey's land taxes, and so agrico—argrik—" She struggled with the word, and embarrassment swept through her.

"Agriculture."

"Agriculture is not an avenue for them." She exhaled gently and prayed that she had used all words correctly, as she had forgotten the meaning of several.

"There are not enough jobs?"

"No, my lord. General Marcus Antonius has founded the union of working slaves; they can be bought and sold easily for any work, and they are bought at a low cost, making the labour wage not enough to feed families."

"When did Marcus Antonius form this union?"

"Two years now, my lord."

"What else?"

"Morale is low. Many are disheartened as they struggle to make their payments. Some turn to crime to gather the coin so that no soldiers come to cut the fingers from one of the family. Such a thing dooms the family. Since cripples cannot work, the family falls to ruin. Many are young and able-bodied, but if unemployment and eviction do not bring their death, then disease surely will."

She felt as if she had spoken enough for an entire week and felt uncomfortable in such a conversation with such a man.

"Is that all?"

"The lower city has been spurned by the Senate, my lord, but they are your subjects also." She pursed her lips tightly for fear of her mouth spouting a river of words beyond her control.

Julius was quiet for a moment. "You have spoken well, Hortensia. I enjoy the company of those with more intelligence than the old fools quarrelling in the Senate, and honesty is so rarely observed. I thank you for entertaining my interrogation."

"Are you well, my lord?"

"You may go."

Hortensia stood at once and hurried from the room with relief.

◆

THE MEN SHOUTED AT POMPEY AND AT EACH OTHER. Julius, Crassus, and Octavian sat quietly, watching the madness of powerful men squabbling like children. Pompey seemed amused by the eruption he had caused with his slander, and smiling, conversed with his delegates. Crassus rubbed at his brow with a calloused hand; the man had a low tolerance for nonsense, but he thoroughly understood the respect he must give the Senate in order for his plans to be approved. Julius knew his mentor had more patience than him to sit through hours of listening to men of spent youth vying for their voices to be heard and ideas acknowledged, seeking comfort in the face of their irrelevance, refusing to admit their time had come and passed and now existing merely as ghosts watching greater men shape the future of an empire that no longer needed them.

Irrelevance and the hindrance of old age were too unpleasant to think on, and Julius at that moment hoped to die in battle, a general's death, before his bones became brittle and his muscles seized. Such a death would require a war in which to fall gloriously, and war would not come if he did not coerce it.

He pushed himself to stand, and soon the room quietened, most of those present likely forgetting the source of their dispute and grateful for the progression in agenda.

The senators and military men of the curia looked to him. He caught a glimpse on Pompey's face of the fury in him that Julius commanded such respect; hate, envy, and resentment haunted the short general's eyes.

Julius spoke. "My good senators, I take your dispute as gravely as I do your devotion and tender care for Mother Rome. However, I believe it has come time for me to announce my agenda. The civil peace of our empire is at stake, and now that the slave revolt has been crushed and I have returned victorious" (Pompey's eyes narrowed) "I intend to mend those dilemmas immediately. Placated people are a prosperous people, and so I wish to implement many citizen aids—"

"Where will the gold for such endeavours come from? You have drained us dry already, funding your military!" came the shrill voice of Flavius from his seat.

"Come now, Flavius, let us speak no falsity in a curia of honourable men. You know well that General Crassus funded the entire campaign to crush the slave revolt with his own coin—sparing no expense, I might add. I have also been informed of the inventory of the treasury, and there is more than enough from the many campaigns in which your four generals have prevailed. I would advise not to insult my intelligence again."

The old senator's face flushed with anger.

"Our empire has been at war for generations," Julius continued. "Much blood has been spilled and many victories attained, but the cost has been the sacrifice of the people and their sons and husbands, plus rationing, eviction, poverty, and disease. We have neglected the ones whom we regard as the pillars we rest our laurels upon. My good senators, those pillars will crumble, and all we have built will topple if we do not preserve their strength and harmony, and thus, loyalty. Rome must be truly great, not just in name and image. I intend to restore peace and prosperity in our great lands, but—it might surprise you to know—it costs gold to gain gold. My agenda for doing so is thus."

Before he continued, he braced himself beneath his confident composure for the objections that were sure to come. "Gold will come from the treasury of Rome and so from all men in this room who serve her."

Stunned faces blinked at him. He held up his hands to placate the greedy wretches—Rome's rats in robes—but the panicked whispering gained momentum.

"We live well beyond our means, and if you truly love Rome, you will care for her organs!" he shouted above the rising hubbub. "Her heart is broken, but we are the wolves that protect her from harm. By doing so, we will allow her to heal and thrive to a magnitude we as mortal men cannot comprehend."

"You want us to feed the diseased whores and their lice-ridden bastards with our own coin?" Flavius shouted toward Julius. "If you care for the scum of Rome so much, Caesar, let them suckle at your tit and stroke your cock for your gold! Next, you will be petitioning to arm the whores and lead them into battle!" A roar of support lit up the crowd.

"You're going soft from watching your men battle for you, Caesar. The cream of Rome's citizens takes precedence over the dregs of society!" A flustered bald senator gestured angrily to the men around him to give their cheers in support.

Only the generals remained silent. Julius could see in their eyes that they knew he was right, and he was relieved that he would have their support. His voice cut through the cheers like a hot blade. "I suggest you retract your repugnant snub, Senator Marullus, for I have killed more men and won more battles for Rome than you've strangled shits."

Crassus stole a glance of Octavian, who sat straight-backed on the ledge of his bench, his attention consumed by the majesty of his uncle.

Julius's voice boomed out, filling the Senate. "Bravery is encouraging growth when the prospect of that growth exceeding your own is not just a possibility but likely. Cowardice is letting other men die when you have more than you need because you do not want the dying man's greatness or wealth to surpass your own. That is not how great empires become great. There must be sacrifice now for wealth to return to you tenfold. During my absence, while I was winning Rome's wars, much corruption has been allowed in this Senate. So, you will allow me this. Although, be warned, this is not a request: I am merely informing you of my plans for Mother Rome.

"Now hear me, senators, for my patience is wearing thin, and I will not repeat myself. I will found new settlements for the veterans of each of our armies. They will receive pensions and low taxes, for many are crippled and cannot work. This is both incentive and respect. The Empire of Rome owns much fertile but unpopulated land; there are, at my councillors' best estimate, twenty thousand poor families with three or more children. They will all be given land—"

An explosion of dispute erupted and caught like wildfire.

"Silence!" Julius roared. The anger that emanated from him seemed to reach the senators seated at every wall. The room became silent. Pompey glanced at Crassus, who leaned informally in his chair, a slight smile on his lip as he listened to his protégé address the Senate of old fools.

"To deal with widespread unemployment, I mandate that large landowners are to have at least one-third of their labourers be freemen instead of slaves." A man shouted about the slave traders who worked for him, and Julius replied without a pause: "It is a backwards world when the slave owners eat better than the child citizens we will later conscript to fight our wars, and by the size of your belly, Senator Lucius, I would say you will not be going hungry because of this decree. I intend to cancel one year of rent for stricken dwellings—"

"You're mad!"

"The boy takes initiative beyond his right!"

Arguments began in small groups, and most shook their fists at Julius. But his attention was elsewhere; he had noticed that an old man in brown robes and worn sandals, who carried his weight hunched forward, had slipped into the curia silently and sat to watch him speak. Julius had reached the end of his very short patience, and his weariness from three years of war flirted with his legendary temper, so with gusto, he continued once more, growing louder, and all felt the weight of his words. Some of the senators gazed toward him with hearts stirred by his passion and conviction. "A snake must shed its skin when it grows, and grow, Rome will. Cool your heads, senators, and when you come to realise the legitimacy of my words, you will already be witnessing the accolades of my foresight."

Crassus suddenly appeared at his side. The old general's voice seemed to rumble through the gut of every man present. "I concur with the decrees of Julius Caesar. He has my support and my share of gold required. Glory to Rome." And with that, he shot a look at Julius, strode across the Senate floor, and made his exit.

Pompey stood almost begrudgingly, and with malevolent eyes, spoke as if the words pained him. "I, Pompey Magnus the Great, support Julius Caesar in his decrees. You have my gold. As I speak for Marcus Antonius in his absence, I declare the same." He then disappeared from the room, a scowl across his face and anger in his step.

All four generals were in support of the agenda, and so Julius had succeeded; he glanced down at his delegates and scribes, who sprawled over
papyrus, making notes of his statements.

Octavian stood, utterly elated by the thrill of such a battle of articulated
wit, and shouted, "Hail Caesar!"

The response from the senators was compliant but lacking enthusiasm, as
was to be expected. The entire Senate erupted into babbling disarray as some
stormed out and some congregated to debate, but Julius, with Octavian in tow,
crossed the room, took the old man in brown robes carefully by the arm, and
led him away from the curia.

When they reached the bright, sunbathed courtyard, Julius guided the man
to sit beneath the shade of a lone central sycamore and seated himself beside his
ageing attendant. Octavian stood several strides from them, waiting patiently.

"Albus, my friend, you are a sight for weary eyes. I trust your balls have
dropped in my extended absence?" He grinned at the old man, who grinned
back, affection lighting up his eyes.

"Indeed, I have the vigour of a young stud. I think I shall join your next campaign if you'll allow it." The heavy creases on the ancient man's face stretched
with his smile, and Julius saw the image of the younger man he had known
when he had been entrusted to Albus's care.

"I'm sorry, good man, but I cannot have you embarrassing my soldiers with
your skill," Julius jested. He noted the lightness in his heart. "How strange that
one old fool can strip me of my anger, fuelled by many old fools. Does that not
seem lacking in sense?"

"Ah, but the trick is to disguise yourself as an old fool." He gestured to the
robes he wore.

"Strategy, Albus. I see I have managed to teach you something after all."

"We must work with what we have. You threw a snake into the fowl pen in
that room. Caused quite a stir."

"They will recover."

"Indeed, they will, but they will not forget," Albus said gently.

Julius stared for a moment into the ripples of a nearby fountain with a
beautiful central statue, the fashioned hands of a peasant woman extending a
basket of carved wheat. "There will be a legacy of Rome. She is great beyond

any other even now, but for a man's name to live on, that is another matter," Julius said distantly, and Albus sighed.

"You have come to the question all men must ask themselves. I do not envy the choices you face, nor the trials that await you as you arrive at your answer. I ask you, though, is insulting the Senate with such potency a step towards the resolution you seek?"

"They are obsolete arse-lickers who cannot accept that their time has passed."

"Everything screams when it is dying," the old man said as if his mind were elsewhere, and the animosity drained from Julius. He noted his delegates, young men in white robes carrying rolled papyrus, flanking Crassus, who leaned against a marble pillar across the courtyard.

Julius looked up at Albus with burdened eyes. "I am happy to see you well, old friend." He turned to Octavian, who stood by the fountain. "See that Albus has all his needs of today met, lad." Octavian nodded dutifully at his uncle.

Julius stood and strode toward Crassus, his muscles stiff and tiredness weighing on his face. As he collected the entourage and made his way down the long hallway, he noticed the true fatigue in his body.

"Your speeches never cease to greatly beguile me. I was certain Pompey would attempt to dispose of you himself in a moment," Crassus remarked casually, with a touch of amusement.

"Let us hope I have reached my quota for speeches. I have tolerated old men for too long. Rome has no use for those who refuse to progress. I have a mind to dissolve the Senate and simply guide Rome to glory myself."

"Be wary of the number of people you antagonise, General. The Senate holds much power still, and the military needs its influence in matters of the people," Crassus warned.

"Then with respect, General Crassus, it is time something is done for the people." Julius halted at a chamber door and turned to the group of attentive young men who had skipped to keep up with his stride. "See that all I have decreed is enforced. Do not fail me. I need to sleep, and when I wake, I want no rebellions or disasters to greet me."

They scattered in several directions, and Crassus leaned into Julius. "War takes its toll on even the greatest of warriors, Julius. Do not forget that we are but men, and the time will come for every man to reap what he sows. I like you, boy, and I will back you, but make sure to heed warnings when they are given."

Crassus stared sternly, then turned on his heel and strode away, leaving Julius to retire to his rooms.

Nights were difficult for Julius as sleep was a realm where no armour could be worn, and no strategy could be predetermined. His dreams were haunted with darkness and death, the deeds of a man who did not have regret, merely the rush of Ares in his veins before and during combat and the low feelings that followed. He would wake at all hours, drenched in sweat. Sometimes his screams would wake servants and himself, but the fading in and out of the dreams was surely the wrath of the gods, for dreams seemed to exist on either side of the veil of consciousness, in a limbo of distorted sounds and images, creatures, and the voices of the dead.

One morning, in the earliest hours, he awoke shouting, his eyes wide with desperation; he sat upon his damp sheets and wiped the sweat from his brow with a trembling hand. *Dreams of such confusion and nonsense should not plague the greatest general of Rome*, he thought.

With frustration growing in him, he decided sleep would evade him until dawn, and he shouted into the half-darkness of his chamber. "Servant!"

He heard one of the night guards posted at his door shuffle quickly down the hall to fetch a servant. When the door opened, he looked up to see Hortensia, her eyes tight from being woken. In the half-light, he could no longer think of what he had called a servant for, for she was of such contrast to his dreams: beautiful in a way that was truly her own and calmingly still, not raging before him with weapons or fangs. He revelled in the solace from his nightmares. He noted the crease of her pillow linen indented on her porcelain cheek and the pale blue colour of her nightgown beneath the brown smock that she'd hurriedly thrown on. Then he noticed that her feet were bare.

"My Caesar?" she asked softly, uncomfortable in the silence under his strange stare.

"I apologise. My night mind has the better of me. Bring me wine and warm water." She turned toward the door. "Also, some bread and cheese." She nodded, and without a word, was gone from the room.

He sat a moment before standing and dressing in a simple linen skirt, shivering from the cold sweat trickling down his back, drying in the breeze from the large, high windows that opened to his balcony. He could see lights of the night folk—whores, bakers, and artists, no doubt—in the lower city. He didn't notice how long he stood and gazed at his beloved Rome, but the soft, cautious voice of Hortensia brought him back to his room.

"General? Can you hear me?"

"Yes, yes."

"Your wine and supper." She gestured to a large wooden table, set upon a rug, with elaborately carved legs supporting its enormous weight, and four chairs of the same fashion sat around it. There, a broad silver platter was laid, laden with grapes, nuts, the cheeses he dearly missed while away, and crusty, dense rosemary bread. "I will return with your hot water." She swept from the room.

Caesar felt the growl in his stomach at the sight of the meal and sank heavily into the chair to feast. As the wine warmed his skin and the herbed bread spread with soft, pungent cheese filled his belly, he felt his irritation melt away.

Hortensia returned to the room with two wooden buckets, which she emptied into the mounted basin in the corner of the room. Then she turned to him. "Is there anything more you require, General?" she asked, standing with each hand clasping a bucket handle. Her hair was braided and fell behind her, with many rogue strands curling over her brow, and her large eyes watched him with careful regard. The sudden longing to not be left alone slithered around his shoulders.

"Are you hungry?" he asked.

She stared at him, not knowing how to answer.

"I . . . I don't know." She shifted awkwardly at the question.

"If you would like to join me, I would enjoy the company." He gestured to the seat opposite him, and cautiously, she surveyed the room and his face, then placed the buckets on the floor, edged reluctantly toward the chair, and sat stiffly. He filled a golden goblet of wine and placed it in front of her, then motioned towards the food as he chewed audibly. "Please, eat."

🌿

HORTENSIA HAD NEVER SIPPED FROM A GOLDEN GOBLET before, and the wine on her lips was sour and overpowering. She sipped more deeply and swallowed loudly.

Julius smiled at her. "Do you drink often?"

"Servants rarely have time for such activities. It is delicious, thank you."

"Have you tried the cheeses?" He turned the cheese patter to face her and pushed it towards her. She cut a piece and tasted it.

She had had cheese but never like this. This was heavenly and unexpected due to its odour; she had never been stationed in the kitchens and wondered if they had sampled many of these luxuries. Surely not, for fear of reprimand, but this moment was exquisite. She tried to contain her delight at the flavours, not wanting to appear like a child tasting sugarcane for the first time.

They ate in silence until Julius drained his cup and placed it upon the table. "Do you enjoy your work?" he asked blandly.

Hortensia froze, but regardless of her feelings, there was only one answer to this question if she wanted to live. "Yes, my Caesar. More so when you are in the palace."

"And why is that?" he asked with slight amusement, and she felt the severity of his powerful gaze. She regretted her words, for now, she would surely have to dig herself from possible offence.

"The staff are happier. You are a generous and kind master. We couldn't want more," she lied, as her mind wandered back to the days-old babe who had died because Brutus would not allow the child's mother to return to the kitchens to check on it during a feast.

"Somehow, I doubt that," Julius said casually.

"It is true, Caesar. We prefer your presence to your absence."

"Why?" he asked again.

She braced herself for the repercussions of the daring comment she had committed to her lips. "Some are cruel beyond punishment, for pleasure," she said, not meeting his stare.

"I assume you refer to my wife, which I would not dispute."

"And others, my lord." Too afraid to look him in the eye, she placed her cup upon the table, bracing to be thrown from the room.

"All in this palace know my expectations for treatment of staff. None would lay a hand without entitled reason. It is a master's right to punish servants as he sees fit for the crime committed. I have chosen my staff personally; they would not intentionally disobey. That is how one ensures loyalty in a world of deception and whispers."

His tone was harder now, and she felt the wine caress her mind warmly. "Yes, master," she said with a small voice, praying to be released from his company.

"You may go. The sun is arriving, and you have duties to attend. I thank you for your company."

Grateful for the escape, Hortensia rose from her chair. As she made for the door, Julius called an order. "Stop."

She paused, nervous, hearing his footsteps approach her. She turned toward him and saw concern on his face, but he took her shoulders and turned her away from him again. She tried with all her might to steady her increasing heartbeat, wondering if she would be executed for a simple miscalculation of manners. She felt the soft and brief touch of fingers against her back, then suddenly he grabbed her arm, and she was being dragged backwards. She gasped with fright and began to shake.

He pulled her to face the mirrored disc where she could see Caesar and herself staring back; her chest heaved with fear, and the perplexed look on his face worried her further.

He turned her body so that her back was reflected, and then she understood. Two small red streaks stained her blue nightgown.

Now his face seemed more a picture of confused frustration. His grasp on her had loosened. He reached to her shoulder and pulled on the fabric ties, letting her gown fall away to one side and reveal her back. Julius gazed for several moments at the fresh wounds and the old scars. He spun her roughly toward him and held her arms tightly, his face inches from hers.

"Who did this?" She remained frozen, and he shook her roughly. "Speak, girl. I have no patience for hesitation!"

"One who punishes for pleasure, my lord." She barely managed to whisper the words as her heart pounded in her throat.

Understanding came over his face, and in a mere moment, he was gone from the room, leaving her standing, half-naked, blood warmed with wine, alone in the chambers of Julius Caesar.

Suddenly sense came over her. She dressed and fled from the room back to the servants' quarters.

◆

JULIUS CHARGED THROUGH THE HALLS OF HIS PALACE, power in his step and the sense of reason eluding him. Anger consumed his mind as the words of Crassus from long ago boomed inside his head:

"*You are indeed a wolf, Julius, for you are ruled by your instincts. You implement your precise hunting skills and go for your prey, or in most cases, enforce your agenda upon the Senate. The wolf can be gentle, but that does not make him a friend, for when he becomes hungry enough, he will tear all who stand before him apart, innocent or not. That is the nature of the wolf. Hear me, friend: Your wolf nature is both a blessing and a curse.*"

EGYPTE

RETURN OF THE FATHER

— XII —

"Ho! Formation to the west!" A soldier's voice rang out as he hurriedly passed Kleopatra's bedchamber. Akela sprang from the bed to run to the terrace. On the western horizon was a dark line like a thick snake, slowly making its way through the city. Her heart leapt, and she let out a squeal as she dashed out of the room, sped down the hallway, and charged up the steps to her own apartment. Once inside, she dressed in her best red tunic, wiggled her feet into small leather sandals, and splashed water from the basin onto her face. Then she ran through the palace, passing Claudius and Neos.

She burst out of the palace, ran down the stone steps toward the trail down into the lower city, and charged along the path. Rounding a corner, she could make out a large figure on an enormous stallion, making its way toward her down the wide road. The rider sat stoically atop the terrifying beast as peasants threw small white flowers at its feet, and behind him, foot soldiers received gifts from loved ones. Some were led away by excited young women; others greeted small children and raised them smiling into the air. The streets were alive with cheering. The warriors were home, and there was much to celebrate.

Akela took off at a run and only slowed as she reached the beast at the head of the caravan. She looked up to the man, who seemed taller than she remembered. The sun burned her, but she craned her neck to see the war hero poised as if he were Ra himself, majestic in his ferocious stature. His stern and unkind face looked down at her, and she felt as though she might cry as she watched it stretch into a wide smile.

He extended an enormous arm, and she felt the ground fall away beneath her. Hoisted onto the moving mountain, she threw her arms around her father's neck and held on as tightly as her thin arms allowed, feeling his wide chest shudder with laughter. Gently, he held her back from him, his rough hands gripping her under her arms, and looked at her; love swelled in his eyes. "I left a beloved child, but I return to a noblewoman. What have you done with my daughter?"

"She got tired of waiting all season for you to return."

"Ah. I should know better than to keep a woman waiting. I have missed my sharpest silent blade." His grin was met by hers.

The trail of military men reached the palace and came to a halt before the pharaoh, who stood tall, decorated in his finest robes and jewels, his crown upon his head and his hands held open in welcome to the returning heroes.

The general's horse stamped its foot in the sand. He dismounted elegantly, reached up for Akela, and placed her on the ground beside him before turning to ascend the stairs, draw his sword, and kneel before the pharaoh. "My sovereign, may you look upon your fighting men and read the victory in your name upon their faces."

The pharaoh swelled with pleased relief. "Welcome home, General Ankhmakis. The gods look upon your courage and drink to your success. Tonight, we will feast, for you bring Egypt and your pharaoh great honour. Come! In my hall, you will tell me of your deeds; wine and shade await you."

The pharaoh turned to address the warriors before him. "You have brought honour to Egypt as the finest Sand Eagles of the city of the Ptolemy dynasty. You have fought bravely and so brought riches upon yourselves and your families. Sitkamose will grant your wages and see that you are fed and celebrated as heroes tonight."

⚜

KLEOPATRA HELD AKELA'S HAND AS THEY MADE THEIR way down to the banquet hall dressed in plain white floor-length chitons, simple gold pins adorning their hair. The large room was lit with many torches burning against the stone walls, and the smell of delicious foods hung in the air. They walked through the crowded room to take their places with the royal family and their companions.

Akela watched her father sip from his goblet as the pharaoh continued what she suspected was a prolonged stream of questions following the debriefing. Neos, Claudius, Isis, and Berenice, who sat close by, listened carefully to their discussion, faces serious and thoughtful.

"Your strategies regarding the savages were right. It was easy to meet them at every advance and disable their defences. They are tough people, but they lack battle experience, and so the capture count is high and promising in quality. We return with more than you asked for, sire."

"Excellent. Tell me of the reports of the foreign army that came to your aid by the coast." The pharaoh's tone was serious and focused.

"My sovereign, it was a strange event, surely arranged by the gods. The Macedon king breached the shores and took the savages from the north, pushing them back toward us, and we crushed the resistance between us. After the battle was won, their king approached and stated his intention to seek a treaty. I invited him to dine with me, and he spoke of the warring and conquest across the seas in Roma and the ferocity in the growing armies of the powerful General Crassus. King Andriscus himself, sixth of his name, yielded Macedonia to the service of Rome, and so they remain in their own kingdom, unharmed, not stripped of their trade or gold but in the service of the Roman Senate. The king, as an ambassador for the great army, came to the west to extend Rome's intentions to me, to relay to you and all Egypt. Rome does not wish for conflict with Egypt, great Pharaoh. They recognise the mighty sand kingdom as independent, and will not attack, but state their intent to conquer Assyria and the northern regions of Gaul."

"And do you believe this to be true, General? Or do you perceive deception in the cunning of Rome?"

"I perceive their gesture to be true, Your Highness. It would not serve them to attack us, for the war would rage for generations and leave both kingdoms drained. Even a warlord of unsound mind would rule against such a venture. I sat with him myself and thought the man to be wise and honest. He is a skilled warrior, and his men respect him."

"You have always been a true judge of character, Ankhmakis. I would trust no other with the task."

"Thank you, sire. If I may add, he has a young son that, if not promised already, could be wed to one of your daughters, should you desire further security in the matter."

The pharaoh thought for a moment, calculating in his cunning and greedy mind, then declared, "We drink to victory. We will continue with conquest in the west and keep a watchful eye on the movement in the lands of the north and east." The well-wined crowd cheered merrily before resuming their chatter.

The general leaned toward the pharaoh once more. "Sire, the Macedonian King, Andriscus, expressed his wish to meet with you himself if you would allow him to visit. He wishes to see the great lands of Egypt and to meet its pharaoh. He will be journeying from the west to the isle of Kretos, and kindly requests permission to breach his fleet in the bay of Alexandria and make the journey to the palace if you agree to receive him."

"So, the snake requests an invitation into the oasis. To observe our defences and report our weaknesses to its flute master? I think not."

"I assured King Andriscus that I would deliver his request to you personally, sire, as a gesture of thanks for his aid in the battle he helped win for Egypt, where he sought no riches, nor slaves, nor payment."

"And so, I must invite a foreign king to my hall in good faith of his intentions?"

"I judge him to be sturdy in honesty and steadfast in his word, Your Highness. If we can learn more of Rome, then we will know of their weaknesses too. If the king reveals ill intent, I will slay him myself."

"It is wise to know one's enemies before they become so. Very well, make good on your invitation, and we shall meet this king. Now, let us feast!"

It was interesting, Akela thought, that this foreign force sought peace with Egypt when Egypt, too, held settlements in Assyria, but she supposed that would be addressed when the Greek king made his visit. She had studied the lands of Greece in her lessons with the old fat scholar and was excited at the prospect of meeting a king from a land so far from hers.

She stared a moment at her father, who seemed grateful to be sitting down and well-fed. His face was as calm as it always was, yet new lines had appeared on his brow, and the weight of much death seemed to rest upon his tired shoulders. He rubbed his weary eyes and stared into his goblet, seemingly lost in memories. Akela wondered if they were pleasant memories or the kind that haunted his sleep and caused him to cry out names and panicked commands.

He glanced up at Akela, and his gaze settled on her admiring expression. He smiled at her yet seemed to remain in his thoughts, eyes heavy.

Akela had barely finished her meal before the general rose and politely announced his retirement to his waiting bed. He was honoured with cheers and toasts as he bowed to the pharaoh and excused himself. He moved to Safiya, who sat at one corner of the banquet table, holding one babe in her arms and chatting to Berenice. He bowed on approach, and she greeted him with a radiant smile. He leaned close to see the child and congratulated her, then moved toward the door behind the royal dining chairs. Akela shot out of her chair, abandoning her plate and goblet, and ran after her father.

The hallway was quiet, and only their steps echoed. "You have been keeping to your studies?" he asked softly.

"Yes. I have studied the land of Greece you spoke of."

"I must take care what words I speak then. You are now grasping their weight."

"The horse master has taught me to ride, and I am very good. I can ride the black Arabian. I have named him Onofria."

Her father let out a throaty laugh. "Of course, you have."

"May I keep him?"

"I will assess if he is worthy of you, then we shall see."

She smiled and took his hand as they walked in silence up to their apartment. The room was warm, and the windows allowed the bright moon to cast light upon the tapestry-adorned walls. The general's chests had been brought up and placed at the end of the bed. Akela ran to change into her nightgown, and the general undressed himself of his heavy military garb, then opened his chest to look wearily at its contents.

Akela entered the room in her nightgown, and her father presented her with a stunning sheathed dagger, the edges of the leather studded with gold pins and the flat sides of the sheath pressed with deep-blue and red gems. The hilt was bound with thin twine for excellent grip, and when she pulled it from its cover, the blade was thin and so sharp that it made a metallic sound against the fabric.

She looked up at him with her mouth agape in awe, and he touched her cheek lovingly and smiled. "Tomorrow, I must see to business in the slave market; we will sit with stew and find some sugarcane plantain pies. Perhaps you will find a pretty necklace you would like. To bed with us, child. Sleep will wait no longer for me."

They lay beneath the linens of the large, feather-stuffed bed, and within moments, her father's large chest heaved in deep rhythm, the sound flowing over Akela like a wave of the great sea. She lay her small head over his arm and drifted off into a dreamless slumber.

❧

THE SUN HAD FLOATED TO THE SKY BEFORE SHE AWOKE, her neck a little stiff from refusing to leave her place on her father's arm, but she found he was no longer lying next to her. He emerged from the robing room in a beautiful dark knee-length tunic and high-strapped sandals, his sword sheathed in a scabbard at his hip. He truly looked like a majestic god of war.

She grinned, and he smiled gruffly at her. "We must be off to see to business soon. Hurry your step, child."

❧

THEY STOOD AT THE EDGE OF THE PROMENADE AS Kleopatra came running around the corner with Kohlis in fast pursuit, seemingly unimpressed by the child's vigour. Kleopatra came to a halt before the tall general, and he bowed low to her.

She beamed up at him. "Welcome home, General. You have been sorely missed by all."

"Thank you, Your Highness. I am happy to return to you. Am I to believe you will be joining us today?"

"If you will allow me, sir. I want to come with Akela. I have a linen scarf and have removed all jewels."

"Then, with your cunning deception, I cannot refuse."

He turned to Kohlis and extended his arm. "I have inquired of your character, Kohlis, and I am met with an admirable report. I am Ankhmakis, and I welcome the kinship of a man with such a respected reputation." The general then spoke a strange sequence of throaty sounds to Kohlis, with an unfamiliar tone of humility—the language of the slaves, Akela deduced.

Kohlis nodded his head stoically to the general and gripped his forearm in greeting. Kleopatra slipped the scarf in her hand around her head and face and tucked it behind her.

"Let us be on our way," the general said and turned to descend the steps, his man Anhotep falling in line a step behind him. Anhotep was an obedient right hand. It was clear that he personally revered the general greatly, but he lacked the physical size of his hero, making him resemble a goat as he struggled to keep in step with the general's great strides. Akela liked the man and enjoyed his scampering to keep up with her father.

The marketplace was as alive as always with daily trading and peddlers carting their wares on old wooden planks pulled by donkeys; goats were herded through the side streets as their masters swore loudly at them and whipped long reeds at their rumps. Coloured ribbons lined the fronts of stalls, strung from rooftop to rooftop. Customers shouted and haggled with shop owners, and bored-looking women sat by sandal-repair stalls, their babes suckling at their breasts.

The celebrations of the returning soldiers had been vast and nightlong. The remains of broken ale flagons and the marks of emptied stomachs stained the streets. Sleeping men sat propped up in the sand, the drink encouraging them to rest where they fell.

Akela held her father's hand as he led them toward the place of his business, through the markets, stopping to buy the two girls some fig tarts that they contentedly ate as they walked. They emerged from the far side of the market to see a worn and sandy trail along which donkeys pulled sunken carts heavy with stone blocks, struggling under the weight of the brick, unkind men whipping their hindquarters relentlessly.

Akela took in the sight of the hundred or so slaves hauling the finely cut blocks of stone on their backs, their ankles bound in iron devices, the sound of the chains ringing out rhythmically. A large, dark man dripping with sweat, his bare feet bound by chains, walked slowly past, a smaller, lifeless man draped across his shoulder. The man did not look up as he passed, his breath heaving under the weight of the body.

The slaves swarmed in great numbers around several large constructions surrounding the enormous monument of a pharaoh with the body of a resting lion. It was a marvel to behold, stretching high into the sky and proudly overlooking the great city of sand. The general made toward an area where many Egyptian soldiers were gathered around large crates of fabrics and metals, sacks of grain, nuts, and dried fruits, and wagons with large cages fixed to them.

Inside were several tired and defeated-looking dark-skinned men and women dressed in dirty clothes, leaning against the bars. They watched the approaching general and children with no interest as a baby began to cry loudly.

Donkeys, horses, and camels stood tethered to many of the carts, and behind them was an assortment of beasts that Akela could identify from her studies as zebras, hyenas, baboons, chimpanzees—even a pacing lion. A weary giraffe stood tall behind the caged beasts, and the girls marvelled at the majesty of such creatures.

Akela looked back at Kohlis, and her smile abandoned her lips as she saw the large man staring at the men and women in the cages; his breath seemed faster, and his spirit troubled. They had noticed him too, their gaze finding him quietly.

The general turned to the giant man and said, "They had a choice, my friend, as did you. All have chosen their sides, and you mustn't harbour shame in yours. I will see that they are fed and sold well." Akela noted deep feeling in her father's voice, but it seemed to have only a slight effect on the conflict within Kohlis. "Take the children to the shade and wait for me there."

Kohlis led the girls to a shaded tent canopy, where a woman handed out wooden cups of wine. Kohlis turned away from the scene where the general stood, and Akela noticed an elderly woman who sat crumpled in a half-shaded cage on the sand, her hair thinning in tufts and small cuts on her scalp where the hair had been snipped. She sat curled around one of her legs, her head at an awkward angle against the iron bars. Her eyes, wide and eerily vacant, bore into Akela, casting a shiver over her under the hot sun.

The old woman's chest heaved in the heat. She pulled herself closer to the cage bars to fixate on the general's daughter. Akela turned to the woman carrying the cups, pulled a copper coin from her waist purse, and said, "Water."

Akela approached the cage and knelt, offering the cup of water. The woman reached out with mangled fingernails like talons, took the cup, and drank deeply, her eyes never leaving Akela's face. Now closer, Akela could see the woman's skin was covered in red and brown spots, and the brown of her irises was faded at their edges. The woman lacked teeth and smelled of sweat and soiled rags.

Kleopatra, with her face wrapped in her scarf, came to kneel cautiously next to Akela. The old woman dropped the drained cup with no regard, darted a bony hand out to grasp Akela's wrist, and then said clearly, in a low, fearful growl, "The snake, the lion, and the eagle within you will each find their equal, but no two shall be one, and so you will forever change the world of men at the cost of wholeness . . ."

The woman's whole body shuddered as her eyes seemed to stare past Akela into an abyss no other could glimpse. "A peasant woman-god will rise. Her spirit is pained and restless. I see rivers of blood staining her hands." She gasped and gripped Akela tighter, pulling her close so that her hot, rancid breath seared through the child's nostrils. The crone spoke faster, in delirious whispers. "Beware the Ides of March. The child in the belly will die with her. The she-warrior who rips a golden wreath from a great eagle rips it also from herself. The martyr's son lives. Poseidon swims with the fury of insult. The tides will call you home, child, atop a throne of blood and sand."

The woman grimaced in suspended pain and then flew back against the far wall of the small cage as if Akela were a fire burning with a blinding light. "The harbinger of a death that must come will bring the fall of kings! The peacock and the isle of turquoise! Two children forever bound by blood and lies and name! It is written! Kill me! Kill me!"

The woman thrashed about in the cage, and Akela reached in to grip her forearm. She felt Kohlis come to stand behind them as she spoke clearly and calmly. "You are safe. There is no death here for you today. Tell me, prophet, do you truly see these things?"

But the poor creature merely sat frozen and muttering nonsense. Kleopatra leaned forward and placed a single gold coin at her bare and dirty feet, then asked gently, "Do you see my future, woman prophet?"

The woman ignored the gold at her feet and answered in a hoarse whisper, never once releasing her fierce gaze from Akela's wide brown almond eyes. "One and the same, child." Then she began to scream louder and louder—a tormented wail echoing from the deepest well of another time—and began thrashing against the iron bars of the cage and howling as she scratched at her eyes. Blood began to run down her face.

Swiftly, Kohlis cast a large black blanket over the cage, and the screams fell silent. Akela and Kleopatra, wide-eyed and open-mouthed, remained kneeling upon the sand. "No more." Kohlis' deep command echoed in the air.

The girls stood quietly, their eyes cast to the ground. Akela's mind raced and struggled to remember anything except the woman's eyes and the hate and fear in her. She wondered what the woman could have seen to terrify her so completely that she would beg for death and claw out her own eyes, but in truth, Akela already knew the source of the fear

It was her.

🌿

THE GENERAL'S BUSINESS SEEMED TO TAKE ALL DAY, AND the sun was beginning its descent as the small party walked back to the palace in silence. The general left to attend His Majesty's council meetings, and Kohlis fell back to do whatever he did once inside the palace and released from his service. The girls held hands tightly while they walked with confused and heavy hearts toward Kleopatra's chamber.

Arsinoe rounded the corner and walked down the hall toward them. Akela felt Kleopatra's hand tense in hers and readied herself for a potential attack from the violent princess, but Arsinoe's bored gaze swept over the two then away again as she passed. Akela stopped and turned to stare after Arsinoe, who seemed to glide gently along the sleek stone floors, but Kleopatra, with fearful breaths, tugged on Akela, and they hurriedly departed.

Once inside the safety of her room, Kleopatra sat on the terrace, her eyes locked somewhere out on the ocean to the north, and Akela leaned against the bed, both lost in thoughts that swam low and shallow as if in murky, uncertain waters.

GREECE

THE OPUS-BLOOM

— XIII —

It had been weeks since her wedding, although it had felt like years inside this prison of a palace. Chrysanthe had been coaxed to rise and try to maintain a daily routine; she had attended few official discussions as Athanasios conducted the business of Kretos and been foiled by Markos at every attempt to steal a blade or fly from a balcony. It was as if he knew her thoughts as they happened, which made her belly uneasy and his presence all the more uncomfortable.

On one particular night, her attendance was demanded at a banquet for some occasion she did not care to know of, and it was Markos who had dragged her kicking and clawing to the hall, Markos who had placed her in a seat next to her husband, and Markos who had intercepted the carving knife she had darted forward to snatch, aiming it for her throat.

Demosthenes had simply howled with laughter, turned to the king, and asked, "What have you done to me, brother?" It was Markos who had dragged her back to her chambers when she was excused, and Markos who had snatched her from her attempt to leap from the high ledges above the palace garden.

She had looked up into his ice-coloured eye many times and found no sympathy, tenderness, or mercy there. He had ordered that her window be boarded up, leaving her alone in constant darkness and unable to see even the great green waves that were so soothing. Every chance for freedom from this nightmare was hindered by the one-eyed giant who seemed not to have a soul. If his death came within her lifetime, she would celebrate it.

Her shame was known around the palace. Many had heard her screams and cries, and many had glimpsed her struggle to walk on the rare occasions she left her apartments, only by order of the king. She could see it on their faces. Some quickly looked away after their pitiful glances, and others lingered on her with malignant stares that rolled over her body, reimagining the vile acts for their own satisfaction. She was accustomed to it now and used the little pride she had left to hold her chin up and go about the business required of her, though the green of her eyes seemed faded somehow when she looked in a mirror.

She was present but not. Since she had lost her voice to her screams many nights ago, she had remained silent and found it strangely calming to simply float like a ghost through the duties of her new life, numb to all feeling or thought.

Lysander had arranged an outing to the lower city for the princess to bestow a royal presence upon the disease-ridden peasants and the great unwashed. He had insisted that it was important for the people to see the more agreeable and patient sovereigns if they were to improve the morale of the impoverished neighbourhoods, which bred livestock and housed several royal soldiers. They would be distributing several sacks of grains and scraps from the palace kitchens, and Lysander was simply thrilled that, finally, he could implement his plan for a united Kretos.

"You will enjoy the orphanages, I think, my lady. They are dirty and cramped, but the children will be happy to see you, I am sure," said Timeaus, as they made their way down the neglected dirt trails of the lower city, where many peasants waited in anticipation. "Perhaps your time with them will encourage a little prince to take hold in your belly. It is surely time for a child now that you are married, a little blessing for Kretos—"

Incapable of entertaining another word from the annoying boy, Chrysanthe threw herself from the wagon, intending to land in the dirt and hopefully break an arm or leg, which could both save her from Timaeus's incessant prattling about his dreams of royal children being born out of love and as well, with any luck, force the physician to declare that in order to heal these bones, she would have to sleep alone for many months, during which time she would throw herself from whatever height she could to break the bones again.

Expecting the ground and the certain pain of broken bones, she found only the large arms of Markos beneath her. She sprang from his embrace and screamed with all the air in her lungs, feeling her throat light with fire and the screech begin to falter as the last of her breath escaped. She stood panting in the ensuing silence, her wide, enraged eyes locked on her guard, venom and violence in her stare. He simply stood before her, taken aback. His regard softened, a trace of pain on his face, more reaction than she'd ever seen from him before.

Lysander stepped in carefully to place a tentative hand on her shoulder, clearly afraid she might become savage and lunge at him, teeth bared and fingers clawing at his throat. But she did not.

The distribution of scraps and sacks of half-rancid grains was a shorter, more thankless ordeal than Lysander had predicted, but all that they had brought had been taken. Chrysanthe did not participate in this staged gesture devised by Lysander. She had no wish to gain regard from the people, for they were just as trapped here on this filthy rock as she was, but she envied them, for they were freer than she would ever be.

She sat upon the wagon as peasants snatched the damaged and stale goods, staring vacantly out to the ebbing waves of the deep harbour, ignoring the constant glances of Lysander and Markos, poised for another outburst of rage.

Timeaus had not taken his eyes off a group of donkeys corralled nearby in the agora. He hunched awkwardly against the flimsy wooden railing with an intense fixation on the mules, who refused to come when he beckoned to them.

The day was cloudy and the sea black and murky. A storm was coming. The boats in the harbour would have to be beached and the sails retrieved to be stowed safely until the storm passed. The livestock would need to be brought under shelter, and extra kindling would need to be hoarded for the cold nights ahead.

Chrysanthe felt the eye of Markos on her back and turned to scowl at him, but she found no trace of surprise, no recoil of embarrassment, nor any intent to look away. She huffed and turned her gaze forward; surely Lysander had given these lice-ridden paupers their dues, and they would depart soon.

But Lysander was engaged earnestly in conversation with several townsmen who remained. The old man's tone of voice was commanding but respectful. Lysander appeared to provide a balance that the people and the palace needed, under-appreciated and often not acknowledged. He portrayed himself to her as a loving father and husband, loyal to his king and dedicated to his work.

In her experience, however, such men did not exist. Even though she had grown fond of the grumpy adviser, she was certain he would prove soon enough that he was merely another savage.

Tired of the day's events already, she pulled her shawl tighter around her shoulders and looked to the mules once more. Timeaus had coaxed one small one to him. Suddenly, he swung a fist with such force and speed at the mule's head that flecks of its blood spattered his tunic, and the air around them shuddered as the beast's scream echoed across the agora. The princess was shocked by the boy's sudden violence, and she could only watch as the young mule staggered to and fro, panicking in its pain.

"You, boy!" the shepherd screeched.

Lysander dashed to placate him. The men argued until Markos's patience expired, and he stalked toward the shouting men and the screaming mule and cast his giant presence over the boy and Lysander.

Unsurprisingly, the shepherd stopped shouting and started to listen to Lysander. Chrysanthe, half-amused, felt that nothing seemed to matter anymore; she climbed off the wagon, her gold sandals sinking in the mud and filth. She lifted her tunic, and without a look back, made to cross the gloomy agora.

A hand grabbed at her arm, and she turned to see Lysander, flushed in the face. "Get back on the wagon, Princess. We are to return to the palace."

"I will walk."

"I must insist, Prin—"

"And I must decline your insistence, Lord Lysander. You may wait for me at the palace gates, or you may join me, which I have no doubt will be your choice, seeing as I am to never be granted a moment without the hot breath of captivity upon my neck." She glared into his eyes and could see the exhaustion that plagued his mind and body; he took a breath.

"As you wish, my lady. Lead the way, and as your servant, I will follow." He dipped his head respectfully and turned back to call for Timeaus to take the wagon.

As Chrysanthe struggled onward through the mud, the wet sludge sinking and challenging her balance, great arms, ever-so-gentle, lifted her slowly from the muck. Her exhausted pride wanted to rage and protest, but she relaxed in the strong and sturdy grasp, allowing Markos to carry her across the agora and place her carefully down on dry dirt. She stood calmly, grateful to be free from the public spectacle of the pathetic attempt to placate the filthy masses of the lower city.

Markos had marched back into the fray to help Lysander through the mud. Before the princess were many stalls, and she found herself staring at one in particular, where a low, poorly built wooden table laden with very small clay pots and tiny vials stood beneath a canopy, from the frame of which hung little corked bottles, on strings, clinking softly in the slight breeze. She found she had approached the kiosk and stared down into the hundreds of serums and pastes that littered the table, tinctures seemingly for every ailment or need, and a strange whisper on the breeze licked the soft hair on her neck and cheek. *Tinctures . . . vials . . .*

Lysander arrived behind her, panting and frazzled from the day's events. Chrysanthe turned to him. "Take me to the apothecary."

"Surely, my lady, the markets have all you should require."

"They do not. You would trust my life to potions passing as perfumes, brewed in farmhouses? Take me to the royal apothecary—and, Lysander, I am in no mood to dawdle." She turned and strode into the shaded city streets.

❧

AT THE DOOR OF THE APOTHECARY, SHE TURNED TO Lysander.

"I will not be long. You may wait for me here."

"You must be accompanied at all times, my lady; that is the—"

Chrysanthe whipped around to stare at him, the fury in her revived. "I am quite certain *you* do not have monthly blood pains, old man, and if it were at all possible, I would very much like to see you endure them as I must. Queen Charis has advised me I am to come to this man for the pain. Your accompanying me would simply be inappropriate." She could feel her nostrils flare and sweat beading on her brow, which in any other situation would have been unbecoming for a lady, but here and now, it aided her cause.

Markos and Lysander stood before her, their faces stunned and embarrassed.

"You may wait for me here." She turned to climb the stairs. The feeling of weight lifting from her was astonishing, and once up the roofless winding stone staircase and out of sight, she leaned her back against the stone and looked up into the cloudless sky for a moment before pushing the door at the top of the stairs open, revealing a small, hunched man, his smock stained and grimy and his wideset eyes staring up at her with what seemed to be caution and irritation.

"I am—"

"I know who you are."

"I very much doubt that, sir. I am not from here; I am travelling from—"

The old grump chortled. "Save your breath, Princess. I do not care what crock-of-falsehood character you have invented."

Chrysanthe's rage bubbled once more as she realised the truth. "You have been ordered to refuse me service."

"Ah, so you are not simpleminded then," the man said dismissively. "That's both a blessing and a curse."

"Do you or don't you supply the queen and the old physician Buchorus with medicines?"

"Aye, but not you. Go quickly from here, and neither one of us need lose our lives."

"Well, then, there seems no reason for pleasantries or pretence. I seek Opus-Bloom, and you will give it to me." She spoke firmly, but the man began to laugh. "My request is not humorous."

"That was a request, was it?" He leaned against the table and shook his head slowly. "And I would have such a thing, would I?"

"You are the healer who has all potions, are you not?"

"I am, my lady. If I *were* to have this terrible thing, and if I had *not* been ordered to deny you service yet you *were* to acquire it, I would be executed."

"You gave it to an assassin here in Kretos, and you will give it to me also," Chrysanthe replied in a cool and menacing tone.

"Princess, you are naive. To believe all things you hear is to be made a fool."

His entitled smile released the anger in her. She stepped toward the closest table and swept her arm across it, sending all upon it crashing to the floor. She snatched up a small clay bowl and launched it toward him. As it shattered into pieces, showering him in shards, she grabbed a heavy, painted urn from another table. With enough time to anticipate the incoming threat, the hunched man dropped to the ground and scuttled through the debris of his wares to take cover. The urn exploded as it crashed into several items on a shelf, sending the entire structure tumbling to the ground, and although she could hear the man shouting, she somehow felt alive with the expression of her rage, the release of her desire for destruction, and she hurled whatever she could snatch at the sheltering man until there were no more weapons in reach and she paused to catch her breath, eyes closed, drinking in the freedom she felt coursing through her, her skin seemingly alive with Zeus's lightning.

Then, suddenly, something struck her, and she found herself lying with her cheek pressed against the stone floor as someone shouted at her.

Groggily, she pushed herself to her side and fell onto her back. Her vision distorted everything into strange shapes for a moment, but as it somewhat returned to normal, she focussed on the terrified man standing over, clutching a length of wood. He stood poised and wide-eyed, evidently in shock at his own actions, actions that had condemned him and his family to death. He knew it, as did she. The fight was finished, and with a lazy grin, she sat up.

"Lady." Tears streamed silently from the man's small eyes. "Lady Chrysanthe, please spare my children and my wife. They—they have no part in my actions against you. Please, I have two daughters, they are only young. I have no right to beg you this; I have nothing to buy their lives with, I—"

"Ah, but you do." Chrysanthe stood and stepped close to him.

"Forgive me. I truly do not have Opus-Bloom. Five nights ago, I arrived to find the door opened and several elixirs moved or spilled or broken, as by a thief."

"You know this thief?" she pressed.

"Aye, Princess. I have never seen his face, but a man like that . . . to seek justice on him is to seek one's own death."

"The name of this man?"

"Princess . . ."

"The name and where to find him, and no man will come for you, *or* your daughters . . ."

◈

CHRYSANTHE HAD BEEN SUMMONED TO THE MEGARON OF Athanasios. The walls were elaborately decorated with trophies of war and the armour of the great warriors Kretos had defeated, her father's armour among them. She had chosen a seat far away from the king's, but at his request, had begrudgingly moved to the place directly beside him. She had eased into her chair gently and winced momentarily as the pain in her groin complained, but aware of Athanasios's close scrutiny, she hardened her face and kept her cold, distant gaze ahead.

They were here to listen to the public's grievances, endless, boring accounts of petty feuds with neighbours and the failed deliveries of adequate dowries from brides' fathers to the husbands. Charis had sauntered in at some point after midday; she had noted the proximity of her husband to Chrysanthe and thrown an expected look of venom at the princess before taking her seat beside the king, stiffly yet gracefully, and immediately signalling for wine. It was then that a farmer entered the hearing space, his hair white, his skin sun-weathered, his eyes tired, and with a significant limp in his stocky right leg.

His grievance was between himself and his neighbour. The neighbour's son had bedded the old farmer's daughter but refused to marry her or enhance her dowry at all, and so the farmer was asking his lord to decree that the two marry, as with his daughter defiled, he could now not arrange a profitable marriage.

Athanasios turned to Chrysanthe. "What say you, Chrysanthe? Should the union be ordered?"

She felt the familiar pang of dread—how stupid of her not to realise there was more to this public embarrassment than merely forcing her presence.

"I do not know the ways of Kretos."

"You need only know the ways of man. Did you not learn anything of counsel from your parents?"

"I learned a great deal from my parents, but not of counsel."

"Well then, as a caretaker for the people of Krete now, what would you have me do?"

"I would declare the two wed. The boy has taken a future from the girl and her family, no matter if they are truly lovers or not, and I am sure an agreement can be made between the two fathers for future payments if a full dowry cannot be paid upon their wedding day."

Chrysanthe glanced at the farmer. "That is, assuming you are truly concerned for your daughter and not for the wealth you hoped to acquire by selling her like a sow to the highest-bidding brute." Her words hung in the air of the hall like a vile smell.

Athanasios' stare lingered on her, and she could feel his eyes sweep over her collarbones and up to her jawline. The snake would strike soon, and she braced herself for what humiliation he had arranged so meticulously for her.

"I disagree with my counsellor," he said. "It is the law on Kretos, as it is in all of Greece, that a peasant man may take any woman he wishes, but it is a woman's place to ask her father's permission to take a husband, which, I am assuming, she did not?"

"No, my lord, she did not," the old man replied nervously.

"Then am I or am I not correct that the girl in this debacle is the culprit who has shunned the law and caused offence?" asked Athanasios with an air of boredom.

Dread swept across the poor man's face as he sank to the ground to kneel before his lord, preparing to beg for the sparing of life.

"The punishment will be death for the girl, for having defied her father, the law, and therefore, her king."

"No!" the man yelled, his voice shaking with terror, his eyes darting among the three royals before him. "Please! She is a good, honourable daughter! She did not mean to offend your highness. She is innocent in this! I know it! Please, my lord!"

"I imagine, like any good father, you wish to take her place for her punishment." The king spoke in a low voice, and realisation of the impending danger dawned across the quivering man's face.

Athanasios remained silent, his soft but violent gaze resting on the helpless man at his mercy, while Charis gestured to a servant for more wine as simply as if she were bored with a court jester.

Chrysanthe remained disinterested and remote, but the man's wide, fearful eyes stared up at her, pale blue and piercing. What was it that he wanted her to do? Don a sword and helm and fight the guards to help him escape? She barely had the strength to walk and clearly didn't have the means to fight off her husband each night. Surely the man knew his death was imminent, and that he would not get to make arrangements or say goodbye to his family.

As the silence grew, a guard quietly stepped forward behind the man and drew his sword; Chrysanthe stared at the kneeling peasant, keeping his gaze on her, hoping that this small gift of distraction, the only thing she could offer at this moment, was enough to ease his fear even a little. The guard brought the sword down heavily in a curving slash, and the farmer's head rolled several paces from his body, which crumpled to the ground and spewed blood over the stone floor in front of her.

Chrysanthe stared, unable to discern the storm of rage within her from the violence, the finality of death, and though she felt as powerless as the peasant had, the guilt of living still whispered to her coldly. Athanasios was looking for weakness, looking to see what he could still break in her, but this, she could deny him. She felt his gaze on her and the hostility of Charis's malicious jealousy consuming the large room like a great, ugly serpent, but she continued to stare with vacant eyes past the gruesome scene, clutching the arms of the chair to keep her hands from shaking with such a grip that her knuckles became pale, and her clenched jaw began to ache.

The king's blatant disappointment was clear; he ordered the mess cleaned immediately to continue the hearings of the day. Excusing the queen and princess, he suggested that they watch the running races being held in the village below from the queen's apartments, and if ever a person thought a king's suggestion was not a direct order, they would be gravely wrong.

Begrudgingly, Chrysanthe eased herself as gently as she could from the chair and followed Charis at whatever pace the pain in her body would allow. The two women climbed the stone stairs to the queen's apartments, which were laden with fruit bowls and decorative vases and luxurious litters of pillows and fine cloth. Charis poured two cups of wine and handed one to Chrysanthe as rain from a sun-shower drizzled steadily past the large windows.

"You may want to find comfort. I expect we'll be here for a time," said Charis, draining her cup and pouring another. Chrysanthe found a soft-looking cluster of pillows and eased herself down into the welcoming comfort, and Charis sat close by, setting two large jugs of wine on the wooden table before them.

"Why do you expect that? Are the races long?"

"The what?" Charis snapped. "Oh yes, they're long and tedious, much like shagging with a flaccid lover." She sighed heavily. "Tell me, Princess, of your Sparta."

The queen's eyes were pools of silent, hardened pain, and now they were the window through which she saw the world. *Ah, so there is something you want to know*, thought Chrysanthe. "Well, it was beautiful when it was still standing," she said with a touch of venom.

"Don't test my patience, girl. You will fast find that I possess none."

"Sparta was fields of barley," she began, feeling her throat tighten as memories played in her mind. "There was a river, spectacular to see, where the night flowers grew and lit up the dark. Sparta was mother to us. The warriors were strong and brave and honourable, the women even more so. The lands were dry, but the crops never failed, the ports thrived, and trade was profitable. The people were happy."

Charis stared at the princess, lost in some other thought under her stoic expression. "Your people loved you?" she asked.

"I would not claim they loved me. They did not know me. I was encouraged to stay within the palace. But I loved them, for they carried Spartan values on their shoulders with pride."

"I hear your mother was quite popular amongst your people."

Chrysanthe felt her back stiffen. "She was much adored, and rightly so. She was well-loved by the people, yes, but whatever respect and honour she was shown, she earned." Chrysanthe kept her eyes hard on Charis.

The princess's dedicated but feeble defiance seemed to amuse the queen. "Love of sovereign does not exist. There is only fear that commands respect. I believe your father was rumoured to have understood that very well." Charis pulled a small green vial from her robe and emptied it into her wine, then sipped deeply. "And he was flayed alive for that arrogance." The queen smiled. "You have such spirit still. Thank the gods for the entertainment in this mundane piss-pool of a place. How is married life? Is it everything you dreamed of?" Her voice was dripping with venomous challenge.

"Let us not feign sisterly affection, Charis. We do not like each other. In fact, I suspect we two do not like anyone in this 'mundane piss-pool of a place.' Ask me what it is that you have been told to ask, and then let us enjoy the sunshine in silence." Chrysanthe sipped her wine deeply, the warm burn trickling down her throat.

"Very well, as you know, you are beholden to King Athanasios, and any treachery against him is treachery against all our family. If you should happen to come upon agents of deceit or if you have reason to suspect such treasonous activity, you are to come to me immediately without delay, is that understood?"

"Of course, Charis. Has there been an attempt on the king's life? Or is there reason to suspect betrayal?"

"Are you or any of your advisers plotting against King Athanasios?"

"No, Your Majesty."

"Has that eel Lysander ever uttered a word of the sort?"

"No," replied Chrysanthe with genuine surprise.

"You do know that, if it is revealed that you have lied to me, I will personally have the pleasure of peeling the skin from your naked body in front of the good people of Kretos. They must see what I will do for them to protect their king from harm, thus protecting them."

"Yes, I understand you will peel the skin from my naked body in front of a fiendish crowd, and the pain will be great, the agony unrivalled. My blood will stain the ground below for years to come, and all children will be told the story of my demise. Yes, Charis, I am clear on your threat." Chrysanthe huffed and gazed out of the enormous window at the minuscule figures running in the rain.

"And what of your servants and personal guard?"

"No deceit to report." Chrysanthe felt her throat catch in its dryness and sipped her drink as calmly as she could. "Why would anyone seek to assassinate Athanasios anyway? You all are such a lovely family." Chrysanthe's expression remained one of callous defiance and contempt, and to her surprise, Charis chuckled at the snipe.

"You have the stomach to establish your place here."

"Then it is a shame I don't have any family left to murder."

"Better to wear the white linens of royalty than the black wrappings of the dead, they say."

"I would challenge that it is better reversed."

"And I would agree."

Silence grew again as both women ruminated on the odd exchange and their unspoken yet clear connection through their suffering, engulfed in the knowledge that, if given a chance, each would murder the other without a thought.

"Strange how the colour of something can change its value." Charis traced the fine gold threads of her robe gently with a fingertip, lost somewhere far away in her thoughts. "A rock of this colour determines who will die, who will live, and who will rule all others, yet it is just a rock. A shiny yellow rock from the ground." She giggled shrilly. "A rock decides our lives." She returned to the present with a whimsical look, and for a moment, Chrysanthe glimpsed the childhood stolen from the queen who now drank deeply from her cup, her eyes and cheeks reddening.

"Queen Matola decorated these apartments—a great beast of a woman, ruthless and depraved. I quite enjoyed the bitch."

"She was the queen before you?"

"No, she was our husbands' grandmother; it was a cruel shame that she couldn't live once Athanasios took the throne. I would have enjoyed her company more than any."

Chrysanthe's mind flooded with images of the creature in Corinna's cage, and she shifted her weight as she tried to shake them from her memory. "She had excellent taste," Chrysanthe lied.

"I doubt she did much designing. We still employ the thread-maker for any royal garments; his embroidery is simply unmatched, as the fool Lakeros would tell you himself." Chris gestured lazily around the room at the many pillows, rugs, curtains, and linens.

Chrysanthe remained silent, trying to conceal the hope suddenly surging through her. That name . . . Lakeros. She knew that name. A tall, slender man by that name had visited her mother in Sparta many years ago, when she was a small child. She recalled that his thick black facial hair had been combed impeccably and oiled daily, his black eyebrows had looked like caterpillars over dark but kind eyes, and he'd dressed with the inspiration of the many places he had travelled to peddle his trade. Once, great rulers had recognised the beauty of his work: kings, queens, lords, and warlords alike had requested he visit them to make for them the finest threads. The man had been humble and soft-spoken, in contrast to the flamboyant colours, cuts, and designs of his clothing.

Lakeros had sat with Chrysanthe in the palace gardens after Kallisto had spurned her request to accompany her and her friends on a trip to the city markets, leaving the princess downcast and sombre. Lakeros had spoken of his own siblings and how his brother had come to accept that he would never fight in battle next to Lakeros, for Lakeros had chosen the path of beauty and peace. He'd indulged the young girl in her questions about his travels, and his words still echoed distantly in the depths of her memory: *Too often, my work is used to disguise something ugly as something beautiful.*

But if this was indeed the same man, what was he doing on such a hideous island as Kretos? Surely the man was too old by now for travelling such great distances to work, but then again, Charis' definition of "employ" might be more suited to the word "imprisoned."

"Is the man arrogant?" Chrysanthe asked innocently.

"All men are arrogant." Charis looked at Chrysanthe incredulously. "But yes, the man has more arrogance than he ought to—too much, especially, for the filthy hovel he dwells in."

Ah, so he lives in the lower city, Chrysanthe thought.

The little prince, Athanis, and his sister, Charissa, wandered up the stairs and into the room with sullen expressions, but not too sullen to prevent Charissa from greeting Chrysanthe with a glare of daggers. The children sat and began to tell their mother of the hardships of the day: their weekly scholarly lessons, a scolding from their father, and an archery lesson with Demosthenes. Chrysanthe found a curious transformation in the little boy; he had seemed smaller, meeker, and more timid when she had first met him. As the weeks had gone by, he had become more and more entitled—no doubt the influence of the king and his villainous brother. There was no wonder in the child's eyes any longer. All innocence was gone.

The girl, of course, only continued to percolate more hate within her, which Chrysanthe knew one day would be released on some poor soul—hopefully, not Chrysanthe. How easy it would be to topple her from the high stairs or nudge her from the ledge of a high window ...

Enough fantasies for one day, Chrysanthe told herself, and her heart was heavy again, her mind numb, her spirit wandering too far away to be coaxed back to her.

"I am bored, and I despise children. I will leave you with the footrace." Chrysanthe stood as fast as her injuries would allow; pain jagged through her, but she hid her reaction from Charissa's malicious gaze and swiftly crossed the room and descended the stone staircase without looking back.

Markos stood quietly at the bottom of the stairs. He fell in step behind her. As she made her way through the hallways, she noticed she was holding her breath and paused to place a hand on the stone wall, steadying her breathing until her shoulders relaxed. She had to find Lysander swiftly, for the afternoon sun would descend soon, and she would need to act quickly.

She rounded a corner of the hallway and saw a young servant boy exiting her room with her bed linens. When she called out for him to stop, he turned toward the command and obeyed.

"Locate my adviser Lysander and tell him Princess Chrysanthe of Kretos requests his counsel."

"Yes, my lady."

Chrysanthe caught Markos's eye and shot a quiet glare at him before entering her room and pushing the great door closed. Now alone for the first time all day, she allowed herself to catch her breath and rip a hunk of bread from the fresh loaf placed on a platter on the small table, along with grapes, figs, and cheeses. Charis's wine was strong, and on an empty stomach, she had felt its effects.

Still chewing on the bread, she bent down to lift the hem of her ankle-length dress and retrieve the small but elaborately embroidered dining cloth that she had stuffed into the straps of her sandal; she folded it carefully, as small and flat as it allowed, and slipped it beneath the brooch at her breast, pinning the small cloth under the fabric of her dress. There was a knock on the door, and drawing a breath, sure of her plan, she opened the door to Lysander and Timeaus. Greeting them with a sweet smile, she stepped out of the room and requested the two walk with her.

"Lysander, I am embarrassed at my childish behaviour in the face of your immense effort to help me during the time of adjusting to this palace life. You have my sincerest apologies. I do hope that you will forgive me, for your efforts exceeded those of any royal advisers I have known."

Lysander took the compliment humbly and quietly with a smile as they continued past the royal gardens towards the main gate into the upper city.

"You have both been good friends to me. I have decided that I do indeed need to know my people in order to earn their trust and respect, and so I request that you accompany me to the lower city so that I may walk among them with new eyes."

The three stopped before the great gate with Markos a few paces behind them. Lysander hesitated, no doubt surprised by the sudden change of heart and preparing to gently explain why it might not be wise, after the events of her first visit, to go to the lower city again without a royal escort of soldiers. Keeping her sweet smile in place, she turned to Timeaus.

"What say you, Timeaus? The honey cakes will be my treat today." She watched his face light up at the promise of such a delicious gift and an adventure outside the palace.

"Oh, my lady! Thank you! If we hurry, we will get them while they're still warm!" Timeaus turned away and called to the guards above to open the gate, and Chrysanthe happily linked arms with Lysander and ushered him forward into the city.

EGYPTE

THE LION CUB

— XIV —

The end of Shemu approached. With the crops fully grown, the fields thick with barley, wheat, and corn were scythed before Aket, the flooding season, when no farming could be done, and peasants tended to their animals or took on building work for the pharaoh.

The vividness of the blue in the sky had begun to dull and grey as the last of the fields were being harvested. Theos kept to himself mostly. Arsinoe seemed to have disappeared completely, which blessed Kleopatra with peaceful days. Isis was scarce, and Auletes was heavily dedicated to his sword practice. Claudius and Neos seemed to spend whole days and nights in the battle chamber with the pharaoh and his war council.

When Ankhmakis was not with them, he spent his time with Akela in the gardens, answering her never-ending questions and explaining the battle strategies and politics of war to her. She delighted in listening to his voice and watching him move small game pieces into formations to show her how he had won famous battles. She imagined him in the world of the game pieces, riding Appollodon, slaying the savage enemies of Egypte.

The days seemed shorter now, and there was much activity in the fields, the pace of winter preparation slowly increasing. Word had arrived at the palace that the Roman Empire ambassador, Macedon King Andriscus, had anchored his ships in the Bay of Alexandria and was approaching the city himself with an entourage of ten men. Akela stood on the terrace of her palace apartment, looking out to try to glimpse the mysterious foreign guests, but their ships were only specks bobbing on the bay.

She gestured widely to the pretend audience below her, dagger in hand. "I have secured victory against the dreaded Assyrian raiders, and they shall bother my people no more!" She paced slowly and proudly the length of the terrace. "Tonight, there shall be a celebration! The wine will flow, and the music will be loud. Baked honey tarts for all!" She paused and held up a hand in response to imaginary applause. "I am humbled to be your queen—"

"How are your subjects today, Queen Akela?" She jumped and spun to see her father leaning against the terrace archway, arms crossed, his face stern but his tone playful.

She grinned. "They are well, Father. There is a shepherd who has lost a sheep and blames the goat man, but the goat man has lost a goat and blames the shepherd. It is a mess."

"Ah. And what have you decreed?"

"The goat man is to give the shepherd one of his goats, and the shepherd is to give the goat man one of his sheep. They will find blessing in the exchange. One will now have goat milk, and the other will have wool."

"Indeed, you would make a fine queen." He gave a small smile. "Now ready yourself for greeting our guests from Greece." He pushed off the archway and turned into the room to don his black-plumed helm and golden gauntlets.

Akela ran to the garment room and slipped on a thin cotton, floor-length dress, elegant and emerald green. She wiggled her feet into simple sandals, and as her father adjusted the leather straps on his breastplate, took delicate sprigs of small white field flowers, and peering into the reflective metal plate mounted on the wall, wove them through her hair.

A few minutes later, her father stepped confidently into the hypostyle, his mere presence commanding respect from the crowd, and Akela followed him. He stepped forward to bow to the pharaoh and then turned to face the far entrance with a face of intimidating stone. Akela paused at the sight of the fully uniformed Egypteian warriors who lined each side of the long reception hall, where the pharaoh sat proudly on his throne. The great room had never had this warrior formation before, and she suspected it was an intentional flexing of muscle ordered especially for the arrival of a foreign king . . . or else there was danger perceived in this visit.

She moved to the side of the small steps where the nobles and companions stood and exchanged a glance with Kleopatra, who sat in her royal reception chair amongst her siblings. The faint sound of heavy footsteps echoed lightly against the high painted ceilings, and hushed whispers trickled through the crowd.

Soon, a small party of leather-clad warriors approached the pharaoh and stopped before him to dip their heads in respect. The men were each tall, broad-shouldered, and muscular, wrapped in intricately designed skirts made of small circles of fabric layered over each other below sturdy sword belts and magnificent bronze-coloured breastplates adorned with depictions of lions and fastened tightly by leather straps. The men wore fine knee-length sandals and golden gauntlets, carried half-moon golden shields on their backs, and held beautiful golden helms at their right sides. The party was a sight to behold. The tanned king stood beside a boy half his height but dressed in the same way as his companions.

🌿

KING ANDRISCUS SILENTLY CURSED TO HIMSELF AS HE walked toward the pharaoh of Egypt, sitting atop an elaborate golden throne, soldiers lining the walls. *Overdressed for a peaceful meeting,* he thought, but it did not surprise him. *Any pharaoh who builds temples to worship himself has an ego.*

The heat in these lands was ferocious, and no winds swept the sand to deliver relief, which only irritated the king further, and hope stirred in him that this meeting would be successful and over swiftly so he could return to Macedonia before Poseidon raged below the winter seas.

He glanced subtly from side to side, counting the fighting men in the room, and gauged that the quality of the fighting he had seen in the west from these soldiers, who outnumbered his own three to one, would be equal to that of his lions. Surely this sovereign of lands of sand would not allow so many nobles and guests to attend if he intended to attack, but Andriscus well knew that men of little wit and much hubris were capable of such stupidity and poor strategy.

As Andriscus came to a halt before the spiteful-looking leader, he forced a warm smile and dipped his head in a respectful nod. "Ho, great Pharaoh of

Egypte!" His voice boomed commandingly through the quiet hall. "I am King Andriscus of Macedonia, and this is my son, Prince Astyanax, fourth of his name and namesake of our legendary ancestor." He gestured proudly to the young boy at his side, who dipped his head toward the pharaoh. "Thank you for your invitation to your kingdom; from what I have seen, it is beautiful as it is prosperous."

The stern general from the beach battle looked as he had when they had first met but was now well-rested and fed. He stepped forward to greet Andriscus respectfully. The Greek king wondered if the man had any personality at all, but he stepped forward to grasp the general's extended forearm. "General Ankhmakis, it is good to see you again and not amidst a scene of carnage. A bath suits you, my friend." He turned again to the pharaoh. "I have come not only to see your great kingdom but also as an ambassador for the great General Crassus of the Roman Empire, who seeks peace between our lands."

The pharaoh almost sneered his bored reply. "I was not aware there was peace to be negotiated."

The man was an imbecile. "General Crassus merely wants to be transparent about his intentions regarding his warring in Assyria and wishes to let it be known that he and Great Rome have no desire to engage in conflict with mighty Egypt. We are here in peace, in the hope we might learn more of each other if we are to be neighbouring empires who wish for no battle or misunderstanding between us."

The pharaoh seemed irritated by Andriscus's speech but replied, "So be it. I will not refuse to extend courtesy to a gracious foreign general. You will be my guests for three nights. We will dine and drink and discuss the intentions of your Rome. Come then. We shall feast."

ASTYANAX NOTICED HIS FATHER'S TENSE STANCE RELAX slightly beside him. It seemed the olive branch had been accepted, and they were to live among the sand heathens for three nights. He hoped the nights were shorter here.

He glanced up to the others who sat beside the pharaoh: a beautiful woman and a hateful-looking woman next to a girl with a scarred face, caked with clay to cover the wounds, a young boy, and two older men. A young girl with a kind face sat next to a hairless boy whose face seemed disfigured, scattered with red raised scars, and who had a walking staff beside him.

Then, standing below the thrones, he saw her, draped in an emerald gown. White flowers adorned her long, dark hair, which fell in waves around her pleasing face. Her eyes, as they flicked up to meet his, were almond-shaped and dark, with a smear of gold on each lid. She did not shrink from his gaze nor coyly look away and redden as girls often did when they saw him. Her expression was curious and regal, almost defiant, he thought.

The kind-faced girl skipped down the steps toward the emerald goddess and took her by the hand, and then they were lost in the now-milling crowd.

Astyanax's father put a hand on his shoulder. Astyanax looked up at him. "You will listen, boy," his father said. "There will be much to learn at this table, and crucial knowledge will often be found in what is *not* said."

The boy nodded confidently, and together, they followed the Egypteian general out of the great hall.

🌿

AT THE BANQUET TABLE THAT EVENING, THE TEN WAR-riors, their king, and his boy sat tall and rigid in their wooden chairs, surveying the assortment of foods laid before them, which they clearly found unfamiliar. Some seemed curious, yet others seemed suspicious and hesitant as the servants offered portions of goat stomach and pheasant kidneys brined with apricot wine. Akela watched one man opposite her at the enormous horseshoe-shaped table inhale several dishes with enthusiasm, seeming not to even taste them. He appeared to experience each taste as the same and ate with gusto while engaged with several scholars who had come to ask him questions of his land.

He belched loudly, and the Egypteians froze with shock, gazing at the man, who noted the confusion. With a large smile, he brought his fist down fiercely onto the table and said loudly, "Your cuisine is excellent, Sand King! I thank you!" And then he continued his feast, draining his cup as his fellow soldiers nodded in agreement.

Safiya, beside the stiff pharaoh, let out a laugh that seemed to melt the hearts of the men present. Nobles clapped at the beaming Macedon man, who raised a pheasant leg toward the queen in cheers. Safiya laughed again and addressed King Andriscus warmly. "Your men are truly refreshing company, Your Majesty. I look forward to learning more of your customs and also, now, of your cuisines."

He dipped his head, receiving the compliment gracefully. "Already, my men and I have observed the many differences between Egypteian architecture and our own, and I speak for all of my party when I say Egypt is truly a marvel of beauty."

Palace musicians began to lightly strum lyres in the far corner as kitchen servants brought several more large platters of meats and cheeses and fruits to the table. Astyanax had been hesitant to try the strange, inflated organs that had been spiced and roasted and set before him, but hesitation was a trait the boy sought to eradicate, and so he carved pieces of each dish for himself. He had especially enjoyed the olive bread with its thick, creamed white lard and had dipped it in a delicious stew of camel meat and barley. The meat was tough, but the spices made it enjoyable.

The servants had filled his cup with wine, believing him to be older than his twelve years, which was understandable as the muscles in his arms and back were well used to the wielding of sword and shield, and his legs were defined from his lifetime mastering the horse. His father noticed but allowed it, and so he sipped happily. His father's conversation with the pharaoh about politics seemed to melt into the music.

The young princess he had been told was named Kleopatra entered the room and took her place opposite him. Though she was pretty, it was the girl who sat down beside her who was the reason for the increased pulse in his chest and his strangely parched mouth—the girl in the emerald dress he had seen in the throne room. He thought he had never seen a more beautiful girl.

Suddenly, her kohl-lined eyes came to rest on him, and he felt the weight of her presence render him unsure of himself. Embracing the new sensation, he held her gaze and smiled heartily. She clearly did not expect the greeting, and the strength in her stare faltered before she dipped her head toward the plate before her. Astyanax thought he saw the hint of a smile play on her lips and resolved then and there that he would talk to the girl, hoping he would find answers to his heart's behaviour. Pleased with his plan, he drank deeply from the goblet.

They exchanged glances twice more before the pharaoh rose from his chair and the room fell silent. A short line of women wearing little more than loin-cloths entered at the end of the hall and stood next to one another, displayed before the audience. They were covered in thin golden chains and jewels and had kohl designs on their skin. Their faces were youthful but ashen, and their eyes looked at the ground.

"Our official business has concluded, and now our guests will be treated to all our great kingdom has to offer." The pharaoh's tone did not match the manners in his wording. He gestured to the half-naked women before them and then addressed the Greeks. "Please enjoy the women of Egypt as you have enjoyed her food and drink; you have travelled far, and I am sure you will welcome the company. Tomorrow we shall show you our great monuments. I bid you goodnight." Astyanax felt the emerald girl's eyes on him; he looked away from the assemblage of maidens and straightened his posture.

The pharaoh nodded to the Greek king and exited the hall through the door behind his chair. The room resumed its chatter. Astyanax looked to his father. He saw the insult on his face, but he held himself tall and called to a servant for more wine. After an acceptable length of time, the Greeks excused themselves to retire also.

None but the loud and full-bellied warrior stopped at the line of young women. As the others exited, he strode confidently up to the girl who stood at the far end of the line, then took her hand gently and gave a small bow; she exchanged a subtle look with the girl next to her, then looked at the large warrior. He kissed her hand, then held out his arm toward the exit archway. With a small smile, she obliged, and he escorted her from the room.

Astyanax was slower to follow his party in their departure, still hoping to speak to the emerald-clad girl, but when he looked back to where she sat, she and the young princess were gone. He recovered from his disappointment and quickly exited.

Astyanax entered the guest apartments after several wrong turns in the palace halls to find his father pacing furiously while his men sat around the room and offered their thoughts.

"The man is sour and joyless, and his dishonourable conduct is not unnoticed!" he spat.

"Perhaps he truly was tired, Your Majesty?" one warrior offered.

"No, Santos. I know it was his desire to speak no more to me, and I know this because if I had the option, I would have retired upon his arrival and simply dined in the apartments rather than endure such lifeless discussion with a sack of rocks!"

Several of the men laughed, and it seemed to soften the anger in the king, who stopped pacing and also laughed into his cup. "We will drink this nauseating king's wine, and see his obscene constructions, and with the mercy of Poseidon, the dark clouds brooding on the horizon will loom nearer, and we will request to make for our ships to be on our way before we are trapped in the bay."

Astyanax hoped the storm would come in swifter winds, and they would be delayed, long enough for him to get to know the girl in the emerald dress.

Upon arrival in the guest quarters, the party had made fun of the strange decorations and elaborate finishings that seemed to adorn every object in sight. They had let out a collective sigh at yet another foreign bed to spend their nights in. They had travelled far for many months; the men missed their wives or favourite whores and the comfort of their own beds and the familiar meals of their homeland.

Astyanax missed his mother, a fair-haired beauty with slender arms and eyes that appeared to have been poured from the great ocean. He did not like that they had been forced to leave her to tend to the kingdom when the Romans had come to charge them with their new duties under the blanket of the Roman Empire. He longed to see with his own eyes that she was indeed safe and well.

As the men settled in their beds around the guest apartments, Astyanax lay down on the comfortable feather bed, with the warm, balmy breeze from the terrace flowing gently over him, and with the face of the girl in his mind, embraced sleep, willing the next morning to come swiftly.

◆

A LIGHT BREAKFAST WAS SERVED IN THEIR CHAMBERS, and the Greek men devoured the food gratefully. They were told that Prince Astyanax was invited to join Princess Kleopatra on a separate outing to see the great river. Andriscus thought for a moment that it could be an attempt to murder the young prince, leaving Macedonia without an heir, but he quickly dismissed the thought, as there was no point to such an assassination and no motivation. He then understood that the pharaoh wished to open the door for a possible union for future political security and silently agreed it to be a wise strategy. He told Astyanax to speak with Kleopatra, to be courteous, and to get to know the princess, and Astyanax promised to oblige his father's command and represent Macedonia proudly.

The Greeks donned their military uniforms once more and made their way down to the promenade to meet the waiting pharaoh and his party, which held twenty or so saddled camels, bright coloured tassels decorating the long leather reins and saddle padding—a magnificent sight. Several people tried to cover their amused snickers at the faces of the Greeks as they realised they were to ride the humpbacked animals. The men shifted their weight uncertainly, but Andriscus spoke coolly. "I thank you, Pharaoh. I shall do my best to stay upon the beast."

He strode down the steps to meet the sitting camel, awkwardly gripped the pommel, and swung a leg over the saddle. Before he could position himself properly, the camel lurched to his feet. The king recovered from the shock and adjusted his seating as a few of his soldiers laughed. The pharaoh glared at the Greek warriors, clearly filled with furious disbelief that soldiers would laugh at their sovereign.

Then the king also laughed. "You laugh now, you scoundrels, but I saw no one else step into the unknown first. Climb aboard your strange horses." He beamed with wondrous glee at the thrill of such a thing, and the smiles disappeared from the Greeks' faces as they accordingly descended the stairs.

The pharaoh, now mounted on his own large animal and flanked by his essential staff and guards, led the way down the plant-shrouded path toward the lower city; one by one, the newly mounted Greeks followed.

🌿

ASTYANAX SPOTTED THE GIRL FROM THE DAY BEFORE standing calmly, dressed in a long light-blue dress that clung to her slim frame—and to her chest, where her body was beginning to develop. Her long, dark hair was braided, and from her ears hung small gold earrings with tiny sapphires at their ends, glinting in the sunlight.

He noticed her attention was distracted by a dull, clacking sound coming from the hedged garden behind her. Astyanax pulled his wit back to his duty for today and saw Princess Kleopatra standing near the girl; she wore a simple white dress, and her neck and wrists were decorated with pretty coloured bracelets. He approached her and bowed, then straightened to meet her plain but pleasantly warm face. Her eyes were light-brown and large. There was innocence there, he thought, and kindness, something he did not see often, and it made him smile.

"Your Highness, Kleopatra, I am Prince Astyanax of Macedonia, and I am pleased to meet you. Thank you for hosting my father and me at your palace. My father tells me you wish to show me your beautiful river today? I am very much looking forward to the honour." Out of the corner of his eye, he saw the other girl turn toward them.

Kleopatra's smile was warm and friendly as she responded. "It is Egypte's pleasure to have you as our guest, Prince Astyanax. We do not receive many visitors, and I am happy to show you the beauty of our River Nile. This is my companion, Akela." She gestured to the girl, who dipped her knees in a curtsy to the prince.

"My brother, Prince Theos, will also be joining us today." She gestured to the crippled boy he had seen in the reception yesterday, who sat upon his camel already with no hint of joy on his face. "As will my guard, Kohlis." She smiled up at the enormous dark-skinned man behind her, who didn't smile in return.

There are a lot of joyless faces in this kingdom, Astyanax thought, but if he lived in a place of such heat, he doubted he would smile either. He nodded to the giant.

"Please come meet your camel. I hope we have paired you with one with an appropriate temperament," Kleopatra said excitedly, making for the beast.

Astyanax noticed Akela was once again focussed on a gap in the garden hedge behind her, and he stepped forward to glimpse what held her attention. He saw a young boy in a small leather breastplate training with a stocky, bearded man, attacking and defending with wooden practice swords. "What do you watch for?" he asked.

She jumped slightly, then turned to face him, and he found himself suddenly very aware of the flow of the blood in his veins and the feel of the air in his lungs. He was not nervous, nor scared, nor uncertain, nor was he out of his own control; instead, he felt great comfort in her intense gaze, as if all that he was stood naked before her, as if she had stripped him of all pretence. It felt liberating. It felt . . . alive.

"Prince Auletes." She glanced back at the warring boy. "His parry is dreadful."

Astyanax stared at the annoyed crease in her brow. *What a strange girl*, he thought, *to have a mind for weaponry when surely she has not herself seen war, nor would she have been educated in such things.* Unable to curb his curiosity, he asked, "What adjustment would you give, my lady?"

She shot him a harsh glance but replied, "Stop him putting so much weight on his right foot." Then she stepped past him and walked away as if irritated by the fighting boy's trivial incompetence.

Astyanax turned sharply and whipped down the stairs to where Kleopatra stood stroking the coat of her camel. She looked up to him and smiled. "Shall we mount our ferries?"

"After you, my lady." Astyanax held out his hand to steady her as she mounted her animal. She thanked him, and he then turned to offer a hand to Akela but found she was not only mounted already but her camel was standing and pacing alongside Prince Theos and his mount.

Astyanax took a breath and approached his own camel. He swung a leg over the saddle, then gripped the pommel with all his strength as the ground fell away below him; the awkward rise of the enormous, humped thing almost made him fall to the dirt. As the great beast settled into its stance with a loud snort, he took the thin leather reins and found he was smiling broadly. The ground was far below, but there was no fear in him, simply a pleasurable thrill, and he let out a laugh, reaching down to pat the coarse coat of the odd beast. He looked up to see the other three children grinning at him. Akela's smile transformed her face.

Their caravan began its journey down a dusty path toward the east. The view was magnificent. The animal's movement felt strange at first, but Astyanax soon adjusted to the rhythm and found it pleasantly calming, as was the low conversation between Akela and Theos behind him. The sun beat down on them as the narrow path began to widen, and Kleopatra slowed her camel to bring it beside his, smiling warmly at him. "Have you been told to be as polite as I have?"

"I have, Princess." He chuckled, and she joined him.

"I'm sure you know more of the politics of kings than I do, but I would wager my weight in gold that this activity will be much more enjoyable than listening to my father boast of his pyramids and temples."

"Then the gods have blessed me this day indeed. Tell me of your River Nile."

"It is a very long river and provides useful transport for the trading boats between Alexandria and Luxor. It is home to many delicious fish, and its waters are steady, making it perfect for relaxing boat rides."

"Is that what we are to do today?"

"Indeed, it is. We have food and drink, and we hope to show you the beauty of our lands. You can see much of Egypte along its shores."

"May we swim in the river?"

"Such a thing is forbidden. Crocodiles and other dangerous animals make their home in these waters, and they will feast on all who enter the river. Crocodiles are enormous beasts with hides tougher than leather, and the grip of their jaws is stronger than iron. They are not pleasant creatures but do not fear, they will not make a meal of you today. Our boat is sturdy."

The shoreline came into view. The water was still and blue against the banks of golden sand, adorned with green shrubbery and tall white flowers among the reeds. As they drew closer to the small but lavish canopied boat bobbing lightly on the water, he saw that there were flowers of striking azure growing in the water. Kleopatra's camel leaned forward to fold itself to a lazy kneel, and suddenly the animal beneath him began its descent. Before he could do more to prepare himself than grip the saddle instinctively, the camel had knelt, and his feet had touched the ground.

Once the party was grounded and ready, they stepped along the small wooden plank to the boat, which was pleasantly larger and more comfortable than it appeared. Astyanax boarded first and extended a hand to Kleopatra and Akela, helping them onto the vessel.

Akela's hand was soft and strong, and her touch thrilled him. What had happened to him? Perhaps the Egypteians had poisoned the food, and her effect on him was a beautiful hallucination? If that were true, it would be a good death, he thought.

Once Kohlis boarded last, the captain and his small crew launched from the shore, and they began a marvellous drift down the river. As they lay across many beautifully embroidered feather-stuffed pillows, servants brought cool drinks to them and placed bowls of grapes and figs and meats and cheeses next to large loaves of dark brown bread. The sun was much more pleasant now in the shade of the sheer canopy that flapped peacefully in the breeze.

Theos requested wine, and a servant leaned forward to fill his cup, but before he could take a sip, Astyanax leaned forward, offering his cup in a toast. Theos looked annoyed at the formality but obliged him. "To the friendship of our peoples." Astyanax smiled, and Kleopatra and Akela raised their goblets to the toast also. As the Greek prince sipped, he flicked his eyes up toward Akela, who to his delight, was watching him too.

"Is Egypt what you had expected, Prince Astyanax?" Kleopatra asked, her sweet voice making the heat of the day pleasant and her large, light eyes inviting open conversation.

"Truthfully, Princess, I did not know much of Egypt before we received sudden orders that we were to land on your shores to request to speak with your Pharaoh, Ptolemy Auletes. We miscalculated our direction, and strong winds on the Aegean pushed us off course. Fortunately, Poseidon took pity on us, and we came across your General Ankhmakis."

"Ah, a welcome turn of fate then! Yes, the general is a fine example of Egypt; he is much decorated, and his courage in battle speaks to his admirable character. He is Akela's father, and his best qualities are mirrored in her." She smiled at Akela, who remained poised but acknowledged the compliment.

Astyanax stared at the girl. *A general's daughter. Free to marry whom she pleases* . . . His heart leapt for a moment until a voice in his head whispered, *But you are not* . . .

"Then how lucky you are, Princess, to have such a companion." He turned to Akela, the cup sweating in his grip. "Your father is a wonder to see in battle. The man has no fear and fluid technique."

"Did you fight him?" Akela asked, straight-faced and without hesitation.

Astyanax was taken aback. "Uh . . . no, my lady, we soon appeared to be on the same side, but I would no doubt be honoured and intimidated to fight such a warrior."

"Fearful?" she pressed.

"I believe I would be, yes."

"Then you are a wise man." She grinned, and he relaxed, as he now understood her game with him. She was smart, and he was out of practice with the subtle ways of flirting.

"You seem to know of technique yourself, my lady. Are the women here schooled in war?"

"I learn from my father. When he is here," she replied, and Astyanax noted a sadness in her tone.

"Then you have access to the grandest tutor." He wished to hear her speak more, all day if he could, perhaps all night also, but his father had given him a specific task, and he would have no kingdom to offer a wife if he did not follow orders now. He turned to Kleopatra. "Your Highness, I saw a great spotted cat within the palace this morning; my father almost drew his sword to slay the beast, but we were informed the cat was a pet?"

"She is Heba. She is magnificent, no? She was a gift from the general, and she is dear to my heart, like my own child," Kleopatra answered, the love for the great cat evident in her smile. She beamed fondly.

Astyanax noticed Theos roll his eyes. "Prince Theos, do you have any pets?" Astyanax asked.

The two girls grew silent and looked cautiously at the boy with the broken face, who seemed unused to questions. "I . . . yes, I have a horse and a python." His expression was one of relief at having survived the interaction, but Astyanax knew there was more to the prince than the prince himself thought and that knowing as much about the royal family as possible was an asset.

"What breed of horse do you keep?"

"An Arabian mare. Their breed is fine-haired, so the saddle does not slip. Her legs are slender, which is not ideal for sand, but the horse is light, so her lean build is redeemed by her weightless glide across the dunes. She was brought from a successful raid in the east. Akela has tamed the brother stallion, and he is a fierce mount." There was a glint of excitement in the crippled prince's remaining eye. "The general's horse, Appollodon, is a breeding wonder to behold! The black stud has shoulders built for the sands. A monster of a thing, each foot bigger than your head."

"You know breeds well, Prince Theos. I would like to see how you find our Grecian fillies. They are sturdy and brave war animals yet have stubborn temperaments. When you come to Macedonia, I will have one waiting for you, and then we shall compare our mounts." He grinned, and Theos grinned back.

"Tell us of your Macedonia, Prince Astyanax," Kleopatra said, and Theos moved closer, now clearly interested and eager for the response.

"It is a large kingdom, Princess. Where would I begin?" he replied politely.

"Tell us of your palace and your monuments," said Theos.

"Well, we have no monuments such as your great structures, but we do have temples dedicated to the gods placed throughout the city. They are grand structures with high ceilings. Tall bronze statues of great warriors of Greece guard the entrances beside large copper bowls where a fire burns day and night. Inside, there are many designs carved on the walls, and on a podium stands a statue of the god, carved in white stone. Priests and priestesses keep the temple, tending to offerings and the public seeking guidance.

"The palace is a marvel, truly. Each tower is fifty steps high, and the roofs are clad with bronze plating that shines in the sunlight. The mountains behind the city reach up into the clouds like mighty giants. The palace itself was designed by a Greek architect who travelled from Athens long before my grandfather was born.

"Lush vines grow through the terraces in the courtyards, and the women wear colourful dresses." He paused. "It is hard to describe one's home to others who did not grow up there. The people are happy, and they love their king. The army is strong, and the soldiers are good men. Macedonian wine is much revered by neighbouring countries, and trade is increasing. The city is crowded with travellers and sailors seeking to make a fortune, mingling on the streets among the merchants and soldiers and smiling whores."

"How are the soldiers good men if they visit whores? Smiling or not," asked Akela sharply, and Kleopatra stiffened.

"I did not say the soldiers visited them," he replied calmly and thought he saw a flash of annoyance in her face.

"Do you think they don't?" Akela challenged in an attempt to cover her mistake.

"I'm sure they do; many of them are very young and making good wages. Would you say a good man cannot visit such a woman?"

"Yes, of course, that's what I'm saying."

"And what of loneliness, Akela?" he asked, and from her face, knew he had judged right that she was often lonely when her father was away. Perhaps he had also told her of the unbearable loneliness a man of war felt following a day of slaughter, something he had heard his own father speak of. "Both women and men get lonely, do they not?" he continued, his voice calm and smooth. "Perhaps there is more to such an exchange of money than we understand, being too young to know of the loneliness of widows or the haunted sleep of battle-weary men?" He kept his voice level and unchallenging.

Akela looked away.

"Perhaps you could tell us of your family, Prince Astyanax?" Kleopatra asked quickly.

"Yes, of course, Princess. My mother, the queen, is very beautiful and well-loved by the people. She tends to their bereavements and requests with care. They say she is the heart of Macedonia, and my father is the lion's head. He can be a harsh man, but he is honourable and has trained me to be so. My younger sister, Lykopis, is a sweet girl with golden hair and a gentle spirit, much too timid for royal duties, Father says."

"How wonderful that you have a sister. I would like to meet her one day."

"I hope you do, Princess."

"I am sorry you have no brothers; I have many to spare." She grinned.

"I will gladly take Prince Theos from your hands. We will breed some fine war stallions and ride them into battle," said Astyanax with enthusiasm. Theos smiled into his cup.

"Ho, hippopotamus!" a skinny servant boy said fearfully and scrambled to the stern, where several spears were stacked neatly; taking one, he looked to Kohlis, who had drawn his sword and was poised low at the starboard railing.

The children climbed carefully to crouch next to Kohlis and peeked over the side at the beast in the water. A wide snout with large nostrils and small, dark eyes floated slowly through the water, observing the boat as it passed, its ears flicking at flies. Astyanax had never seen such a creature; he wondered why the men drew weapons upon sighting it.

Kohlis's tense stance was released as the animal swam leisurely past without interest in the party, and all returned to standing to look out at the majesty of the river. Kleopatra and Theos began a conversation about the hippopotamus and its diet.

Astyanax spotted flowers on the riverbank and found that he could not look away. "What are they?"

"They're beautiful, aren't they?" Akela smiled. "The tall, white, curled ones are called arum lilies, and the ones in the water are blue lotus or azure lotus."

"They are truly beautiful."

"Egypte is rich with much beauty," Akela agreed.

"Yes, indeed it is. There is so much colour here—so much yellow."

"Do you mean gold? Have you not seen gold before, Astyanax?"

Akela giggled. His name on her tongue melted like honeycomb, and he smiled. "Gold is plentiful, yes, but the colours in Macedonia are cooler, like the great ocean."

"I have not travelled the ocean. Is it perilous?" she asked inquisitively.

"It is. Poseidon can be a spiteful god, and his temper can smash ships upon rocks, killing all aboard, or his breath can sweep vessels far off their courses. It is dangerous, yes, but the adventure, I promise, is worth braving the storms." He smiled warmly at her, and she seemed to mirror the look in his eye.

She turned away to look toward the riverbank. "I suppose if you are to be king one day, you must know much of the world. You must know your enemies and your friends and the progress of the modern kingdoms so you may better serve your people," she said seriously.

"Do all handmaids think this deeply of kingdom politics?"

"General's daughters do. Perhaps the gods intended me to be born a man. If I were, I would fight you right now for your kingdom," she threatened playfully.

He laughed loudly. "Somehow, I don't doubt it. What if we avoided a war and simply shared the kingdom?" He did not know what he was saying now and felt as though he'd dropped his only weapon in the river and floated helplessly in her presence.

"Are you asking for a Macedon queen?" she asked bashfully, and he noted the change in her demeanour. She had been strong and defensive, but now she glanced up at him with warmth in her dark, almond eyes, her essence sweet and girlish.

He let the question linger in the air and turned to look out to Egypte. He had not thought much on marriage, for he did not meet girls his age whose company he enjoyed. The young women of Macedonia, although beautiful and respected, seemed ill-intentioned or simple-minded. They lacked intelligence and spirit. "I . . . have much gold and jewels to offer a bride." He frowned as he reached for words.

"What would I do with gold?" Akela asked, disappointment in her tone.

"Whatever you like, I suppose." He felt hot in the sun, his mouth dry, and he decided to speak for fear that she would hear the thudding in his chest. "If I asked you to marry me, would you come with me to Macedonia and be my people's queen?"

He watched her smile slowly fade, and she dropped her gaze. "Do princes in Macedonia have the privilege of choosing whom they marry? General's daughters hardly seem a suitable match. I have nothing to give you."

"I have gold enough for the kingdom, but that was not my question," he said seriously, and she met his gaze with mild confusion.

Then the boat shuddered with the thump of wet wood. They gripped the wooden railing of the vessel and looked to the port bow, where Kohlis was speaking to a fisherman in a boat that had drawn up close to theirs. They moved to the port side, where Kleopatra and Theos stood chatting.

ꙮ

THEOS SAW THEM APPROACHING. "THE MAN'S SAIL IS stuck, and his catch is too heavy for him to take to the oar," explained Theos, gesturing with his goblet.

"Kohlis will fix it," Kleopatra said with a bored sigh, and she wandered away to fill her cup. Akela followed her.

Astyanax grinned as the giant Kohlis, who with the two boats roped and secured together, bickered with the old fisherman. The old man flailed his arms in a panic at Kohlis's large feet stepping onto his deck, apparently very fearful that the mountain of a man would sink his vessel. They argued loudly over each other, with Kohlis first trying to placate the man and then pushing past him, moving with care toward the sail and beginning to assess the problem.

"Your kingdom is vast with entertainment," Astyanax said to Theos as the old man, now clinging to the rudder, eyed Kohlis ruefully.

Theos smiled. "Yes, the days are certainly not dull. There are always strange sights and theatrical accidents."

"Is that what happened to you? An accident?" Astyanax asked softly.

Theos tensed, and his eyes suddenly turned cold and lifeless. "A slip of the tongue, rather."

"I did not mean to offend."

"Strangely, I have never been asked that question. It is common knowledge in this kingdom what happened to me. But the truth is avoided, as if it didn't." Theos stared blankly at Kohlis, heaving on the base of the smaller boat's mast. "The harshness of my appearance was a gift from my father, by his own hand. We must all accept the pharaoh's gifts. Am I now not a handsome prize for a wife? The children cower. Why shouldn't a woman?"

Astyanax took in the words and anger brewed in his belly at the thought of a man beating his child with the intent to end the young life. He steadied his voice. "You will know the truth of a woman then, whether she truly loves you for your nature rather than your position, and that is worth more than any amount of gold or a handsome face."

"Love is of no importance here. I remain ugly and crippled, and that is all," Theos said.

"That is not true, Theos. Love and hate in men speak loudly in the silence around them. There is much love in you. There is pain also, but the love in your nature speaks loudly. Looks will fade; love will not. I do not worry for your heart, my friend." Astyanax clapped Theos roughly on the shoulder.

A screech sounded high and shrill. Everyone on both boats turned toward the sound to see Akela and Kleopatra perched on the bow of the boat with several bees investigating the smell of their flowered perfume. They swatted at the air feverishly, the bees unrelenting.

Both girls fell backward into the river. They surfaced, splashing and panicked, the weight of their dresses pulling them down. Kleopatra screamed. The closest servant awkwardly leapt to the bow and jumped into the water, then swam behind the girls. The tethered boats were still drifting at a steady pace down the river, and the children's distance from the vessel was growing.

Astyanax unhooked his scabbard and raced along the deck of the boat, stepped up onto the wooden rail of the bow, dove off into the water, and began to swim toward the girls. By the time Kohlis had flown over the portside beam and surged to the bow, rocking the whole vessel in his haste, the servant and Astyanax were keeping the splashing girls afloat and were kicking with gusto back toward the boat.

Kohlis spun around to the boat-master and bellowed, "Bring her to the starboard side, you fool!"

The wide-eyed man began to pull at the tiller as Kohlis threw a rope to Astyanax, who caught it with one hand, clutching Kleopatra in the other. Kohlis heaved on the rope, and when close enough, he reached down, grabbed Kleopatra's arm in his large grip, and hoisted her onto the deck. He reached down a hand for Astyanax, but the Greek remained in the water, his eyes fixed on Akela.

"Take the hand!" commanded Kohlis, urgency in his voice, but Astyanax refused. Kohlis drew in the rope and cast it out again toward the servant trying to keep Akela from slipping below the surface, the weight of her dress clearly draining his strength. Then the servant shrieked and immediately began kicking with all his strength toward the boat before he dipped below the water and his grip slipped from Akela

Akela looked around her for the man to surface again, but seconds passed, and she knew Astyanax could see the panic in her eyes as she reached for the rope but struggled to grip it. Astyanax kicked himself off the wooden hull and sped toward her.

The servant surfaced abruptly, his eyes wide with terror, and spluttered as he tried to breathe. Astyanax reached Akela with speed, and with one arm securely wrapped in the rope, drew her to him in a tight hold, then extended his foot toward the screaming man, who grabbed it. Then they were speeding through the water toward the boat, pulled by Kohlis.

They reached the bow, and Astyanax hooked an arm around Akela's thigh and lifted her for Kohlis to pluck from the water as if she were a wet cloth. Astyanax, one hand holding onto the wooden rail, pulled the man toward him so that Kohlis could lift him free, but suddenly, the man disappeared below the surface again.

Acting quickly, Kohlis took Astyanax's arm and hurled him from the river onto the wooden deck. He sprang to his feet and darted back to the bow to see the man surface once more. Kohlis leaned far forward over the bow, his hand extended, but as the frantic man reached for the hand, a great shape surged through the water toward Kohlis. To Astyanax's shock, Kohlis balled his hand into a fist, and with all his force, brought it crashing into the beast's eye, knocking it back to the water. The man was out of reach and looked up as the face of a water demon, eyes yellow and dead, deeply set in armour, appeared behind him.

Astyanax was sure the creature was the god of death, with an abomination of teeth in its long snout and spiked armour trailing down its back. As he stood staring, his heart in his throat, another beast appeared. Then another. The pleading man and the soulless monstrosities quickly disappeared for the last time beneath the murky surface. The man's screams were cut short as the water before them began to thrash violently, flashing with scaled tails. Suddenly, the water calmed, and the air itself seemed to quiver in the presence of such horror.

Astyanax found he was gripping Akela's arm, but she did not move; she was, like all of them, frozen in shock and shaking.

🌿

THE PHARAOH'S VOICE RIPPED THROUGH THE AIR, echoing around the hypostyle, and seemed to move through the children who knelt before his throne. Akela thought the man's face might melt away with the anger seething from him.

The general stood beside the pharaoh, no trace of a loving father upon his face. Beside the general stood King Andriscus, his expression that of a man fighting with himself to control his rage. A very fearful Kleopatra sat clutching the hand of Theos on their royal chairs, and the composed figure of Kohlis knelt patiently before the pharaoh, a small pool of blood forming below him from the five angry lashes across his naked back.

Akela knelt next to Astyanax on the cool floor. Her knees were beginning to ache against the hard ground, more and more with each passing minute, but she dared not move or look up to meet the terrifying stares. There were several conversations that seemed more like arguments among her father, King Andriscus, and the pharaoh, and it was a considerable time before the pharaoh addressed her directly.

"And you, child. You have endangered the lives of royal heirs, you stupid girl. Do you know the punishment for such incompetence?"

She drew a fearful breath to defend herself, but another voice answered the pharaoh instead. "It was I, great Pharaoh. I beg the mercy of Your Majesty for my carelessness and stupidity. I did not know the magnitude of the dangers within the River Nile. I did not imagine such creatures to exist, and it is ultimately my ignorance that caused the accident. For that, I hold the deepest regret and anger at myself. Akela swam to protect the princess, but my naive foolishness led to the gruesome outcome."

The pharaoh turned to Theos and Kleopatra and stared questioningly. Slowly they nodded, and his eyes swung back to narrow on the Greek prince. "If you were any other man's son, I would have you whipped to your death, naked in the slave market, and leave you for the vultures to feast on your eyes. Do you understand, boy?"

Astyanax nodded.

"Your father has shown bravery and courage coming to the aid of my empire, so you may keep your life. If I have learned anything, it is that a father is not responsible for the disappointment of his sons. He will decide your fate. Such are the trials of a king with sons." With that, he swept from the room and disappeared from the hall.

King Andriscus stormed forward and collected Astyanax, hauling him away. Akela looked up to see her father walking away. Theos looked as though his father had speared him through his gut and stared blankly at the ground.

Kleopatra sprang from her chair and ran to Akela, kneeling down to embrace her friend. "I'm so sorry, my sweet friend." There was pain in Kleopatra's voice.

"No, I am sorry. Are you hurt?" she replied.

"No, sweet sister, are you?"

"No."

"Let us retire and dine in my chambers," Kleopatra said firmly. She pulled Akela to her feet, but she struggled to walk from the pain in her knees.

AKELA SAT MISERABLY ON THE TERRACE OF HER APART-ment, wrapped in a light woollen shawl, pulling it tighter in the cool breeze that now swept through the city from the sea. She watched the three large Greek ships sail into the low fog that hung above the waves, the dull sun still glinting off the brass finishings on their decks. The news had come from the Greek king's shipmaster that storms were developing, and if they were to make it back to Macedonia before winter, they must sail immediately. Whether that was true or not, she did not know, but she knew both kings were eager to be relieved of each other's company in the palace, and the Greeks were gone before dawn.

She sighed. A feeling of shame and loneliness had rested heavily on her spirits since the events on the River Nile. The look on the servant's face as he faced his doom haunted her nights. Her father had spoken sternly to her, more sternly than he ever had before, and when they said goodbye to the palace guests, the mood was sombre and tense. She had looked upon Astyanax with his black eye and cut lip, and she had wanted to reach out to touch his face and say she was sorry, but she had no farewell for the prince, and the weight of words unsaid was heavy.

She had been shocked as any when a merchant from the docks had arrived at the palace requesting an audience with Prince Theos. When Kleopatra and Akela had followed Theos to meet the merchant in the dirt forum outside the palace, they had arrived to find a sun-hardened, gruff, uncomfortable-looking man holding the leading rope of a lean, dark, towering mare. The children gasped at the majesty of the great animal as she pawed the ground, her pelt glistening in the hot sun. She was a beauty to behold, and just as Astyanax had described: slender-yet-muscular long legs, a lean body, and a powerful back.

The uneasy merchant thrust the rope into the hands of Theos. "From the Macedonian boy, a gift for Prince Theos," he grumbled.

"The Macedonian *prince*," Akela corrected sharply, but the man ignored her. "Name's Kallistias." He nodded and turned to make haste back to the port.

The three children glanced at one another as they admired the snorting beast, and Akela saw Prince Theos smile as he had not since the beating of his body and spirit.

🌿

THE RAINS HAD BEGUN, AND ALREADY A BARLEY FIELD IN the far south situated close to the riverbank had flooded, and two oxen had perished in the waters. The rains were welcomed by all and provided the flourishing city with much-needed moisture for the crops, the animals, and the water collectors, who stored water in wooden barrels and kept them in large water houses away from the heat in case there was a particularly long summer.

Akela had opened her winter chest to retrieve her shawls, which the women wore with their longer, thicker winter dresses, and had found a brooch amongst the fabric that had belonged to her mother. She fondled the brooch in her hand, remembering it with her fingers. It was the shape of a discus, embedded with tiny red stones and with the eye of Isis carved into the middle. She vaguely remembered the shape of her mother's hands, her fingers long and slender and her wrists lean and delicate. She did not remember her mother's face but recalled only her hands and her perfume.

Sometimes on calm days in the summer, the breeze would carry the scent of the marsh flowers through the palace, and she would remember her mother faintly. The woman had screamed often, shouting nonsense in tongues, and had locked Akela in chests and closets in their small home. She had never hurt Akela, but there was hurt in her mother that Akela and her father could not ease, and so one morning during one of her mother's violent episodes when she had been a danger to Akela and herself, the general had had no choice but to take a dagger to her heart.

Akela recoiled at the memory of how afraid she had been of her mother waving a glowing hot poker wildly in front of her. Her father did not speak for days following, and since then, his eyes had been haunted with the guilt of his broken heart. Perhaps it was because he hadn't been able to save his wife, or because he'd taken a mother from Akela, or simply because he had taken her life, believing that insanity was no life at all.

Akela pinned the brooch to her dress and shivered in the cool breeze that rolled in from the north, sweeping the palace and bringing sand into the open hallways. But it was not the breeze that made her shiver; she sensed in her gut that dark days would descend upon Egypt before the winter solstice fell, and that the rains were the beginning of it all. It seemed to Akela that the fates laboured carefully at their loom, pulling threads and stitching doom, and that great destinies had been set in motion.

🌱

KLEOPATRA SMILED AT HER BROTHER, WHO SAT ACROSS from her, poring over parchments covered with ink markings and hieroglyphs. Even with the mutilation of his body, Theos still had a quality of calmness or awareness about him that she enjoyed. Her brother had always been dear to her, and his voice reading to her comforted her greatly.

"You have always been the smartest of us all, brother," she mused, resting her elbows on the wooden table. She saw his mouth curve into a half-smile as he read. Even with the tightened and repositioned flesh of his cheek, his smile was still handsome. "I believe you know it, too."

"Well, I wouldn't disagree. Someone's got to do it if you're a lost campaign."

Kleopatra feigned offence and huffed in boredom. The study hours had been long of late, and the fat old scholar Taros seemed to delight in giving his students further work. Kleopatra was thinking that she might go blind and her ears might fall off if she was given yet another assignment when suddenly Akela burst into the room, out of breath.

"Your father has guests, and you will want to see these ones. Come, Theos!"

The three raced through the halls toward the hypostyle, coming to a stop at the edge of the hall, where a small crowd of noblemen, members of the palace commons, and the pharaoh's war generals had gathered. The room was eerily silent as the three youngsters pushed their way through the audience, and several footsteps were heard on the marble floor.

Before the pharaoh stood eight enormous warrior women. Their armour traced the shape of their breasts, they wore skirts of animal hide, and their boots were of stretched and hardened goatskin, adorned with studs and dark-coloured stones. Some had enormous horned bows and quivers of long feathered arrows wrapped around their bodies. Some had swords—one had two blades that formed a cross behind her back—and one strong-legged woman with a large flat nose and short neck had two smaller knives strapped down each boot, as well as countless more fixed to her waist belt. Many carried spears, and the menacing warrior who led the party wore a modest bronze crown, a band across her brow, and a strangely curved dagger in her belt. All the women assessed their surroundings, clearly taking in the apprehension and uneasiness of the audience, yet the less-than-warm greeting did not seem to faze them, and their expressions remained stern, hardened, and menacing.

"Great Sand King. I am Queen Thalestris of the Amazonian tribes who dwell far beyond your western settlements." Her voice was deep and strong, and the grace in her stature was a thing of beauty. "My daughter, Xanthippe."

She gestured to the very attractive, large-eyed woman standing behind her. "And my generals, Mimnousa and Toxaris."

The strong-jawed one with stocky legs and fat fingers nodded sternly at the pharaoh, and the other, with a girthy waist and astounding height, merely stared unblinking at him.

The warrior queen continued. "We are a small army making our way across the great desert toward Myria, where our sister tribes under Queen Thermodosa defend their lands against the Assyrian barbarians in Lydia and Phrygia, and also go to aid our allies in Gaul, who are under attack by Roman centurions. Greetings to you, Queen Safiya. I knew your father, and he would be proud to see the queen you have become."

Safiya nodded in respect.

"On our travels, we have heard of your mighty kingdom and present ourselves with peaceful greetings." The pharaoh remained silent and staring. Thalestris continued as if this were a common response to her presence. "I am told your city is a trading hub too vastly unique to be passed by without a purchase. Beyond my desire to meet such a king, I would like to request a specific trade with Your Highness."

Kleopatra looked toward her father to find his expression one of contained uncertainty and shock, and it amused her that he could be thrown by the existence of such beastly and intimidating women. Safiya sat beside him, her face a picture of thrilled curiosity. Next to her, Berenice tried to hide her disgust at the abominations before her, and Neos and Claudius sat on the pharaoh's other side, mouths slightly agape. Isis, Auletes, and Arsinoe were nowhere to be seen.

"I am glad to hear of the grand reputation of Egypte's prospering trade, but you have travelled far to help tribes that are facing great odds . . . I have heard that the Empire of Rome is laying siege to Assyria and its surrounding lands," the pharaoh finally replied.

"I do not believe a Roman garrison has ever come up against an Amazon force before, and if they had, they would have cowered like shivering children. We are aiding our sisters in their defence of our birth-right lands, and no *man* will take them from us. If these pompous Roman infants with swords decide to attack the northern tribes, we will mount their heads on spikes and boil their ribs to build our huts."

The room was silent, and the pharaoh looked as though he might find an excuse to back out of the hypostyle. "What specific trade request?"

"We require excellent-calibre breeding stock, and the slaves we have seen in your city are of exquisite variety. Your slaves are strong and would provide us with agreeable seed for strong offspring. We have brought many exotic spices from our lands and many treasures from our travels. I would ask that we agree upon a price for six good breeding slaves first, and then I would request to explore your great city and discover its wonders. But now, we are hungry and must rest."

"It is customary to dine with royal guests," Safiya said with a smile.

"Indeed," the pharaoh said. "You will stay in our guest apartments until we reach an agreement on your requests. Come then; we shall feast so you may rest." He rose and stood a moment uncertainly before striding away, leading the guests to the banquet hall.

Kleopatra glanced at Berenice, whose face was pale. She stood shakily, and Safiya stepped forward to take her hand and lead her gently out of the hall. Kleopatra and Akela exchanged looks of wild curiosity, but then Kleopatra's eyes followed the departing Berenice again, and concern nudged her thoughts.

"I've never seen Father so flustered . . . ever," said Theos with a wide-eyed grin.

Akela grinned back at him. "We're not missing this feast, and I could eat a camel."

"You two go ahead; I'll be right behind you," said Kleopatra, incurring an inquisitive look from Akela, but Theos took her hand, and they departed to the dining hall.

Kleopatra passed through an arched doorway that led into a dark hall with a stone wall to the left. On her right, pillars held up a gazebo that led out to a small garden oasis with lush ferns. At the end of the hall, she could make out the figure of Berenice, doubled over and coughing, and Safiya holding one of her arms to keep her on her feet.

As Kleopatra approached with careful steps, she saw a small pool of vomit at Berenice's feet. "Berenice?" Kleopatra asked in a small voice, and both women looked up to see her.

"Come, child." Safiya held out her hand, and Kleopatra took it. "Your sister isn't well—too many marinated olives, perhaps. We will get her some water and put her to bed with a wet cloth for her brow."

Kleopatra took Berenice's other arm. Her sister's skin was cold and sticky with sweat, and her head lolled. Her legs carried her only as far as her bed, where Safiya and Kleopatra lay her down. Kleopatra fetched wet cloths and brought them to Safiya. The queen dripped some of the cloths with an assortment of oils and laid one across Berenice's brow, one behind her neck, and one across her chest. Berenice's breathing began to calm, and Safiya quietly pressed her fingers around parts of her belly.

"What are you doing?" Kleopatra whispered.

"Sometimes bellies are fickle things."

"Will she be all right?"

"Oh yes, child. She will be as normal in a few hours. Now go and join the feast. I will stay with her."

"Can I stay awhile? She wouldn't leave me if I were sick."

"You are right, she wouldn't," said Safiya gently. "Of course, you can."

AS THEY ATE, AKELA AND THEOS STARED AT THE BAR-barian women who sat at their banquet table. The night was cool, and the breeze nipped at her ankles, but Akela noticed that the rugged women didn't seem to feel it. Their armour was fascinating, and their weapons well-made and beautiful. She had never seen a female wear armour before, and now it seemed as though she could not imagine life before this. Her eyes drank in every detail, from the studded-leather shoulder garments to the animal-skin skirts.

She noticed that Queen Thermodosa had several dark-coloured jewels set in her leather headband. Most of the women obviously had two bulges in their breastplates, but one had a simple, flat chest plate, and Akela wondered if she were, in fact, a man who enjoyed dressing as a woman warrior. Perhaps she had no breasts at all, as she herself did not. *But you will have them soon,* she reminded herself. Their faces were wide, as were their noses, and their jaws strong like a man's, but their cheekbones and eyes were truly those of beautiful women.

She found them remarkable, and to her shock, jealousy flashed in her chest. These women were fierce, and even men shrank in their presence; they appeared to only need men to breed, and they had surely known great glory in battle. If she had been born a boy, she would have fought in many battles with her father by now, at the age of twelve, and could have perhaps asked to spar with one of the giants.

"I don't know what to make of them," Theos whispered.

"They are magnificent," Akela answered in awe.

"Only you would think that. They won't be magnificent when they kill us all in our beds."

"They will be magnificent even then."

"The great Montu has placed so much potential in the wrong bodies," Theos snapped.

"The curious proof sits before us that the war gods can bestow their gifts on any kind of body they please," Akela countered angrily.

She'd clearly taken Theos by surprise. "I am glad you are in your body—you have a pleasing body . . . you . . . um . . ."

Theos stumbled into silence. Akela rolled her eyes, and with an annoyed huff, stood abruptly and left the hall.

She dragged her feet and slapped them childishly on the hard, flat marble floor of the vast hallways, pouting to herself and trailing her fingers along the wall. *One day, I will be a soldier of Egypt, and I will fight with Father and cut down our enemies.* Her thoughts crept away from her, and she stopped when she heard a shrieking laugh ahead of her. Looking up, she saw a young woman and the boy who held her hand; they were laughing about something, and the sound was beautiful to hear.

Then the girl turned her head to look at the boy, and Akela's heart stuttered to see the face of Arsinoe. She threw herself against the wall and hoped the shadow of a pillar would be enough to hide her presence. She saw the boy lean in to kiss the princess, then take her hand and scurry off down the hall ahead.

Akela stared after them as they disappeared quietly out of sight and then stood a moment, shocked by the unfolding of events. As she made to continue on her way, Isis rounded the corner to her right, and she stepped backward immediately into a curtsy. "Your Highness."

"What are you doing, girl?" Isis questioned sourly.

"I'm retiring for the evening, Your Highness."

"You're always lurking. What are the beasts like?" she asked, nodding in the direction from which Akela had come.

"They have the frames of men and well-made weapons. They have proved respectful, and the queen enjoys them greatly," Akela replied respectfully with a dip of her head.

"The bitch would enjoy a pile of camel dung greatly if it made itself acquainted. And what of battle plans?"

"I am sorry, Princess, I do not know of these matters." Akela braced for a slap to her face, but Isis merely discarded her answer and continued down the hall. Akela wasted no more time reaching Kleopatra's room.

❧

WHEN AKELA AWOKE, THE DARK CLOUDS OVER MEMPHIS had cleared, and the blue skies lifted her spirits greatly. She stretched out lazily in her bed and sat up, already feeling the rumble in her belly. She pulled on a light-blue dress in tribute to the sky and opened her door to make her way to the kitchens for breakfast, but as she rounded a hallway corner, she halted.

A figure stood at the end of the bright corridor, sunlight glinting off his armour and the sword in his hands. As she stepped cautiously closer, he smiled at her, and her heart leapt with joy; she ran toward Astyanax as he opened his arms to receive her, wrapping her in them and embracing her tenderly. The scented oils in his hair were as familiar to her as if she had seen him yesterday, and his deep chuckle shot happiness through her in an instant. She withdrew from the embrace, smiling wildly at him. "I have thought of you often; I didn't say what I wished to when you left. I am sorry that I could not find my words," she whispered into his neck.

"You are forgiven, my queen."

"I'm not a queen."

"You are now," he said, and her brow furrowed slightly at his words.

"What are you doing here? I thought you would not return to Egypt for many years."

"I am here to help you end this dynasty, my love." He touched her face gently.

"I don't understand . . ." She pulled back, trying to make sense of his words, and saw that his breastplate and his sword were drenched in blood. Tiny specks of it had sprayed his face, and some had spattered his golden blond hair.

"You will be queen now." He gazed at her lovingly, but his stare felt like a stranger's, and she felt that something was very wrong.

"Whose blood is this?" she asked, trying not to let her voice shake.

"It is all of theirs. There is no one left., I have seen to it." He suddenly held up the severed head of Kleopatra, her vacant eyes staring far beyond Akela, whose knees began to shake

She stumbled backwards. "What have you done!" she said, choking on her words.

"What you wanted me to do!" Astyanax replied, his face darkening with anger. "So you could be queen!"

"I never wanted this! This is madness!"

"Love *is* madness, little girl!"

"Get out! Get out!"

Astyanax began to scream with rage, a sound that seemed to echo through the halls and reach deep within the palace. Below his screams, a low rumble grew louder by the second, and suddenly, behind him, a great wave of blood surged with great ferocity around the corner and flooded the hall, enveloping him and crashing down on her . . .

ᴪ

AKELA WAS RIPPED FROM HER DREAMS BY A MAN'S muffled shouting as he swept down the hall outside the bedchambers, his rage-filled tirade fading as he moved farther from the door. Kleopatra stirred next to her but did not wake. Akela lay frozen stiffly in the bed, her heartbeat quickening as she waited for the heavy door to be kicked open, at which time she would have to face what terror entered, but time passed, and no one burst through to accuse her of crime and demand justice, no enemies came like shadows with murderous daggers, and no palace guards came to retrieve them.

Wiping the sweat from her brow, she drifted back into the warm embrace of slumber.

✦

"ARE YOU SURE HE'S NOT HERE?" KLEOPATRA WHISPERED to Akela as they sat eating breakfast in the great banquet hall, assessing the young men who sat at the far tables with the noblemen, palace councilmen, and generals.

"I don't know. I didn't see enough of his face. He was taller than her, and now they are all sitting," Akela replied with slight frustration.

The hall was buzzing with the day's agenda for the council, and there was still much chatter and many cautious glances directed towards the Amazon women, who sat stiffly at the breakfast table, ripping pieces of bread with their teeth. Isis, Claudius. and Neos were engaged in a seemingly serious discussion with the queen's daughter, Xanthippe, who seemed nearer to their ages and more welcoming to interaction than her tribal sisters. *Much too serious for so early in the morning*, Akela thought. Then memories of her nightmare swiftly chased away her appetite.

"I wonder if she's with him now?" suggested Kleopatra.

"Daylight wouldn't be the cleverest, but then, Arsinoe is unnervingly clever at any time of the day or night," Akela replied, wishing for silence on the matter.

"Well, if a boy can soften her rotten heart, then I like him. I suppose that is telling of her behaviour lately." She smiled delightedly. "No more watching my back."

"Never assume your enemy will change," Akela recited in a tone much like her father's.

"Not everything is a battle strategy, my friend. We are women. We fall in love," Kleopatra gently chided.

"Everything is a battle strategy, including love. People are animals, and animals kill to survive. Love is yet another obstacle to survival." Akela felt sweat bead on her forehead, her recent dream seemingly influencing her unrest. She watched intently as Isis and Xanthippe spoke.

"You are maddening sometimes," Kleopatra snapped, and Akela pulled her attention away from the heated discussion across the breakfast table.

"Where is everyone else?" she asked.

"I don't know," Kleopatra replied, irritation in her voice. "Maybe we should ask if Berenice will teach us to weave silks today?"

"We'd have to find Berenice first," Akela pointed out.

They exited the hall, making for Berenice's quarters, but walking down the hallway towards them came Theos, the remaining parts of his face a picture of fear, as it had been the day his body was broken.

"What is it, brother? Are you hurt?" Kleopatra asked as she reached him.

"Berenice is with child." His voice was shaking. "Father has been informed and unleashed his rage. Last night, he ordered the man responsible found and executed; it seems he had fled the city already, but before dawn, the man was discovered, and General Ankhmakis carried out the execution."

"What?" Akela felt her chest tighten and her hands tremble.

"But there were discussions of her marriage to the Kretan prince Demosthenes . . ." said Kleopatra with worry in her throat.

Theos nodded solemnly. "Father is furious. She can no longer be used to secure an alliance if she's been defiled, and to birth a bastard child . . . I fear for her, sister. Truly." Tears welled in his eye.

"All will be well, Theos," Akela said as firmly as she could muster. "Safiya would never let your father hurt Berenice. She will most likely be punished for it, but he will not hurt her."

"Like he wouldn't hurt me? Like I was punished?" His words hung in the silence. He gathered himself, and this time, his tone was soaked in sorrow. "Father is with the warrior queen now, negotiating their slave trade, and he has proposed an unusually generous deal preceding a 'delicate' proposal—a solution to this problem. The queen has accepted his request to take Berenice to Myria with them. She is to leave today, and Father has ordered that no one is to see her before she departs. I have tried, but guards are posted at her door." His voice seemed to quiver as he spoke the painful truth aloud. Akela and Kleopatra stood with mouths agape. "I am sorry, sister, I know how dear she is to you. If it were you in her place, my heart would truly break." He turned away to hide his tears.

"I would never leave you, dearest brother," Kleopatra said, stepping forward to embrace him, her voice weak. "What are we to do?" she whispered as they wept.

◆

THE MORNING SEEMED TO SLIP AWAY SWIFTLY AS
Berenice sat on the terrace of her rooms and looked over Egypt for the last
time. Her heart ached, and her eyes stung from weeping through the night.
Two large saddlebags rested against the end of her bed, containing any possessions she wished to take with her. Servants had packed them with jewellery
and perfumes and dresses, but she had ripped the bags apart with her hands,
and the contents had spilled across her room. Two new bags were brought, and
she had chosen to take with her two books, a comb for her hair, her winter
cloak, and just a few tunic robes.

Her parrot screamed loudly, most likely feeling the tension in the air, she
thought. Her arms felt heavy, hanging at her sides, and her lips were dry from
sobbing. There was no will left in her now. She had accepted whatever fate
awaited her and would endure as much of it as the gods demanded before
the sweet release of her death. The realisation that her love was gone was
too painful to face, and even though she resisted, the memories of last night
insisted on playing out again and again before her eyes.

⚜

THE PHARAOH HAD FLUNG HIMSELF FROM HER QUARTERS
after Safiya had pleaded sense with him, and the rage in the man was a terror
to behold. He had left her chambers with Safiya making haste after him, and
Berenice had sunk to the floor and through her sobs had begged the gods to
whisk her lover swiftly from the city and onto the ship she and Safiya had paid
for his passage on.

Hours passed, and her hands trembled when there was a rapping on the
door; she called out to grant entry with a hollow voice, and when the door
opened and in stepped General Ankhmakis, his face grave and his gaze full of
pity, her heart ripped in two inside her chest.

The general stepped forward and knelt at her feet. "It was swift, Your
Highness, and my blade true. I would not let him suffer." His voice echoed
in her quiet apartment the way it would in a tomb, heavy with the weight of
his conscience.

Fighting back tears, Berenice weakly pulled herself to her feet and stood
before the general, fighting for control as she straightened her back. "Thank

you, General, you have done me a great kindness." Despite her efforts, her voice gave away her grief.

"I have arranged for his body to be kept at an apothecary in the lower city, and I have two men waiting outside who will escort you there if you wish to see him and make funeral arrangements," the general whispered gently into the stillness of the room.

"Very well. I will go now."

❧

SHE HAD LOOKED UPON THE FACE OF HER LOVER, THE father of her unborn child, for the last time, his bloody wounds covered for her sake. She had paid seven gold coins to the man who had agreed to embalm him properly and bury him with respect somewhere where flowers grew. She touched his cold face for the last time and kissed his cold lips, then returned to the palace before dawn to accept her fate.

Now, as she stepped purposefully across the promenade, her chin high and her gaze locked ahead of her, she passed the pharaoh and Safiya, whose babe cried in her arms, and then passed her siblings, feeling their gazes—but the only gaze that hurt was little Kleopatra's.

Berenice strode to the horse to which her bags had been affixed and mounted the beast elegantly, uncomfortable in the unfamiliar saddle. The pharaoh remained unwavering in his regal stance, and no words were exchanged.

Kleopatra pulled the latch on her necklace and ran toward Berenice's horse. She reached up to offer her the gold Egyptian coin on a thin chain, but Berenice ignored her. She nudged her horse to walk.

Her boot knocked Kleopatra to the ground.

❧

KLEOPATRA SAT IN THE DIRT, TEARS STREAMING DOWN her face. The grey muscular legs of a horse halted in front of her, and she looked up, squinting in the sun. Queen Thalestris reached down a large man-like hand, and Kleopatra placed the coin in it; the queen gave a small smile and rode on without a word.

The line of horses moved slowly in the sand toward the coast, where the terrain suited the animals better and they could travel faster, ten large male slaves in chains being led behind them with an array of expressions on their faces.

Once the royal party had returned to the palace, Akela appeared next to Kleopatra and placed a gentle hand on her shoulder. "This will not be the last time we see her, surely. When we travel, we will visit her, and she will show us her new life."

Kleopatra wiped her face with her dress. Within moments, the royal promenade audience had dispersed silently. Akela helped Kleopatra stand, and they returned slowly to their apartments.

❦

"BUT I DO NOT UNDERSTAND, FATHER. WE ARE PLANNING to attack those lands." There was temper in Neos's voice as he wrestled with his urge to pound the war-chamber table with his fist.

"Then we have merely lent these slaves, and upon our victories in Assyria, they will be returned to us. This is why you will never be pharaoh. You are too short-sighted. You simply lack intelligence, and it is hard to believe that you came from my seed," the pharaoh spat viciously.

Neos held onto the last of his patience and went on to argue further, only to be repeatedly made a fool of by the pharaoh.

The council had spent most of the day discussing the information they had gathered from the Amazons of the battles and territories of Assyria and its current state, deciding whether to go ahead with the planned invasion or pull back their soldiers from the eastern settlements, which would avoid a war they could not possibly win. The pharaoh's wishes bordered on the absurd, and the council argued at every turn.

Claudius rubbed his weary eyes and finally stood quietly and left the room.

The afternoon was warmer than the previous day's, and the air smelled of salt; there would be a storm on the ocean that night. The hall was quiet as he leaned first his back and then his head against the sandstone. His thoughts of war and strategies cleared, and instead, his mind wandered to the memory of the round-faced girl whom he had been arranged to wed. Those plans had been dashed when he'd learned from a messenger that the princess of Kypros had perished from disease out there across the stormy ocean.

He had only met her once, when his army had held a settlement in Tripolis on the eastern coastline. He remembered an un-noteworthy character, plain and homely. But she had been a sweet girl with an agreeable nature, young, and with good hips for birthing children. He had been disappointed to hear of her death, for he had grown accustomed to the idea of marrying and having sons. *A daughter would be nice too*, he thought. But now was no time for thoughts of dead princesses, not when his father planned for Claudius to take his army east and hold their settlements there in savage and unpredictable lands for no reason other than pride.

Claudius knew the unnecessary loss of life would be great and not an easy feat to come back from, as sons of Egypt had dwindled in the warring of recent years. Claudius sighed; he was tired of war, tired of responsibility, and wished for sleep.

He lifted his head and opened his eyes to find Isis standing before him, her arms crossed and eyes narrowed and hateful. "Sister," he acknowledged.

"Has he decided that we shall make war in the east?" Isis asked sternly.

"You know I cannot speak to you of such things. You are not part of the war council. Father will make any official announcements."

Claudius began to walk away, but Isis persisted. "You treat him as if he is a god and me as if I am mud under your sandal," she spat, but he did not turn back. "That is not how you treated me under you before, Claudius. You should've said you wished for a compliant whore!" she screeched with daggers in her voice.

He spun around and was in front of her in seconds, his eyes ablaze with rage. "I loved you, sister—all the gods knew of my love for you, my desire for you—but I do not anymore."

"Because you got bored."

"Because you spew bile! You love out of spite, and what love is that? You are not capable of it. Your heart is rotten, and your gentleness gone."

"I would have loved our child had we been blessed with one. I would have learned love. You would love me still." A rare vulnerability shrouded the accusation.

"Have you bled?" He asked bluntly.

She stared at him a moment, searching for any kindness in his eyes. She found none. "No."

"And you never will; the gods have declared you are not a woman. You are all hate, sister. If we had had a child, it would have hated the world enough for us both, but we did not because you cannot, and now it is done." Claudius turned on his heel and stormed away down the hall.

❧

"I'M GLAD THE KYPROS WHORE IS DEAD!" ISIS SCREAMED after Claudius, but he did not return. Fear erupted in her, and she sank to the ground, her emotion overcoming her. Panic nudged the depths of her heart. She knew the servants had been ordered to report when her first blood came, but it never did, and if she could not bear children, she was no use to her father's alliance plans. In fact, she was certain she was a threat to his ego. If she was infertile, it would reflect poorly on his seed quality, and barren princesses were either sent away to temples to study the gods or sacrificed at the first harvest festival of the season.

Isis felt the fear replaced with seething fury once more as thoughts of her father's disgust consumed her, and the pain of her brother's rejection twisted her love for him into spite.

❧

THE RAINS HAD COME SWIFTLY, AND THE WINTER HAD been long and unusually gloomy, with clouds and sandstorms catching many unprepared peasants by deadly surprise. The storms would bring great whirling winds of sand and throw them against the palace walls until they passed over the royal residence and left the open halls under layers of fine golden granules.

Theos had taken to Berenice's pet bird and had cared for it since she had departed. He, Kleopatra, and Akela often sat in her apartment in silence, still in the empty sadness of her absence. Isis was rarely seen around the palace, and Claudius and Neos seemed confined to the war chamber with their father, the general, and the war council as plans were becoming finalised for Egypte's armies to march east and south, as well as a regiment of soldiers to the west to reinforce Egypte's authority and presence. Auletes was dedicated to his studies and only paused to practice his weapons skills. He seemed just a child, but he had begged to go to war and fight with Claudius.

Arsinoe had been spotted on rare occasions, humming as she glided down the halls. Her hair now hung freely and was adorned with pretty gold pins; her scent now was of desert flower perfume. Akela had seen her with the boy three more times; they kept to the shadows and seemed to disappear silently, but she had seen him hold her hand, and in the shadows of the gardens one night, he had slipped his hand beneath her dress as he pinned her against a wall, and they had kissed. *What strange behaviour,* Akela had thought. *Who would want to keep company with such a wretch as Arsinoe?* It made no sense; the princess was evil.

She looked up at Kleopatra, lying glumly on Berenice's bed. "Perhaps we could watch Heba catch rabbits today? I am sure she would like our company."

Kleopatra gave no response, and all Akela could do was climb onto the bed beside her friend and embrace her until they drifted off to sleep.

❦

THE AFTERNOON WAS CLOUDY WHEN THEY WOKE, AND the air thick with humidity. No linens felt comfortable, and her hair sticking to her skin irritated Akela greatly. She sat with Kleopatra in the royal gardens. They had taken to short walks with Heba every day to escape the glum mood of the palace. Theos, having spoken to Neos, told them that plans for the coming wars were decided, and that in the strongholds in the east, disease had ravaged the lands through Marqesh all the way to the western coast on the mainland. Both sides had taken great losses, and ultimately the Egypteian settlements had been overcome and their territory lost. Surviving soldiers had retreated and fallen back to the land held in Sidon.

It was clear that, with the loss of numbers and no reinforcements to spare, their campaigns in the east were over, yet the pharaoh remained adamant the east would fall to him. Claudius had convinced his father the remaining Eastern settlements were secure, so they would let the Assyrians war amongst themselves and with Rome, doing much damage to each other, before Claudius would return to take back the east. Neos was to march south to conquer the heathen enemy there, Claudius would accompany him, and with both armies, victory would be swift, leaving Claudius to then march east to return those lands to the pharaoh. The general was to leave for the west again and secure the settlements there, and knowing that her father would leave again for many months, Akela was gripped by sadness once more.

Theos had also relayed that Claudius was becoming impatient with the persistent nagging of Isis concerning the coming wars and that their father had noticed the princess's misplaced interest in such matters, having her thrown out when she had made it past guards to where the council met. Akela had never liked the bony and small-faced Isis and knew full well that Neos was the only royal who seemed capable of tolerating her presence. She shivered at the thought of Neos himself, who made her unexplainably uneasy.

Small birds flitted around the royal gardens as Heba half-heartedly pawed at the air where they swooped, teasing her. Kleopatra and Akela lay on the grass staring at the sky, the clouds moving fast. The low rumble of the churning ocean set a peaceful tone.

"I wonder if there will ever be a time without war," Kleopatra said, more to herself than to Akela.

"Most likely not. Men seem to revel in it. Savages." Akela sighed.

"I don't know what order I would give if I were queen and Egypt were under attack," Kleopatra said glumly.

Akela laughed. "We wouldn't last a day if you were queen," she teased.

"You underestimate me," Kleopatra said with irritation.

Akela's laugh faded. She rose and to sit beside her friend. "Do you disagree?"

"You can be very cruel sometimes, Akela."

"Yes. I can. But I do not underestimate you, Kleopatra; I merely recognise your strengths. That is the wisest strategy in any play, and you, my friend, have no stomach for war. You are kind and merciful. You desire peace in a world hungry for death." Akela spoke gently, and Kleopatra's shoulders sagged. "There is a place for you in this world, but I do not think it is on a throne, and I thank the gods for that, for I would die before losing you to the many cunning forces who wish for power through your death."

"What will become of me?" Kleopatra asked with sorrow in her voice.

"You will marry some foreign prince and travel to strange lands, and you will have many sons, and they will protect you, and yours will be a lifetime of figs and happiness. Claudius will be pharaoh after your father. Isis and Arsinoe will be wed before you are, and so there will be few demands for your duty," Akela said reassuringly.

"Would you come with me if I asked for you as my handmaiden?" Kleopatra looked into her eyes.

"Of course. We will never be apart, my dear friend." Akela smiled and hoped her words stayed true.

"Do you wish to marry?" Kleopatra asked casually, and Akela's thoughts brought her the memory of Astyanax and his strong grip around her as he'd lifted her from the river into the safe hands of Kohlis, but she pushed his face from her mind.

"No. I will have no children and no husband; I will fight for Egypt with my father."

"I would like to be in love. Like Isis and Osiris," Kleopatra said wistfully into the breeze.

"I have no evidence that love is of any use to ambition. Perhaps it is enjoyable, but I do not see the point. You can still produce children when you are not in love."

The silence grew, but neither were uncomfortable. They watched Heba rub herself against a large, leafy plant and then collapse in the shade.

Soft footsteps approached. Theos came to stand before them and then crumpled to his knees. His face was ashen, and his ravaged skin seemed drained of colour. Akela frowned as she noticed Theos was not blinking.

"Are you not well, brother?" Asked Kleopatra, concern in her voice.

He stared fearfully at her, and when he spoke, his voice shook. "Please forgive me, sister. I look to you for solace." His words hung in the air as Akela's heart sank; something else dreadful had happened.

"I love you, brother. I will always welcome you with kindness. Now tell us what the matter is."

"Isis and several members of the guard have been murdered," Theos said. "Father claims to have discovered a plot against his life led by Holis, one of the general's captains, and they have been slain."

"Holis would never do that!" Akela said, shocked. "He is an honourable man and loyal to my father! This cannot be!"

"I wish it were not so. I am sad to tell you that it was your father who was ordered to slay the traitors."

Theos looked at Akela with pity in his eyes. Akela could not believe his words. Her father trusted and respected Holis and knew his wife and children well; to execute him would have been a blade to her father's heart.

"You say Isis is dead?" Kleopatra urged.

"Yes, sister. Poison. It seems she was indeed implicated in the plot against Father. He wanted the focus to be on Holis and his men, but she was poisoned in her room and is to be buried without respect in the southern palace garden."

"The garden? This can't be." Kleopatra's eyes widened. "She is a princess of Egypt; she is surely to be laid to rest in the royal tomb."

"Father is furious and has disowned her, declaring her a scourge upon the kingdom to be buried like a peasant in the dirt. Sister, I am full of fear for my own life. Father's rage is murderous, and the anxiety of waking each day twists my stomach and grips my throat. I cannot eat or sleep, and I fear he will kill me also."

Theos began to sob, and his body sagged into Kleopatra's arms. She and Akela held the terrified boy. Akela felt the wetness of his tears on her dress and noticed his whole body trembled in their embrace.

"Father will not hurt you, dear brother; I will not allow it," Kleopatra said. "You will keep to your studies, and he will be preoccupied with the coming wars. Hush now. All will be well." Her words were soothing, but her glance to Akela was less so. Isis had sown the seeds of suspicion in their father's mind, surely now to sprout further, leaving all their lives hanging in the balance.

⚜

CLAUDIUS DESCENDED A TORCHLIT STAIRCASE, HIS sandals barely gripping the slippery stone steps. Carefully, he made his way down to a long, chilled, and musty-smelling room, where several men in long beige robes with their hands and heads and faces wrapped in cloths milled about in the darkness.

Claudius tightened the fabric around his own face and approached the naked body of Isis, lying on a stone slab with several trenches carved into it. At a basin in the stone beside her head was a small hole, dripping blood to a bowl beneath it.

The robed men paused where they were, acknowledged the prince, and bowed deeply, glancing hurriedly at each other. Claudius came to stand next to the body and stood gazing at his sister's peaceful face. A strong emotion clenched in his chest, and suddenly his legs felt as though they would not withstand his weight. He closed his eyes and attempted to steady his breathing, thankful for the fabric over his mouth covering his silent grief.

He looked at her once more. *Merely sleeping*, he told himself. "Oh, my love, you never did learn to hold your tongue." He took her cold hand in his, trying to steady his throbbing heart. There were cuts on her body, for the robed men had already begun burial preparations, and the smell of the embalming amber hung sharply in the air.

He beckoned a man to him, and he scurried before the prince, bowing low. "Did she die quickly, leper? Tell me truthfully."

The man's eyes seemed hesitant, the skin around them peeling horribly beneath the tightly wrapped cloth. "No, Your Majesty. The poison. There was not a large dose, or the eyes would have bulged and the tongue swollen." The man spoke low, between ragged breaths. "But there was enough to end her and the babe."

Claudius' stomach lurched. "The babe?" Claudius truly felt as though the man had slapped his face, and anger flared in him.

"Yes, sire. The princess was with child, early still, but the seed would not have been carried to birth."

"Why not?"

"The womb is compromised, Your Highness. I suspect many a seed has been planted but forfeited also." The man's watery eyes watched the prince beadily, and Claudius found his breathing shallow as he stared at Isis's stomach. He thanked the man and swept from the room without another word.

GREECE

THE LADY'S HOPE IN LAKEROS

— XV —

The honey cakes were especially good today, sweeter and stickier than she remembered. Timeaus had eaten his as fast as Zeus' lightning, then at her request, had finished the rest of her cake also.

The day was warm and the breeze slight as they made their way past the many stalls that lined the main road leading to the port far below. Vendors peddled fine gold and silver jewellery, barrels of spices, roasted meats, and arrays of colourful garments and cloth. With their elated mood, the arrival to the lower city was timely, and the contrast in status was jarring; here, several peddlers lay in the shade of their stalls, and the houses had many visible cracks and poor design. The roofs were tiled with incompetent clay plates; their lighter colour and rough texture suggested there had been too much rock in the mixture. Many of the outhouses were poorly maintained, their sewage spewed out onto the street with a putrid odour, and donkey faeces lined the streets, simply swept aside to the edges.

The three wandered into the bustling marketplace, its perimeter lined with stalls under fabric tarps. Markos followed paces behind, scanning for danger, though his size did not allow for stealth.

Chrysanthe swept her gaze over the many stalls and dirty-faced children scampering around the marketplace like rats. There were stew and soup stalls, bakeries, garment stalls, butchers, blacksmiths selling farming tools, and prostitutes shading themselves, taking a break from the sun—and then she saw the seamstresses in the far corner, next to an alley. "I should like to look at the wares," she said and immediately made for the other side of the market.

She reached a dismal jewellery store where a short, grey-bearded man with no teeth sat. She smiled at him, and he returned the grin, gesturing a dirty, calloused old hand over the pitiful display of odd designs. As Lysander appeared at her side, she leaned in close, feigning interest in the man's trinkets. She had to be careful about her plan; she knew no royal family would welcome a foreigner into their fold without planting a spy within her immediate staff. By her judgement, Markos wasn't good for anything but imitating a walking brick, and the maids did not ask enough questions to be spies. That left Lysander, and she was determined to outwit him in this most important bid for freedom.

She thought of asking Lysander to go fetch her a new dress appropriate for palace wear, but he would insist they make such a purchase where garment quality was high. She would have to be smarter and fast.

As she glanced around for viable options, a large, well-dressed man with a curled red beard and many gold rings on his fat fingers stepped toward them. "Lysander, you dog! What are you doing here, old man?" His voice boomed around the market, but not a soul seemed to notice.

"Kolossis, you grow fatter by the day!" Lysander greeted the man, but the irritation in his voice was not lost on Chrysanthe. She took the opportunity and slipped away to the neighbouring stall, where several women of all ages sat slouched over pieces of fabric, working their needles and thread.

One woman looked up. Her eyes were tired, and her dark hair was almost all grey. Chrysanthe slipped her hand into her dress, swiftly unclipping the brooch, and retrieved the dining cloth to present subtly to the woman. "Do you know where I can find the tailor of these threads?" the princess whispered.

The old woman leaned to look at the cloth, then looked up at Chrysanthe with a smile and shook her head.

A fat younger woman with prominent black chin hairs snapped her head up at the quiet interaction and waddled over, followed by a very tall and extremely thin young woman. Both looked at the cloth. "That there's my work," said the fat woman. "I got them fancy dining cloths, them child clothes, bathing cloths, shit cloths." She gestured gracelessly to the many piles of terribly embroidered cloths before her, then ran her gaze over Chrysanthe, taking in the quality of her gown, her perfumed hair, and the bulging pouch at her waist. "Seven silver coins for one or two gold coins for three." She attempted to smile with the air of a savvy businesswoman, but Chrysanthe's gaze hardened at the audacity.

She quickly moved to the next stall, glancing back to make sure Lysander was still occupied. The elderly woman at this stall sat without grace upon a stool with a cup of wine and her needlework before her; her face was sour, wrinkled, and puckered, and her old skin hung from her face and arms as if it were a loose undergarment, an effect made more prominent by the shadows of her tattered awning.

"Please, do you know where I can find the tailor of this work? His name is Lakeros," Chrysanthe said.

The woman squinted long and hard at the fine gold embroidery; she made mumbling sounds, seemingly to herself, and then began to cough violently, a harsh phlegmy hacking.

Chrysanthe knew the cough had drawn attention and her desperation surged; she could hear Lysander initiating farewell to the red-bearded acquaintance, and she knew her window of hope was fast closing. She looked around as subtly but as quickly as she could for any other seamstress stalls in the marketplace but found none and stood planted to the ground, watching her minuscule chance for freedom melt away into the mud.

Then she felt quiet eyes on her. She looked up to see a young, tired-looking woman with long dark hair, a babe suckling at her breast, stepping toward her from behind the coughing crone. The young mother laid a hand on the old woman's shoulder compassionately and glanced at the dining cloth herself; she did not smile, but nor was she hostile. She simply leaned forward as if tending to her wares. "Eastern edge, by the wheat mills, large windows," she whispered as the babe stirred in her arm.

Suddenly, Lysander was at Chrysanthe's side, clearly irritated at being cornered into a conversation he cared nothing for. "The gall! What an absolute goat of a man! What have you found, and do you plan on purchasing further?" he said with irritation.

"Your lady has good taste, my lord," the young mother said to Lysander, her expression never changing but her demeanour gentle and caring.

Lysander hardly acknowledged the woman and turned to the princess. "My lady, it would be wise to make our way back to the palace. It is not safe here after dark."

"Do we not have Markos?"

"Yes, Your Highness, but I fear even the giant would be no match for a crowd."

"You believe a crowd might attack us, Lysander? That sounds as though you have little faith in your people."

"You have shown your face; now let us depart." He growled the order.

Chrysanthe reached into the pouch at her waist. "Yes, Lysander. I have made my purchase; we may go," she said aloud for show. He seemed relieved and looked around for Timeaus.

Chrysanthe placed two gold coins on the rickety stall table. "For your little one." She met the woman's brown eyes, and the secret was kept. Then Chrysanthe placed another gold coin next to the other two and glanced at the old woman half-slumped over the table, her mouth hanging open and her eyes shut, breathing with a strained wheeze. "For medicine."

Chrysanthe turned on her heel and stuffed the cloth into her coin pouch, reaching Lysander across the marketplace, chiding Timeaus for the boy's curiosity about a group of men gambling. Many stalls were closing for the evening as the four made their way toward the path leading to the upper city. Markos had appeared and was closer to her than usual.

As they passed a stall selling perfumes, with several garlands of flowers displayed before it, Chrysanthe stopped and stared, bending down to smell a large pink bloom.

"They are beautiful lady, as you are. Which do you favour?" Timeaus appeared at her side and gazed up at her with pure curiosity.

She pointed to an orange and yellow flower with long thin petals.

"Why don't you buy some? I am sure the aroma would be welcomed when you wake each morning?" He grinned as she looked down at him once more, reminded of the innocent childhood she would never know.

"They will only die, Timeaus, a constant reminder that I cannot, and I cannot bear my heart breaking again."

The boy was silent as her words lingered in the air, as were Lysander and Markos, for they knew it to be true and without resolution. The chilled breeze began to swirl as she glanced toward the docks, where the pale bodies of four slaves swayed, suspended from the rope around their necks. "I envy them."

All turned and stared, caught by the moment of unexpected introspection, and she felt Markos's ice-blue eye fixed on her. He seemed deep within his own thoughts—if a brute like that was capable of thought. She hoped one day she could provoke him to run his sword through her heart. *A faint possibility*, she thought, and turned to lead the way up the path to the palace.

⚘

THE PALACE HALLS WERE QUIET, AND THE NIGHTS WERE becoming colder; the candles' flames flickered in the draft that slipped through the cracks in the boards covering Chrysanthe's chamber windows. Theophila had tended to the princess's slow-healing wounds with foul-smelling pastes and oily, stinging tinctures. Of course, these remedies did nothing for the deeper wounds on her spirit.

She would be adequately recovered soon and deemed fit once again for attempting conception, though she knew conception of sons was far from the mind of Demosthenes when he came every night to violate her. She had pinned her last hopes on the foreign tailor she had met a lifetime ago, and she had sent Theophila away to find Timeaus and request that he bring her cheese and bread and a jug of wine.

The princess paced the dreary room, becoming more anxious by the second. Time passed painfully, and she felt as if it had completely stopped before there was a soft knock on the door. She opened it and smiled down at Timeaus, standing aside for him to enter.

"I'll take my supper at the table," she said loudly, glancing up to see the one eye of Markos glaring with vehemence at the boy's back. She closed the door on the giant and turned quickly to Timeaus as time was precious. He had set the platter and the jug upon the small table; she took his arm and pulled the boy across the room into her small garment alcove. She took both his shoulders in her hands and bent down to face him.

"Listen to me now, Timeaus," she whispered urgently. The boy remained still, staring at her. "I have a request of you that I cannot ask of another; this palace is not a safe place for me to speak freely. Your help tonight is vital to my life. Will you do me this favour as my friend?"

He nodded quickly.

"You must go to the lower city tonight. *No one* must see you; that is very important. You must not be followed. Keep your pace hasty and your presence undetected." She took the folded dining cloth from the shelf beside her and handed it to him. "Take this and conceal it in your tunic. You must find a man, a tailor who lives on the eastern edge of the port by the wheat mills. The home will have large windows and most likely be separate from other dwellings. Give this to the man there and speak of its urgency. Do not linger. Return immediately to your quarters and go to sleep. We must never speak of this again—and, of course, you have only to ask a favour of me in return. Do we have an agreement, my friend?"

"Yes, my lady, I will do as you say. I will not fail you," he answered with dutiful innocence.

"Thank you, Timeaus." She retrieved two gold coins she had concealed on the shelf and placed them in his small hands. "Take these; they will aid you, should any obstacles arise. If none do, then keep them for yourself."

"That is many honey cakes, my lady," he said with wide eyes, and she smiled before ushering him to the door.

Timeaus was gone, the night was quiet again, and the letter concealed within the cloth was on its way to Lakeros; now all she could do was kneel and pray to the messenger god Hermes to swiftly guide her last hope to an old friend in the hands of a mere child.

⚜

CHRYSANTHE WOKE AS SHE DID EACH MORNING TO THE occasional flapping of wings and gentle cooing of the doves that slept overnight in the alcove the wooden boards had made of her window. She noticed as she stretched out her body that no bruises ached and no flesh pulled against stitching, and dull panic roused in her belly.

She knew the heart of Lakeros. He was an honest and compassionate man, and he'd loved her mother dearly. *But time turns the heart of men, and he is, after all, a man*, she thought as she rose from her bed and crossed to wash her face in the full basin. The nature of his gender could not be denied, but the hope that clung to the thread of life within her breast spoke louder than her fear of betrayal by a man who had shown her such kindness so many years ago. Now her hope was all she had.

If there were to be a rescue, it would be under cover of darkness. If she could feign injury for only one more evening, she could keep Demosthenes from her chamber just long enough to receive the plan from Lakeros and prepare for her swift departure.

She hid the faith in her heart from Isidora and Theophila as they redressed the healing wounds and laid a pale-yellow tunic over her that fell to her ankles, braided thin gold wire into her crimson hair, and decorated her with extravagant gold jewellery. Once the joyless physician had entered to assess her condition and been successfully fooled by Chrysanthe's committed theatrics, she departed with Markos in tow for the kitchens, the hub of palace gossip, to inform the cooks that she would be taking her supper in her chambers that evening and would like an abundance of cheeses, breads, and fruit, as she was feeling particularly ravenous. She knew from the subtle looks exchanged between several servants bustling around the large, hot room that no questions would be raised at this request, as with sudden cravings, it would be assumed that she was pregnant, not planning to escape this godforsaken pit of Tartarus or die trying.

She thanked the cook and had turned to make her exit when Timeaus bounded up to her, a small leather coin purse a new addition to his attire. Quickly, she ushered Timeaus away from the kitchens and toward an alcove in the hallway where an old relic of a vase stood pitifully upon a stone pillar, and looked back toward Markos, who stood far enough away he could not overhear, though his eyes were trained on the boy like a lion on a stable rat.

"I have done what you asked of me, my lady," Timeaus said cautiously.

"And you were not followed?"

"No, Your Highness. I was very quiet and very fast. None could have been faster."

"That is very good, Timeaus. Did you see the cloth into the man's hands?"

"Yes, Princess. I asked if he wished me to wait, but he sent me away. I came straight back and went to my bed exactly as you asked." He studied her face, which she schooled to an expression of soft inquiry that she hoped did not betray the now rapid beating within her chest.

Lakeros had received her plea, and understanding the gravity of the request, would not have risked a reply that might be intercepted, for the stakes were already too high to allow the slightest complication. If the grand escape were indeed to happen, it would be swift, at the first chance presented, and any attempt to inform her of a plan would be time wasted.

It was decided; she would retire to her chambers that evening, gather essential possessions, and wait for the rescue. "Thank you, my friend. I am truly grateful for what you have done for me." She smiled and embraced the boy.

"I wonder, my lady, if you would accompany me to the bakery for breakfast." His smile was large, taking up most of his face and encroaching on his hopeful eyes.

"It would be my pleasure, and I would quite like the excuse to shirk my summons to sit at court today for as long as it is possible." She grinned at him, and they made their way toward the lower floors, through the royal gardens, and toward the large southwestern gate to the upper city, with Markos trailing as usual.

Chrysanthe laughed as the boy theatrically retold the tale of the pig that had escaped and terrorised his father when Timeaus was little. As the gate opened for them and they exited the palace, the story reached its peak, and Chrysanthe laughed loudly.

A strange and unpleasant scent whisked past her. She had braced herself for the usual bustle, noise, and chaos of the upper-city streets but found it absent. Instead, her laugh echoed through deserted alleys, somehow seeming inexplicably inappropriate. At that moment, the snake in her belly curled tightly into itself.

Turning toward the empty streets, the sun felt like ice on her skin, and the laughter sounding from her belly only moments before melted away into the breeze. It seemed as though time had ceased to pass as she stared up into the face of horror.

Suddenly, the tightness in her belly released in a nauseating convulsion, and she vomited on the ground. Raising her head once again, she felt her heart rip slowly and excruciatingly apart within her breast as she stared up into the face that she knew was Lakeros.

What barely resembled a body was nailed by its hands to a length of wood supported by roughly erected posts. The sagging corpse had been gutted, its entrails pulled out in a sickening display, organs exposed, a length of intestine wrapped around the neck in sick jest. Deep lacerations were scattered across the body where strips of flesh had been peeled back and left to hang, several toes had been severed, one foot barely remained attached to the body, and the arms had been set alight for flames to spread where they would. The man's face was contorted into a silent scream. The tongue had been cut from his mouth and discarded in the dirt next to his manhood and his ears. An unnervingly large pool of dark blood had soaked into the dirt below the hideous display, where pieces of charred flesh congealed in clumps under the hot sun.

She looked for eyes that had long melted from their charred sockets, the same eyes that she vividly recalled from that hot day in Sparta so many years ago. She stared into her friend's face, frozen in agony by the death he did not deserve—the death she had condemned him to—and her knees buckled. She sank to the ground and vomited again, her body purging her of every hope she had for freedom, replacing it with insurmountable, guilt-plagued grief.

Her breath began to catch in a strange, shallow rhythm as the gravity of the peril before her seeped into her consciousness. She noticed Timeaus watching her with a curious expression, and in her dazed state of delirium, she thought she saw excitement in his eyes. She swung towards him. "Were you followed, Timeaus?"

The boy's eyes had glazed over; now, he seemed in a state of shock. "No, my lady. I did exactly as you told me. Exactly."

Chrysanthe grabbed the boy's shoulders and shook him violently. "How did this happen?"

Timeaus recoiled at the anger, fear on his young face. Chrysanthe released her grip and hung her head, feeling his small hand rest cautiously on her shoulder. "There is a spy among us, Timeaus."

"Surely not, Princess. Who would wish to spy on you?"

"The queen? The king? Demosthenes? Lysander? Corinna? Name a soul in this dreadful place, and they are surely seeking to rob me of myself."

"Well, it is certainly not Lysander. He is too good a man and a fine adviser," Timeaus said firmly, but Chrysanthe knew that snakes disguised as twigs might go undetected and prove fatal. Lysander was indeed clever, ever the masked strategist motivated by elevation of status, and only those higher in position had the power to grant him his desire.

She looked up to realise that the shade cast across her was the enormous figure of Markos, who stood still as stone, his gaze fixed on the monstrous display. Suddenly, he turned to look at Timeaus, and Chrysanthe did not recognise the rage in the giant's one eerie eye. In only two strides, Markos had reached Timeaus, grasped him by his golden hair, and thrown him several feet. The boy tumbled into the dirt, landing heavily on his shoulder and letting out a cry, before scurrying backwards, staring up at his attacker.

Markos then took a length of wood resting against a pile of discarded building materials and raised it to strike the boy, who threw his feeble skinny arms over his head and cowered, bracing for the blow.

"Stop!" Chrysanthe had pulled herself to her feet and reached Markos' side in an instant. The giant turned to look at her but did not lower the wood; his vehement stare pierced her weak assertion of authority, and no further words were needed. She scowled at him, reached down to pull Timeaus to his feet, then pushed him toward the open palace gate. Needing no persuasion, the boy scampered away, and her despair returned in a sickening wave, overwhelming her reasoning, desperate to spill violently from her into the world.

"He is a child!" she screamed hoarsely, then threw her body at the brute, pounding with unrelenting fists at his body, blindly hammering as tears overcame her vision until she realised the wetness that covered her hands was her own blood, seeping from her strikes against his copper breastplate.

Large hands closed gently but firmly around her wrists, and she did not resist their restraint. Instead, she sank her weight into the giant's grip and let him lower her to the ground. The silence between them seemed deeper than that of the noiseless city streets, empty of people but full of the stench of death.

Just as Markos shifted his weight as if to speak, the faint metallic sound of several swift armoured feet grew closer. As the many royal soldiers arrived, they silently surveyed the scene. Then one spoke. "Princess Chrysanthe, your presence is requested immediately in the royal court; King Athanasios will wait for you no longer." The man was clearly taken by surprise at the violent execution he had been confronted with, but his tone was serious.

"Requested implies choice," Chrysanthe mumbled vacantly, staring at the dirt in which she sat.

"You have angered the king with your tardiness, and I am to relay that the daughter of the first peasant waiting to present his bereavement to the court has paid the restitution for you." The gravity in his low voice told her all she needed to know, and all resolution left her. Chilling numbness spread like a winter mist through her bones, and she felt her spirit leave her body, the last light in her extinguished. Athanasios had won, and so she was a princess of Krete.

She did not feel hands lift her from the ground, nor did she attempt to run. She did not bother to greet the royal members of the court as she was placed by callous-handed soldiers into her seat before the council. Markos approached Athanasios and leaned to speak into the king's ear. Demosthenes was seated next to his brother and cocked his head to listen. After a brief moment, the king's eyes, strangely with no anger in them, flickered toward Chrysanthe, who stared into oblivion, and as Markos drew back, Demosthenes chuckled harshly. Her entrance was merely a breath lost in the wind, and Athanasios resumed discussion with his brother.

"Does she seek to force our hand? The cunt of a hag is a delusional hysteric. I do not remember when she wasn't," Demosthenes said with casual annoyance.

"She seemingly has no desire for further wealth or lands. The victory against Sparta placated her whining, and she has asked for no other spoils," Athanasios replied.

"But the whore still feeds from the treasury at our expense like a leech. There are no dowries for barren corpses, so what use is she to us?" Demosthenes asked dismissively.

"Her ships, brother. Her people are thieves, pirates, and cutthroats—"

"Armies follow whoever pays them, which would be us in her absence, or they're executed," Demosthenes growled, scratching his groin. Then he grabbed a large helping of fruit from the platter set down by a servant between the brothers.

"We cannot integrate condemned men and murderers into the populations of our main cities. With your small mind, Demosthenes, tell me what you think would happen." Athanasios was clearly the more intelligent of the two and working to contain his irritation. Demosthenes growled loudly, sending little ripples of fear over Chrysanthe's skin; it was the voice that came for her body in the dark.

"So, we kill her," Demosthenes said with chilling casualness. He spat grape seeds at the ground, several catching in his beard, unnoticed. "She's a bitch, anyway. I know you hate her too."

"Every woman is a bitch to you," Athanasios replied, sounding almost bored with his brother's inability to fathom consequences in royal strategy.

"Aye." Demosthenes grinned and winked at Charis, whose cold, dead stare seemed to look through him.

"Kill her if you like but know that her army of bandits will then become your charge. There are fewer Kretan women to warm your bed in the western city," Athanasios warned as he briefly glanced toward the council before him, still whispering and discussing this day's agenda. The king's words gave the thick-minded prince pause, betraying his priorities. "Selene will be married to the King of Castos," the king added firmly to Demosthenes.

"That old pig's arse is still alive?" Demosthenes seemed both surprised and entertained.

"For now. He holds the trading routes to the southern Attica islands."

"And when he chokes to death on one of his seven chins?" Demosthenes reached to take a leg of meat from the platter between them and proceeded to eat loudly.

"Then she will marry the king's son. As is their tradition," replied Athanasios. He received several pages of papyrus from a court servant and began to read.

"Isn't the boy an infant still? He can't yet fill his prick to secure our two kingdoms with an heir."

"Selene is perhaps the cleverest of us all. She will do well," the king replied, distracted.

"I have no doubt she will. How is it that both our sisters are harlots?" Demosthenes chewed the hock of meat, generously spilling it down his front. "They live the lives of princesses without care or duty while we fight wars and secure the future of our family."

Violence flashed in the king's eyes before he spoke. "Selene will serve her duties in due time, brother. The studies of the Bahariyya Temple are no easy feat."

"Do they teach the virgin princesses at this *Blah-ria* how to ride a cock to please their husbands?" Demosthenes jeered. "I could perhaps journey to this temple and be of assistance in this scholarly matter?"

Charis suddenly exhaled loudly, which seemed to convey the impatience of all present.

"We may need Atlas for dealings in Zykanthos or further north in Thessaly," Athanasios continued as he sifted through the papyrus he held.

"I forgot that Aristokles had a daughter. A plump arse, if I remember. I'd invade Zykanthos for the chance to bend her over his throne. That Queen Eirene, though . . ." Demosthenes seemed perplexed for a moment. "Strange witch of a woman."

"Pace yourself, brother. King Castinos arrives this evening to discuss the further protection of Rome's oceans and deliver payment for this summer's patrol."

"That fat bastard. You'd think he was pregnant."

"As long as he can drink for two, then I have no qualms." Athanasios handed the papyrus back to the council servant, who dashed away obediently.

"Ah, I like this plan."

"Many agreeable terms have been set with the generous flow of wine," Athanasios said, his attention now drawn back to the council. Demosthenes grunted in agreement.

"Then I can expect that, when you are summoned in the morning, I will find you asleep where you fell?" Charis shot at her husband, who ignored her snipe.

"Aye, you can, my frigid queen," Demosthenes taunted. "I will be his bedfellow this evening, most likely long past dawn. Thirty jugs of wine should suffice to dull our minds to your existence."

Charis glared at Demosthenes as he grinned, meat caught between many teeth.

Which means Demosthenes will be occupied until the early hours also . . . Chrysanthe thought.

Her eyes wandered toward the far open doors. The body of a small, fair-haired girl lay in a pristine pool of blood, the sun glinting off the undisturbed surface, by the entrance of the megaron, at the feet of a soldier guarding his post, whose distant and hauntingly pale face Chrysanthe recognised as Thianis. The dark circles below his eyes had drained colour and much of the life from his skin, and the young man's lips were set slightly open as he took shallow breaths, his gaze avoiding the child's body at his feet.

Chrysanthe simply looked away. A voice deep inside whispered, *"It is only more blood. None can hurt her now."* Then envy steeped in guilt stirred in a distant cavern within her. She would have traded places with the poor child in a heartbeat.

224

Demosthenes declared his hunger, then stood and passed gas loudly. He paused to linger beside Chrysanthe, reaching to caress a length of her flaming russet hair.

"I have missed the warmth of your body, my love." The foulness in his tone should have sent shivers over her skin, but to her, they were now only words, only sounds amongst an ocean of mere existence. "I have been a husband simply lost without his wife, and I have dreamed of our carnal reunion." Receiving no response from her, he gave a low chuckle and lumbered away to make his exit.

"We begin!" The deep, powerful voice of Athanasios boomed across the megaton, startling her.

A small, spindly man appeared in the doorway, holding his farmer's hat in his hands, his eyes wide as he took in the sight of the dead child. Carefully and nervously, he approached the thrones and stated his tribulation.

The morning sun crept toward the west, morphing into its afternoon glow, as many men and women came to speak before their king of their ailments, hardships, and disputes to be settled. Prisoners awaiting their judgement were also brought forward. As the sun faded, it looked as though the little girl were merely sleeping upon a crimson pillow.

Then came a man, one of the few remaining of the shackled men who had been standing at the back of the room against the wall. One of the royal guards kicked him forward, and he stumbled toward the king, where he sank to his knees. His wrists were bound, his body lean, with layers of sinewy muscle under sun-darkened skin, and his eyes malignant crescents glaring out from under handsome dark curls. There was the hint of a smile in the corner of his mouth.

"What is your crime?" asked Athanasios.

"Rape and murder, my lord."

"Was the woman married?"

"No, my lord."

"Did she mean you harm?"

"The girl agreed to trade me one of her chickens. A fox attacked her coop in the night, and all the chickens perished. A fox's meal is not my concern. I am still without a chicken."

"Yes, she would have still owed you the bird. So, you took another payment?"

"That was the price I saw fit."

Athanasios stroked his long black beard as he thought, then turned his attention to Chrysanthe, who had not said a word since she had arrived in the megaron.

"What do you believe a fitting punishment to be for this man's crimes, Princess?" he asked, and she looked up at him, startled from her trance. In his dark brown eyes, she knew a plot of more sinister magnitude was brewing. She did not care what happened to this man. She had no care for anyone on this filthy island, but indulging the king seemed doable now that her spirit had died.

"One hundred lashes from fellow townswomen, bloodletting, and genital mutilation until death," she answered, with no heart to her words, and the audience fell silent.

Then came booming laughter from Athanasios that lasted until he had exhausted his breath. "Dear girl, this is not Sparta. We are not savages!" With a truly entertained expression, he turned back to the prisoner. "You were well within your rights. A stock trade is a trade. You may go." Still grinning with genuine amusement, he turned to Charis, only to be met with the coldness of her cold, blank stare. The palace guard moved forward to collect the man, who grinned terribly at Chrysanthe as he was hauled away.

She knew the request for counsel was not in earnest and that the criminal was most likely employed by the king as it seemed anyone here committing crimes was doing so with either the knowledge of the king or in his employ; this man would return to his life in the countryside and go on to rape and murder several ill-fated women, never facing punishment for his atrocities. There was no retribution, no salvation, for the people of Krete, no justice for such brutal crimes. These lands would forever be ruled by the wolves of mankind.

It was clear now why her mother had forged a council of both sexes and had carved her own image of power from the shadow of her husband. The young died, the innocent were savaged, and women were the property of men whose minds only festered with hate, blood, greed, death, power, and lust. There was no war to be won here, nor had she the strength for it, even had she cared for the fate of anyone, including herself.

Without a word or discharge from her king, Chrysanthe stood and made her exit, moving swiftly but with no panic in her breast, for what was there left to fear? Pain would come. She had begun to live within it now. Death was to be embraced, should the final blessing ever find her.

Mid-stride in the deserted palace hallway, there was a cracking pain in the back of her skull as she was shoved against the sandstone wall, and suddenly the face of Athanasios appeared, towering over her, his angry, heaving breath hot on her cheeks and his enormous body pressing hard against her, pinning her to the wall.

"Your disrespect speaks volumes of your intelligence," he hissed. "I give you food and shelter. I clothe you, protect you, adorn you with jewels and gold, and you show me no gratitude, no respect."

"You cage me like an animal, and you dress me in the clothing of dead mistresses and gold you've slaughtered entire cities for. It is curious how your so-called 'protection' is no better than your brother's depravity." She pushed herself against his grip, only to feel his huge body push back, the breath forced from her lungs by his enormous weight.

"You ungrateful whore!" Small flecks of saliva pattered her face.

"And who's making is that?"

His furious eyes searched hers for something; the man's true desires were masked, and she knew a masked man was a dangerous one.

"It is not a woman's place to question her king's decisions nor embarrass him before his subjects."

"Then perhaps a king should select better counsel than a woman he well knows will question him."

She watched rage flicker through him, but he only grinned unnervingly. "You are a resourceful little cunt, aren't you?" he breathed, his face inches from hers. "You will be broken until you know your place, and perhaps one day your chamber door will open, and the cock that slips into you will be your king's, as is his right."

His black eyes glistened, and her skin crawled with the threat, but still, no fear came. "I can feel your small prick now and finally understand the queen's eternal dissatisfaction. Perhaps even more so, Corinna's." Her blood pumped faster. Could she coax him to kill her?

Athanasios heaved her toward him in his grip, then rammed her back against the wall. She felt the injured lower left rib crack once more, sparking pain in several directions.

In a disturbing instant, his temper was replaced with control. "There will be no death for you here, Princess. Your husband will use you as he pleases. Your life is not his concern." The bottomless pools of darkness that glared at her faded into a sickly, relaxed smile as he released his grip, and her feet returned to the ground. He stood in the fading light of the hallway, his breath becoming even, running a large hand across his beard as he smiled, then turned to walk briskly away.

Chrysanthe wished for death and for escape, and her own rage stabbed her chest as if she had been speared by a lance. She stepped toward a vase mounted upon a decorative pillar. She picked it up, surprised by its weight, but still, she hurled the pottery with all the might her injured rib would allow.

The vase fell short and shattered across the marble floor far behind the departing king. His laugh echoed through the corridor, and she stood watching him, unsure what to do now, until he rounded the far corner and was gone.

MYRIA

MARCH OF GHOSTS

— XVI —

The sun had streaked the Mediterranean sky with purple and orange as it descended slowly beyond the mountains, casting shadows on the fringes of the valleys and chilling the early evening air, before the two children cleared the treeline surrounding the valley where the Myrian tribes of sister warriors made their home.

Upon bursting from the undergrowth into the burning fields in the wet valleys, Euryleia stopped, her face soaked with tears. Bremusa slowed from her run to an ungraceful stop as the brave heart in her chest clenched uncomfortably in its racing rhythm at the sight of the many elders in long grey robes, aided by younger sisters, stacking tied bundles of branches and kindling against the sides of enormous wooden pyres, the height of a full-grown stallion, with shallow pits below them.

A grey-robed elder helped a small girl climb up onto one pyre, then passed up a heavy clay pot for the girl to pour thick, dark oil carefully over as much wood of the structure as she could reach with her small arms. The enormity of the loss settled into Bremusa's comprehension as she gazed across the field. Thirteen pyres reached up from the earth like small wooden mountain. Each could hold the bodies of sixty warriors. On the eastern edge of the pyres, a strangely shaped structure was being assembled from long lengths of wood, a group of sisters piling large stones beside it.

On the far north side of the wetlands, beyond small clusters of trees, evening fires released their grey breath in clouds toward the sky above the dark mud walls of huts and homes on the outskirts of the enormous village. Households were scattered across the many valleys, but the queen and her council resided in the central village, where all were called when the gong was sounded.

Pressing on, passing hurriedly through the shallow marsh, the two young Amazons, now reduced to children in their hearts, rushed toward the village, where cheers, shouting, and war cries could be heard from the centrum. The village was already bustling with cooks hauling sacks of grains and vegetables over their shoulders, off to start cook fires as there would be many mouths to feed, and healer sisters dashed through the bustle, laden with all the medicines, bandages, and tinctures they could carry.

Bremusa pulled Euryleia toward a nearby hut, took the small dagger from her belt, cut the rabbits and pelts from their waists, and dropped them at the hut's door before they shot off toward the centrum. The crowd of Amazons was vast, and the two had to weave through the ranks to push toward the front.

Scanning the faces frantically, Bremusa spotted Echephy standing on the left flank of the assembly, her long, tanned legs giving her a better view, her arms crossed tightly, and her usually mischievously relaxed demeanour replaced by a deathly, stoic face, fixated on the centre of the attention. Echephy was only a few years older than them but looked and carried herself as if a seasoned warrior; Bremusa often found comfort in the company of such a friend.

As they approached, Echephy caught sight of Bremusa and Euryleia and beckoned them to her. When they reached her, she guided them to climb up upon the scaffolding of a low structure amongst the perimeter of dwellings, from which they were able to see across the centrum.

An unrecognisable human head, missing its eyes and several lengths of matted hair, its mouth agape, stood propped on a stake planted in the dirt to the far left of a large group of warriors. One wore the adornments of the queen, and she addressed the crowd with words Bremusa could barely make out.

"It is the queen's counsel, and my belief, that my blood sister's rule is no longer the path for our tribe. Her decisions in battle have been called to question, and her abilities to protect our sisters from unnecessary losses have declined."

The queen seemed familiar. Bremusa thought that when their army departed the village all those years ago when she was just six years of age, she had perhaps been too young to recall the face of their fierce queen, Korypis, but more chilling than the strange tension thickly seeping through the tribe, or even the uncertain rule of their nation, were the eerily still giants that each stood a head taller than the amazons of Myria: true soldiers of Artemis, skin darker than a moonless sky, expressions absent of fear or curiosity, monstrous limbs thick with muscular superiority. They stood as if rooted to the ground.

The creature that stood to one side of the Amazonian queen as she addressed the gathered tribe was draped in dark robes and lengths of strange, striped skins beneath fastened leather belts that supported the many facets of her oddly shaped foreign armour—an armour that fitted perfectly to her wide, muscular shoulders and long torso. Her lips were thick and prominent, pursed to match her unfriendly face.

Bremusa felt a ripple of unsettling dread in her belly, for behind the colossal god that seemed to be the foreigners' leader was gathered a crowd of the same kind. She found that the harder she looked, the more pairs of menacing eyes she located. They blended into the darkening forest as if they were the embodiment of the macabre spirits that roamed these woodlands, wailing in the night, looking for their sisters. These warriors had seen death. Some, perhaps, had been blessed by Ares himself, a great honour that also came with great, violent obscenity. Some seemed to have brought death with them.

Perhaps death walked and supped amongst them this night.

"What is she saying? I can't hear," Euryleia grumbled restlessly.

Echephy turned to her, her face paler than usual. "Go and start a cookfire in the far corner. I will find you."

Euryleia must have sensed something sinister in Echephy's words. She hesitated where she stood, looking up to Bremusa, perched on a higher wooden beam.

Bremusa was transfixed on the dirty little blonde girl at the queen's side, earth smudged upon her face, her bright blue eyes like sapphires even from this distance. The little girl's skin was deeply sun-touched. By her rigid and tense expression, she had never laid eyes on the Amazons, and Bremusa wondered what she would think if she saw her sisters for the first time.

Looking around, the blue-eyed child took in the village and its inhabitants. Fear churned in her face, but there was courage there, the defining trait of a true Amazon.

"Go!" Echephy hissed, and Bremusa looked down into her eyes, where she found no kindness, only desperation and harsh command. Bremusa took Euryleia's extended hand and jumped from the scaffolding to the earth. They pushed back through the crowd with haste.

By the far treeline of the village centre, Bremusa and Euryleia claimed a ring of stones set in the earth and began their cook fire, easing it into strength with tufts of dried undergrowth and small twigs, with large logs at the ready. Nursing the flames into life, they carefully watched the dispersing crowd as hopeful faces searched for the ones they longed to find. Some friends and family were reunited after too long. Some sisters held other sisters as they wept upon the ground.

A sudden move caught wide attention as a stocky, bald sister with cuts on her scalp and an eye bruised purple and black cleared the crowd at running speed and collided with a thin, slender woman, with long, dark hair down to her waist, and both crashed to the ground, rolling in the dirt in a passionate embrace. A short cheer went up at several cook fires, unnoticed by the pair, who had torn each other's clothing from their bodies and begun to make feverish love to one another.

Horses were being led through the centrum toward the outer stables to be washed and fed. Amazons lifted belongings and leather saddlebags from their backs and made off in various directions for a hut to claim before the fast-fading light eased into the dark evening.

"Bremusa," Euryleia whispered, and with her eyes, guided her friend to what she saw; a monstrous beast the height of two warriors, with long, thin, bony legs and an extended neck, moving slowly and awkwardly yet still majestically as it was led to a halt before a small tent. There, it lurched dangerously as it folded its seemingly incapable legs beneath it and knelt upon the ground. Two sisters helped a cloaked rider dismount from the beast's back, revealing a small leather saddle between two mountains upon the animal's back.

The hunched figure seemed to need the aid. The dark hands extending from the robes gripped tightly for support as the rider disappeared into the small mud hut. It seemed they had many foreign guests tonight, and the uneasy feeling remained thick amongst the assembly, though the visitor of most interest proved to be the humped creature, as village sisters flocked to it with inquisition and wonder.

A ZEALOUS MOAN ERUPTED AS THE THIN, DARK-HAIRED sister in the dirt reached the zenith of her joy and lay filthy in coital bliss upon the ground that had been made mud by their sweat. Euryleia took no notice, instead keeping her attention fixed on the returning warriors and the uneasy faces of those who had remained in the village. She recognised few of the returnees from her memories. Some smiled, some were sombre, and some were cautious. Many were severely injured. Older cook sisters and healer sisters scuttled about the village, distributing meat and bread as well as stopping to cleanse and dress wounds.

One old healer, her back hunched under the enormous weight of her satchel and her ample bosom, knelt by an injured sister, a gaping gash in the warrior's leg oozing thick sludge. The crone reached for a length of iron resting in the heart of a burning fire and quickly yet precisely pressed it firmly down upon the wound, forcing a guttural screech that sounded throughout the village but stopped no conversation nor drew a single weary gaze. The slight smell of burning flesh wafted on the breeze as it passed the far cook fires and dispersed.

Bremusa held a flat piece of wood out as an old cook sister distributed an agreeable portion of rabbit and pheasant before quickly limping on to the next cookfire. Placing the wood on the ground, Bremusa removed the dagger from her belt and began to hack small chunks from the meat, dropping them by handfuls into the large metal pot propped upon the blazing fire. Euryleia added assorted herbs from small bowls, and the steam from the stew began to smell appetising.

Footsteps approached, and they looked up to see the tall, dark-haired Echephy leading the dirty blonde child by the hand to sit on the ground before the large logs placed around the fire pit. At first, no one spoke. Euryleia caught the glance of the grubby young thing and gave a joyless half smile.

Echephy stared into the flames for several moments before she spoke. "These are my dear friends, Bremusa and Euryleia," She gestured to them. "My friends, this is Lykopis. She has travelled far to be with our tribe. I am told my blood sister Tarthos has returned with the army, and the new queen has tasked her to instruct Lykopis in the ways of war. She is now our charge."

"But she's a child . . ." said Euryleia.

Echephy looked up to meet her gaze. "In war, there is no such thing."

Euryleia saw the child's face cloud with worry, made even more pitiful by the streaks of tears that had cut through the dirt on her gaunt little face. "Some stew will warm you up. How many years are you, Lykopis?" She reached for a bowl, filled it with stew, and handed it to the girl.

"Eleven," she meekly replied as she accepted the bowl and attempted to sip the steaming contents hungrily.

"You are very small for the age of eleven, and you are much too thin. We must fatten you up."

"Mother says I am quick and small, and that is an advantage." Lykopis grinned, and Euryleia returned the smile as she handed bowls of stew to Bremusa and Echephy.

"Then all foes should fear the cleverness of such a woman."

◆

"WHAT HAPPENED BEFORE WE ARRIVED TODAY? I DO NOT recognise the sister in our queen's place. Tell me I am mistaken, Echephy." Bremusa spoke quietly. They kept their heads down, apparently focused on the stew in their bowls, but in reality, cautiously assessing the sea of tribe sisters and newcomers.

"War is coming," Echephy whispered. "You were lucky not to witness the execution of Queen Korypis. It is her blood sister Thermodosa who leads us now, and it was she who accused Korypis of weakness and misjudgement, costing them victories and the lives of many sisters. It was she who struck the head from the body and displayed it to claim her position. No one dared question the act, as we do not know what six years of warfare held for the Myrian army. We *do*, however, know that there was no trial." Echephy stared into her stew quietly.

"I remember her now, Korypis's sister," said Bremusa, lost in thought. "And so, the two flanking warriors are her daughters?"

The shock in her voice was matched by Euryleia's. "Dienomache and Anaxilea?"

"Indeed," Echephy answered. "They have welcomed the spirit of war and assumed their duties with the ease of a pond ripple. They are not the sisters you remember. They are true daughters of Ares."

"How did you get the wound on your cheek, Lykopis?" Euryleia asked then, and all seemed grateful for the change in conversation.

"I caught my foot while walking and caused a warrior to stumble. I was hit for my carelessness. Do not worry for me; my brother hits me much harder." She smiled.

"Well . . . we'll get some paste for the wound before we sleep."

A large figure approached them and dropped several full saddlebags by the logs before catching the flying embrace of Echephy with a small chuckle. The sisters held one another tightly in silence, and it was clear that Echephy was attempting to stifle her weeping from joy.

Once they finally released each other, Bremusa extended her forearm to the warrior. "Tarthos, my heart sings at your safe return."

"You have become a fine woman, Bremusa. It is good to see you," Tarthos said as they gripped one another's wrists in greeting.

"Welcome home, sister," said Euryleia, and they embraced briefly.

"Sweet Euryleia, your beauty has only grown over these years."

"Sit, sister, you must eat, and there is much we must ask." Echephy gestured to the ground by the fire. Tarthos removed her thick copper breastplate and bright-red scabbard and dropped them to the ground, then sank to sit. Bremusa felt Euryleia tense and knew that she, too, recognised that the sword in the red scabbard had seen the death of many, even on this day.

⚜

ECHEPHY HANDED TARTHOS A FULL BOWL OF STEW, AND she ate hastily. Echephy surveyed her dear sister, noting the deep creases on her brow that had not been there six years prior, the raised scars that covered her exposed skin, and the deep and defined muscles that complemented the sheer size she had grown. Most grievous was the haunting vacancy in the eyes that had transformed the sister she had known into this stranger.

Harrowing death seemed to grip her heart then, the pain of grief flooding her—grief at the loss of the life she had once known. Her beloved sister was gone, replaced by a soldier with no concern other than fighting until she could not. Her throat tightened as she looked at her friends around the small cookfire, and she shuddered at the thought of all that the imminent war could rob them of.

After finishing a second bowl, Tarthos wiped her mouth with the back of her hand and belched loudly before leaning back to rest against one of the surrounding logs.

"Tell us, sister, all that we do not know of your return," Echephy asked in a low voice, and all leaned a little closer.

Tarthos's shoulders sagged as she drew a solemn breath. "We made it down the coast unopposed, and whatever quarrel folk had with us was quickly settled by the skill of Korypis; we were strong, prepared, a sea of mighty Amazon come to wipe from the Earth those who sought to destroy us . . . but we were not prepared for the death contraptions of our cunning enemies.

"We arrived in the Bay of Miletus, where the Roman pigs had already breached the shores and established a foothold in the forest. As we rode down into the valley to meet them with our blades, enormous, mountainous rocks flew from the woodlands and rained down on us from the skies. It was as if they were hurled by Zeus himself." Tarthos closed her eyes a moment before she continued. "Our sisters barely had time to scream before the boulders blocked out Apollo's sun and brought their swift deaths. We retreated quickly but not quickly enough, and the loss was greatly felt. We were able to capture a Roman scout, from whom we learned the death contraption was named 'Ballista,' seemingly the child of Rome's 'Catapulta,' after their leader's lover, Calpurnia. There was no denying that the gods had smiled on Rome.

"We set up a camp in the valley beyond, where there was much terrain for our army and much cover for our scouts. The Romans came at us every day for months . . . years? . . . I do not recall. I dreamed of their faces, all those I killed, all those I lost, screaming as I woke, until slowly, the dreams became fewer. Eventually, I did not dream at all, and the screams of the dying were only a river of blood to wade through, cleaving and clawing.

"We raided surrounding villages for supplies that soon dried up. We were making enemies, and several Roman spies had infiltrated Stratonican and Cibyran settlements and learned our position and numbers. Eventually, we had no choice but to retreat towards Sagalassus, where we were not received as friends. The Assyrians drove us back, but we were funnelled through a pass into a smaller valley where the lands were marshy, and no food grew. With the Roman-aided Stratonican horde to our south, the bastard Assyrians snapping at our flanks, the Roman swarms in our noses, and the Laodicean mountains to our north, we were trapped. We could not

take the horses north to attempt the sharp rocky passes—they were too steep—
and without the horses, we could not carry our injured.

"The assaults came from all sides each day, and none could be described
as anything short of slaughter. Rock rained from above, gouging the earth as
it crushed us. Each day's light brought the sound of clashing metal and our
sisters screaming, and then came the darkness. The food was scarce, and the
Cibyrans had piled rocks across the river Marsyus. We were starving.

"Korypis gave the order to begin executing the injured. Instead of funeral
rites for our brave sisters, we were ordered to pile the bodies as walls. The
remaining army was to slip out of the valley in the darkness and attempt the
dangerous mountainside in hopes there was a pass through which to escape."
Tears were streaming down Tarthos's face as she paused. "We killed them. I
killed them, to save them from the Roman blade, and once the night was empty
of their screams and my hands soaked in their blood, like fierce lions of Ares,
the Afrikaan army launched its poised attack on the enemy, laying siege to all
three surrounding camps. Once we rallied to join forces with them, victory was
swift. We were saved and escaped before the enemy could regroup."

Echephy reached out to place a hand upon the shoulder of her sister, who
only slumped forward, letting the tears run like a stream from the tip of her nose.

"As we departed, I remember looking back to the valley below. It looked
as though an entire forest had been razed to the ground, logs piled upon each
other, not a space between them—a forest of bodies, rotting in the sun. I admit,
sisters, I do not know what will follow now."

The silence amongst them seemed louder than all the cheering, moaning,
celebrating, and conversation that carried across the vast sea of village cookfires.

"My heart bleeds for you, sister," said Euryleia.

"As does mine," Echephy echoed.

"Mine also, dear Tarthos," whispered little Lykopis, placing a gentle hand
on her arm.

Tarthos placed her own hand over it affectionately. "Do not bleed for me.
Bleed for our sisters who died without reason, without dignity . . . who did not
return to see Myria before Elysium."

"They are here as our sisters?" Bremusa asked, staring across the fires at the
mass of warriors who sat stoically, barely moving as they ate from bowls with
their fingers, the strange aromas of their food wafting on the breeze.

Lykopis responded. "Yes. They are sisters from Afrikaan, a vast land of many peoples, a land in turmoil far beyond Egypt. You see their queen? She is Thalestris, a warrior of great skill and strength. I was ferried from Cyprus to the shores of Maltus and given to her to be brought to Queen Korypis. We faced many foes along our journey, though none, I am sure, as terrible as those faced by Tarthos." She squeezed Tarthos's hand lovingly. "Thalestris was sent by the Afrikaan Queen Tederrenium to aid their Myrian sisters as they had received word of a Roman horde sweeping the Aegean to the west."

"The Roman scum is bold, more serious a problem than we were led to believe," said Echephy. "Korypis would never have us abandon Myria."

"Would Thermodosa?" Bremusa countered, and they shared a concerned glance.

Echephy then turned to Tarthos and nodded toward the Afrikaans. "How many are they?"

"Several thousand. The majority on horseback—fifteen cavalry regiments, I would guess. Their skills lie in sheer strength, the javelin, archery, and hand-to-hand combat, but they are also proficient with the sword."

"Who are their strongest?" asked Echephy.

"The terrifying warrior beside their queen is Xanthippe, daughter of Thalestris, and the closest five to her at any time are the queen's guard. They are the fiercest fighters I have ever seen," replied Tarthos with awe in her voice. "Thalestris is an honourable queen and a fierce ally, though she knows the risk they take by coming to aid us. We are flanked on all sides by strong enemies, and the Amazon queen in the north is waning in strength."

"What was that animal? The one carrying mountains upon its back?" Euryleia asked Lykopis, who grinned.

"That is called Kammel. It is the war horse of Egypt. The pharaoh, Ptolemy, gifted several to Queen Thalestris as she passed through their lands seeking to purchase slave men."

"We had more, but we ate some great meat from those bones, tough but tasty. Horrible beasts, though; they just spit and shit," sniped Tarthos.

"Then the cloaked rider was Gypto?" asked Echephy.

"Princess Berenice," Lykopis said. She smiled, but there was sadness in her eyes.

"Iphito is her name now," Tarthos snapped. "She was not happy about it, but she insisted that she be allowed to bless the beasts before the meat was carved. Strange girl. Hardly speaks, purges her belly a lot. Can't be good for the body."

"She is ill?" queried Euryleia.

Lykopis nodded solemnly. "She will not eat nor speak."

"And the bastards, they are the Gypto slaves of Thalestris?" said Bremusa, more statement than question, disgust seeping through her words.

"Yea, sister, that's them," growled Tarthos. All looked to the far-left outskirts of the enormous clearing, where several large Egypteian men, hands in chains and metal collars around their necks, sat in the dirt of the treeline. "Those, too, are exotic beasts from Egypt, also a gift from their pharaoh. We did not eat them, though. They're more useful alive."

"Prisoners for what purpose?" whispered Euryleia.

Some seemed content and rested against tree trunks, some watched carefully with calculating eyes, and some were jovial with each other, apparently pleased with their situation. One attempted to scratch an itch on his back but made such noise and irritation with his shackles as he pulled on them that the man next to him lunged, and a small scuffle broke out, cheered on by both prisoners and Amazons, until the giant queen stood abruptly, took only a few strides to them, and brought a thick club down on each, ceasing their brawl. The men were all similar in build; large, wide-shouldered, and muscular. None seemed weary from their journey, suggesting excellent stamina.

"Breeding, of course," said Tarthos. "Gyptos and Afrikaan cocks are said to be thrice the length and girth of any Greek man's. I am told some sisters even ride them for pleasure. I would like to try."

"Foul!" said Bremusa, loudly disgusted, and Tarthos chuckled.

"You will need to if you are to bear a strong daughter," poked Echephy.

"Bremusa desires no seed in her belly to slow her race to the battlefield," teased Euryleia as Lykopis and Echephy giggled.

"That is wise, Bremusa." All snickering ceased at Tarthos' tone as her words sliced through the air. "All who are able are to begin training immediately to prepare for the coming wars; your bodies must be ready. There is no sense in fighting hindered by the wreck of motherhood. Should we fall, our entire nation will be wiped from existence."

❧

THE MOOD BECAME SOLEMN ONCE MORE. EURYLEIA'S gaze came to rest upon the tall, thin, dark-haired girl and her returned lover wrapped around each other by the warmth of their cook fire, holding one another tightly as they stared quietly into the flames.

Euryleia knew the elation in their hearts at their reunion could not eclipse the sorrow of sisters absent. The rites of passage would be held soon that evening, and no soul present would escape the heavy weight of loss, though, at this moment, they had much to be grateful for.

❧

ALL STOOD GATHERED AROUND THE THIRTEEN WOODEN structures perched upon the marshlands below a sea of stars sprayed across the night, some still cautiously assessing each other but all humbled by the sight of their slain sisters, wrapped in clean white fabric, merely sleeping as they prepared to depart for the Elysian fields.

A group of elders in their long grey robes held freshly lit torches, standing before Queen Thermodosa, who held the rope lead of her giant auburn warhorse Colossus, taller than the titan Thalestris herself. Thermodosa's daughter Anaxilea stepped forward and presented her mother with a long, ruby-encrusted dagger. She took it and handed her daughter the rope before turning to the vast tribe before her and raising the dagger to Olympus.

"This night, we will send our sisters to the eternal fields of Elysium, where they will enjoy the spoils of their victories and be praised for their bravery and sacrifice. They will hear us sing their names, and they will know that, in the pain of parting, we thank them for their glorious death and are eager to unite with them upon our own arrival. May Ares and Artemis look down upon their daughters and see the courage of their sisters who fought like lions for their glory and their love."

The Amazons pounded fists to their chests in fierce approbation as their queen turned sharply, and in one motion, slid the dagger deeply across the stallion's throat. Blood began to pour into the large crucible below. The beast staggered and lurched as it attempted to escape, but the queen's guard of terrifying warriors stepped in to steady the horse as the stream of blood began to wane. Then his body was released to the ground.

Thermodosa knelt by the steed and laid a soothing hand on his nose as he snorted once more, then lay still. The war cries and cheering of the immense tribe quietened, and several members of the queen's guard stepped forward to drag the beast's body to the base of a pyre.

The ceremony commenced. A group of elders dipped smaller bowls into the crucible and dispersed toward each pyre, where they began a chilling chant against the wailing tune of an elder, who painted the queen's face with bloodied hands. The old, grey-cloaked Amazons each dipped a hand into their bowls, and as the tribe joined the mournful melody, flicked the blood across the bodies upon the pyres. Oil was poured upon the horse's body, and elders touched their bright torches to the bases of the pyres, which quickly blazed into glorious reverence, reaching their orange fingers to the sky above, roaring loudly against the howling chords of the death song of their people.

Bremusa felt the great heat upon her cheeks as she watched the bodies of her sleeping sisters consumed by hungry flames. Across the flaming field, she saw the rock-based structure catch fire and burn deep but low to the ground; night-touched sisters cast powder from small clay pots into the orange and red tongues, honouring their Afrikaan dead. She felt almost weightless in this striking moment, as though she were travelling with them to their destination, and in many moments, she thought she saw the souls of warriors dance amongst the blaze, released.

The magnitude of their sorrow had taken all words from the mouths of those present. The pain of such a colossal loss of life would surely never be fully healed in their hearts; the profound grief would be felt for generations. The flickering light of the tall flames licked the watching, sombre faces and danced across the ground in wondrous majesty as the eerie evening breeze carried the chorus of haunting hymns across the valley to echo off the rock faces.

◆

THE SHORT WALK BACK TO THEIR HUTS SEEMED A journey of many nights. Not a word was spoken. Euryleia led Lykopis by the hand to a large stone- and mud-walled hut, roofed with bunches of tightly fastened branches and with an animal skin hanging across its entryway, where Bremusa waited. She pulled back the skin for them to enter, and Lykopis was surprised to find the interior quite pleasing to the eye. Beds of skins and furs were placed around the edges of the space, with loose belongings near each one. A clay jug of drinking water sat by the large tree trunk that seemed to support the structure from its centre, where other small pottery was also stored. She knew these kinds of structures in Macedonia as *mitato* shelters, but these were clearly built to withstand the strong winds that swept through the mountains and into the valleys, and the chill of winter, and intended to provide a more permanent dwelling than poorly constructed *mitatos*.

Euryleia led her over to a low deer-hide bed piled with sheepskins. As Lykopis settled into the cocoon of immediate warmth, Euryleia reached for a small clay pot, and with her fingers, swiped up a portion of clear green sap-like paste and applied it gently to the wound on Lykopis' face.

"I asked Hera for a sister many times," murmured Lykopis, eyes closed, succumbing fast to exhaustion.

"And Hera answered you with thousands," Euryleia said, and Lykopis felt her pulling the sheepskins up over her and tucking them around her.

Her final thought was that, strangely, coming here felt like returning home, and all fear melted from her heart as she tumbled into slumber.

EGYPTE

THE ABSENCE OF ISIS

— XVII —

It was peculiar that life simply continued, not so much as if Isis were not dead but as if she had never existed. The halls were seldom busy with servants, and the gloom kept most confined to their rooms. When exchanges were had, the tone was now nervous and on edge, and when servants delivered meals to their chambers, Akela and Kleopatra observed their worried glances around the rooms and eagerness to retreat. There was not much to be said; they could only wait until the palace resumed its war-chamber meetings and the pharaoh emerged eager to continue preparations for the campaigns that loomed at the end of winter, which fast approached.

Ankhmakis had not spent much of the winter improving Akela's archery skills as he often did, dedicating many hours to honing her technique, endurance, and range, and the absence of her favourite activity with him was felt deeply in her spirit. When her father was away at war or at home but spending entire nights with his soldiers in military preparation, Akela awoke as she usually did next to Kleopatra. She dared not let her father know that she barely slept in their apartment within the palace, but the girls' friendship was deep, and there was much comfort in each other's company in times as uncertain as these.

Akela stirred and vaguely registered wetness beneath her; she sat upright and pulled the linen away to find that she sat in a small patch of dark blood. Confused because she had felt no pain of a wound, she then panicked that somehow she was dying, her mind leaping to the possible causes for her sudden demise. Then she recalled a faint memory of her old maid Rheusa, who had died many years ago but had informed Akela and several noblemen's daughters briefly of the transition into womanhood and the bodily changes it would bring.

Dread slithered down her spine. Her first blood had come, and she was now a woman, but the pharaoh would be informed of the proof in the princess's bed as her own, and Kleopatra would be deemed ready for marriage at almost thirteen. If the pharaoh were to find out that it was, in fact, Akela's blood, he would have her whipped for her disrespect for sleeping in the princess's bed. She steadied her breathing and shook Kleopatra awake.

"What is it?" Kleopatra sat up groggily.

"Forgive me, Princess, I do not know what to do." Akela stared into Kleopatra's eyes with fear.

Kleopatra looked down at the patch of blood. "You are a woman!" She gasped with glee, but as the situation dawned on her, Kleopatra's eyes widened. "Oh..."

"What do I do?" Akela felt close to tears, but to her surprise, Kleopatra's face focused. She sprang from the bed and ran to the large chest in the far corner of the room, throwing it open and fetching fresh sheets.

"We will change the linens and burn the soiled ones; help me strip the bed and then clean yourself up."

They hurriedly ripped the linens from the bed and removed the second layer, which the blood had also soaked through. Then, working on each side of the bed, they fixed the new linens in place and pulled the thicker blanket neatly into place. They stared at the bed a moment before Akela leaned forward and roughed the linens up to look slept in, then both girls gathered up the bloodied sheets.

The sun was coming up, and the chatter of Kleopatra's chambermaids echoed softly down the hallway as they approached her door; the two girls exchanged a terrified look, then suddenly, Akela dropped the linens she held, reached for a sandal that lay by the bed, and held it out before her.

The chambermaids' voices had reached the door. Kleopatra dropped her own share of the linens, snatched the sandal from Akela, braced herself, and slapped the sandal hard against the middle of her own face. Then, as the door handle turned, Kleopatra tossed the sandal back beside the bed and clambered into it. Akela yanked the linen up to Kleopatra's face, then turned to see two chambermaids enter, their faces sinking into shock.

The maids rushed forward and pushed Akela out of the way, pulling back the linen to inspect Kleopatra's face.

"My nose is bleeding again. I got so warm while I slept," Kleopatra said indistinctly to the scowling older maid.

The maid whipped around to face Akela. "What happened, girl?" she asked coldly.

"There were no rags, so I took linens from the chest. I am sorry, Maid Keris; I didn't know what else to do."

The old maid looked around the room, her upper lip and the tuft of black hairs above it twitching. She seemed to find nothing suspicious and turned to tilting Kleopatra's head backward and pinching the bridge of her nose.

"You'll be the death of me, child," she grumbled at the princess.

"Sorry, Maid Keris," Kleopatra said through her blocked nose.

⁂

THE MAIDS WERE GONE, AND BREAKFAST HAD BEEN brought to Kleopatra's room. Her nose had stopped bleeding, and she sat dabbing it with a wet rag. They picked at their assortment of cut fruits and bread with cheeses, but neither was hungry, both realising that no matter who had bled today, they were close in age, and soon they would both be women.

"Thank you," said Akela quietly.

Kleopatra gave a warm smile. "You would have done it for me, and besides, I would very much not like to be sent away to marry yet. A bloodied nose is far preferable." She gave a cheeky grin, looking ridiculous with the wet cloth still stuck up one nostril.

"But it will happen soon, won't it?"

"Yes, I suppose it will, but we will not be separated when it does," Kleopatra assured her.

"What if your father forbids me to stay with you? He does not like me very much."

"Father doesn't like anyone very much, but this he will not deny his favourite daughter." She grinned again.

"I pray that you are right, my friend." Akela smiled weakly.

"I will bleed soon but not today! Unless it is from my face." She chuckled at her own jest. "So, let us revel in our cleverness and find my cat. I wish to spend no more time with Keris; she is an old witch." She huffed. "If the babies hadn't been born, we'd still have lovely Rhema."

"Yes, those disrespectful babies." Akela grinned, and Kleopatra laughed.

Then a young servant girl entered the room again with fresh water jugs and began to pour them into the bathing basin she had been filling for Kleopatra to wash. The girl's eyes looked distant, and her shoulders tense. Akela noticed the girl's hands shaking as she struggled to keep the pour from the jugs steady.

"Let us hope that is all the blood we see for a long time," said Kleopatra, retiring the wet rag from her face. Taking in Akela's expression, she followed her gaze to the servant girl, who finished her pour then stood, still lost in her own thoughts.

"Good morning!" Akela yelled, and the startled girl jumped backward, her foot knocking over a clay jug, which smashed on the floor as she fell ungracefully onto her rear end.

She scurried to her feet quickly and bowed very low toward the princess. "I am sorry, Your Majesty, I did not mean to—I wasn't thinking. Please forgive me! I am sorry, please, my princess, mercy, please." Her voice was desperate and meek.

"There is nothing to forgive. It was my friend's fault for scaring you. You will not be punished." Kleopatra smiled warmly at the girl, who hurriedly bowed and turned for the door, only to find the old maid Keris waddling in with two more water jugs. Upon seeing the shattered jug, she put down the ones she held and raised an open hand to slap the girl, but Kleopatra's voice filled the room, louder than Akela had ever heard it before.

"Keris! I command you to stop your violence."

Akela stared wide-eyed at the princess, seeing the determination on her face. As the shocked Keris lowered her hand, Kleopatra said, "You will not strike this girl now or ever. Do you understand me?"

"Yes, Your Majesty." There was a touch of anger in the old woman's reply.

"I scared the girl; it was my fault. Let her be about her duties," Akela said to Keris.

Keris scowled at her. "If there is trouble, it is always around you, you stupid little girl. Look at the mess you—"

"Silence!" Kleopatra said firmly, and this time Akela looked at her in disbelief. "Remember to whom you speak, Maid Keris. Akela commands the same respect as all the noblewomen you serve, and you will address her as such. Am I understood?" She sat poised and tall as she waited for the stunned maid's answer.

"Yes, Princess Kleopatra, you are understood. I offer my deepest apologies. I forget my place." Keris bowed low, emptied the two jugs she had brought into the basin, gathered up pieces of the broken one, and then scurried out of the room without another word.

Akela turned to Kleopatra with a gaping mouth. "Who was that? Have you been possessed by past pharaohs? I am shocked, dear friend. Truly, I am bewildered!"

Kleopatra laughed groggily. "I believe I may have lost quite a bit of blood, Akela." She sank back into her chair, giggling loudly. "Everyone is so tense." She peeled open a fig and sucked on the fruit happily.

"Do you smell burning?" Akela asked curiously.

"No. Though I can't quite smell anything right now." Kleopatra took the wet rag from the table and dabbed her top lip again to check for any blood.

"Perhaps the kitchens are cooking a boar," Akela speculated.

"I hope so! Safiya loves roasted hog. We should visit the babies today. Claudius said they've been moved to the top eastern apartment in the hope of more sunlight in the rooms."

"Let us hurry and wash, then. What do I wear? I don't feel any different." Akela felt confused.

"I will wrap you with blood linens the way Berenice showed me; they do not show beneath your gown."

Freshly washed and dressed, Akela walked a little awkwardly at first but began to adjust to the thick weave of fabrics between her legs that wrapped securely around her hips. She turned back every five steps or so, nervous that she might have left a trail of blood behind her, but each time, it was not so. The undergarments seemed to feel larger than they appeared, and soon she became confident and excited by the little secret. The girls giggled as they scampered through the halls, Akela answering Kleopatra's questions about the new sensation.

They bounded into the hypostyle with the vast mosaic floor and made for the exit onto the promenade ahead. The entrance to the staircase leading to the eastern apartments was to the right. They had not seen the babies for many weeks as Safiya was keeping them warm through the chilled winter; although winters in Egypt were not deathly, the coolness still was not ideal for infants.

As they made their way across the decorated floor of the hypostyle, they passed a group of three servant women huddled together. One was carrying a lidded basket. The second had an arm around the third, whose face, Akela noticed, was wet with tears. A fourth servant came rushing after them, struggling under the weight of a bag of flour over her shoulder, panic in her step and her hurried breathing.

"Perhaps if the servants had less fear of a whipping, they would work with less anxiety; it is rather souring to the spirit when they're scuttling around scared all of the time," Kleopatra said as they approached the promenade, the eastern-staircase door in sight.

The burning smell hit Akela again. "We are nowhere near the kitchens," she mumbled, confused, as they stepped out into the dull sunshine.

"What did you say?" Kleopatra said, glancing at her, but Akela had stopped, frozen in horror, staring at the far side of the promenade. There in the sunlight hung two bodies, strung by their necks from a beam, their hands and feet bound, blackened and charred all over, smoke wafting from the corpses as they swayed gently in the breeze.

There was not a living soul on the promenade save the two girls, and the scene on such a beautiful day was terrifyingly eerie. Kleopatra doubled over and threw up her breakfast on the ground several times. Akela stood glued to the spot, unable to move; the blackened faces, frozen in mid-scream, stared toward them with eyes they no longer had. Small piles of black had accumulated on the ground beneath each one, and Akela's stomach churned as she realised their skin had melted from their bones and dripped from them. She reached down, grabbed Kleopatra by the arm, and dragged her forcefully toward the eastern staircase entrance.

They climbed the stairs without slowing, eager to find the safety of Safiya. Coming to the top of the stairs and the thick wooden door to the royal apartments, they stopped to catch their breath. As they calmed, they heard a low, deep voice speaking on the other side of the door. Both girls hitched up their dresses, knelt on the floor, and leaned their ears to the crack where light came through.

"Do you believe the boy was innocent?" Safiya was asking in a concerned tone.

"One would have to define the many facets of innocence and how much of young romance remains innocent," Claudius answered with a heavy sigh.

"You say she claimed the two robbed her of a jewel?"

"Yes. She accused them of fooling her and stealing the necklace, but the boy claims she slipped it into his tunic once he was arrested. I spoke to a servant who said Arsinoe and the boy shared a romance that ended, and he took up with the other girl. I suspect she was unfortunate collateral. It was Arsinoe who chose the form of execution, and I regret that the couple was not slain before the fires caught." Claudius sounded exhausted.

Kleopatra locked wide eyes with Akela; the wrath of Arsinoe had finally cost lives, and there was no doubt of her taste for blood.

"I worry about her impulsive rage and for the other children," said Safiya.

"As do I. I have no choice but to leave these worries with you, my queen, as I prepare to march my army south to aid Neos with his campaign. I am happy the babies are well; I wish you good health, Safiya, and may the gods be with you while war wages all around us."

Footsteps approached the door. Akela and Kleopatra scrambled to their feet as the door lurched open. The tired eyes of Claudius took in their tear-stained faces. He gave a sympathetic smile and bent to level with them.

"You two stay together. Do I make myself clear?" Both girls nodded. "War reveals much character of the ones around us, but remember, not all war is fought with weapons on a battlefield surrounded by an army." He looked at Akela, his worried eyes speaking to hers, and she understood the riddled warning: There would be battles fought here at the palace while the warriors were away fighting theirs, and that meant strategy if they were to see the next winter. Her brow hardened. She gave him a curt nod, and he disappeared down the stairs.

🔱

SAFIYA BECKONED THEM INTO THE ROOM, AND THE GIRLS spent the afternoon lying on either side of her as she fed and rocked her babies. Kleopatra could hear Akela's steady breathing as she slept against Safiya's side. The two babes likewise slept quietly in their bassinets, gurgling occasionally.

Kleopatra clung to Safiya's other side as the queen stroked her head softly in silence. Steadied by Safiya's rhythmic breathing beneath her head, she shed a hushed tear for the poor souls who had suffered today at the hands of her sadistic sister.

Kleopatra could remember being younger, with still unstable legs, trying to keep up with Arsinoe, who charged through the palace at incredible speed. She had watched Theos and Arsinoe race and recalled her heart's desire to one day race her sister, who fed her figs and took her hand when she could not find her way. That sister had melted away several years ago, and Kleopatra only knew that Father had said he could not find a suitable match for Arsinoe because no one wished to marry a goat-faced sow.

Kleopatra did not understand the insult at the time—she had thought Arsinoe very beautiful—but now, nearing womanhood herself, she understood that the terror inflicted upon Arsinoe by their father was more than skin deep. Kleopatra recalled the memory of her father's cruel and humiliating laughter as he detailed the ugliness of his least-favourite daughter in front of the small group of subjects gathered before him as he sat upon his throne.

Seeztui, the palace surgeon before being replaced by the scholars responsible for saving the life of Prince Theos, was an unnervingly skeletal man with a partial nose and eyes seemingly closer together than was usual. The terrifying man was rarely seen in the palace as he dwelt in the dark confines of the apothecary below the royal healing rooms, where he was permitted by the pharaoh to conduct his extended study of the body and its functions under the guise that his findings would see Egypt recognised as the pioneering originator of new medicines and techniques.

Kleopatra was sure the weaselly waif of a man truthfully enjoyed the mutilation of bodies and relished the opportunity to sift amongst the entrails of his experimental corpses. He was a man who raised the hairs on her arms, and she could not imagine spending extended time in close proximity of his deathly stink as Arsinoe had been forced to do. The reptile-like surgeon had listened intently to the pharaoh as he had explained the unattractiveness of little Arsinoe's face as the poor girl stood in front of her father, humiliated before the small audience. Kleopatra had stood apart from the scene, watching nervously from beside the pillars of the large throne room, waiting for her sister to be released from summons to resume their game in the gardens.

"The eyes are very large; there is no shape to them," the pharaoh said flatly as he inspected Arsinoe, her chin in his hand, "and the nose is long like a crocodile." He turned to an elderly, tired-looking adviser and asked, "Would you agree to marry your son to a crocodile, Pausiris?"

The old man took in the question, almost missing the mockery in the pharaoh's voice, before shaking his head sternly.

"See? None of my other children have the nose of a vile creature. Where is Kleopatra?"

Kleopatra felt her stomach tighten and heat prickle over her skin at the mention of her name in the cool but dangerous tone of her father.

"Where is the child?" The pharaoh was becoming angry, and Kleopatra stepped hesitantly into view. The pharaoh pointed to her, wearing a thin smile. "You see? The nose of a princess that will fetch a fine husband of great position and bring more prospect to the glory of Egypt."

The sickly reptile eyes of the physician locked on Kleopatra, and her instincts were to back away from him, but his steps were swift as he darted forward to snatch her at her arm, pulling her closer as he stared down his half-nose and inspected hers. His strong, bony fingers dug sharply into her skin. She was convinced his ragged fingernails would pierce the flesh of her arm. She struggled against the grip, trying to retreat from the putrid smell of rot on his breath. As he clasped her face in his claws, she found herself eye-level with his neck, and there saw transparent, crinkled skin with a greenish hue that made prominent the dark spots and peeling flesh. Wounds that appeared old but recently opened festered on the skin's surface, and as the man drew strained breath, his chest heaved, and there was a rattle somewhere deep inside him. Upon completing his observation of Kleopatra's face, he released his grip, leaving a throbbing bruise in its wake, then strode to Arsinoe and dragged her screaming from the room.

The audience had looked on, some in shock, some undisturbed, and some seemingly delighted. For the many years to follow, Arsinoe was sliced and sewn and dug at and scraped at as the terrifying man endeavoured to create a new face for her that would resemble Kleopatra's. Every few months, Arsinoe would be subjected to this torture, disappearing for lengths of time, then resurfacing with new wounds or modifications to her face and body. The enthusiasm of the physician when presenting his methods to the pharaoh was unsettling but did not seem to faze His Majesty, who simply looked bored as the man explained how he had used forceps of his own design and metal clamps to attempt to shape the princess's nose, how he had used the venom of a bee to try to plump her flat breasts, and how he had fed the girl animal lard from the kitchens in an attempt to fatten her up and disguise her angular shoulders and slim, boyish frame.

Arsinoe, desperate for the affection and favour of her father, became despondent as her spirit slowly succumbed to the pain inflicted upon her. Eventually, the light in her went out, and the creature who remained was one of suffering, violence, and malice.

And so, Kleopatra had lost a sister, and Egypt had been robbed of a fine young princess.

GREECE

WORTHLESS LAURELS

— XVIII —

Chrysanthe had retired to her room for the evening with no desire for food nor wine nor the will to live; her mind burned with images of charred flesh peeling from festering muscle in the hot sun, and her own screams echoed inside her.

As she sat on the edge of her pitiful excuse for a bed, she felt the presence of Markos, standing guard outside the heavy chamber door. She had begun to sense him now. His proximity at any time remained undeclared but never unnoticed. He was a silent shadow, never too close and never too far—a condition to her servitude in this hell. She was a true murderer now, her friend's innocent blood on her hands. Perhaps that was their bond.

Staring blankly at the boarded window with her foggy mind rummaging through half-formed thoughts and abandoned hope, she wondered if the one-eyed giant had a family, perhaps a wife or a daughter. Did they know of his brutality or of the heinous pigs who paid his wages to keep a princess alive and imprisoned so that she could be humiliated, tortured, and raped?

She found herself delighting in the vision of him tied to a burning cross, his skin bubbling with red blisters as his screams filled the air, but she flinched as the vision began to flicker, and instead of Markos engulfed in flames, she saw the contorted face of Lakeros. She gasped, and suddenly the vision was gone, the screaming cut off, and she sat, once again, alone in the lonely, dim room.

She pulled back the bedlinens, the weight of the day's heartbreak upon her shoulders, and collapsed into the bed. The hours passed as though time had slowed, allowing her mind to replay images of Lakeros and his fate more times than she could bear.

Suddenly, muffled shouting echoed through the hallways. She sat up and jumped from the bed to cross the room and press her ear to the wooden door. There was a loud crash as what sounded like a platter clattered to the floor. Something—a goblet, perhaps—bounced down the hall before coming to rest.

She heard footsteps running away from the door. Could Markos have left his post?

Her heart began to skip. Did she dare open the door? What if the threat within the palace was greater than the wrath of the king or the ruthlessness of Markos?

It remained silent outside her door, so she eased it open and leaned out to look down the hall, where she saw Markos disappearing around a far corner with a troop of Kretan soldiers. She stood frozen, presented with an opportunity yet without a plan to seize it. But the chance might never come again, and suddenly her resolve was unquestionable.

She darted to retrieve her darkest cloak from its hook and secured it tightly around her. *What is the plan now? What will you do, run to the edge of the island and wait for them to catch you? Or make off into the sparse forest where wild dogs and boars will rip you to pieces?*

What a horrible way to experience the last moments of life. She shuddered in the silent darkness and noted that she could hear no more running of soldiers. The attack must have been thwarted, and Markos would return quickly, thinking she would still be sleeping.

Then it came to her: Phrixos. She stepped toward the open door, then realised she had no gold with which to pay the murderer. Hope began to slide down her throat toward her stomach. How many times could she bear the feeling of her freedom being snatched from her?

Her body felt weak and spent, but at a faint whisper in the air, she looked around, poised to defend herself. She found no one there; perhaps it was just the wind whistling through the wooden boards of the window.

Then she heard the whisper in her head: *"Laurels. Worthless laurels."*

And then, she understood. She lunged toward the thin wooden box standing on a pillar by the far wall, where Theophila stored the princess's formal jewels. She knew she could not open the box without a key, so she picked it up and held it above her head. She paused, listening intently. She could still hear no one, so she brought the box crashing down upon the stone floor.

Now lying strewn across the stone amongst the splinters of wood were several bracelets and rings. She snatched up the ruby-encrusted diadem. "Worthless laurels," She whispered in the darkness. Snatching up several small pieces of jewellery, she shoved them inside a small bag that she stowed beneath her cloak. Then, carefully pulling the heavy door shut, she made off through the dark halls toward the palace gardens. Far away within the palace, she could hear the shouting of orders and the faint footsteps of the soldiers' heavy boots; she did not know how long it would be until Markos discovered her deceit and hunted her in the night, so an unpredictable route was crucial.

Arriving at the palace gardens, she could see torchlights in the far hall, and looking up, saw that the soldiers posted at the walls had weapons drawn, but their attention was focused on the torches. Feeling her way along the edge of the palace walls, which were smothered by creeping vines, her hand pressed through the dense and thorny stems against the rock wall until finally, several paces on, she pressed and found no wall. Quickly, she pulled the mass of thorned leaves and branches back enough to push herself through, then hurried down the dark passage she had walked once before, on the morning of her wedding, ushered by maids, her hand against the curved stone wall.

Hushed voices began nearby, and for a moment, her heart clenched painfully. A young boy was speaking to an older man. Could it be Lysander and Timeaus? The sound was muffled, and the voices unclear. She strained to hear them.

"I have failed, Master."

"Yes, you have."

"She was not in her chambers, but the bed was warm."

Were they talking about her? It made sense that there would be a plan in place to remove her from her rooms in the event of an attack. Most likely, Charis and her children were somewhere secret also.

"Go now, boy, melt into the night."

Suddenly, men's voices echoed down the narrow passage ahead of her, and she stopped. She squinted her eyes to focus on where she thought the end of the passage ought to be, and not too far to her left, saw the glow of a torch begin to grow; they were coming down the hidden passage.

She spun around and pawed at the wall the way she had come until she found the first exit, tightly tucked into the stone. She pushed with all her desperation and felt the secret door shift stiffly, but it did not open. With the voices of soldiers growing nearer and panic thumping inside her chest, she threw her weight at the wall in the darkness and burst through, stumbling to get her balance before stepping out of the slim shadow cast by the guarded wall above. Whipping around, she pushed the door back and slipped an end of her cloak between the door and its frame, easing it into place.

She could hear the faint and muffled steps of heavy boots passing by. She leaned her ear against the stone, listening for the war party to pass. Glancing back to the scene atop the wall, she saw that two soldiers had come to the ledge. As long as they hadn't seen her, she was safe.

The moaning sound of iron hinges screeched into the night; one palace gate was opening, most likely for men to investigate a sound below or for a routine patrol. Whatever the reason, if they came, she would not escape.

As she hurried to form a plan, a peasant from the upper city stumbled into the light of the torches, apparently after a night of heavy drinking. He was supported by his young son, the boy's frame sagging under the man's immense weight. They were occupied, but surely, they would pass too close.

She spun around, pressed her ear to the stone, and listened for footsteps, but heard nothing over the pounding of her heart. It was painfully clear that the only option was to return the way she had come. Hopefully, with the element of surprise, she could dash through the group of soldiers and outrun them down the passage.

The drunk man stumbled closer, and the time was now. She yanked at her cloak, and the stone budged toward her, enough for her to get her fingers into the small grooves and pull it open, fling herself inside, and pull it shut behind her.

She found herself wide-eyed in complete darkness, her heavy breathing the only sound. Looking to her left, she saw the tail end of light disappearing around the curve of the passage; they had passed, and she was alone, undetected. Forcing herself to move, she dashed onward, one hand against the wall, guiding her.

The second door was easier to find now that her sense of touch was heightened. The ridge of the battlements above cast a shadow that reached the outskirts of a thick forest. From there, she was able to slip quietly into the upper-city residences and navigate the dark alleys toward the eastern lower city, where she sought the red-roofed tavern at the very edge of the district.

By the time she caught sight of the dark-red tiles in the moonlight, her throat was burning, and her legs ached so deeply she wondered if she had ripped the muscles from her bones. *What if he is not here? You have come this far on hope, on a chance. Then what?*

She crept through the darkness toward the back of the tavern, keeping to the treeline, and came to a deserted clearing, where stray cats searched for scraps. She crouched and strained her eyes to scour the shadows for a sleeping man or possibly a door ajar.

Her eyes focused on a hunched figure, draped in long, dark clothes, sitting unmoving in the shadows against the tavern wall. All at once and without a sound, the cats scattered, darting out of sight, and she watched as another cloaked figure entered the clearing, approached the hunched figure, slowly eased it to stand, and then led it over to a wide seat, partly shaded from the moonlight. Then the two simply waited, still and silent.

Chrysanthe's tongue was dry in her mouth. She would have to accept that it was the stupid idea of a desperate little girl to attempt to find a man she knew nothing of. She carefully eased herself up and made to turn back.

"We meet for a third time, child of Sparta." A deep, calm voice sounded gently in the night air, and she froze, the strange tingling of destiny trickling down her spine. There was no walking away from this. The man she had come to find had found her. How? She did not know.

She steadied herself and made her way down the small slope, stepping out of the shadows and coming to stand before the two figures. Their faces were cast in shadow and hood, but the man's frame was thin and tall, and she could see he was cleanshaven.

"How did you know I came to find—" she began.

"*How* is an inapt question. *When* would be more precise, but I will forgive you this, child, as you will one day forgive me." The stranger spoke with ease and apparent unclouded confidence.

Chrysanthe suddenly felt very aware of the night air almost vibrating around her, the sense that the goddesses of fate, the Moirai, were present here on this night for this strange meeting, and the providence of their attendance clung as dew to the blades of grass and bark of the trees.

"The third time, you say?" she asked, her mouth dry with the uncertainty of the divine decree of this rendezvous.

"The luxury of time is not ours. Ask stronger questions. Where is your big friend?"

The reality of how truly alone she was now bit at her senses. "He is not my friend. I have none."

"A princess with no friends?" he asked slyly. *How did he know who she was?*

"I . . . I come to find Phrix—"

"What use have I for worthless laurels?" The second figure's voice sounded as if stone dragged against stone, and Chrysanthe stared into the face of an old crone who had adjusted her hood and leaned into the moonlight. The hag's eyes were pale and seemed clouded over like the moon behind clouds; there was no trace of kindness in the wrinkled face, where a toothless, joyless grin seemed to pull at the side of her mouth as she observed the shock on the princess's face at her words. Her thin fingers protruded from the cloak that shrouded her plump old body, and her white hair trailed in long strands down her front.

Chrysanthe wondered if she had been tricked or had wandered into a trap. How could two strangers possess such knowledge of her? She fumbled for a reply as she felt the man's heavy stare assessing her, and her silence seemed to irritate both strangers.

"What use have I for girl's trinkets? I cannot trade royal jewellery in the markets, and if I were to melt the gold to coins, do you not think that soldiers would torture every blacksmith on Kretos for the name of the thief? Why do you not simply throw yourself into the river? The speeding water would surely kill you, and some poor farmer would find you and take what he could from you to feed his family."

The man's accent was strange on the ear. He had a point.

"I had not thought of—" she began meekly.

"Our logic lacks when we are filled with the stubborn resolve of youth," the man said. He chuckled softly. "And how would you like it done? An arrow is precise, but a dagger is quick. Poison is a messy choice, though certain."

"How ever death comes, I will welcome it," said Chrysanthe. She sensed the man grin, and as he removed his hood to reveal a shaggy, unkempt mess of hair, she met his slanted black eyes, glistening with an animal-like wildness—eyes she had met before . . .

"Perhaps one hundred lashes, bloodletting, and genital mutilation?" he continued.

"You are the man from the king's court. The rapist and the murderer," she breathed.

"I have been a man of many courts, and I am very glad not to have been dealt the punishment you suggested," he replied, and she knew he was playing with her. "Do not believe all that you hear, Princess; even less of what you see with your own eyes."

"I cannot leave this rock unless one of us is dead. You can choose if you wish. I have no preference, be it my husband, the king, or myself," said Chrysanthe.

"It is neither of our destinies to take your life," the old woman mumbled from the shadows.

"Demosthenes is not my kill, and the death of our king will be the deserved revenge of another. Denying that retribution would be akin to denying you the chance to slay your father," the man said.

"I am of higher status than you, and I demand that you—" Chrysanthe blurted, with frustration brewing in her throat.

"It is not your time, storm rider," the decrepit old crone interjected, coughing heinously behind the assassin.

"You have been brought here not for death but for the saving of a life not your own," the man said quietly. "Mazterra sees all. Our hearts scream our fears, our love, our desires, and our sin."

"Remember this, girl," the woman's voice cut through the air. "Innocence will only survive through a single window of ice in a dark sky."

"You will not help me," she stated and feared she would cry from her anger.

"No," the man said, without emotion.

"Destiny approaches." The hag chuckled, her laughter setting off a wretched cough.

Chrysanthe's skin seemed to prickle in the night air, a familiar sensation she knew too well, and she became acutely aware that she was being watched. Hopelessness entwined with fierce anger rippled through her as she turned to see Markos step silently out of the shadows toward her. His stance was calm, and his one blue eye glistened in the pale grey light above; his long ropes of matted hair were tied back with a piece of leather, revealing blood sprayed across his tunic and breastplate.

"Forget the name," Phrixos called after her, and she turned to see him helping the old woman to hobble away. Then the two cloaked figures were consumed by the shadows of the nearby buildings.

She stood a moment, staring after them, refusing to let the hope die inside her once more. Markos merely waited for her to regain herself and turn to walk past him, her head held as gracefully as she could manage.

The journey back to the palace was tiring. Her wounds still ached. Every time she stopped to lean against the wall of a building or breathe through the pain, Markos would pause and wait silently until they continued. When they reached the palace gates, there seemed to be double the soldiers needed on the walls, Athanasios no doubt taking precautions against a second attack.

Markos pulled the hood of her cloak over her face and approached the gates; they opened, and he pulled her inside. Turning the corner toward her chambers, they were faced with a troop led by Athanasios stomping down the hall; they stopped abruptly as they met the princess and the giant.

"What is this?" Athanasios asked, his eyes darkening as they narrowed on Chrysanthe, and she felt ashamed of her fear. She had wished for death for so long, yet now, in this moment when it might come to her, she feared it.

Without hesitation, Markos spoke; the deep, formidable sound was foreign to her ears. His thick accent dripped through the air. "After the war-room slaughter, I returned to my charge. If intruders stalk the castle, she is safest in hiding."

He did not bow or address the king formally, and she could see it irritated the blood-soaked Athanasios, but the giant was of such value to him that it continued to be begrudgingly overlooked. Whenever Markos was reminded to bow, he would bow obediently, feigning surprise that he had forgotten to address the king as required by this land's customs. It was one of the few pleasures that graced Chrysanthe's days on Kretos.

Athanasios seemed satisfied and relieved that he could continue with his troop toward whatever urgency required him. Chrysanthe and Markos stepped aside to let the soldiers pass, and they were gone in mere moments.

As Markos pushed open her chamber door, she scowled at him, but she let him pull shut the great wooden door behind her and then slid into the bed to fall gratefully asleep within moments.

◆

AS IF NOT A MOMENT HAD PASSED, SHE WOKE TO A LARGE hand pressed across her mouth, pressing her lips into her teeth until she could taste blood. Her eyes sprang wide in the darkness, searching for sight, to no avail. The body on top of her was heavy and reeked of wine and garlic, and she began to kick her legs feverishly at the intruder.

"Tell me you have missed your husband's cock," Demosthenes breathed into her ear, his hot, breathy chuckle ripping through her like a dagger, fuelling the struggle of her body against his. As she squirmed in his grip, the chance for rebellion presented itself, and she bit down with all her strength. Blood leaked from his hand, drenching her face and flooding her throat. His furious yell filled the small room as she coughed for air and tried to blink the blood from her eyes, but a sickening crack sounded against her skull, sending a warm sensation down her body to her toes, trickling out to her fingertips.

She now lay still, her mind spinning and waves of nausea billowing in her stomach. The sounds of her husband's animalistic grunts began to fade along with the bodily sensations of him pounding against her flesh, and she felt herself slip beneath the surface of a warm swell, the heavenly water consuming her.

◆

WHEN SHE WOKE, SHE CAREFULLY PUSHED HERSELF TO sit and found her body was stiff but free of pain. She sat on a patch of lush grass, dressed in fresh, plain linen, and looking around, she realised she was surrounded by piles of treasures. Glittering crowns and goblets and enormous rubies perched on mountains of dulled gold coins stretched for miles around her into eventual darkness and up into the heavens that seemed too black to possibly be day.

"Are you wanting passage, child?" A soft, raspy voice asked, and she spun to face an elderly man standing half-submerged in the vast, dark, glistening lake before her. His limbs were unnaturally long and grey in tone, and he looked as though he could scarcely hold himself to stand. There seemed to be no meat or muscle to him. His skin stretched almost painfully over his skeleton, his back was hunched, and his clothes were frayed, but his smile was warm and kind as he gestured to the old wooden boat suspended upon the water beside him.

"I . . . I suppose I do. Forgive me, sir, how did I—"

"You washed up on my shores this morning, you did. You must've come from up-river, happens a lot; those currents are strong." He smiled, and her confusion seemed to melt away. "Come, Princess. You've travelled a long way, and there are those expecting you. Best not keep them waiting." He winked, and she noticed the strange shape of his eyes, friendly but almost catlike.

"But I don't have—" she began, realising she did not have her coin purse at her hip, but the old man's long bony finger extended out before him, and upon following his gesture, she looked down to find a simple golden ring around her wrist.

"It is yours if you will give me passage, sir."

"Then let us depart." He smiled warmly.

Chrysanthe stood and approached the riverbank, her dress trailing along the grass. She slipped the gold bangle from her wrist and placed it in the old man's outstretched hand. His long fingers closed around it, then dropped it to the water, where it disappeared below the dark surface. The man chuckled softly at the surprise on her face, then bowed theatrically and extended his hand again to help her into the small boat.

She lifted the hem of her dress with one hand and took his with her other; his papery skin was like ice in her grip, but strangely, it did not burn her, and with one elegant dip of her toe into the cool water, she stepped up into the vessel. It was a small boat made of weathered dark-red wood, with little room for more than two passengers and a bench for the captain. A high, curved rod sprouted from the bow. At its end hung a lantern flickering with gentle candle-light, casting a soft golden glow.

Chrysanthe sat down and looked up when she heard a wet thud land on the small deck. The man had one foot on the deck, but the unnatural length of his leg left her mouth agape; he appeared not to notice her as he pulled himself into the vessel, standing taller than three men. He shuffled in his place, shaking water off his long legs before stepping backward onto the rower's bench under the lantern, which barely cleared his stooped head. He settled himself upon the bench, with both knees folded tall on either side of him as if he were a toad. He grinned at her once more, then took a wooden oar from the hook on the bow and used it to push off gently from the riverbank. They drifted peacefully across the rippling dark waters. Occasionally Chrysanthe would glimpse a golden shimmer beneath the lapping water.

"It is very peaceful here. You are lucky for such serenity." She closed her eyes and listened to the silence.

"Aye, Princess. It is not lively in these waters. It is what I prefer," he said contentedly, with a hint of pride.

"Do you live here alone?"

"Aye."

"Do you not get lonely?"

"I have my gold to keep me company. Each piece has stories, secrets they whisper to me of the deeds of men, the travels of coins, the blood spilled for the possession of them."

"Forgive me once more, sir, if I speak out of turn. You have much gold here, enough to buy kingdoms if you wished, but your tunic is battered and ragged. Is there not a seamstress in the next village to sew you a replacement?"

He chuckled. "No, my lady. There are no villages nearby, so I make do." He kept his eyes on the far shore.

"I find myself with an abundance of linen I do not need, and I would be glad to cut you a length of mine for a new tunic." She ran her hands across the several layers of her dress, then looked up for his reply, only to find him regarding her curiously, the smile gone from his lips, his eyes wide with animal-like attention.

"You do not know me, child, yet you would gift your clothing to a poor ferryman?"

His strange eyes only amplified his puzzled state, and Chrysanthe averted her gaze, her mood becoming sombre. "Please do not judge me, boatman. I have not been kind to others; I have lost myself in hatred. I have no use for more than I need, and you, sir, are kind. The linen is yours if you want it." Her voice was heavy.

"Ye have already been judged, and not by me," he replied, his voice low and serious. "Keep your cloth."

They stared at one another for a moment before the sound of disturbed water splashed gently further out on the lake. The ferryman's eyes flicked in an instant to the source.

"Are there fish in the river?" Chrysanthe asked excitedly.

"Aye. Many fish." His voice was quiet and cold again.

The oar glided gracefully through the water as Chrysanthe leaned over the side of the boat to look for the fish. The ripples were mesmerising, and the rocking of the wooden vessel on the gentle, silken surface was hypnotic; as the swells of water rolled away, she caught glimpses of gold. The bottom of the lake was littered with coins, jewels, statues, and cups revealed for mere seconds. Her gaze drifted further to a shape, a shadow it seemed; she concentrated on making out the figure in the water until the ripples passed, and it turned to look at her.

Their eyes met. The creature's unnerving green eyes were like those of a feline, with vertical slits of black peering dangerously at her. Its skin was grey and sickly, and she noticed that it, too, was rowing a red-wooded boat with an oar and a passenger. She stared down at herself in the reflection for only a moment before leaning back into her seat and looking up with wide eyes at the old man, who stared back at her with meaning before returning to watch the riverbank drawing nearer.

"Perhaps it is best that we speak no more, lest we disturb the herring."

Silence fell over the dark waters. She did not feel fear, nor was she unsettled; she was sure of her safety. A strange sense of knowing had sunk into her bones, and when her mind began to wander, it was gently nudged back to the present, as if nothing else mattered but the here and now.

The boat gave a little shudder as the prow eased into the mud of the riverbank, and the ferryman pointed behind her with a long bony finger.

She turned to see the most beautiful woman standing on the shore. The woman's skin seemed to glow in the darkness around them. Her yellow hair fell in ripples down past her hips, and she wore an elaborate white dress that glittered with embossed gold.

The woman—the goddess, she somehow knew—smiled at Chrysanthe and waited patiently on the shore. Chrysanthe thanked the boatman and carefully disembarked. He pushed off from the bank without another word and drifted silently away into the darkness.

Chrysanthe approached the golden goddess, transfixed by the light that seemed to emanate from the beautiful creature. The woman smiled, held out her hand, and without a word, led Chrysanthe down a dirt path into a thick forest. The trail was winding, with many forks in the road. She wondered how the woman kept her bearings.

As they journeyed on, the forest around them became a maze of tall, thick red rocks higher than any palace she had seen. They wove through the dusty labyrinth, avoiding the sharp edges of the stone, then briefly passed through a dark cavern where a gale raged and snow flurried in terrible ferocity; the woman didn't release her hand. Gradually, their surroundings shifted into the thick, lush greenery of trees and undergrowth, and they approached a large shimmering shape that appeared to be a wall of water, rippling gently in the serenity of the forest.

The woman gestured to the strange watery shape, and Chrysanthe approached with overwhelming curiosity as if the water called to her in a language she did not know but understood. She stared at the glittering surface, and there behind the ripples was a scene of grass and sunlight she could almost feel on her skin. Below an enormous willow tree, its many fingers swaying in breaths of wind, sat a woman whose deep-red hair came alive in the sunlight, as did her own. Her heart leapt, and she stepped through the water and placed both feet onto the grass as the woman under the tree stood and turned toward her.

The face of her mother was more radiant and more exquisite than Chrysanthe could recall, and still, she did not believe the stunning vision until she had flown across the grass and flung herself into her mother's tight embrace.

What felt like hours had passed as they had spoken endlessly, their feet in the cool pond where fish chased one another and water lilies sprouted before their eyes. Chrysanthe now lay her head on her mother's lap in the shade and began to cry as Apollia sang softly and ran her long fingers gently through her daughter's hair under the limbs of the willow weeping in the breeze.

The princess's gaze rested on her mother's other hand, where a wooden ring was wrapped around a slender finger. On it was a strange shape she felt she knew but could not place: a jagged carving in dark wood. She reached out to touch it.

"It is not your time, little storm rider. Look for the single window of ice," whispered the queen of Sparta, and suddenly, Chrysanthe was wrenched backwards as if being pulled by an invisible rope.

Her feet could not touch the ground. The green pastures and trickling river sounds began to melt away, and she was pulled with resounding speed backward through the caverns, onto the bank of the dark river, where, as she passed, the boatman held a lifeless sailor in his arms on the glistening sand. He looked up, and she saw that his face was that of a demon, distorted and inhuman. His hands had become long claws, and his sharp needle-like teeth dripped with blood from the neck of the pale sailor. The creature merely watched without reaction as she was pulled away across the dark lake and thrust at full speed into the mountains of gold, which tumbled down to consume her and block out the light.

❧

IN A GROGGY HAZE AND DIZZYING NAUSEA, CHRYSANTHE became vaguely aware that she was lying on cold stone. She coughed, and the unmistakable taste of blood in her throat invaded every breath. As she struggled to open eyes that seemed swollen shut, she thought she caught a glimpse of one pained, ice-blue eye above her, then strong, large arms slipped behind her back and beneath her knees, lifting her with shocking ease. He paid no attention to her naked body. She did not understand the man, but perhaps savages like him were only complex to her because of the ultimate simplicity of brutes. The pain as her body was moved was unbearable, and all judgements of character bled away along with her consciousness.

❧

A NEW WARMTH GREETED HER CHEEK AS SHE STIRRED, and she recognised the joyous kiss to be sunshine. She felt the familiar, heavy flow of the Hellsmint herb in her blood, dulling the pain. She could hear whispers nearby as Isidora and Theophila bustled quietly around the room. She moaned as she attempted to move, but her limbs felt as though they were made of stone, and each breath was at great cost to her strength. She felt a rough-skinned hand take hers, and she slowly eased her swollen eyes apart to find Theophila had appeared at her side and was leaning close.

"You've come back to us, Princess," she said with a sweet smile; there were dark crescents below her soft eyes that spoke of her tiredness.

Chrysanthe stared up at Theophila with bruised and terrified eyes as she tried to speak. What fresh hell was this? Had he finally killed her? But only rasping sounds escaped her lips.

"Hush, child," came a familiar voice. "You have been badly injured, and now it is time to rest. Do not fuss. We won't leave you."

Chrysanthe glanced at Isidora, who had appeared beside Theophila, the permanent scowl on her face replaced by concern and genuine pity. She gave Chrysanthe a slight smile, the sympathy in her face foreign but warm.

Chrysanthe noticed the boards of her window had been taken down, and the fresh air rolling over her exposed body cooled her fever in such a blissful way that she wondered if perhaps this was life after death. A breath caught in her throat, and suddenly she jolted with a cough; pain spread through her bones like a wave of fire, and desperate to be free of the agony, she attempted to sit up once more before both Isidora and Theophila leaned forward to push her gently but firmly back to the bed.

"Save your strength and try to sleep. Our enemies hang from their necks at the castle walls. All is well in Kretos," said Theophila in a soothing tone.

"Many bones are broken, Princess; you must be still for them to set," Isidora commanded softly.

Chrysanthe thought she heard someone shifting nearby, but it was impossible to turn her head and see. Before another thought could pass, a burning smudge of herb wafted under her nose, and she slipped away to nothingness.

❧

WHEN MORNING CAME AGAIN, THE FIRST LIGHT WAS dull on Chrysanthe's cheek, and the stench of stale blood permeated the bed linens and thickened the air. She opened her eyes slowly, her sight adjusting to the cloudy daylight; winter was descending upon them quickly, and soon storms would crack with the ferocity of Zeus, flashing his rage across the skies. Buchorus's morose face stared back at her, the last remaining tufts of hair on his almost bare head were now strikingly white, and there seemed to be even deeper creases in his old face. His eyes, usually formidable and sour, now watched her with a hollow bleakness that he didn't attempt to hide.

"Buch—"

"Do not speak. Listen to me, for I will not repeat myself no matter how injured you are. Lakeros was a dear friend to me, and I am certain it was me he would have intended to reach in orchestrating your escape. I have seen many atrocities in my long life, and the suffering across generations never truly ends. The wounds on the mind are far greater than those of the body. You have slept for three nights. You are young, but your strength is fading, and you will not survive another beating. You cannot eat, the jaw is too injured, and soon you will not have the strength to heal. The body wishes to die, but the spirit does not." He drew a heavy breath, then sighed. "If it is death you seek, I will help you. Oftentimes, it is the appropriate treatment. Hemsbane." He raised a small green vial in his hand. "Or I can prop you at the window, but do not fall until I am gone, as I will not be punished for your selfishness. Which is your choice?"

He looked at her, his expression unchanged. She felt her pulse quicken beneath her skin but kept her breath steady, and holding his gaze, she said, "Hems . . . bane." He nodded curtly and pulled the small cork from the green vial, stepping closer to lean over her and prop up her head.

"The taste is horrid, but you must swallow quickly, or the death will be painful." He positioned the vial above her lower lip, and visions of her mother standing in a field of green, smiling with open arms, swam before her as she parted her lips to welcome death.

The scent of the Hemsbane was strong and violent in her nostrils. Faint bells sounded, and her mother withdrew her extended hands, then turned her back on Chrysanthe and began to walk away as the deep, booming bells grew louder. Buchorus began to pull away, listening intently to the metallic echoes with his mouth agape. He corked the vial just as the heavy door swung open and in stumbled Theophila.

"Prince . . . Demosthenes . . . is dead." She struggled to relay the message through ragged breaths and leaned back to rest herself against the sandstone wall as Buchorus flew from the room in an instant.

Having been so close to her freedom, her sweet release from this hell, Chrysanthe watched Buchorus sweep from the room, her hopes of peace leaving with him, and her head lolled to the side, where beside her, on a small table, was a single yellow flower placed in a chipped piece of pottery: the same flower she had seen only days before in the marketplace, the softest yellow, the colour of the harvest corn in the Spartan crops. Timeaus was a sweet boy, and she would not forget to thank him if he visited, for what other friends did she have in this wretched place?

Theophila's words slowly trickled through every part of Chrysanthe's mind, like water bypassing every rock and dam built to protect her from her reality, and slowly seeped into her bones and her heart. Suddenly, her spirit reared in her, and the true revelation of the prince's death was realised. Her heart soared, tears streamed from her eyes, and she began to laugh. Theophila appeared at her side with an expression of confusion but then took the princess's hand as her laughing settled, and she looked up at the old woman with eyes of joy.

The flustered maid smiled grimly. "No one must see your glee, Highness, please. For all our sakes, contain your elation. You must sleep and rest. Isidora will bring you breakfast soon. You must eat as much as you can, for the prince must not win this battle you still have left to fight."

Not long after Theophila had departed the princess's chambers, the heavy boots of soldiers could be heard running through the halls, and shouts echoed every now and then as the kingdom of Kretos responded to the death of their prince. Before long, Isidora entered, carrying a wooden tray on which was a cup of water and a small, steaming bowl. She closed the door behind her and approached to place the tray on the table beside the bed, then helped prop up Chrysanthe.

The bread soaked in broth was warm and tasty, only hurting a little as she swallowed, and she managed to eat a good portion before the pain in her throat became too much. Isidora piled bloodied and soiled linens and rags into a woven basket, then came to remove the tray from her lap and help her ease back down into the bed.

Isidora sat gently at the end of the bed, watching Chrysanthe carefully; her usual scowl was nowhere to be found, and there seemed to be a question on her lips. But pain ebbed throughout Chrysanthe's body, and closing her eyes, she relaxed into the pillows to ease the discomfort, her breathing heavy and strenuous.

🌿

ISIDORA SAT IN THE DULL LIGHT OF THE COMING DAY and gazed at the distorted purple shapes covering so much of the princess's exposed skin, the thin layer of sweat on her brow, and the strained heaving of her chest as she fought to breathe.

Isidora thought nothing of royal women. Their purpose was clear and simple: produce healthy heirs and many of them, no matter the cost to their own health. Any injuries sustained during the pleasing of their husbands in the act of conceiving said heirs were necessary for the kingdom, but what she had seen these last three days and nights had displaced something inside her. Her beliefs seemed no longer acceptable. The savagery was disturbing, and as she sat with her spirit struggling to reconcile her reasoning with the unspeakable damage she had witnessed, she saw her sister's face upon the princess and quickly wiped the tears from her cheek.

The scene played again in Isidora's mind: She had entered the princess's chamber on the second night after Demosthenes' attack, and what she had seen had made her drop the basket of fruit she carried. It had tumbled to the floor, and a battered apple rolled to gently nudge the naked body of the princess lying on the floor, her whole left side bruised purple-black and blue-and-green.

Isidora had approached her quickly and knelt down. She had stared at the severity of the wounds, the unnatural shape of the princess's wrist and two of her fingers, the deep and angry bite mark that had pierced the skin of her flank. The ribs were visible from starvation, with much swelling and bruising across them. Then the maid had seen lengths of golden-red hair scattered in clusters around the bed and on it.

All animosity and hatred had drained from her as she pictured her sweet, fair sister Gytheya in the princess's place, and she'd begun to gently tend to Chrysanthe. Her wrist and fingers had been broken from the attempt to flee the bed in a suspected fever dream and would need to be reset a second time by the physicians.

Chrysanthe had stirred in Isidora's arms and looked up at her with panic, gripping the maid's arm tightly. "She hunts in the moonlight, and her steps make no sound! He comes for us all! The boatman, he waits!" Chrysanthe had shivered and begun to struggle, but Isidora had held to her tightly.

"Yes, Highness, but now is time for resting." She had soothed and rocked until the damaged body relaxed in her arms.

Isidora was pulled from her memory as Chrysanthe opened her eyes.

"Is he really dead?" she asked weakly.

"Yes, my lady, he is."

"I thought it was a dream."

"Perhaps it is a dream, in a way," Isidora said, the compassion in her voice betraying her hardened heart.

"He is dead, and I live. I live." And with that, Chrysanthe's eyes closed once more.

MYRIA

A DANCE OF CARNAGE

— XIX —

The day had begun early, and already the air was thick and humid with the changing of the seasons. Bremusa felt the warm sun on her back as she shovelled mud into pails with her sisters in the marshlands south of the burning fields, where the land was wet and uninhabitable.

The village was a flurry of activity. Orders had been given to make various adjustments to accommodate the new sisters and begin preparations for the combat training that would last through the winter. They had been tasked with fetching the clay to repair the huts for the foreign tribe sisters to make their homes in and settle into their lives in Myria.

The weariness in Bremusa's body struggled with the effort of the task, and she straightened to stretch her back, yawning widely, her gaze coming to rest on the still billowing clouds of smoke that rose from the collapsed mounds where the funeral pyres had stood tall. It was sobering to see the remains of the pyres in daylight.

Bremusa scolded herself as she knew her fatigue was her own fault; the burial rites had gripped her deeply in a way she could not explain but had ultimately kept her from sleep. She had slipped from her hut that morning, hours before the sun rose, to make her way back to the burning fields.

Bremusa had sat upon a damp fallen tree. The ground had been thick with dew, and there had been a blissful peace across the valley. She had let her mind wander. These fields were sacred, and it was common when one stared into the ripples of heat from the fires to catch glimpses of their sisters dancing with Dionysus.

Bremusa had felt the bite of jealousy that her sisters now knew the answers to all questions posed in life, the completion of duty, the love of the gods, and the confirmation of their purpose. It was rare that she doubted her purpose as her love for Euryleia, which if measured, would surely surpass even that of any god and their legendary affections, but if they were separated in battle or by distance and Bremusa could not protect Euryleia, or was killed while away from her, would Bremusa join her sisters in the Elysian Fields? Or would she have failed her charge and be cast to the Asphodel Meadows, where souls resided if they did not achieve greatness in life, serve their purpose, or accomplish any other recognition that would set them apart and earn themselves a place in Elysium?

The air nipped at her skin, and a shiver touched her as she imagined such a place as described in a poem by Odysseus, a great pirate king of legend:

"There are meadows that I can't describe,
the landscape as level as seen in dreams,
or visions where nothing is thought of but the moment.
It is not clear, and memory exhausts itself,
omitting something. Silence is a part of it,
and distance reaching in a small space.

Since there are few instances in the world of such a thing,
it fills our sleep with a pattern for Elysium.
Our friend Achilles walked in these same fields.
There in the whiteness of flowers where we could not go, he thought of us,
pained by death beyond our speaking."

It was a haunting ballad in the stillness of the waking valley. Even the great Achilles, who surely believed in his purpose, was sent to reside in the misty grey meadows of great and eternal unknowing.

Bremusa sighed, her cold breath a brief cloud before her. She watched the still body of an Amazon who lay sleeping where she had fallen before the remains of a destroyed pyre and wondered if it was this collapsed sister's wails that she had heard through her broken sleep, howling to Artemis of her grief.

The faint, low bellow of a horn sounded deep within the village, and Bremusa's body snapped to attention. Her world was waking, and this day would reveal what faced them and how they would prevail. Perhaps she would be recognised for her efforts in labour for the tribe and acknowledged by the queen herself.

With hope invading her heart, she leapt from her perch on the log and dashed back along the forest trails toward the village, merging onto a larger common trail at great speed, precision in her agile step. Without slowing, she turned sharply around a bend in the dense forest.

A great crack resounded as she bounced backward and crashed to the ground. As she sat blinking in shock, sitting in the dirt, a cool voice pierced her bewilderment. "Are you often this unskilled a runner?"

Bremusa looked up into the formidable face of Thermodosa, flanked by her guard. "You will answer," she commanded.

Bremusa scrambled up, fumbling with her dagger, which had fallen from her belt to the dirt, finally sheathing it and standing stiffly before the intimidating leader. "Nay, Queen. Please pardon my error." Bremusa felt her heart pounding at her ribs as if fighting to burst free from her chest.

"Would an enemy pardon your error and let you stand?" With thin, grim lips, the queen's deeply scarred face was jarringly angular and unpleasantly sharp-featured, framed with masses of thin, matted braids, beads, and small pieces of metal and feather woven intricately within them. She was lean but strong and tall, with large, calloused hands. "I will not ask again, infant."

"No, Thermodosa, they would not."

"Are you to be a cow for breeding or a sword in the heart of my enemies?"

"A sword, Queen. The mightiest of weapons in the army of Myria, thirsting night and day for blood." Bremusa watched as Thermodosa smiled, and soft chuckles came from the warriors at her back.

The queen drew her sword from her hip and turned it to offer the hilt to Bremusa. "Show me."

Bremusa knew what her commander was asking and knew that, should she refuse the order, she could be cast out of the tribe or have her throat slit by a queen's guard. An Amazon's life belonged to their queen, to do with as she pleased.

Bremusa took the handle of the blade and tried to hide her struggle under its immense weight. Gripping it tightly, with both hands, shifting her weight to her back foot and bracing herself, she lunged forward, angling the blade toward the queen's belly, but her hesitation betrayed her attack, and with flagrant ease, Thermodosa leaned only slightly. With her hand, she parried the tip of the blade, slapping it out of Bremusa's grip. Her other hand shot out to slam into Bremusa's exposed ear with extraordinary force, causing a sickening crack and two smaller snaps as her entire body collided with the trunk of the thick tree to her immediate right.

Bremusa felt her body crumple, and she fell to the ground, her head echoing with the deafening screams of harpies. As she opened her mouth to speak, not knowing what could possibly be said, she threw up down her front, the vomit streaked with a stream of blood coming from her nose.

She was vaguely aware of the queen, who bent with ease and retrieved her weapon. "Exhale on a lunge," the queen's voice said firmly.

Footsteps trailed away, and Bremusa's world faded gently into darkness.

◆

ECHEPHY AND EURYLEIA HAD BONDED QUICKLY WITH little Lykopis, caring for her with patience. Bremusa nursed the tender flesh of her arm and watched the three girls inspect a trail of bull ants, teaching Lykopis about the insect and its dangerous bite. The girl learned quickly, a good skill to have, thought Bremusa, though her skinny arms and delicate frame would be useless in battle. The girl was small for her age, and Bremusa was sure Lykopis had not yet had her blood.

The deep pain in Bremusa's shoulder flared, and she dropped the small spade she held and the scoop of mud along with it. Anger rose in her throat, aggravated by the incessant ringing that had barely dulled since the deafening blow to her ear.

"Enough! There is work to be done!" she snapped at the group. The joy fled from the three girls' faces as they returned quietly to their work, but it was not long before Lykopis continued with her endless questions.

"When all tasks are done, your time is your own?" she asked hopefully.

"Yes. When Bremusa is in one of her more agreeable moods, we swim in the lakes or lay on the grass, hunt, fornicate, sleep. You may do as you please if the work is done for the tribe."

Bremusa scowled, and Euryleia smiled as Lykopis' cheeks flushed, casting her gaze bashfully to her work. "Women are open lovers here," she said.

She glanced only for a moment to Echephy, who met her stare, but she, too, looked away quickly.

"Yes, it is encouraged," Euryleia said. "Strong bonds between us all encourage the fiercest fighting in war, and for a tribe to survive in a world of men, we must be strong. We celebrate when the moon is whole. There is much wine and meats and lovemaking." Euryleia giggled. "Though sisters who have not had their blood merely enjoy the food."

"Or make off with a donkey's load of corked wine." Echephy grinned mischievously.

"One winter solstice, Echephy drank three water kins full of the ceremonial wine, danced all night, fell upon her cookfire, then vanished," Euryleia told Lykopis. "An elder discovered her asleep amongst the goats two days later!" She dropped a shovel full of mud into her pail.

"And it took until the next winter to get the stink off her," jabbed Bremusa.

"Never has an Amazon had a truer friend than the simple goat," Echephy mused playfully. "I defend myself. There is no business that Karthdia should have with the brewing of such potent wine! Though I would drink it again and dance into the loving arms of Dionysus, who only commends my debaucherous splendour." She bowed theatrically . . . to the amusement of Lykopis.

"Such freedom here," Lykopis said, a note of sadness in her voice, noted immediately by the others.

"Freedom is yours now." Echephy held her gaze; the distance between them might as well have been absent. Bremusa subtly observed their moment, a moment seemingly lost on Euryleia, who struggled greatly with retrieving her shovel, stuck deep in mud.

"You three have not spoken of your families—or rather, your mothers, I suppose," Lykopis continued.

"These are all our mothers," Euryleia said happily, "and we are all their daughters."

"Tarthos is my blood sister," Echephy said. "Our fathers died in villages east of the mountains in Assyrian raids many years ago, and our mother was a great warrior in the queen's guard. She fell protecting her queen. Tarthos tells me stories of her might of spirit and skill with the javelin," she finished proudly.

"Tarthos says my mother was very beautiful and died to give me life," chimed in Euryleia.

"No sister remembers quite clearly my origin, but I am told my mother is dead," said Bremusa with indifference, barely looking up from her work.

"The ones you see are our family." Euryleia managed to pull free her shovel and stumble backwards.

There was a pause before Lykopis spoke. "It is good there are no fathers or brothers here."

"Tell me of your brother, Lykopis. Is he handsome stock?" asked Euryleia wistfully.

"Handsome, yes. Astyanax is Father's favourite. He is strong and skilled with his sword. Mother says he will make a magnificent king, but I think he would make a magnificent latrine pot."

"You are a princess?" Echephy asked, shocked.

"I suppose no longer. I am Amazon now!" Lykopis beamed widely.

"Harrah!" shouted Bremusa and Euryleia briefly, brandishing their tools, but Echephy remained mesmerised by Lykopis's smile.

"I am not the only foreign royalty who has joined you," Lykopis said with concern. "I am worried for Berenice. She is ill, and I cannot think of a remedy."

"The one who rode the mountain-backed beast?" asked Bremusa, and Lykopis nodded.

"Iphito, Tarthos says," said Echephy.

"I suppose she is Iphito now, yes," replied Lykopis. "She will not eat nor speak, and her skin has become dry and rough. Oils seem to soften the damaged surfaces, but they must be applied daily, and with each day passing, she grows weaker. I fear she does not want to live."

"She is a Gypto?" asked Bremusa.

"Queen Thalestris brought her from there; they say she has not spoken a single word."

"Tell us more of Thalestris," Echephy demanded.

"There is nothing more I can tell you than what has been said already. The journey to Myria was long. I know no more of her than the strong leader she presents and the great respect her presence commands within her tribe. When we reached the surrounded Myrian army, I was sent to safety with Beren . . . with *Iphito.*"

"Is Macedonia a great distance from Egypt?" interrupted Euryleia, as she hoisted a wooden rod onto her shoulders, a full pail of mud swinging at each end.

"It is a journey over vast seas, yes, but I am told the heat is comparable to my father's kingdom. I was sent to the King of Kypros to wait for the Afrikaan tribe to journey up the Assyrian coast to Tarsus, where I was given to them. My father's trade ships frequent Egypt. They return with wonderful spices and meats."

"And what does your father send to Egypt?" asked Euryleia, following Echephy carefully through the mud toward the trail back to the village.

"Macadamia nuts and olives mostly."

"We will collect Iphito a platter of such and see what her preference is. Bremusa will hunt her a rabbit," Echephy decided.

"I will?"

"Yes, you will feed your sister, Bremusa," Euryleia mocked a scolding tone, "and if Iphito is not partial to rabbit, then I suppose it is more for us!"

"An Afrikaan warrior poached Iphito a pheasant one evening, but she retched onto the ground at the sight of it," Lykopis said miserably.

"Oh," Euryleia said, deflated.

The small party of mud bearers trudged slowly back to the heart of the village, where there was much activity and movement. Old, grey-cloaked sisters led groups through the village. Weaving through the crowd, out of the sea of people emerged Lapis, a joyless, short old crone with roughly cropped grey hair that oddly matched her robes and a scowl upon her face as if she were born with it. The old woman spotted the girls and barked a command at a cluster of Afrikaan sisters sitting spiritlessly on the ground nearby, who responded slowly. As they stood, Bremusa watched them become almost twice her size; with their long, slender, ebony-skinned limbs, large lips, and strangely styled hair, they were truly a sight of exotic magnificence.

Lapis pushed past Bremusa roughly, with no regard for anyone, babbling loudly in the old tongue as she continued down the road that led to the western living quarters. Bremusa felt the weight upon her body begin to ease and turned to see only the belly of the Afrikaan warrior above her, who lifted the wooden rod clear of Bremusa and onto her own shoulders. Then, in a few large strides, she caught up with Lapis as she rattled down the road. The other tall warriors followed, the other rods with pails upon their backs, carried with elegant ease on powerful frames.

"Not ones for conversation, are they?" Echephy said.

"You have Mother's shield and daggers?" The low power of Tarthos' voice thickened the air, and Bremusa turned to see the agitation in her stance, her face a picture of unrest as she came to stand before the small group of sisters. Dressed in battle armour and fully armed, she towered over them, an impressively striking Amazon warrior.

"Yes, sister, why do you—" began Echephy.

"And your blade is sharp?"

"Why should blades be sharp if there is to merely be training?" Echephy asked.

Tarthos' expression darkened. "Sharpen it," she hissed before she turned and strode away with purpose, leaving uneasiness behind and prompting Bremusa and Echephy to lead Euryleia and Lykopis quickly away toward their huts.

☙

APOLLO HAD BEGUN TO PLUNGE HIS BLAZING CHARIOT deep into the precipice of the mountainous horizon, leaving the sky streaked in soft orange and purple, a gift for his dear sister, who would enjoy it as she brought the moon. Already, many torches burned brightly across the expanse of the low-levelled hippodrome, a dirt arena where generations of Amazons had trained and been born of the agony and paid tribute with blood spilled. The wooden walls were a low corral below simply constructed platforms where armour-clad Amazons stood or sat on various levels, their eyes fixed unwaveringly on a duo of warriors sparring roughly in the dirt. Cheers and jeering would erupt as one made an advance or displayed an impressive move.

At the entrance to the ramshackle half-stadium, Echephy bent to tighten the straps of Lykopis's ill-fitting leather chest guard; the girl's wide eyes nervously took in the terrifying sight. "I can loose a steady arrow, but I do not know the blade," Lykopis said with worry in her voice.

"Can you now? That I'd like to see," replied Echephy, distracted with the fastenings.

Euryleia came to stand next to Bremusa and slipped a rigid hand into hers. Bremusa looked at her friend, sporting a fine, bronze-plated cuirass and a short sword at her belt that clearly burdened her with its weight. "You will not fight today. It is merely a demonstration," she said quietly.

Euryleia squeezed her hand tighter with affection and smiled sincerely. "One day, though." The true fear in her eyes bled through her smile.

"One day. Not today," Bremusa reassured her.

Euryleia smiled once more and leaned to place soft, gentle lips sweetly on her cheek before leaning back. "Thank you." Euryleia squeezed her hand within their tight embrace, then stepped toward the stadium scaffolding, following Echephy, who had pulled Lykopis up behind her, ready to find a seat.

Settling almost halfway around the arena, on lower benches close to where the titan queen and Thermodosa sat in large, grand chairs, the four sisters began to observe the display of back-and-forth combat. The fighters were experienced warriors of perhaps twenty years, skin marked with proof of their familiarity with violence. One was a Myrian Bremusa did not recognise. The raised scar she bore reached from her shaved bald crown down her face and descended her chest to trail below her clothing; her eyes were mean, and her sturdy weight struck at a sickening speed. Her opponent was an excellent match, with quick reactions and precise counterstrikes; her Herculean frame and lengthy arms were proving a difficult obstacle for the short sword held by the Myrian, who took a hilt blow to the jaw and a swift kick to her lower leg, causing her to stumble and struggle to recover.

Echephy leaned forward to join Bremusa in resting her forearms on the wooden railing. "Is the Myrian injured?"

"She's nursing her left ankle. The right must be her dominant—there's no other way she still stands."

"And she's going for the weakness. Clever."

In three swift movements, the Afrikaan had skirted a thrust from the Myrian, slipped behind her, and pushed a foot into her injured ankle, and then shoving her weight against her adversary, dropped the Myrian to the dirt, where she lay as small clusters of cheers and hails sounded from the stadium benches.

The Afrikaan leaned down and took the forearm of the fallen Myrian, smiling as she pulled the defeated warrior to stand and helped her limp from the arena past another two who had engaged in their own brutish conflict. The spirit of the crowd began to grow as favourites challenged champions and sisters quarrelled over outcomes; tensions rose and fell, and young warriors were called on to test the fruit of their practice.

Bremusa knew one of them: Pestelle, a girl her own age, with thick legs and a short torso. The girl had lower-quarter attack advantages and stamina to match. Bremusa had sparred with her. As she watched Pestelle begin a match and execute sequences they had learned, Bremusa could see the adjustments each warrior of varied stature, height, weight, and strength would have to make in order for those maneuvers to succeed. It was almost beautiful to watch something she had only just begun to understand performed as if it were a dance of carnage, gliding across blood-soaked sand.

Suddenly, Pestelle was on the ground, clutching her left shoulder. Her Myrian combatant stepped back to allow a one-armed warrior to rush forward in aid. It was their cicerone, Millettisse, a proud and serious woman who cared deeply for her daughters and sisters, and once they could walk on their own, led the youngest daughters in battle training. She was a fierce legend to them all. Although approachable and goodhearted, when challenged or irritated, her deformed and damaged appearance accurately reflected her dangerous nature.

Bremusa felt uneasiness creep into her belly and glanced toward the queen's podium, where Thermodosa leaned to a young warrior beside her, speaking closely into her ear. The young warrior's sharp eyes flicked to Bremusa, glinting dangerously in the light of the flickering torches. Her stomach tightened around a knot of dread.

Sure enough, the young Amazon, bearing an excellently fashioned aegis and wearing copper-plated boots, effortlessly hopped the scaffolding of the arena and landed with pristine balance in the dirt. As the warrior stepped closer, Bremusa recognised the faint face from a childhood long lost: Anaxilea, the queen's youngest living daughter. Her posture expressed true experience yet slightly subdued confidence.

As the Amazonian princess—the friend she once knew—came to stop and glare at the four sisters in the crowd, something slightly brushed Bremusa's leg, and she looked down to see sweet Euryleia's hand trembling. She looked back to the arena to see Anaxilea raise her sword and point at Euryleia. Euryleia began to try to stand on shaking knees.

It was time to show the courage Bremusa had prided herself on and carried with her since finding she had basic skill with a blade and that her build was advantageous in combat. Bremusa reached a hand to Euryleia's shoulder and pushed her back down to her seat. Then Bremusa stood. Though she was certain her wavering knees revealed her fear to all, she forced her body to comply. With the wide eyes of her sisters on her, she climbed roughly over the wood railing, praying to Artemis that her sword would not slip through her grip from the sweat beading on her palms.

As she landed on the dirt of the arena, fear gripped the back of her throat, cutting off her air, but forcing deep breaths from her belly, she coaxed herself to steady presentation before Anaxilea and drew her sword.

Anaxilea turned to look at her mother. The queen nodded, honouring the trade of Bremusa fighting in Euryleia's place.

Immediately, Anaxilea lunged at Bremusa, who barely raised her blade to block the blow brought down from above. She stumbled forward and spun back to face Anaxilea, who had already reset her footing and begun advancing once more. Bremusa tensed as Anaxilea came at her from the side, only managing to deflect the strike with sheer luck and shoulder strength.

Anaxilea whirled the blade around, and again Bremusa's only save was to blunderingly turn into the attack. Anaxilea's weapon met strong metal, and she was forced to sidestep and adjust. The focus in the princess's eyes was that of a cougar hunting a mountain mole; the mole was no match for the cat, who knew a thousand ways to kill it, while the mole had only just realised the cougar was no friend.

Anaxilea charged again and then again, Bremusa barely countering the assaults but somehow taking minimal damage and remaining standing, though the sword in her hands was becoming heavier by the moment.

It was then that Anaxilea feigned a right step. Bremusa leaned to meet the attack, but the princess changed her direction suddenly, allowing no time for

Bremusa to anticipate the blow of a powerful fist that crashed like a horse's kick into her right side, sending breathtaking pain shooting through her ribs. She doubled over, then felt her legs kicked out from under her. As her belly hit the dirt, she struggled to breathe, feeling pressure in her lung. Coughing the dust from her mouth, she rolled onto her back with great effort, vaguely aware of more pain from a point on her shin.

Anaxilea stood over her and looked down. "To have a weakness as clear as yours is to know that one's death is close. She is pretty, but she will not live to see your accolades." Her voice was cool and tempered but laced with threat, and Bremusa followed Anaxilea's gaze as the warrior looked up into the crowd, where Euryleia sat watching, still as marble, with fear on her face.

Realisation tickled through Bremusa as Anaxilea stepped toward Euryleia, and with every piece of her body that was not frozen in shock, she wrenched herself from the ground, took two great strides, and then launched herself into Anaxilea's back, toppling them both to the ground. Anaxilea shook off the assault like water from an eagle's back, stepped toward Bremusa, half-rising from the ground, and brought the back of her hand down heavily on Bremusa's face. She followed the blow with a well-positioned kick to her gut, and as she clutched her belly, curled in the dirt, she believed she would truly spew her organs.

"Now, regret your failure." Anaxilea stepped with purpose toward where Euryleia sat on the benches. The image of Euryleia in her place, lying there in the sand, parts broken inside her, heaving half breaths as her sisters watched from afar, danced before Bremusa as a dream does before waking.

Knowing Euryleia's blood would mix with her own in this soil before the torches were spent hurt her in a new and unfamiliar way. She tasted the copper of her blood running down her throat from her nose, and a rage ignited, blazing and consuming her very flesh. With every muscle screaming and a bone somewhere in her side scraping against another, she pushed herself to stand. Then absent fear of any consequence, she surged across the arena and brought her true weight down on Anaxilea, this time holding tight to her adversary as they tumbled across the earth.

Scrambling on top of Anaxilea, Bremusa brought a heavy fist down upon her chest, making the princess jerk beneath. The girl recovered in time to block the second blow with an armoured wrist, allowing her to sneak a jab to Bremusa's injured rib.

Anaxilea was able to push herself free, and they both scrambled up. Anaxilea rushed Bremusa head-on and punched her jaw. Bremusa returned almost immediately, and in close range, saw the opportunity to inflict tremendous damage; she lunged forward, crashing her forehead into the bridge of the princess's nose, causing a river of red to gush from her nostrils. Bremusa took advantage of Anaxilea's moment of shock and disorientation to deliver a punch to her breast that caused a recoil but seemed to only fuel the warrior in Anaxilea, who spat blood from her mouth and twisted expertly to kick the legs out from beneath Bremusa, sending her to the ground once more.

From the dirt, Bremusa kicked Anaxilea's ankle with such brutal force that she fell beside her, only to reach an arm out, grip the collar of Bremusa's breastplate, and bring a ruthless knee over into her stomach, sending nausea coursing through her. Anaxilea climbed upon Bremusa, dripping blood heavily onto her face, and delivered a punch, but her effort was waning. Bremusa's head lolled to the side from the blow, and in the brief moment that her vision returned, she focused on the dull bronze shield lying beside them. Without conscious thought, she reached for the small, sturdy disc and heaved, wrenching it up through the screeching pain of her ribs and slamming it with savage brutality into Anaxilea's face. The princess fell beside Bremusa, whose vision had begun to blur once more as she lay bleeding onto the earth.

❦

THERMODOSA'S LIP TWITCHED, AND SHE STOOD, SWEEP-ing her gaze across the arena with pride. "It is the new age of Amazon, where there is no divide of sisters! The Myrian shoulder draws a mighty bow aimed to rain fire down upon our foe, and the Afrikaan arm sends a merciless spear through their wretched hearts! The new breed of Amazon will slaughter our enemies for generations to come!"

The crowd erupted into a storm of cries and cheers. The match was done.

In the benches amongst the roaring Amazons, three daughters of Myria, mouths dry and hearts pounding, watched their sister lie broken yet valiant beside a bloodied princess of Myria.

"A destiny has been set into motion that will not be undone . . ." Echephy breathed without really knowing why.

EGYPTE

ARSINOE'S LIES

— XX —

Egypte's legions, armed and mighty, marched toward the south, the sun glinting off their armour as they led the caravan of pack camels and goats and wagons. Neos and Claudius had descended from the palace, handsomely adorned in traditional Egypteian armour as the pride of Egypte; two experienced princes departing to conquer barbarians in the south and claim the land for Mother Egypte.

Kleopatra had watched her brothers, their faces hardened, clear the length of the promenade toward their waiting mounts, passing the still-hanging bodies of the unfortunate victims of Arsinoe's wrath that she insisted remain for several days. A grim beginning to a campaign.

Kleopatra waited until she could see the faraway specks of her brothers reach the heads of their armies, and the masses of soldiers began their journey south. General Ankhmakis would ride west with his fierce Sand Eagles in two days' time, the delay to give time for all supplies to be loaded and packed in the lower city, as the priority was to send the larger army south first.

The scene on the southern horizon left the princess's mouth dry, and worry whispered to her. *"Where is safe now if not with Claudius? When the general leaves, will even the palace be safe?"* With her brothers, Berenice, and soon, the general absent, Arsinoe would be free to rain her terror down upon those who spurred the hateful demon in her.

Kleopatra wandered through the eastern palace halls and thought perhaps she would find Akela and Theos and see if they would join her in the gardens since the sun was growing brighter each day now that winter passed behind them.

Suddenly, she could not breathe, and the sound of her gurgling efforts echoed in her ears. In the midst of her shock, Kleopatra realised she was lying on the ground with Arsinoe straddling her, her hands gripped tightly around Kleopatra's throat. Kleopatra beat weakly at the deathly grip, staring with terror into her sister's hungry eyes, where she found only exhilaration and triumph. The pressure on her windpipe was immense while the passion of Arsinoe's loathing fed her strength, and the precious moments seemed to trickle past.

Kleopatra's cheeks flared with heat, and her pulse throbbed harder yet slower against Arsinoe's clamped hands in the last efforts of life. Her mouth opened in a fruitless gasping reflex, and her tongue began to swell as she felt her eyes bulge. The tiny pops of blood vessels rang in her skull. She seemed to watch her own blurred death from above, seeing her skinny legs kick at nothing and her thin arms claw feebly at her attacker. As her muscles began to fail and her body felt the cold of the stone beneath her melt away, she became vaguely aware that she was dying.

She saw the figure of Heba dart forward and swipe at Arsinoe, hissing fiercely, but all the spots on the cat's magnificent body melted into black. The pressure in Kleopatra's head was uncomfortable, but the calm sensation that flowed through her took the fear from her as she descended—it was like stumbling off a cliff in pure darkness into the sweet relief of death.

♦

KLEOPATRA OPENED HER EYES SLOWLY, WINCING AS HER eyelids struggled against the bulge of their sockets, to find the face of the demon physician Seeztui leaning low over her, breathing his revolting breath onto her face. She truly was in the underworld, and the punishment for all her wickedness was to endure the same torture he had inflicted on poor Arsinoe for all of eternity! She began to speak, but hot fire ripped up her throat, and instead, she released an agonising moan, which brought a hideous grin to the surgeon's emaciated face.

"You cannot speak, child. Your wounds are severe, and you will take time to heal. There is a bamboo rod inserted to help you breathe, and you must lie still if you are to relax the muscles enough to recover. I would have liked to have studied the internal trauma of such an affliction, but alas, next time."

He smiled wryly, and after subsequent time adjusting to her situation, Kleopatra surrendered to the reality that she had no choice but to lie there for many days. But she was alive.

The old man rubbed a sticky balm across her throat with his spindly fingers and wafted a burning herb beneath her nose. Quickly, the pain began to melt away, and so too did the world.

⚘

WHEN SHE AWOKE ONCE MORE, HER SHOULDERS WERE stiff, and her neck muscles were throbbing so intensely she was sure their pulsing movement would be visible to any who observed her. Her mouth was dry, and as she attempted to swallow around the bamboo apparatus, she winced. Her eyes seemed less swollen, and blinking had become manageable, although her sight was still a little blurry, and there was a red hue to the edges of her vision.

"Can she speak?"

"No, sir, she has much damage to her throat," Seeztui replied.

"Will she recover?"

"Yes, of course. My methods are superior," the physician snapped.

Kleopatra tested the movement in her fingers and found that the muscles up both of her arms felt strained. She suspected it was the result of her attempts to pull on Arsinoe's hands.

How could her sister have done this? Had she truly intended to kill Kleopatra? Surely not—perhaps she had been bitten by her monkey and been driven mad?

"No," a voice said. "*She would have murdered you sooner had she had the chance.*"

Kleopatra's mind wandered to Akela. She wished her friend could hold her hand and read to her to pass this dreadful time of pain and slow healing, and she wondered why her friend had not come to visit her.

Then the general's face came into her view, and as he leaned over the princess, the deep worry in his eyes expressed his concern. "I am sorry this has happened, Princess. I pray for your swift recovery. I am told you are strong. I believe it. I have posted guards at your service, and so you are not in further danger." He gave a weak smile that did not reach his eyes.

Kleopatra groaned slightly in acknowledgement, and Ankhmakis withdrew from view.

ꙮ

AKELA AND ARSINOE KNELT BEFORE THE PHARAOH ON his golden throne, his face a picture of fury.

"My children have brought me more irritation than any slave in my kingdom, and now they attempt to murder each other. Have none of you any potential?" The pharaoh glanced at Theos and Auletes with disgust before looking back at Akela and Arsinoe. "Arsinoe, you say the girl struck you as you attacked Kleopatra?"

"Yes, Father. The bitch struck me with an urn—"

"You lie!" snapped Akela.

"Silence!" boomed the pharaoh.

"She struck my head, and the urn smashed, and that wretched cat attacked me as I lay helpless. The cat and the treacherous witch must be punished, Father, and the law states it must be death." Arsinoe's voice dripped with feigned innocence as she pressed on the bloodstained fabric over the wound on the back of her head. Akela's skin burned with her fury.

"Just as the law requires execution for the attempted murder of a princess such as Kleopatra?" The pharaoh seemed amused.

"You are right, Father, as you always are, but I'm afraid the tale has been skewed. I was merely playing a game with little Kleopatra, and this vermin wretch must have mistaken it for an attack." Arsinoe shot a glare sideways at Akela.

"Unfortunately, Kleopatra is unable to testify to your claim as it seems her throat is sufficiently assaulted. And you girl, what say you?"

His eyes rested on Akela, and she felt the weight of his animosity toward her, but she had to fight for her life. "Arsinoe lies to Your Highness, for she wishes to cover the grudge she harbours against Kleopatra. I did not attack her and never could. I do not have violence in me, sire, and to do so would bring shame to my good father and his position. He and I are both your loyal servants. I merely came upon the scene, where it appeared the mount and vase had toppled, and I called for help." Akela hoped her voice had remained strong and certain.

The general looked as though he would draw his sword and slaughter all if Akela were to be found guilty, but he remained poised as stone.

The pharaoh stared at the girls for several moments. Akela felt dread creep into her chest; he could not let the crime go unpunished. Harming a royal family member was of the deepest offence, and if he did not order her death now, Arsinoe would ensure justice would be done later.

The look on her father's face broke her heart. His daughter, all that remained of his family, was to be executed before him. The disappointment in his eyes stabbed her deeply. She wanted to run to him and hide in his arms from the man who would soon drag her away to cut her head from her body . . . *But every warrior dies*, she thought, and perhaps her father would fall in the west this time, and she would wait for him so that they might journey the dark road together.

Theos stared morbidly at his feet, and Auletes sagged in his chair, boredom on his face, but Safiya could sit silently no longer, and with a straight back and elegant tact, she spoke. "My love, I wish to speak to the character of the general's daughter. The girl is gentle and mild-mannered, and I do not believe her capable of such violence. She has seen justice done by your great hand and understands that such a crime demands execution; she is an intelligent child and loyal to you, just as her father is. The cat was clearly there, and such an enormous beast could easily topple the stone mount and urn onto the Princess Arsinoe. Surely there is justice to be done here with no bloodshed."

Akela thanked the gods for Safiya's ability to calm the pharaoh with her presence as none had been able to since Kleopatra's mother had died. Safiya laid a loving hand on the pharaoh's, and he took it ceremoniously, then straightened with renewed authority.

Akela watched the pharaoh. She was certain he did not care if she lived—or Arsinoe either, particularly—but her father was about to depart for his crusades in the west, and the battles were crucial to their stronghold on the territories bordering the expanding Egypt. He huffed in irritation, but clearly, his wife's doting nature pleased him.

His terrifying gaze rested on Arsinoe. "The cat will be slaughtered as the culprit; do not waste my time with childish disputes again." He looked to Akela. "Were you not the general's daughter, you would be executed without further discussion, do you understand?"

"Yes, Your Majesty," she replied with a bow of her head.

"This is madness, Father!" Arsinoe screeched. "The harlot could have killed me. She cannot simply go unpunished!"

The pharaoh shot her a malicious stare. "Hush, you ugly child, or I will kill you myself for your insolence! Your pharaoh has spoken, and the matter is finished." He stood and strode swiftly from the room.

Arsinoe scrambled to her feet and paused to glare down at Akela before she stormed away. Ankhmakis embraced his daughter tightly, and she clung to him, her heart pounding in her breast.

He took her arm in a hard grip and led her from the room through the eastern halls in tense silence. They passed servants sweeping up the toppled stone mount and the shattered clay urn, and, glancing across the garden, Akela spotted the camouflaged face of Heba watching the activity in the halls. Just then, a guard shouted and launched a spear at the cat, but it missed her and embedded itself in the body of a tree. In a second, the great cat had launched itself from the foliage, darted from the garden, and disappeared. A group of guards chased after her, and Akela hoped Heba knew that now she must be gone from the palace forever. *Farewell, my friend.*

🌿

THAT EVENING IN THEIR APARTMENTS, THE GENERAL shouted at Akela until the sun began to descend, his face flushed and his eyes weary from his anger. Abruptly, he stopped and sank into a chair, resting his head in his hands, and Akela lifted her head. She hesitated for a moment, fear still in her from his lecture, but then stepped forward, laid a gentle hand upon his shoulder, and then knelt before him. She knew she had shamed him, and she was determined to earn back his love. She reached up and gently pulled his hands away to see tears streaming down his face. She was shocked, as she had never seen him cry before, and she felt guilt that it was she who had brought such anguish to him.

He looked into her eyes and reached out to hold her shoulders firmly. "I am sorry, my love. My anger masks my fear, as today I could have lost you forever." There was pain in his voice. "You are my sun and my courage and my heart. Your death would be my death. One day, you too will know the dread of a parent. You are dear to me, more so than any other, and I would gladly give my life for yours, but gods give me strength, for you test my nerve."

She threw her arms around his large neck, and they embraced.

He withdrew and looked at her once more. "I leave soon, and I have much to organise. I must secure your safety while I am gone. I have sent for Kohlis. He is charged to protect you and Princess Kleopatra day and night; stay close to him and stay away from trouble. That is a command, soldier."

There was a rap on the door, and the general opened it to reveal Kohlis. The general stepped out without another word and left Akela and Kohlis to stare at each other silently before Akela strode past him down the staircase. He fell in step behind her.

The healing rooms were dim and smelled strongly of undiluted wine and the musty bay leaves and sage that were burned to hide the stench of blood and decay. Akela made her way to the chambers reserved for royal patients and came face-to-face with two armed soldiers. They looked upon her face and then stepped aside to let her and Kohlis pass.

Safiya sat next to Kleopatra, holding her hand and speaking to her gently. She turned to Akela as she approached and embraced the girl warmly. "My heart is glad that you are well," Safiya said before she swept from the room.

Akela looked back at Kohlis, who moved to stand just outside the door. Then Akela approached the damaged princess. There was a length of bamboo inserted in her throat at an unsettling angle, and there was a large pillow under her neck so that her head tilted back, allowing the throat to heal properly. Kleopatra's eyes were swollen and bloodshot, but when Akela moved closer and leaned over her friend, they locked on hers and released silent tears down the sides of her face.

Akela took Kleopatra's hand and squeezed it tightly. "I am here, my sweet friend. Kohlis is here too, and so are Father's guards. We are safe from the witch. I am so sorry that you are in much pain, but you are strong, and you must spite her by surviving." Akela gave a reassuring smile. "I suspect Safiya relayed the trial of this morning to you in which Arsinoe insisted on having me executed. She would have succeeded if it weren't for the queen. I spoke of Arsinoe's lies and hatred of you and my innocence of the crime."

Kleopatra looked at her with grief in her eyes.

Akela leaned close to her ear and whispered. "Of course, I did it, and I would do it again." She leaned back to grin mischievously at the princess, who closed her eyes tightly and squeezed Akela's hand through strained breaths. "Your father has declared that Heba is to be killed for her part in the crime."

Kleopatra's body tensed in panic, and her wide eyes screamed at Akela.

"Do not worry, I have already seen Heba escape the guards. She is clever and will not be caught."

⚜

SAFIYA WATCHED GENERAL ANKHMAKIS STRIDE AWAY down the hall, and their conversation played over in her mind. Both were gravely concerned for the safety of his daughter and the Princess Kleopatra with his departure due the following morning and Arsinoe's apparent murderous resentment of the two girls. She ran her hands over her pale-yellow dress, smoothing the fabric, then turned to the door, knocked softly, and entered.

The pharaoh sat on his terrace amongst a litter of colourful embroidered pillows, dressed in his night robes and resting a goblet of watered wine in his hand as he looked out over his beloved Egypt.

Safiya glided elegantly over and sat next to her husband. "Are you well, my pharaoh?" she asked softly.

"My children age me as each day passes. Their nonsense will be my downfall," he replied blandly.

"Certainly. They are *your* children," she teased, and a faint smile played on his lips. "You are a stern father, but children need discipline. They will thank you for it when they are strong leaders because of it."

"It appears none learn from discipline. Few have value, as most are useless as flies on camel shit."

She laughed gently, and it seemed to soften him. "Are you well?" he asked almost awkwardly.

"I am, my love. My body has recovered, and the babies are strong like their father."

❧

WHEN SAFIYA SMILED AT THE PHARAOH, HE FELT THE warmth of her gaze, which often evaded him in his daily royal duties.

He was reminded of the day she had arrived at his palace, only a child of sixteen. She had knelt before him dressed in a yellow dress, with a delicately embroidered yellow veil over her face. He had stepped forward, expecting to lift the veil, look upon the face, and curse at the plainness of the girl he was to marry to replace the loss of his true love, but had been surprised when she'd looked up at him and smiled, her fair hair falling in cascades down her chest and her smile youthfully radiant.

Not a day had passed when he had not mourned his second wife, Kleopatra V, and he knew that no other could take her place in his heart, but Safiya had pleased him greatly since their union; she remained quiet as a woman should, she offered no offence when she spoke, she had delivered him another strong son, and all who visited the palace were enamoured with her compassion and wit, which gave him respite from the incessant prattle of lesser kings.

She had called him "my love" when they had wed, and at first, it had irritated him, for there was no love in royal matches. Only in the rarest cases did an arranged match turn to a tolerable union, as with his Kleopatra V. He was sure the gods had sent her to him to confirm that his reign as pharaoh would be one of great renown. Safiya, however, seemed to truly love him. The feeling was uncomfortable, but he told himself there were worse wives. At least this one did not screech like a harpy about trivial women's concerns, nor did she resist his advances. In fact, she embraced them and reveled in the pleasure with a grace he had not known before.

"It pleases me that you are well. The perils of childbirth are known to all, and you have proved resilient for future births." He nodded, confident in his analysis.

"I am honoured to bear your children, sire," she said. "Your other children are growing, though. Kleopatra has begun her blood, and she is now a woman."

"She has? Excellent. She is most promising to fetch an advantageous match, but she has much to learn still; the child's manners disappoint, and she lacks discipline in her studies."

"She is indeed a great asset to the empire, husband, though I must agree that her discipline is lax," Safiya said. "You considered a union with the Thracian king's son?"

"Until the wretched invalid married him to a whore princess of Sparta he'd been hoarding in his monastery until her blood. That bay of Thessaly will be advantageous for trade, and apparently, that is worth more than honour." He sipped his wine scathingly.

"Who do you suggest now?" Safiya took his arm lovingly and looked at him as though hanging on his every word for another of his brilliant strategies.

"Kyprus. Claudius's bride-to-be died at a very inconvenient time, but the alliance must be made still, and thank the gods the incompetent king has a son. Although the boy is young, he will be expected to marry at the end of the season, and the position of Kyprus is crucial for my navy if we are to hold the coast."

"I see. How clever you are, sire. I did not think of that."

"Do not falsely favour me, woman. I need no flattery," he grumbled and pulled his arm from her.

"I am sorry, Your Majesty, I merely wish to support you as best I can. Forgive me; I am not seasoned in politics and strategy," Safiya said softly.

"Kyprus. Yes, I have decided. I will send word immediately." He softened, uncomfortable in his harshness in response to her clear naivety concerning the matters of men.

"The Greeks on Kyprus worship the goddess Demeter, do they not?" Safiya asked.

"I do not care what false, impotent god they sing hymns to as long as their port is wide and their coin purses deep."

"If Kleopatra dedicated herself to serving their god, perhaps it would entice them to offer a fast agreement of marriage?"

"I see no value in the child wasting time on such menial endeavours when her purpose will be to breed. Your opinion is not welcomed in this matter, woman."

"Very well, my love, you are right. I only speak because my father mentioned many years ago that the Kyprus king wished for an alliance with Athens. The Athene king's daughters know the worship of Demeter also, but are said to be as ugly as donkeys, unlike Kleopatra."

His thoughts swam as she spoke, calculating once more. "The filthy cowson! Of course, he wants to trade with Athens! But Egypt is a far greater empire and not overrun with Roman heathens. No king wants ugly heirs." He paused, deciding. "If it is indeed an enticement for Kyprus to secure this alliance, Kleopatra must study Demeter. The child will excel, and when the goat-shagging Greek looks at her, he will see the greatness of Egypt, and he will not deny me."

"There is a grand temple of Demeter in your uncle's western kingdom of Cyrene; he would gladly take Kleopatra, and his priestesses of Bahariyya would guard her diligently," Safiya suggested.

"How do you know of this, wife?" He eyed her suspiciously.

"Upon my arrival for our union, I requested the appropriate papyrus of Egypt from Alexander's library and read all that I could. I wished and still wish only to please my lord, as is a wife's duty. As it is also a wife's duty to nurture the heart of a pharaoh who grieves." She spoke gently and placed a delicate hand upon his chest above his heart, then looked up into his face with the true love she had for him.

Her loving nature had often confused him. The woman had never wavered in her devotion, no matter his mood or extreme anger. It was true he still grieved the loss of his Kleopatra V, but in the emptiness of her absence, the young and agreeable Safiya had quietly and dutifully planted seeds in the barren soil of his spirit, and somehow had inconspicuously watered them, seemingly for no gain of her own, merely for the betterment of himself and Egypt. He felt affection for his young, kind wife, even if he did believe her kindness to be extreme weakness and even if his affection for her was only a fraction of what he had harboured for his Kleopatra V.

"Let it be done," he said, as his wife rarely asked for his attention or expense, and after all, she was a woman. Surely, she would know of the many more subtle attributes that made a young princess an enticing bride and an advantageous match.

❦

SMILING INWARDLY, SAFIYA SAID, "I PROPOSE THE GENeral's daughter attend her there also—if she is to be the princess's handmaiden, an education would be a grand statement for Egypt." She saw the irritation flicker in her husband's eyes at the request, but she continued. "Egypteian royalty must be nothing less than impressive."

The pharaoh's ego was prone to insult, but her experience with her own father's hubris had sharpened her tactics. The pharaoh's eyes now gleamed with the grandeur of his vision for Egypt. He seemed to taste it in the air.

"Indeed. All must see the undeniable splendour of the Pharaoh XII Auletes." He seemed lost in the romance of his self-admiration, swigging his wine generously.

"I will send the children right away, as soon as Kleopatra is well enough to travel, and then the preparations for your agenda can begin."

Pleased with herself but wishing to win back her favour with him after her minor aggravation, she leaned in and whispered, "Now, let us make another son, my love." She slipped her hand beneath his robe, and the Pharaoh grinned in compliance to her carnal appetite.

🌱

AKELA'S TEARS DRIPPED ONTO THE HOT STONE OF THE promenade as she watched her father lead his army west, little more than specks on the far horizon, and she wondered if she would know when the day came that she stood up upon this stone watching him leave for the last time.

She straightened her back and tightened her jaw; her father would be disappointed if he saw her weeping like a child. Warriors did not weep, for their fate was already written and in the hands of the gods.

Brushing the tears from her flushed cheeks, she turned back toward the palace and passed her personal guard, who waited for her in the shade. He was tall and lean, with strong arms and a stern face. *Not much of a chin*, she thought, but he was attentive, and Akela enjoyed his silence.

The guard fell in behind her, and the irritation that she had to be followed and was consequently never alone flared in her core, but she quickly squashed it.

She swore to herself. She was not afraid of Arsinoe, and to kill the bitch had been her intention, but after the initial blow, she'd realised she was not sure how to tell if someone was dead; the princess hadn't been moving, and she'd wondered if she had been successful. Relief had flowed over her, but then she had seen Kleopatra with bruises and bulging eyes, lifeless on the ground, and all further effort went to helping her. Akela promised herself that if the opportunity arose again to kill the murderous bitch, she would seize the gift.

Rounding a corner, she saw Kleopatra sitting in the garden with a green shawl around her shoulders and Kohlis standing silently nearby. *For such an enormous, imposing man, he is terrifyingly quiet,* she thought.

"You are walking?" Akela asked with surprise in her voice, and then she bounded toward Kleopatra, who smiled at her friend's arrival. "And the bamboo is gone?" Akela bent to inspect the princess's throat carefully. "Wonderful! The swelling has gone down significantly. Seeztui might be a genius after all."

Kleopatra took Akela's hand gently and looked up at her with compassion in her eyes.

"Let us be without sadness today, my friend," Akela said to her. "Father has gone to fight for the glory of Egypt, as I will, one day. It is an honour. You must concern yourself only with your healing."

They sat in the shade in peaceful silence, and the pleasant afternoon passed by uneventfully.

⚶

SEVERAL DAYS HAD PASSED SINCE THE GENERAL'S DEPAR-
ture with his army, and the palace had settled, but with an uneasy tension in the air. The servants no longer chattered amongst themselves. In fact, they were hardly seen at all. The pharaoh spent much time in his war chambers adjusting plans as messengers came from each of Egypt's campaigns. Arsinoe was nowhere to be seen, Theos never left the palace scripture room, and Auletes was dedicated to his sword training, determined to be the warrior his father dreamed of.

Safiya divided her time between caring for her babies and visiting Kleopatra, observing her recovery with a watchful eye. No one had seen Heba since the attack on Kleopatra, and it sat heavily on her heart that her dear friend and beloved pet had been chased from her home and must live amongst the shadows of the peasant city, careful not to be seen.

The girls had spent most of their time indoors while Kleopatra recovered from her injuries; the healing had been slow and painful, but according to

Seeztui, the progress was excellent. Akela had spent the days reading to her, and they had been brought paints and papyrus.

The moon began to rise in the dimming sky, and broth and goat milk were brought to Kleopatra's rooms. She winced slightly as she carefully swallowed the soup, its warmth soothing the aches in her throat muscles and welcomed greatly by her belly. Finishing the entire bowl, she then sipped the thick goat milk as she sat at her wooden chamber table next to the terrace. The night was warm again, and the familiarity of the temperature allowed her to relax a little.

She eyed Akela enviously—the girl slept, sprawled across the large bed, snoring faintly. Kleopatra's dreams had been haunted since surviving the violent attack on her life, and she dreaded sleep. When she finally slipped into slumber, her dreams would quickly become red-hued. Surrounded by strangers with distorted faces, she ran down a long hall, fearing for her life, but when she sucked in air to scream for help, no cry sounded, and none who passed her could hear her pleas.

Another night, her hands had been bound with curtain ropes, and she had been slowly laid inside an enormous bathing bowl until her whole body sank beneath the water; there was no air, and she drowned, again and again.

The night hauntings were enough to wake her violently and drench her in sweat until she became so worried for what awaited her that she resisted sleep for as long as she could. Her muscles were beginning to release the tension in her throat, and she could even speak, after a fashion, now seeming a luxury that she had taken for granted.

Finishing the goat milk, she rested her head against the arm of the beautifully carved chair, smiling to herself at the sound of Akela's contented, sleeping breaths, and looked out at the moon until she slipped gently into her first dreamless sleep.

❧

THE CHAMBER DOOR SWUNG OPEN ABRUPTLY, AND Kleopatra jolted awake where she had fallen asleep in her chair and swung around to see Safiya and Kohlis stride into the room with three servant women who began sorting through the robe closet and the drawers. Kohlis handed them one of two large sacks made of camel hide.

Akela sat bolt upright with such a start that she tumbled off the bed clumsily, cursing as she collected herself on the ground.

"What has happened, Queen Safiya?" Kleopatra croaked out groggily. She wiped her tired eyes sleepily.

Safiya pulled both girls to her. "Listen to me now, children, for I will speak quickly and only once. You are not safe in the palace; there are forces greater than Arsinoe that wish you harm. I cannot protect you and my babies as well.

"You are to travel to my uncle's kingdom of Cyrene, which stretches narrowly down the western desert, and study with the other priestesses at the oasis temple of Demeter. The matron will know who you are but keep your birth name between closed lips." She stared at Kleopatra, and the princess nodded. "You will take two sacks of belongings and one small chest between you; I suggest you take simple gowns and garments, sturdy sandals, and a few trinkets.

"Akela, if you wish to retrieve anything from your own apartment, Kohlis will take you now; there is a caravan waiting at the promenade to take you to the temple. It will take you a great many days, but your guardian has been given gold for your food and drink. You will not stop along the way, and you will not speak to anyone. Do you understand?"

Both girls nodded, exchanging panicked glances; then Safiya embraced them tightly and stood. "Now pack your effects with haste, little ones. The sun comes, and you must be gone with the dawn breeze." The queen swept from the room as quickly as she had entered.

For a moment, Akela looked at Kleopatra, then servants took the princess by her hand and pulled her to the closet, where they began hastily showing her garments for her to choose. Akela turned to Kohlis, who gave her an affirming nod, and they ran from the room through the palace to Akela's apartment.

She burst into her room, panic gripping her chest. Had her father fallen in the west already? Had Arsinoe hired the best assassins with a mountain of the pharaoh's gold? Had the pharaoh himself decided that the two were no longer in his favour? Or had Isis been right, and enemies were on their way to attack the palace?

Her eyes darted around the room. She ran to open her drawers and snatch at things she wished to take. Kohlis handed her the sack in his hand, and she began to fill it with essential items. She had never been very sentimental with possessions and was thankful for it at this moment; she did, however, retrieve the bejewelled scabbard that sheathed the dagger her father had given her. She snatched up her mother's small golden brooch and reached behind the stand behind her father's bed to take a full leather pouch of coins. If he was truly dead, he would not return for them, and he had said to take it if she were ever in need of it. Now seemed an appropriate time.

She dropped the pouch in the sack, and Kohlis drew the strings closed around her effects. The two made for the door, and Akela closed it without glancing at her father's bed for fear her heart would break in her chest. Now was the time to be strong. She was determined that Arsinoe would not have the satisfaction of Kleopatra's death, no matter who it was that threatened their lives here.

Their strange means of transportation waited patiently at the end of the promenade, where two large horses with enormous, broad feet and strong legs pawed at the sand. The trunk was loaded at the back of the cargo shelf. Akela had never seen a litter with sturdily built walls that moved on wheels before; typically, transportation for royals was luxurious and carried by slaves, but this was a very small room with four wheels and a rickety door.

Safiya urged them into the enclosed chariot with their camel sacks and another bag of fruits, dried meats, and bread. The confused and fearful girls peered out of the window as dawn began to announce itself, and Safiya removed Kleopatra's unwilling hand from hers, tears quietly staining both their faces.

The chariot jolted into motion, pulled by the powerful sand horses, and began to trundle forward. Akela looked at Kohlis; his face was tight and concerned. It softened for a moment, and he dipped his head respectfully to Akela, and then she knew: They were not returning to Egypt.

Akela and Kleopatra held each other close as they watched the palace slowly become distant and shed tears for the only home they had known as they watched the beautiful orange and pink tones of Egypteian dawn begin to stream through the palms into beautiful daybreak over the empire.

🌿

KLEOPATRA WAS EXHAUSTED FROM HER MANY SLEEPLESS nights and still had healing to do, and so she slept for many hours, with her head resting on Akela's lap as Akela watched the world outside the window change from day to night, from sand to grass, from day to night, from grass to sand, and so on. She tried not to think of her father. She wished Safiya had explained the danger to them, but she took comfort from Safiya's promise to write to them once they arrived at the temple.

Their guardian was a man around her father's age with alert eyes, who wore a long cloak even in the hot sun and a brimmed straw hat. When they stopped to relieve themselves or to briefly rest the horses, he would get down from his seat behind the mares and stretch but never said a word.

After many dawns, the chariot wheels dipped into a short ditch and then rolled onto harder, smoother ground. Kleopatra sat up, and both girls peered outside to see a busy marketplace in a flurry of movement. Heavy open barrels of spices and nuts lined stall fronts with garlic hanging from their canopies, and people haggled loudly. A sweaty man roasted whole rabbits over an open cookfire, and the sour-looking woman next to him scraped offcuts of the rabbit meat into a large metal bowl that bubbled over a healthy flame. Children climbed onto crates that housed clucking chickens. Three whores with faded and slightly dirty gowns cackled enthusiastically at a jest amongst themselves, a fat one gesturing theatrically with the wine cup in her hand. The smells were sensational but strange. Even the scent of the livestock was different.

The chariot continued until they cleared the market, and the bustling crowd melted away to reveal sandy alleys and a wider road that travelled the outskirts of the city. They watched as the homesteads and shacks became larger community buildings, from which men with long grey beards who wore long white robes emerged in conversation. They saw fields of goats and several bathhouses and other buildings before they came to a stop before a grand structure.

The temple was spectacular: grey in colour, with tall, thick columns supporting the heavy roof. The stone of the entrance was beautifully carved from top to bottom, and the temple walls were high and stretched widely around what Akela suspected to be gardens and quarters. It was truly an enormous edifice. The bronze statues of the goddess Demeter and her daughter Persephone, mounted on podiums on either side of the steps, stood twice the height of Kohlis, fierce and foreboding.

Akela heard the driver climb from the chariot and unload the trunk, so she opened the door to step out into the sunshine before the temple. She helped Kleopatra down to join her, both stretching their stiff legs as a short, plump woman wearing full, dark-blue robes trotted down the stone steps toward them. Her robes were matched by a veil draped across her face so that only eyes were visible. She carried fabric in her hand, and as she reached the girls, she held a length out to each of them.

"We preserve the modesty of our faces at the temple of Demeter," she directed sternly. "The priestesses are faceless as we serve the goddess equally and completely." The girls took their fabric and fixed it over their heads and faces.

The old woman looked over them as if assessing livestock, and Akela noticed she had a prominent mole upon her brow that had sprouted a dark hair. "You will call me Matron Dadkera. You will obey each rule of this temple with respect and without question. You will not retort, you will not cause distress or discord to others, and you will not sow corruption in the hearts of lambs. During worship, we remain silent, and the entire temple is a place of peace. Breakfast is at dawn. There, daily duties are assigned. You will accept and complete them without complaint. Supper is at sundown. You will serve the goddess until the day you are called away. Come now, and I will show you to your room."

The matron turned on her heel and ascended the steps as the chariot departed. Both girls stood for a moment, glancing around them, confused, waiting for servants to carry their chest and satchels. The matron realised no one had followed her and turned to the girls.

"By Hera, what is the delay?"

"Where are the servants to carry our effects?" Akela asked, and the matron laughed, a coarseness in her cackle.

"We are the servants, child, of the goddess Demeter. There are none here lesser than any other. Bring your possessions, and do not keep me from my duties any longer."

She continued up the stairs as the girls looked at each other, then at their belongings. Akela realised they would be carrying them inside themselves and saw the same realisation on Kleopatra's face. The strange new reality began to settle on Akela like a blanket of ash. Suppressing frustration and helplessness, she felt a pang of homesickness.

They each slung a camel-hide satchel over one shoulder, then moved to either side of the small trunk and lifted it, swaying a little before edging slowly with the cargo up the steps into the temple.

The halls smelled of stale air and burnt sage. Not a single soul was in sight, and the journey to their appointed room seemed to take all morning as they made their way carefully up several sets of stairs. Akela's leg muscles felt tight from the climb, and her arms ached from the weight of the chest.

They rounded a corner to find a long, dim, grey-stone corridor and the matron standing before a door waiting for them, an impatient scowl on her wrinkled brow. Sweating, they passed through the door and set the chest on the ground with a grateful sigh of relief.

Akela looked around at their new home. Kleopatra looked as stunned as she felt. The room was the size of a robe closet. One narrow bed was wedged roughly into the corner. A simple wooden table and two worn chairs sat next to a very small fireplace. Two small robe hooks were hammered into the crumbling wall, and faded linen curtains flapped gently in front of the tiny square hole that served as a window, too far up the wall to show anything but a sliver of sky. It was a miserable sight, and the brick smelled strongly of rot and dampness.

"We are to share this . . . cot?" A hint of Akela's frustration echoed in her voice, and the matron's eyes narrowed at her.

"The priestesses sleep four to a room, but with the Pharaoh's *generous* donation to the temple, it was requested that you two not be separated and have your own quarters. Do not be late for supper; food will not be kept for you." And with that, she waddled out of the room and down the hall.

Akela stepped forward and quickly shut the door, then turned to Kleopatra, who looked as though she were ill.

They sat in the cramped room on the hard lumpy bed in silence. No tears came. They offered no words of comfort to each other. They simply sat in the silence of the space staring at their feet as the hours trickled by and the loneliness of exile swelled uncontrollably in their chests.

το τέλος

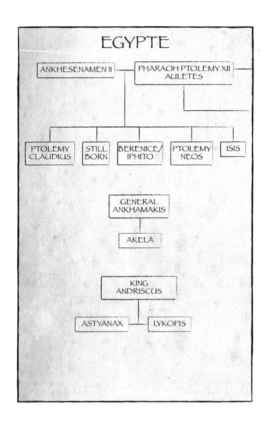

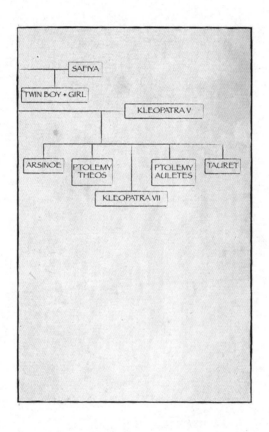

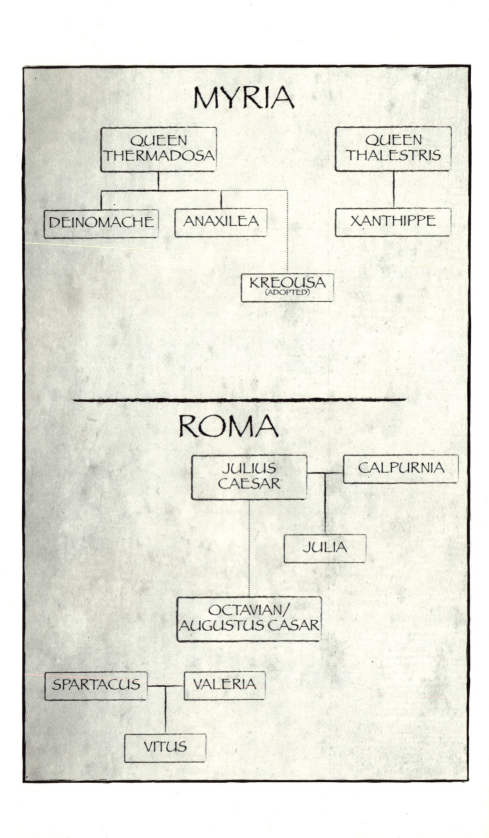

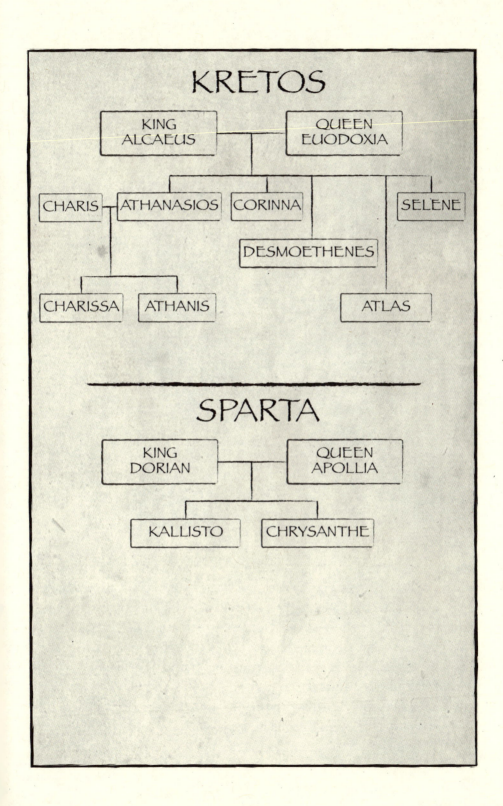

KRETOS

KING ALCAEUS — QUEEN EUODOXIA

CHARIS — ATHANASIOS CORINNA SELENE

DESMOETHENES

CHARISSA ATHANIS ATLAS

SPARTA

KING DORIAN — QUEEN APOLLIA

KALLISTO CHRYSANTHE

ABOUT THE AUTHOR

E. A. JACKSON GREW UP ON A VAST VINEYARD IN RURAL Western Australia with many animals including two peacocks & acres of forest to expand her imagination. As the only child of a Greek family, her bedtime stories each night were those of the famous Greek myths & legends—Noting that those stories & a beaten-up shoebox of *Xena the Warrior Princess* DVDs she received from her aunty one Christmas, has had a major influence on her morals, values, perspective & imagination. She studied Buddhism at a young age & attended Steiner school before kindergarten; a German educational program focused & centred around the circle of life & spiritual development. Encouraged by her family, she has loved to write & tell her own stories since childhood, with an inclination toward romance, heroes & epic tales of glory & passion. That love of storytelling led her to become an actor & screenwriter. Armed with a degree in Scriptwriting for Film & Television & a Bachelor of Communications, her passion for cinema & storytelling impelled her to a decade long career in Vancouver, Canada where she currently resides acting, writing & teaching. Now in 2022 Jackson publishes her first ever literary works, with book one in *The Aegean Series: Snake of the Nile*, where four ancient empires orchestrate what we now know as history, at whatever cost.

Printed in Canada